Also

BAD
SEED

SHARON
SALA

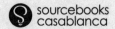

sourcebooks
casablanca

Published by Sourcebooks Casablanca, an imprint of Sourcebooks
P.O. Box 4410, Naperville, Illinois 60567-4410
(630) 961-3900
sourcebooks.com

Printed and bound in the United States of America.
BVG 10 9 8 7 6 5 4 3 2 1

Chapter 1

Philadelphia, Pennsylvania
Mid-January

IT HAD BEEN SNOWING SINCE DAYLIGHT.

A true cold day in hell for the gang at the warehouse who'd just been arrested.

A light at the end of a tunnel for the hostages who had been but a day away from being trafficked to foreign countries.

For Harley Banks, it was just the end of another case, but one she needed to witness to be able to sleep at night. The horror of knowing women and children were disappearing monthly from this site was the stuff of nightmares. She wouldn't let herself think of how many had been packed into shipping containers and loaded onto ships bound for other countries, or how many had died before the ships ever reached port, or how long it had been going on.

Today was the culmination of long weeks of investigation, and she was just another face in the crowd as she watched federal agents bringing out men in handcuffs.

The line of ambulances waiting to transport hostages stretched past the second block.

As she was watching, her phone signaled a text. Satisfied that she'd seen enough, she turned and headed back to where she'd parked. By the time she was in her car, the snow was coming down hard. She started the engine to let it warm up, and then checked the message.

> Well done. Final payment has been sent to your account.
> W.C.

Harley nodded to herself. If Wilhem Crossley was satisfied with her work, then she was satisfied, too.

Being a private investigator was her job. Corporate crime was her specialty, which is why Crossley had hired her to find out what was happening to his import shipments. Being a CPA only added to the skills she often needed to do her job. The audit had been a tricky one. It had taken her a while to figure out that while the invoices were there showing the shipments had arrived, and there were records of every payment that went out to the companies who'd shipped them, the goods had never reached the warehouse. Crossley thought he was being robbed, and he was, but not like he'd expected.

After checking out the validity of the companies shipping products, it didn't take Harley long to figure out the goods were ghost buys. Invoices from foreign companies that didn't exist. Payments going to offshore accounts that were shell companies all belonging to a crime syndicate, and the mole they had planted in the Crossley company just happened to be Maury Paget, one of Crossley's accountants. Crossley had trusted the wrong people, and Harley uncovered their scam. Even though Paget had been identified and arrested, they suspected someone else was running it, but she'd never uncovered a name. It bothered her, but Wilhem was satisfied knowing they'd turned over everything they had to the authorities, and left them to find the boss.

After receiving the text, Harley pocketed her phone and looked up. They were bringing the hostages out now. She couldn't see their faces from this distance, but she could see the way they were clinging to their rescuers, and the ones who were coming out on gurneys, and the children who were being carried out. One thought went through her mind as she put her seat belt on.

Today, I made a difference.

Then she put the car in gear and drove away, unaware she'd been targeted in any way.

———

Wilhem knew what was going down this morning, and yet his son, Tipton Crossley, who was co-owner in the company, didn't even know about the missing money, or that he'd hired an auditor to find out. Now, Wilhem had waited too long to tell him and, at this point, could say nothing. The feds had cautioned him not to alert anyone else about the discovery or the ensuing raid until it was over.

Tip was in China on a buying trip and was going from there to Japan. Wilhem consoled himself with the fact that even if Tip knew, there was nothing he could do about it, but his night was sleepless. The raid was going down at this moment, and he owed Harley Banks far more than the money she'd earned.

He rubbed a hand over the top of his bald head as he stood looking out into their garden. It was already blanketed with several inches of snow, and more was coming down. What a miserable day all around. He couldn't save the hundreds of women who were already gone, but maybe they could save these before it was too late.

———

Phil Knickey had been living his best life as a professional hockey player until he'd crushed both his knees and his dreams in a car crash eight years ago. After that, his whole life went downhill, until he found a new gig—being the man bait for a gang involved in human trafficking.

It wasn't hard. His name and face were still known. Women still flocked to pro athletes, even the broken ones. And once he had one hooked, the moment she headed to the bathroom, there were others waiting to make her disappear. It was money in the bank.

And, Phil knew tomorrow was shipment day. The

women in holding were being shipped out, and today, it was all hands on deck getting them ready. But Phil overslept and was late leaving his apartment. To make it even more frustrating, snow was slowing his travel.

He was less than three blocks from the docks and at a red light at an intersection waiting to turn, when a phalanx of black vans, dark SUVs, and three armored SWAT vehicles rolled through the light with ambulances following, all heading for the docks.

His heart skipped. It could mean nothing, or it might be everything. Within seconds, Phil was on the phone to Ollie Prine, Mr. Berlin's right-hand man. The phone rang twice before Ollie picked up.

"Hello?"

"Ollie, it's me, Phil! Are you at the warehouse?"

"Almost. Why?" Ollie said.

"I'm three blocks away and just saw a small army of black vans, dark SUVs, and three armored SWAT vehicles heading toward the docks. Have we been made?"

"Oh shit! I don't know, but don't come in unless I give you the all clear," Ollie said, then hung up and backtracked to a safe distance away to watch.

To his horror, Phil's hunch was right. Before Ollie could alert the men on the ground, federal agents were swarming the warehouse by the dozens, with SWAT teams leading the way. He sped away from the docks, calling Berlin as he went. The phone rang repeatedly, to the point Ollie thought it would go to voicemail, and then the call was picked up.

"What?"

"Boss, it's Ollie. We're being raided as I speak. Phil and I got away."

"How the hell did this happen?"

"I have no idea," Ollie said. "The only unusual thing at the company offices was an auditor on-site, but I think it's over."

"What? An auditor? Why?"

"I have no idea, only that the old man had one on-site for the past three weeks."

"What's his name? Would you know him on sight?" Berlin asked.

"It's a woman, and yeah, we've seen her. She's a looker."

There was a long moment of silence, and then Berlin gave an order.

"Go back to the area. If you see her anywhere on-site, then that means she knew this was happening and she's way more than an auditor."

"Yes, sir, and if she's there, what do you want me to do?" Ollie asked.

"Follow her and make her sorry."

"How sorry?" Ollie asked.

"Dead sorry," Berlin snapped. "Then let me know when the job is done."

"Yes, sir," Ollie said.

The call ended. He turned at the next block and headed back to the warehouse district. The area had already been cordoned off, so he parked outside the perimeter, jumped out, and headed toward the gathering crowd, keeping an eye out for a tall woman with long, black curly hair.

The moment he saw her, he ducked into an alley to watch what she was doing, and when she finally got in her car, he shifted gears.

Make her sorry, Boss said. *Dead sorry.* He could do that.

Shivering from the cold, Ollie watched her drive past him, then went running toward where he'd parked to follow her. He came around the corner on the run and then skidded to a stop. The car was gone! Either someone had stolen it or towed it, and he was afoot in a snowstorm.

He began cursing a blue streak as he headed up the street to a local bar, and as soon as he was out of the weather, he called for an Uber. He had no option but to wait. An hour later, he was still waiting and at the point of going to heist the first vehicle he found empty, when his ride finally showed up.

"It's about damn time," Ollie said, as he slid into the back seat.

The driver glared. "You're lucky I made it. There's a foot of snow on these side streets. Whada'ya want from me, dude?"

"Yeah, yeah, sorry," Ollie said.

"Where to?" the driver asked.

"The Logan Philadelphia at One Logan Square."

The driver rolled his eyes and eased back into the

streets with the wipers aimlessly swiping at the still-falling snow.

———————

Unaware of the danger on her trail, Harley was already on her way to catch a flight. She'd checked out of the hotel when she left this morning. Her luggage was in the rental car, and she would return the car when she got to the airport. But her drive was hampered by the weather, and by the time she got her luggage checked and her rental car returned, she was running to the gate to catch her flight. She made it with minutes to spare and didn't relax until she was in her seat, on the way home to Chicago.

———————

It was past noon by the time Ollie's Uber dropped him off at the hotel, but he'd done his homework. While he was riding, he'd texted the wife of a friend, who was a maid at the hotel, and after some coaxing and the promise of a hundred dollars, she reluctantly gave him Harley Banks's room number.

Ollie finally reached the hotel, jumped out, and entered behind a party of five getting out of a shuttle. He went straight to the elevators and up to the sixth floor, then headed down a long hallway, looking for Room 645. But when he got there, the door was propped open, and there was a cleaning crew inside. His heart sank.

"The woman who was in this room. Where did she go?" he asked.

One of the maids shrugged. "She checked out this morning."

His gut knotted. Berlin wasn't going to like this. Ollie headed back to the elevators and, as soon as he was inside, sent a text.

She checked out before the raid. No idea where she's gone.

His phone rang within minutes. He answered as he was walking across the lobby.

"Hello?"

"What the hell happened?"

"Snow happened. For all I know, she'd already checked out of here and went straight to the airport."

"Then make it your business to find her," Berlin said, and ended the call.

Ollie frowned. The boss was a cold bastard, but he paid good. As long as he didn't get on the wrong side of him, he'd be okay.

———

It was late afternoon by the time Harley got back to her apartment. She paid the cab driver, grabbed her suitcase, and hurried into the building.

The security guard on duty in the lobby recognized

her and smiled. "Welcome back, Miss Banks. Travel is pretty nasty right now."

"It sure is, but it's home sweet home for now, right, Danny?"

He grinned. "Yes, ma'am. Welcome home."

Harley ignored the moment of loneliness as she headed for the elevator. It didn't say much for her personal life that her only welcome home was from the building security guard.

A short while later, she had stripped down to her lingerie and was putting her travel clothes into the washing machine. As soon as she had it running, she headed for the shower. It was part of her homecoming routine— washing away the negativity of where she'd been.

Later, she downed a bowl of cereal, then headed for her bedroom. Throwing aside her bathrobe, she crawled between the sheets, rolled over onto her side, and closed her eyes.

———

It was just past eight o'clock the next morning when Harley woke. The last thing she wanted to do was get out of her warm, comfy bed, but she had things to do. After a quick wash in the bathroom, she wadded her long curly hair up into a topknot and fastened it with a banana clip, then dressed in an old cable-knit sweater and a pair of sweatpants and headed to the kitchen with her phone.

Two cups of coffee and another bowl of cereal later, she was curled up on her sofa, going through missed messages. One from the federal agents who'd debriefed her. Most of them were things she'd respond to later, except the ones from her mother. That she wanted to get over with. They weren't exactly estranged, but neither of her parents approved of her chosen career and prodded at her constantly for the decisions she made.

Her father, Jason Banks, was a NASA scientist, and her mother, Judith, was an accomplished screenwriter and playwright. They had a penthouse in New York City, a villa in the south of France, and owned a small vineyard in Calabria, Italy.

Harley was a genius with technology and numbers, but that was of no importance to her parents. It wasn't a showy career. It garnered her no fame. Harley also had no significant other in her life, and had chosen to live in an apartment in Chicago. They had nothing against Chicago, but it wasn't New York City. She knew they didn't approve of her adult life, but she'd mostly gotten over letting it bother her.

She wasn't callous enough to ignore her mother's calls, but talking to them did require fortification, so she peeled the wrapper off a piece of chocolate and popped it in her mouth. It was melting on her tongue as she picked up her phone, scrolled through her contact list to her mother's name, and punched the call icon. Judith Banks answered just as Harley's chocolate was melting down to the chewy caramel center.

"So, you finally found time for me," Judith snapped.

Harley sighed. "I've been on a job for the last three weeks. I flew out in a snowstorm, came home in a snowstorm, and went straight to bed. I just woke up. I will not apologize for the need to rest. I just finished a successful case in which I discovered where my client's missing funds had gone, uncovered a human trafficking ring, and was responsible for finding the location of forty-four females who were being held by human traffickers readying to ship them all off somewhere overseas. I found out from one of the agents this morning that they were all on the national missing persons list, and eleven of them were under the age of twelve."

Silence.

"Are you still there?" Harley asked. Then she heard a sigh.

"Yes, I'm here. I was just thinking how ugly your chosen profession is."

"You think a face without makeup is ugly. You don't know the depths of ugly, but it's damn sure not me or my job," Harley snapped. "Are either of you sick?"

Judith flinched. "No, but—"

"Did you go bankrupt?"

Judith snorted. "Of course not!"

"Are you getting a divorce?"

Judith gasped. "No!"

"Is someone threatening you?" Harley asked.

"No! What's the matter with you?" Judith asked.

"Since you have no interest in my contributions to

world peace, I was wondering why the hell you even called."

Judith sighed. "I'm sorry. I didn't mean to—"

"Yes, you did mean to, Mother. You are a broken record when it comes to me. You think belittling me will bring me to my knees and I'll come running home. Good to know you're both well. I'm soul-weary. Today, I'm going to have a massage, and eat pizza, and sleep when I want to, or until I get a phone call about the next job, whichever comes first."

She disconnected the call, laid her head back on the sofa, and swallowed past the lump in her throat. *Why, God? In all the world, why did You choose those people as my parents? What do You expect me to learn from them?*

Quiet wrapped around her, easing the momentary pain of their rejection. She was still leaning back with her eyes closed when she felt as if she was being hugged, and then a different thought rolled through her head. *Maybe they're the ones who were meant to learn from you.*

Tears rolled, tracking down her temples and into her hairline. She swiped at them angrily as she bolted up from the sofa and walked to the windows overlooking Lake Michigan. It was snowing, and she was congratulating herself for taking the red-eye last night instead of waiting to travel today. At least she was safely tucked in for the duration, however long this snowstorm might last.

But the loneliness of her life was obvious. She stood with her forehead pressed against the glass, feeling the cold against her skin, and wondered what it would be like to be loved. Truly loved. Without reservations. Without expectations of anything but loving in return.

———

February: Jubilee, Kentucky

It was a little past 1:00 p.m. when Brendan Pope sped past Bullard's Campgrounds on his motorcycle. The day was brisk, but the sun was shining, and speed always made him feel like he could outrun his past.

He'd been riding since just after daybreak and was finally on his way back to Jubilee. Once he'd passed Bullard's Campgrounds, he knew the highway was a straight shot into town. There was nothing in front of him but a long ribbon of concrete bordered by bar ditches full of tall, dried grass and ancient pines pointing straight up to heaven.

All of a sudden, a huge plume of smoke and debris appeared in the distance, like something had exploded. He frowned, worrying about what might have happened, but as he rode closer, he saw a red charter bus sliding sideways on its side, and what appeared to be a moving van barreling into the field beyond it. It took a few seconds for him to realize he'd just witnessed a head-on collision.

He was less than 200 yards away now and flying, but he knew response time was imperative so he began to brake, then pulled over to the side of the highway, tapped into his phone via the Bluetooth in his helmet, and called 911.

"Jubilee Police. How can I help you?"

"This is Brendon Pope. I'm out on the eastbound highway between Jubilee and Bullard's Campgrounds. I just witnessed a head-on collision between a charter bus and a moving van. The bus is on its side and smoking. The van is off the south side of the highway in someone's field. I'm about two hundred yards away, riding in now. Hurry. This bus could catch fire any second and I don't have a fire extinguisher on my bike."

"Sending all units now," the dispatcher said, and Brendon disconnected and gunned it toward the wreck.

He was about forty yards away when he parked on the opposite side of the highway, hung his helmet on the bike, and got off running. The windows he could see on the side facing up had most of the glass missing. And because the bus was lying on the loading side, the door was blocked.

He could see some of the passengers trying to climb out of the shattered windows and onto the side of the bus, and he ran to the exit door and yanked it open. Almost immediately, passengers began spilling out of the door and running to get away before the bus caught fire, while others staggered only a few yards before falling down—nearly all of them bleeding in some form or fashion. Brendan was helping the injured down when he spotted movement on top of the bus and looked up.

One young man had crawled out through a broken window, and with obvious injuries. Blood was gushing from a wound in his leg, and jumping down was no longer an option.

"Here!" Brendan yelled, and held up his hands.

The man hobbled to the edge. "I can't jump!"

"Sit down and slide. I'm tall enough to ease you down, buddy. I won't drop you. I promise!" Brendan said, then watched as the man dropped down on the frame between two broken-out windows and, with his legs dangling down, slid right into Brendan's arms.

Within seconds, Brendan was helping him to a place of safety. He didn't know how long it would take for the ambulances to arrive, but this guy was going to bleed out and die before that happened, unless he did something about it.

He grabbed a short, sturdy stick from the side of the road, pulled the bandanna out of his pocket, knelt down beside the man, and began to make a tourniquet above the cut.

"What's your name?" Brendan asked.

"Alex Fallin. My sister is Josie Fallin. She's performing at one of the music venues in Jubilee."

Brendan paused long enough to take his phone out and handed it to him. "My name is Brendan. I work at the Serenity Inn. Call her to let her know what's happened, and maybe she can be waiting for you at the ER."

"Thanks, man," Alex said, wincing as Brendan cut the pant legs of his jeans all the way to the gash on his leg, then made the call as Brendan was applying a tourniquet.

To add insult to injury, it began to snow.

———————

Josie Fallin was onstage doing a practice set with her band when her cell phone rang. She'd left it on the piano without putting it on Mute and waved at Trinity, her assistant, to answer it.

Trin grabbed it and hurried backstage to talk.

"Hello?"

"Uh…who's this? I need to speak to Josie. It's an emergency."

"I'm Miss Fallin's assistant. Who's calling?"

"Oh, hi, Trin. It's me, Alex. I've been in a wreck. I need to—"

"Oh my lord, honey! Hang on!" Trinity said, and rushed back onstage and thrust the phone in Josie's hand. "It's Alex! He's been in a wreck."

Josie gasped, waved at the band to stop. "Alex! Where are you? Are you okay?"

"I'm…oh shit, man…that hurts. Sorry, Sis. There's a guy putting a tourniquet on my leg. I'm…"

"Oh my God! Are you hurt bad? What happened? Where are you?"

"We were right outside of Jubilee when the charter bus I was on just got hit head-on by a moving van. It rolled the bus over onto its side. This guy…" He groaned again. "I'm getting dizzy. I need to let him talk," he said, and thrust the phone back in Brendan's face. "You do it, man. I'm gonna pass out now."

Josie was in hysterics. "No! Alex... Where...?" And then all of a sudden there was a soft, deep voice in her ear.

"Miss Fallin, my name is Brendan Pope. I live in Jubilee. I witnessed the wreck and pulled your brother off the top of the bus after he got himself out. He has a deep gash in his leg just above the knee. I've got a tourniquet on it, and ambulances are already beginning to arrive."

"Where is he? Where did this happen?" she cried.

"Between Jubilee and Bullard's Campgrounds, but you can't come out here. They'll be putting up roadblocks and setting up a triage for a whole lot of injured people on-site. Maybe you could go to the ER and meet him there when they bring him in?"

"Yes, yes, I will. Oh my God! Thank you for saving him. Thank you!" she cried, and then hung up and told her crew. "Bad wreck just outside of town. A moving van hit a charter bus head-on. My brother, Alex, was on the bus. I have to get to ER."

———

Alex was trembling and going in and out of consciousness. Brendan could tell shock was setting in as he pocketed his phone. He had to get him to an ambulance.

"I'm sorry, buddy, but this is gonna hurt. There's no time to waste and I've got to move you. Just hang on to me as best you can," Brendan said. "What do you weigh?"

"About a hundred and fifty pounds, more or less," Alex said.

Brendan nodded. "I got you," he said, scooped him up in his arms, and started walking toward the arriving police units as fast as he could.

Police officer Doug Leedy saw Brendan coming and ran to help. "Brendan! What the hell? Were you in this wreck? Are you okay?"

"Yes, I'm fine. I witnessed the wreck. I'm the one who called it in. I just pulled this guy off the roof of the bus and got a tourniquet on his leg. He has a really bad gash. Looks like it might have nicked an artery. He's gonna bleed out fast if they don't get him to ER. His name is Alex Fallin. He's Josie Fallin's brother."

"Oh man! On it!" Doug said, and ran for a couple of EMTs who were just getting out of their ambulance. They came running with a gurney, loaded Alex on it, strapped him down, and headed for the ambulance.

Brendan breathed a sigh of relief when the young man's life was no longer in his hands, but the screams and shouts and the cries for help were coming from all directions now. He guessed there were people still trapped in the bus and ran back in that direction, but when he looked inside, the people who were still there were either tangled up in the crumpled seats and lying

on windows they'd once been looking out of or uncon-
scious. He turned to look for help and saw a rescue
squad from the fire department approaching and
moved out of the way. Part of the team headed to the
smoking engine with fire extinguishers, and the rest of
them piled into the bus to aid the victims.

Brendan turned around, thinking it was time he got
out of the way and let the experts do their job, when he
noticed a child's stuffed toy lying on the shoulder of the
road about ten feet away from the undercarriage. One
wheel on the bus was still turning slowly, and luggage
was scattered all over.

He hurried over to get the toy and, as he bent down,
heard what sounded like a child's muffled sobs. His
heart sank. "Ah, man…please don't let this kid be in
pieces," he muttered, and jumped down into the ditch.

Within seconds, he saw a little boy, no more than
three years old, sitting up in the tall dead weeds rocking
back and forth, bloody, dazed, and crying.

Brendan couldn't tell if the child had been thrown
this far or if he'd somehow exited the bus with the
others, then walked away from the smoke and fell into
the ditch. He squatted down in front of the child and
held out the stuffed toy.

"Hey, buddy, is this yours?"

There was recognition in the little boy's eyes as he
grabbed the toy and clutched it under his chin. Brendan
picked him up, and when he did, the little boy laid his
head on Brendan's shoulders and started sobbing.

The sound broke Brendan's heart. "Hey, little guy… it's okay. You're gonna be okay. I've got you. My name is Brendan. Can you tell me your name?"

"Want Mommy," he sobbed.

"Then let's go find her. We'll find Mommy together, okay?"

He climbed out of the ditch with the toddler and started walking toward the ambulances already lining up on scene.

———

Police officer Wiley Pope was Doug Leedy's partner. He'd just learned about his brother's part in the rescue, but he didn't see him anywhere. The highway was littered with people lying down, and others staggering about in confusion, all of them cut and bleeding.

Police officer Aaron Pope was with his partner, Bob Yancy, setting up roadblocks. Some cars were beginning to line up behind barriers, while others were turning around on the highway and going back the way they'd come.

Aaron knew Brendan had made the 911 call, but knew nothing else about rescuing Josie Fallin's brother from the wreck. He was talking to their police chief on a walkie when he saw Brendan walking through the crowd, blood all over his clothes and hands, and carrying a bloody child in his arms. "Gotta go, Chief. There was a kid in the wreck," Aaron said, and headed toward his brother on the run.

"Brendan! What the hell? Are you hurt? Who's the kid?" Aaron asked.

"No, no, I'm not hurt. I called in the wreck and just found this little guy in a ditch a few yards from the bus. I don't know his name. He just keeps asking for Mommy."

Aaron didn't hesitate. "Come with me," he said, and hurried them to a waiting ambulance.

Brendan repeated the story to the paramedics and gently handed the child over. "There's likely to be a woman in that bus frantic about her baby. Make sure somebody tells her he's been found."

"I'll make sure all of the rescuers know," Aaron said.

Brendan nodded and started to walk away when Aaron stopped him. "Where are you going?"

"To get my bike and get out of everyone's way," Brendan said.

Aaron frowned. "I can't let you ride your bike through here, but I'll help you push it through the roadblock."

"Understood, but I can push it. You do what you need to do. Just make sure someone lets me through," and then he took off at a lope to where he'd parked his bike, toed up the kickstand, and began pushing it up the shoulder of the highway while the snow continued to fall. Once he passed the roadblock, he put his helmet back on, started the engine, and rode the rest of the way home.

Adrenaline was crashing as Brendan pulled up into his driveway. His feet were dragging as he parked in the garage and went inside, took off his biker boots and the black leather biker jacket he'd been wearing and cleaned off all the blood, then stripped and dumped the rest of his bloody clothes in the washing machine and started it to washing. He wanted a hot shower and some clean clothes. After the noise and screaming at the wreck site, the quiet of his house was a relief, and after all those hours on the road, it felt good to be out of the cold.

Chapter 2

BRENDAN WAS FINALLY OUT OF THE CHAOS, BUT THE work was just beginning back at the wreck site. Roadblocks and orange traffic cones were up. Fire trucks were still on-site aiding in rescues. Ambulances were running hot, taking victims to the hospital, then coming back for more. Four ambulances from nearby Bowling Green soon arrived on the scene to help transport the injured. And in the middle of all that, highway patrol cars began to arrive.

The snow was falling heavier now, but the interior auxiliary lights were still working inside the bus, which aided the rescuers tending to those still trapped inside. Broken glass was everywhere.

The moving van was in a field, a good twenty-five yards beyond the highway, with the contents of the trailer strewn around it. Someone's worldly possessions were in bits, just like the people being pulled out of the bus.

The driver of the van was sitting on the ground, dazed and bleeding, as a trio of firemen ran into the field to get him.

The screams from the tourists still trapped on the bus had gone from cries for help and shrieks of pain to a growing silence. It was the silence that worried the rescue workers most.

The police now had the two-lane highway completely blocked off to traffic from both directions, and highway patrolmen were manning the locations. Every police officer in Jubilee was at the scene, including Chief Sonny Warren, who was directing traffic for the ambulance drivers.

Wiley and Doug wound up inside the bus, helping the EMTs get people on stretchers out by sliding the stretchers along the framework of the overturned seats, using them like a stationary conveyor to get them to the rescuers waiting on the ground.

A couple of men from the rescue squad were near the front of the bus, trying to free a young woman trapped beneath a pair of seats that had been crushed down on top of her. She kept going in and out of consciousness, and the only thing she'd said since they began working with her was a repeated plea to find her baby.

When Wiley heard that, he realized she must be the mother of the little boy Brendan found.

Firemen were using a Jaws of Life to try and pry the crushed seats up enough to remove the trapped woman when she regained consciousness again, and the first person she locked eyes on was Wiley.

"Did you find my baby?" she asked.

"Can you tell me your name?"

"Lisa Hamilton. Have you found Davey?"

"Davey is your son, right?" Wiley said.

She reached for her head. Blood was everywhere. It scared her to think what might have happened to her son, and started to cry. "Yes. He's three years old. He was sitting in my lap holding Fuzzy, his toy tiger. He is wearing a red plaid jacket and denim pants. He doesn't have a hat. He'll be cold."

Wiley recognized the description. "Ma'am, he's already been found, and he was sitting up and awake when they found him. He's been taken to ER."

Her eyes were tear-filled and wide with shock and panic. "You swear?"

"I swear. It was my brother who found him," Wiley said.

"Thank God," Lisa whispered, and passed out again.

A few minutes later, they had her freed, on a stretcher, and were carrying her to a waiting ambulance. She was the last passenger to be removed.

———

As the day waned, Wiley checked in with his wife, Linette, who was a nurse at the hospital.

"How's it going, honey?" he asked.

"It's a nightmare," Linette said. "I've already agreed to work a double shift. The workload is crazy, so I won't be home before sometime tomorrow."

"I'm going to be really late, too," Wiley said. "Dani has a thing she has to go to and won't be home later. I'm going to call Brendan and get him to take Ava up to Mom's. She can spend the night there."

"Thank God for big families," Linette said. "I love you. Be careful."

"Love you more," Wiley said, then made a quick call to Brendan. The phone rang a couple of times, and then Brendan picked up. "Hey, Brendan, I need a huge favor."

"Name it," Brendan said.

Wiley quickly explained the situation, and then asked the favor. "Can you please get Ava and take her up to Mom's for me?"

"Absolutely," Brendan said. "I never pass up a chance to get an earful from my favorite little sister."

Wiley chuckled. "You'll get that, for sure, and thanks. I owe you."

"Brothers come free. I'll head that way now," Brendan said, and disconnected, then went to put on his boots and get his heavy coat. He grabbed a blanket on the way out the door and threw it in the back seat, and headed to Aaron and Dani's house.

It was still snowing, but not as heavily as it had been. Between the heater in the car and the windshield wipers, it kept the windows clear, and by the time he got to Dani's, his car was also warm—certainly warm enough for one tiny little blue-eyed blond.

Ava knew all about the switch-up. She wasn't both-ered by any of it anymore. Her brother Wiley, who she called Bubba, was her rock, but after two years of being absorbed into the Pope family, she also knew her other brothers and their wives were always there for backup when the need arose. She was a different child from the starving, frightened child she'd been when she first arrived.

She was standing at the window, watching for sight of Brendan's SUV to come into view, when Dani came up behind her and gave her a quick hug.

"Sugar, I'm so sorry I have this silly meeting back at school tonight, but BJ is going to take you up the moun-tain to Grandma's house, and when Bubba and Linette get through helping with the people who wrecked, they'll pick you up from there and take you home, okay?"

"We're supposed to call him Brendan now 'cause everyone calls him that at work," Ava said.

Dani grinned. "Yes, I know, but sometimes I forget, because he was BJ first to me."

"Like Wiley was Wiley until I called him Bubba," Ava said, and then shifted gears in midconversation. "I love going to Grandma's house."

Dani was still smiling. She was used to Ava's chatter. "And Grandma loves having you."

Ava nodded. "She'll have cookies."

Dani nodded. "I bet you're right." Everyone in the family knew that Shirley Pope always had cookies or something equally good to snack on. "Oh, there comes Brendan now. Go get your backpack and coat."

Ava took off running as her brother was getting out of the car, and Dani opened the door before he had time to knock. "Come in out of the cold," she said.

"Thanks, Dani. The snow is really coming down. I may have to park the bike until spring."

She shuddered. "I don't know how you've been riding it all winter."

He shrugged. "Close to work. Easy to maneuver in traffic. And the kitchens are always hot because of ovens and grills. I warm up in no time. I'm feeling sorry for the people injured in the wreck and the emergency and police who are still out there. I think all of the people have been transported, but they'll have to wait for a commercial-grade wrecker to deal with that over-turned bus, and it's getting dark. I know they're anxious to get the road cleared."

Dani nodded. "Aaron called me a few minutes ago. Told me to watch out for emergency vehicles coming and going on my way back to school."

At that point, Ava came running. "I'm ready!"

Brendan swooped her up in his arms. She was still the tiniest thing, and he was the tallest Pope. They made quite a pair.

Ava hugged him and then leaned back enough to look him straight in the face, her forehead wrinkled with concern. "Are you ever afraid to be this tall?"

He grinned. "Nope. Are you afraid up here?"

"Maybe a little," she said.

"Why? You know I'm not gonna drop you."

"My feet can't touch the floor," she said.

He winked. "Yeah, but mine can. See?"

She looked down the length of his long legs to his size-thirteen boots standing firmly on the floor, and then up at him, and nodded.

"Are we going to Grandma's house now?" she asked.

He nodded and then glanced at Dani. "I'll add my caution to Aaron's. Drive safe, Sister."

"I will. The same to you two."

And then they were gone.

Ava was in the back seat, tucked in warmly beneath Brendan's blanket, talking about school and Mikey Pope all the way up the mountain.

Brendan already knew the two were buddies, but every other word out of her mouth was Mikey this and Mikey that. It made him smile, thinking of how random it was that they'd even found out they had a half-sister, and what a blessing she'd become to him and his brothers. But it was Wiley who saw her first as the waif she was. She had turned on every protective, parental gene in his soul, and he made it his business to become her legal guardian.

She'd come to them as starved and neglected as a child could have been, distrusting of everyone and withdrawn to the point of believing that if she was quiet enough, she could disappear. And now she was a little magpie in the back seat, giving him a play-by-play of the last twelve hours of her life.

Brendan was approaching the turnoff to his mother's house when he realized Ava had quit talking. He glanced up at her in the rearview mirror.

"You okay, sugar?" he asked.

Ava nodded. "Do you think Grandma will have cookies?"

He chuckled. "Ever since you came into our lives, Grandma always has cookies."

Ava almost hugged herself with delight. "Because she loves me?"

"Because she loves you so much," he said.

The impact of those words went straight to Ava's love-starved little heart. She'd suffered too much too young and didn't forget, but she'd finally learned to trust, and that was what saved her.

"We're here," he said, as he turned off the blacktop into the drive.

Shirley Pope had turned on the porch lights, and the security light on the pole in the front yard gave them plenty of light to see by as Brendan parked.

He grabbed Ava's backpack as she got out and bolted for the steps. Moments later, Shirley Pope was standing in the doorway with her arms open.

"There's my girl!" Shirley said, and picked her up and hugged her, then winked at her youngest. "Come in where it's warm, Son. Thank you for bringing her up. Wiley called about the wreck. Such a terrible thing. I hope to God there were no fatalities."

Brendan shut the door behind him as he walked in,

dropped Ava's backpack on the sofa, and shed his coat as he followed them into the kitchen. Amalie, Sean's wife, was setting the table. Ava already had a cookie, and he didn't wait for an invitation to help himself.

"Isn't the snow beautiful?" Amalie asked, as she looked up at him and smiled.

Brendan gave his sister-in-law a quick smile and a wink. "It sure is, honey," he said. They all knew how much she loved the snow.

"Coffee's fresh," Shirley said.

He got a coffee cup from the cupboard, filled it, and then took a quick sip. "Good stuff, Mom. Is Sean in his office?"

"Can I take Sean a cookie?" Ava asked.

"Of course," Shirley said.

Ava grabbed another cookie and took off running.

Brendan glanced at his mom and at the delight on her face. "She's sure made a difference in our lives, hasn't she?"

Shirley sighed. "The blessing we didn't know we needed. On another note, what do you know about that wreck? Wiley mentioned something about a bus full of tourists and a moving van."

"I witnessed it. I'm the one who called it in. I pulled a young man off the top of the bus who had a bad cut on his leg. He's Josie Fallin's brother."

Amalie gasped. "*The* Josie Fallin?"

Brendan nodded. "I'm hoping they got him to surgery in time. He was bleeding pretty bad. I even found a little boy in the ditch who'd been ejected from the wreck. It's been a day," he said.

Shirley's mouth dropped. "Good lord! I had no idea. Well, you know you were there at that moment for a reason, don't you?"

He nodded. "Yes, ma'am. And I got a very desperate hug from a little boy when I pulled him out of the weeds."

Shirley's eyes welled. "Bless his little heart. How will they manage in the dark?"

"I think the only thing they're still waiting on is a commercial tow truck with a lift to get that bus rolled back over, but they have floodlights."

She sighed. "Of course. But you know me, I'm bound to worry. Now, go say hi to your brother. I'm making steaks and baked potatoes. You're invited to supper."

"I better be," he said, and kissed her on the cheek and then left the kitchen.

Ava was sitting in Sean's lap at the computer and, with his instructions, learning how to play a game he'd pulled up, when Brendan walked in.

Sean looked up. "Hey, BJ. How's the hotel business?"

"We're supposed to call him Brendan," Ava muttered, without taking her gaze from the computer screen.

Sean grinned and ignored her.

"The hotel business is sketchy," Brendan muttered.

Sean frowned. "What do you mean?"

"I don't trust the manager Ray hired, and his daughter, who lives with him, is a royal pain. I can't go anywhere in the hotel without her popping up out of nowhere. She's a nutcase. I'm sick of her and her father."

Sean frowned. "Has anyone talked to Ray about them?"

"Nobody wants to worry Ray. Stress is the last thing he needs. Liz is there. She's still the go-between for her dad and knows what's going on about most things, so we leave it up to her to share what she thinks he can handle."

"What are you going to do?" Sean said.

"Put up with Larry, and ignore the daughter until I can't," Brendan said. "Enough about all that. Hey, Ava, what are you playing?"

Her eyes were still glued to the computer screen and the moving figures. "A game," she muttered.

Sean wiggled his eyebrows at his brother and took another bite of the cookie Ava brought him.

Brendan left them to it and returned to the kitchen to help his mom and Amalie finish supper.

"Want me to grill the steaks?" he asked.

Shirley handed him a pair of tongs. "With my blessing," she said.

Amalie elbowed him teasingly. "You're handy dandy in the kitchen, little brother. You're going to make some woman happy."

"Cooking is only one of my skills," he said.

Shirley blushed.

Amalie laughed.

Brendan grinned. Women didn't scare him. In fact,

now that he thought about it, nothing scared him much anymore.

––––––––––

It was very late by the time the road had been cleared and Wiley was finally headed home. He'd already talked to Linette and asked her to check on Lisa Hamilton and her son, Davey, and to see if Alex Fallin had come through surgery okay so he could let Brendan know.

Linette was staying at the hospital, taking a double shift to help cover the influx of injured patients, and his mom had already called to tell him she'd put Ava to bed, so he was going home alone. He would stop by the house early in the morning with clean clothes for Ava, then take her on to school.

The drive up the mountain felt longer than usual, but someone had graded the road, making the drive a little easier. By the time he pulled up to the house, all he could think about was a hot bath.

He walked into the old two-story house that had once belonged to their great-aunt Ella Pope and headed for the kitchen, grabbed a bottle of beer from the fridge and then went upstairs. He took a quick sip of the beer as he started the bathwater, dumped in the bath salts, and then went back to his and Linette's bedroom and stripped. His uniform was as muddy and bloody as he was, but a trip to the cleaners would fix that. He stepped into the tub with his beer, sank down into the hot water, and closed his eyes.

———————

A few days had passed since the raid on Wilhem Crossley's warehouse and his son, Tipton, was on his way home from the airport. Wilhem had skipped going to the office today so he'd be home when Tip arrived.

A few minutes later, he heard a car pull up in front of the estate and looked out. It was Tipton, all bundled up against the cold, getting out of a cab. Wilhem went to the door to greet him. "Welcome home, Son."

"Dad! Man it's good to be home!" Tip said.

"And it's good to have you home," Wilhem said as he closed the door.

Tip dropped the luggage and gave his dad a big hug. "The trip was very successful. The Hong Kong market is booming, as is the one in Osaka. Oh…I also have some great reproduction pieces coming in from Greece."

"Good, that's good, but we have to talk," Wilhem said.

"Sure thing," Tip said, and then saw the frown on his dad's face. "What's wrong? Are you okay?"

"It's not me; it's something to do with the company. I'll have Borders take your luggage up. Get comfortable, and then meet me in the library."

Tip frowned. "This sounds serious."

"About as serious as it gets," Wilhem said. "Have you had breakfast?"

"Not yet."

"I'll ring Cook to bring some rolls and coffee to the library," Wilhem said. Father and son parted company in the foyer, only to rejoin each other in the library a short while later.

Tip entered, poured himself some coffee, grabbed a sweet roll, and took a bite before moving to the blazing log in the fireplace.

"So, what's up?" he said as he took his first bite.

Wilhem shoved his hands in his pockets and began to explain. The look on his son's face went from shock, to disbelief, to anger.

"What the hell, Dad? How did this happen right under our noses? Oh my God. Are we in trouble, too? Do the feds believe we had anything to do with all that?"

"No, no," Wilhem said. "I suspected something was off but couldn't put my finger on it, so right after you left, I hired an auditor specializing in corporate crime who soon found the money trail, what had happened, and then where the money was actually going. We are the ones who turned all of this over to the authorities, so we're in the clear."

Tip was in shock. "It was someone within the corporation, wasn't it? Had to be. How could they hide our money when—" He stopped. "Oh my God, it had to be someone in accounting to be able to juggle accounts like that. Am I right?"

Wilhem nodded. "It was Maury Paget. He agreed to testify for a lesser charge."

"Where's the justice in that?" Tip shouted. "He gets off easy for robbing us blind? How much money? How much have we lost?"

Wilhem sighed. "Millions."

The shock on Tip's face was evident. "Oh my God. Are we in trouble financially? I can sell Mother's estate. She left it to me when she passed. We hardly ever use it."

"No, no, Son. We're not in that kind of trouble. We're still comfortably solvent, but it was a big hit. Paget swears he'll give up everything he knows, but not before he gets a deal from the justice department. And this does involve federal authorities, because the kidnapped women were being shipping out of the U.S. bound for foreign ports."

Tip dropped the sweet roll in the trash. "I'm sick to my stomach," he muttered. "Why didn't you call? I would have come home."

"The feds gave us a gag order. No mention of anything until after the raid, and even then, there was nothing you could have done. Nothing I could have done. Had it not been for Harley Banks, it would still be ongoing."

"Who's he?" Tip asked.

"The auditor, and he's a she."

"Oh. Right. So, where are we legally? Are we in limbo until the trial, or can we continue to do business as usual? I ask because there will be shipments arriving within the month."

"We're clear, but we'll have to unload at a different warehouse. The one we've been using is still considered a crime scene."

"What a mess," Tip said. "Well, we'll do what we have to do. We'll unload the new shipments at the other warehouse until we get the big one back."

Wilhem slumped into a nearby chair. "I'm glad you're home."

The exhaustion on his father's face was evident, and in that moment, Tip saw the age on his father's face and wanted to cry. He dropped to his knees in front of Wilhem's chair and hugged him.

"Don't worry, Dad. I've got this."

———

Days after the wreck outside of Jubilee, Brendan had still not mentioned his part in the rescues to anyone at work. In his mind that was over, but there was still unrest at the Serenity Inn, beginning almost from the day of the new manager's arrival.

Ray Caldwell, the owner of the inn, had been in Boston for over five months now, recovering from open-heart surgery.

Larry Beaumont, the new manager, came with a respectable résumé and unforeseen baggage—a twenty-four-year-old daughter named Justine, who took to living in the hotel penthouse like she'd been born to it. Once she figured out that she had the run of the hotel, the spa, the massage therapists, the hotel beauty salon, and room service from the hotel kitchens, she abused every aspect of those services.

Unfortunately, Justine's résumé was not as spotless as her father's. She'd flunked out of one college and was kicked out of another, and had done two stints in a rehab for alcoholics. She'd just moved home with Larry when he was offered the position in Jubilee, so she happily packed up and came with him. Who wouldn't want to live in the penthouse of a five-star hotel?

But after arriving, she'd balked at going to work anywhere within the tourist community. In her mind, she wasn't serving the public in any way. She was meant to be the one being served. And, she hadn't been at the hotel long before she caught a glimpse of the most gorgeous man she'd ever seen.

Finding out he worked at the hotel was icing on the cake, and learning he was the head pastry chef, even better. His name was Brendan Pope. He was someone with cachet and a good salary, plus he piqued every sexual instinct she had. The only problem was, they were more than five months into their stay, and Brendan Pope had turned down every blatant invitation she'd given him.

Two days ago, she'd been standing out on the balcony, having morning coffee and wishing she'd put on a coat before she'd come out, when she saw him come speeding into the employee parking lot on his motorcycle.

Brendan Pope. Obviously late for work! The main dining room would be packed today and tonight because of Valentine's Day, and he wasn't on the job!

When she saw him dismount and finger-comb his hair after taking off the helmet, she got hot, which angered her even more. She was angry at being rebuffed and was looking for revenge. Maybe she needed to apply pressure in another area, so she picked up her phone and called her dad. The phone rang twice and then he answered.

"Hey, sweetheart. Happy Valentine's Day. Did you see the pink roses I sent to you?"

"Yes, I did, and thank you. You are such a good daddy," she said, and then pretended concern as she continued their conversation. "A few minutes ago, I stepped out on the balcony for a bit of fresh air and saw your star pastry chef just arriving for work. He's late, and considering the holiday and all, and at the rate of what he's being paid, I would think that shouldn't be happening."

"He's not late. He asked for the time days ago. Personal business. The staff is perfectly capable of standing in for him for a few hours."

She frowned. "Oh, well, whatever then," she said.

Frustrated that she couldn't get Brendan in trouble, she soon disconnected.

The moment Larry's call ended, he went back to his computer to check inventory records and see what was on request for reorders.

It had been Larry's decision to change a couple of vendors Ray Caldwell was using. Larry had a cousin in the wholesale business, and one of his lines was single-use bars of soap and travel-size bottles of shampoos and lotions that hotels and motels used as complimentary toiletries. The products were cheap and came in simple plastic vials, rather than the clear plastic with the hotel name and logo on the labels from the vendor Ray used. He also changed their meat purchases to a wholesaler he knew. The meat and cuts were of a lesser quality, but Larry made the same deal with him that he'd made with his cousin.

In return for him giving them the business at the Serenity Inn, they would upcharge their own cheaper products to the same amount Ray had been paying before. Then the purchasing department would think nothing of it, pay the bills as usual, and Larry and the wholesalers would split the extra profits.

This way, Larry was getting two monthly bonuses under the table without anyone knowing. He'd done it a time or two before and never been caught, and he liked knowing he had a nest egg besides his regular salary.

―――――――――

Oblivious to the fact that Justine Beaumont had just tried to tattle on him, Brendan entered the staff entrance of the hotel. He thrived in his chosen field, but his job had become complicated since the manager's arrival.

He'd become the focus of Justine Beaumont's fancy, to the point it was nothing shy of stalking. She wouldn't keep her hands off him and stalked him throughout the hotel. She lurked in the staff hallways trying to catch him coming or going, and jumped in elevators with him at every chance. He'd been semi-patient at first, then began ignoring her completely, up until last month when she waylaid him again in an elevator.

He had been waiting for the staff elevator and checking messages on his phone when the car finally arrived. The door opened. He glanced up, saw it was empty, and walked on, still reading the message. Just as the doors were closing, he heard footsteps and turned to see Justine slip inside.

"That was close," she said, and gave him a look.

He pocketed his phone the minute he saw it was her, and when she headed toward him with a smirk on her face, he knew from past experience that he was going to have to fight his way out.

"How about a little quickie? We could always stop

the car," she whispered, and put her hands on his chest and leaned in to him. She was reaching below his belt when he grabbed her wrists, spun her into the corner, and pinned her hands above her head.

The tone of his voice was flat and as emotionless as his expression. "What's the matter with you? No means no."

She laughed. "I want what I want. A fight just makes everything better."

"You're not getting anything from me, including that fight. Grow the hell up," he said, and turned her loose.

She turned on the tears, and slipped the whiny baby tone into her voice. "Why are you so mean? I just want to be friends," she said.

"I'm not mean, and turn off the tears. They're fake and so are you. You don't want a friend. You want to get laid and that's not happening. Not with me. You've been stalking me for months like some hooker on a street corner trying to score an easy fifty on Saturday night. I'm telling you for the last time…leave me the hell alone."

Her face was twisted with rage as she pulled a knife out of her pocket and swung it at his face.

Shocked, he jumped back. The knife missed his face, but left a long ugly scratch down the side of his neck.

He knocked the knife out of her hand and slammed her against the back wall of the elevator just as the doors opened.

Justine was screaming obscenities and scrambling for the knife when he punched a random number on the panel and leaped out just as the doors were closing. He could hear her screaming and cursing as the doors went shut.

He was holding a handkerchief to his neck as he walked into the kitchen.

"Brendan! What the hell?" Chef Randolph cried.

"Justine. Swung a knife at my face and missed," he muttered.

"Oh my God! That does it! Someone needs to tell Ray about this!" he said.

Brendan shook his head. "No, that's the last thing Ray needs to know. Her father is the one who needs to tie a knot in her chain, but he's oblivious."

"Go down to the break room. I'll make a call to see if the EMTs will make a house call," Randolph said.

Brendan nodded, but skipped the elevator and took the stairs down. He was in the break room when the EMTs arrived.

"It's not deep, but I probably need a tetanus shot, and I can't work in the kitchen with an open wound. Can you bandage me up?" he asked.

"Do we need to know how this happened?" one of the EMTs asked.

"Probably not," Brendan said. "And whatever you do, don't tell my brothers."

After that, he started taking the stairs to evade her. And that was a month ago. Now when they saw each other, if looks could kill, Brendan would already be dead.

   None of the staff liked her. She stomped through the hotel demanding this, and complaining about that, and then obviously repeating her complaints to her father. Larry would appear soon afterward, chiding them for mistreating the guests, when in truth, he was referring to his daughter's imaginary mistreatment.

But today, Justine Beaumont was the last thing on Brendan's mind as he hurried into the staff entrance, stored his helmet and jacket in his locker, and then took the staff elevator up to the floor where he worked.

   Within minutes, he was in the baking area, suited up in a snow-white chef's jacket and baker's cap, overseeing the fresh batches of breads and rolls coming out of the ovens, making sure there were plenty on hand for the noon crowd, and starting more dough to rise for the dinner crowd tonight. Once he was satisfied all that was in progress, he began checking the quality of various desserts for the dessert carts and pulling pastries from the coolers to put his finishing touches on them for tonight. It was business as usual, with waiters coming and going with orders, and the staff from room service coming to pick up orders to be delivered. They were racing to get the orders ready for a table of twelve when they got a room service order from the penthouse.

As always, the picky details of what Justine wanted to eat irked Thomas Randolph, the hotel's chef de cuisine. She'd just ordered shrimp puttanesca, even though it wasn't on the lunch menu, and pecan pie, which also wasn't on the menu.

Chef Randolph banged a pan and cursed aloud. And when one of the kitchen staff went to the pastry area about the pie, Brendan just shrugged it off.

"We don't have pecan pie on the menu anymore, and haven't had it for nearly a year," he said. "Just call her back and ask for another choice."

"She's not going to like that answer," the waiter said.

"She is not our problem. The diners waiting for their orders are our main focus," Brendan said.

"Yes, Chef," the waiter said, and headed for the room service area to call her back.

When Justine got that message, she cursed out the woman who'd called her and hung up, then grabbed her cell phone.

Chapter 3

LARRY BEAUMONT WAS ON THE DOWNSIDE OF A chicken salad sandwich when Justine's number popped up on caller ID. He rolled his eyes, wondering what was wrong now, wiped his hands, and answered.

"Hey, honey, what's up?"

Justine was screaming and crying in his ear, making no sense, running her words together, and all he could make out was something about the kitchen staff refusing to bring her lunch order to the penthouse.

"Justine, darling…slow down, take a breath, and start over. I can't understand what you're saying."

Justine wiped her eyes, blew her nose, and turned on her shaky little-girl voice.

"Daddy, I ordered lunch through room service as usual, and they just called me back and said I couldn't have what I'd ordered and to pick something else, and I don't want something else," she wailed. "I just wanted what I ordered. Nobody likes me here. Brendan Pope is hateful. He won't even speak to me. The staff is mean to me. I hate this hillbilly town. I hate these mountains. I don't know why we came here," she wailed.

Larry frowned. "Just calm down. I'll go speak to them."

Justine shifted into a whisper. "I'm sorry to be a bother."

"You're not a bother," Larry said. "I'll bring your order up myself in a while, and we'll talk."

"Thank you, Daddy," she said. She was smiling when she disconnected.

Unaware of his daughter's deceit, Larry stormed out of his office and took the staff elevator up to the dining room and down the hall into the kitchens.

He came in shouting, bringing the entire room to a shocked halt. "What the hell is going on in here? My daughter ordered a simple meal from room service, and you refused to fill her order? Somebody better have a real good explanation for that."

Chef Randolph threw his hands up in the air and shouted back. "There is a good explanation! We have a room service menu! She ordered food that was not on the menu. She ordered food that's not even on the dining room menu. Half the time what she wants is not even in stock in this kitchen."

Larry blinked. "What did she order that was so outrageous?"

"She wanted shrimp puttanesca made with ziti pasta, not linguini, not spaghetti, and pecan pie, and at this moment, we have two-thirds of the tables in the dining room full of diners waiting for the food we do have on the menu!" he shouted.

Larry frowned. "Well, what kind of shrimp and pasta do you have on the menu?"

"Fried, and the only pasta on the menu is spaghetti and meat sauce, which is on the children's menu. This is a tourist destination in the mountains of Kentucky. Not Rockefeller Center!" Randolph shouted. "There are a dozen other very tasty entrées she could choose from." And then he turned his back on Larry and began slicing off servings of prime rib to be plated.

Larry was still struggling with an answer when he spotted Brendan Pope on the far side of the kitchens and started toward him with renewed indignation.

"Brendan Pope! I want to talk to you!" Larry shouted.

Brendan was piping strawberry gelée on tiny cheese-cake tarts.

"I'm listening," he said, without looking up.

"You will look at me when I'm talking to you!" Larry shouted.

Brendan took a deep breath, and straightened up to his full height. Now Beaumont was craning his neck and looking up just to meet Brendan's gaze.

"I'm looking. Now what?"

Larry was shouting again. "Why can't Justine have a simple piece of pecan pie?"

Brendan's eyes narrowed. That moment of being shouted at was Clyde Wallace all over again, yelling at his sons every day of their lives. And for Brendan, being confronted like this again took every ounce of control he had not to punch Larry. Instead, he took a deep breath and answered.

"She can't have pecan pie because it is no longer on the dessert cart menu. Therefore we do not randomly make pecan pie, and I might add, this was Ray's decision, not mine."

"That's Mr. Caldwell, to you, not Ray. He's your employer, not your buddy," Larry snapped.

Brendan took a step toward Larry—so close now he could see the balding spot in the crown of Larry's head.

"No, he's not my buddy. He's part of my family. He's an uncle to my cousin, Rusty Pope. Liz Devon is Rusty's first cousin. So, yes, we call him Ray. And it was *Ray* who made the decision to quit offering pecan pie over a year ago because of the nationwide drought that sent pecan prices soaring, and it was no longer cost efficient to serve them, so your daughter can make another choice. We have fine desserts here."

Larry was dumbfounded. He had not known about the familial connection, but he wasn't finished with Brendan.

"That's as it may be," Ray muttered. "But Justine says you are mean to her. Rude to her. Won't talk to her. I'd like to know why."

Brendan looked up. Even though everyone was still racing around the kitchen filling orders, now they were doing it in silence. He knew they were listening. And they all knew she'd been chasing after Brendan for months, and they'd all suffered their own incidents with her.

"I'd rather not say. Just let it go," he said.

Larry frowned. Now he was angry and suspicious. "I'm not letting anything go. The least you could do is be decent to her. She doesn't have friends here."

Brendan refused to comment, but Anthony, his head sous-chef, wasn't as reticent. He liked Brendan, and he didn't like seeing him put on the spot like this.

"Brendan isn't going to speak up for himself because he's too much of a gentleman, but nobody ever accused me of that, and I don't mind telling you exactly what we all know. Your daughter won't keep her hands off of him. We've seen her grab his ass and crotch so many times it's become embarrassing. She stalks him every-where. We've all witnessed it. A month ago he came in to work bleeding from a slash on his neck. Your daugh-ter cornered him in the staff elevator and tried it on him again, and when he told her no, she pulled a knife and tried to cut his face. He dodged. Chef Randolph called the EMTs to tend the wound, and if you look closely, you can see the red place where it's still healing. She's a freak. He's made it more than plain to her that he's not interested, but she won't take no for an answer."

Larry was horrified. He knew his daughter was spoiled, but he'd never witnessed this behavior, so he wouldn't let himself believe it and brushed Anthony off.

"I wasn't talking to you," he said.

But Anthony wasn't through. "No, sir, but you came in here shouting at us and throwing accusations around, so you now have to hear the answers to the questions you asked. And there's more. Justine slapped Ronnie, the clerk in the gift store, and she did it in front of customers, and left Ronnie in tears."

"She's hateful to all of us," a waitress said. "She thinks just because you're the manager that it has given her the power to speak for you. She goes through the dining room at rush times, criticizing waitstaff in front of diners and ordering them around. We sincerely hope those aren't your wishes she's putting forward, because you're about to have a mass staff walkout if it continues."

Brendan was in awe of the people who'd spoken up for him, but he could stay silent no longer. "Look, Larry, don't blame us if you don't like the answers you received. But you need to realize that since your arrival, she has single-handedly destroyed the morale of this workforce, and as far as we're concerned, she's your problem, not ours."

Larry's face was flushed with anger. "How dare you talk about—"

"You asked," Brendan said.

"I don't believe you, and you could at least be willing to interact with Justine. Talk to her. Be nice to her. She doesn't have any friends here and she's—"

Brendan's patience snapped. "What the actual hell? She tried to cut my face! Did you really just order me to...I don't know quite how to say it...succumb to her charms?"

Larry's face was as red as his tie. "How dare you talk—"

Brendan had had enough and was now standing toe-to-toe with the man, shouting back.

"No, sir! How dare *you* suggest I cater to her wishes. You sound like her pimp. She's made coming to work a living hell. Stalking is a crime, and I have two brothers who are officers on the Jubilee police force, and Ray would be very unhappy to learn what has been going on here, so keep her away from me, and I suggest you keep her out of your business, too."

Larry was speechless, embarrassed, and suddenly seeing the situation he was in. He didn't need people looking into his little sideline. He turned around and headed for the exit with his head down.

"So do I fry shrimp or not?" Chef Randolph snapped as Larry walked past.

"No," he mumbled and kept walking.

The moment he was gone, the noise level resumed.

Brendan picked up the bag of piping gelée and went back to work. Orders came in. Orders were going out. And Larry Beaumont was on his way to the penthouse.

He rode the elevator up in silence, but he was shouting his daughter's name as he walked in the door.

Justine heard the roar and rolled her eyes, but didn't budge from the sofa where she was sitting. "What is the matter with you, and where's my food?" she asked, and then gasped in shock when her father yanked her up by her shoulders and began shaking her.

"What's the matter with me? The better question is, what's the matter with *you*?" he shouted. "I have hotel staff ready to walk out because of what you've been pulling."

Justine's eyes welled. "I don't know what you're talking about. I told you Brendan hates me."

"Oh, he said nothing about you. Not even the fact that you tried to cut his face. He refused to say a word. It was the rest of the staff that came to his rescue. Where the hell is that knife? Have you been putting your hands on him? Have you been accosting him in the halls? I can check security footage in elevators and halls, so don't lie!"

Justine's stomach knotted. She'd never thought of that. She let the tears roll. "I didn't mean anything by it. I was just flirting a little."

Larry glared. "Flirts don't slice up the guys they're interested in. Even once with your hands on him is out of line. Doing it repeatedly is called sexual assault. If he'd been doing it to you, he would already be in jail. And speaking of jail, he has two brothers on the Jubilee police force, and he is related to Ray Caldwell and his daughter, Liz Devon, our event coordinator. He's fed up enough to press charges if it doesn't stop, and I'm on the verge of being fired because of you!"

"We should have had this information sooner," she muttered, swiping away the fake tears with both hands.

Larry stared. "What are you saying?"

She shrugged. "I would have steered clear of him, that's what."

Larry was dumbfounded, and it showed. "So, you're

not sorry it happened, just regretting you've been found out. Is that what you're telling me?"

Justine should have been warned by the sudden quiet in her father's voice.

"You can't blame me. I'm bored here," she said.

"Did you slap the clerk in the gift shop in front of customers? Did you chastise our waitstaff in front of customers?" he asked.

"So what? If you don't keep people in line, they get sloppy," she said.

Now Larry was shouting. "That's not your job. You don't work here. I do. You have no authority here at all. If I hear about one more incident that you're involved in, I will put you on the plane with a one-way ticket back to Dallas. You can live with your mother. You're just like her."

Justine froze. "I'm not living with her."

"Fine! You're twenty-four years old. You can live where you want, but it won't be under my roof." He shook her by the shoulders. "Do. You. Understand?"

Justine twisted out of his grasp. "You don't talk to me like that."

"I just did!" Larry said, and headed for the door.

"What about my lunch?" she shrieked.

"Pick something from the menu or do without!" he shouted back, and slammed the door behind him.

Justine was in shock. Something told her that she'd just lost the edge of ever coercing her father into anything again.

Larry got back to his office, dumped what was left of his chicken salad sandwich in the garbage, pulled a bottle of whiskey from the bottom drawer, and poured himself a shot. He downed it like medicine, returned the bottle to the drawer, and then buried his face in his hands.

This might have been one of the most humiliating days of his life. Justine was out of control, just like always, only now she was too old to punish. He couldn't ground her anymore. He couldn't take away her privileges, and he didn't know how to get rid of her. He couldn't even call his ex-wife for advice because Justine was just like her. She would think the ass-grabbing was funny. She would call her daughter fiery for swinging a knife at a man. She was just as demanding as their daughter. He was still bemoaning his fate when his cell phone rang. He scrubbed his face with both hands and then answered.

"Hello."

"Larry, it's me, Joe. Just letting you know I sent your cut for the month to your Dallas account."

Larry breathed a quick sigh of relief that it was the meat wholesaler and not another problem about his daughter. "Thanks, Joe. Much appreciated."

"Oh…hey, I'm the one who's thanking you. We just received a new order from the hotel purchasing department. It'll ship out this week with the regular invoice enclosed."

"Perfect," Larry said. "Have a good day."

With this bit of good news to go on, Larry disconnected and went back to work.

━━━━━━━━

Justine needed to make peace with her father and the sooner, the better. But instead of using her cell, she used the landline in the room and punched in the number to his office.

Unaware it was Justine calling, Larry answered on the second ring.

"Hello, this is Larry."

She took a loud, shuddering breath and turned on her little-girl voice...the one that sounded like she'd been crying.

"Daddy, I'm sorry. I'm really, really sorry. None of that will happen again, I swear."

Larry sighed. "I've heard this before and you've reneged every time. I don't have time for any more of your drama. I'm about to leave the office. I have a meeting with the event coordinator."

"Fine. Be like that," she snapped. "I'm going for a drive."

"And I'll see you at dinner," he said, then disconnected and hurried out of the room.

Justine grabbed her key card, boarded the penthouse elevator, and headed back down to her father's office. She needed a little information about Brendan Pope and knew it would be on the job form he filled out. She couldn't get into her father's computer, but there were hard copies in the files in the back room. It wouldn't take long to get what she wanted there.

After Larry stormed out of the kitchen, Brendan went back to work, but it felt like he'd just gone ten rounds with Clyde Wallace. The only thing missing was the actual beating his father delivered afterward. The blowup with Larry Beaumont was long overdue, but it had done a number on Brendan, as fighting always did. He shut down.

He'd gone through all kinds of kitchen drama during his years in New York. He'd had asshole roommates, chefs that needed to be on Prozac, and had a thousand complaints and failures heaped upon him to get to the skill level he was today. He had confidence in his ability to make magic in the kitchen and was still searching for that one woman who felt like a keeper. But never in his life had he ever dealt with someone like Justine Beaumont. There was an odd glitch about her that went beyond her irrational behavior. Definitely the bad seed of that family. Something was definitely wrong with her, and he wanted out of her whirlpool of drama.

He guessed Larry lit into her good after his trip through the kitchen, but there was no way to know how she would react to being called down. His gut instinct was that she was going to find a way to make him the scapegoat, but time would tell.

By the time he finally left the hotel that night, he was emotionally exhausted. He drove through the streets of Jubilee and thought of Alex Fallin and the little boy he'd found in the ditch, and imagined the mother's relief when they were reunited. He knew from Wiley that Alex's surgery had been successful and that the little boy had been reunited with his mother. It felt good to know he'd helped make that happen.

By the time he pulled up in his driveway, he'd turned loose of everything to do with the hotel. All he was thinking about was a hot shower and some downtime. He aimed the remote at his garage door, and as it was going up, he glanced over at his front door and thought he saw something taped to it. He pulled into the garage and got out. The garage door was lowering as he went through the house to the front door.

There was a note taped to the door that had been written with a black marker. He didn't recognize the writing, but the message was both brief and angry.

I'LL MAKE YOU SORRY YOU WERE EVER BORN

The moment he read it, the hair crawled on the back of his neck. Justine Beaumont! It had to be her! But how did she know where he lived? And what did she mean by this threatening note? He knew she was capable of almost anything. What the hell would she do?

He took a picture of it still taped to the door, then got a plastic bag from the pantry, removed the note with a pair of tweezers, and dropped it in the bag. If this was how she was going to play it, he needed to start covering his ass and, starting today, report every uninvited move she made.

He ate supper standing up at the kitchen island, still stewing about all of the events of the day until good sense prompted him to let Liz Devon know what was happening.

He went to get his laptop, then sent her a detailed email, including the harassment he'd been putting up with from Justine and of how she'd been treating staff. He didn't like the feeling of being a narc, but Liz was her father's eyes and ears while he was still in recovery, and she needed to know what was happening, too.

After it was sent, he got ready for bed, set the alarm for his usual 4:00 a.m. wake-up, and crawled into bed.

———

Liz Devon didn't think this day was ever going to be over, and then finally it ended. She didn't even remember driving home until she was walking into the penthouse of Hotel Devon. The fact that she was married to the man who owned Serenity Inn's biggest competitor had never been a conflict of interest for either of them, but her father's heart attack and then the ensuing heart surgery had scared all of them. She was already worried about Larry Beaumont's managerial skills at her dad's hotel, and the meeting she'd had with Larry this afternoon only exacerbated it.

She still had a headache from the stress of the fight that had ensued and kept going over the incident, thinking if she'd been in the wrong.

It all began when Larry walked into her office without knocking, then sat down without so much as a greeting.

———

Liz was on the phone with Josie Fallin, discussing the upcoming event at the hotel and just learning that Josie's brother was one of the passengers on the charter bus that crashed.

"I can only imagine how terrified you must have been to get that message," Liz said.

"It was horrifying," Josie said. "Our parents are deceased. Alex and I only have each other. I don't know what I would have done. Alex must have had an angel watching over him, because the guy who witnessed the wreck also saved him from bleeding to death. Alex said he works at your hotel."

"Really? I haven't heard anyone talking about it. Do you remember his name?" Liz asked.

"Yes, Brendan Pope. I remember because it's the same last name as the mountain above Jubilee."

"Oh wow! He's the head pastry chef here. He'll be the one in charge of the baking aspect of your event."

"That's wonderful! I'll get to thank him in person," Josie said.

"He never said a word about this to any of us, although I shouldn't be surprised. His people aren't the kind to toot their own horn about anything. Anyway… back to the reason I called. I'm just confirming the number of attendees again before I make up the seating chart. Are we firm at two hundred?"

"Yes," Josie said. "That's how many RSVPs we've received and the cutoff for replies has come and gone."

"Okay then, we're good to go. Thanks, and our best to your brother."

"Thank you," Josie said, and disconnected.

Liz was still thinking about Brendan at the crash site when the door to her office opened abruptly and Larry Beaumont walked in. She looked up, a little taken aback by the rudeness of his behavior. He plopped down into the chair on the other side of her desk, gave her the quick once-over as he leaned back, then started talking.

"So, I hear we've scored a big event. Tell me about it," he said.

Liz shoved a lock of her dark hair behind her ear, adjusted her reading glasses, and pulled up the file on her computer.

"Josie Fallin is hosting a big event for her fan club and—"

Larry immediately interrupted. "Who's Josie Fallin?"

"The big country star who's headlining at one of the

music venues here. She's been here for a month and will be here for next three months before going on tour."

Larry rolled his eyes. "Oh. One of those hillbillies."

Liz glared. "That hillbilly, as you call her, is worth millions. Her fan base is worldwide. I think you need to keep that opinion to yourself."

Larry flushed, but said nothing.

"Now, back to business," Liz said. "We've been given a generous budget to set up the event exactly as she wants it, right down to specific food, decor, and special merchandise that she's furnishing for giveaways at the gathering. I'll be putting in the orders today so that we'll be sure to have it all on hand in a timely fashion. It's been scheduled for two weeks hence, which should give us ample time."

"Oh, just give me a list and I'll do the ordering," Larry said.

Liz frowned. "No, sir. I'm the event coordinator. That's part of my job."

Larry leaned forward, slapped his hand on the arm of the chair he was sitting in, and raised his voice a good two octaves.

"And I'm managing this hotel, and I know where to get the best deal for—"

Liz interrupted. "Josie Fallin didn't ask for the best deal. She asked for the best. It's her money we're spending, and she's paying us handsomely for it. I know what she wants, and we're not sacrificing quality."

Larry stood abruptly, shouting now. "You don't have the—"

Liz stood to face him, shouting back. "You forget who you're talking to, mister. My father owns this hotel. He hired me to do this job, and he's damn sure never going to fire me. And yes, I do have the authority to do the ordering for all the events I coordinate. I know how to do my job, and you just overstepped yours."

Larry turned and walked out of her office as abruptly as he'd entered, slamming the door behind him as he went.

And now, hours later, Liz was sick to her stomach still thinking about the shouting match. Turmoil bothered her. Turmoil on the job was even worse. And this wasn't the first time she and Beaumont had an argument, but this was the ugliest. She was beginning to wonder why he'd insisted on controlling something outside of his responsibilities. She was thinking about the wisdom of calling her dad when her laptop signaled a new email. When she saw it was from Brendan, she opened it.

Horrified beyond words at what she read, she felt as if she had no options. Now she *had* to call her dad. This was still his hotel, and he needed to know what was going on and make changes, if necessary. But not tonight and have him worry to the point of not being able to rest. First thing tomorrow would be soon enough.

She sighed, closed her laptop, but stayed at her desk, staring off into space.

Michael Devon was in the elevator on his way up to the penthouse. He'd just finished a dinner meeting in a private dining area of the hotel and was ready to see Liz and catch up on their day together.

As he walked into the quiet, all the hassles of the day fell away. The place smelled of lavender and cinnamon. He smiled, guessing Liz had indulged in her favorite lavender bath salts, and the cinnamon was most likely from her penchant for the cinnamon rolls from Granny Annie's Bakery downtown. He loved Liz deeply, but he was also worried for her and about his father-in-law, Ray.

"Liz, honey! I'm home," he called out.

She answered. "In the office!"

He took off his tie as he was walking and draped it over the doorknob to their bedroom before moving across the hall into the office, then took one look at her pale face and slumped shoulders and hurried to her, fearing the worst.

"Sweetheart, what's wrong? Is it Ray?"

She stood up and walked into his arms. "Yes, and no, but not what you think. There's trouble at the hotel... even more than I knew about. I just got an email from Brendan and found out even more. It's gotten to the point that I'm going to have to tell Dad, but I dread it. I don't want to make things worse for him."

Michael hugged her closer. "Let me get out of this

suit and I'll meet you in the living room. We'll talk, and if there's anything I can do to help, you know I will."

Liz was close to tears. "Thank you, love. You're the best." She followed him out of the office, but when he went to change clothes, she headed for the wet bar in the living room, poured each of them a glass of wine, and was waiting for him when he came back.

Michael sat down beside her, leaned over, and kissed her full on the lips, then stroked his finger down the side of her face.

"We don't do this nearly often enough," he said, and then picked up his glass of wine and took a quick sip. "Okay, talk to me. What's going on?"

Liz cradled her wineglass in both hands, debating about what to share, and then sighed. Michael was her father's competitor, but he was her husband. He would never betray her confidences.

"It's Larry Beaumont, the manager Dad hired. As you know, his twentysomething daughter came with him, and it appears that she's been running roughshod over everyone for months, throwing her weight around with all the staff when she has no business interfering. They're at the point of rebellion. Brendan emailed me this evening. The daughter has been harassing him to the point that it's come to sexual harassment and stalking. He has rebuffed her attention and she's angry. He found a threatening note taped to his front door when he got home tonight. It was unsigned, but he suspects it was her. He's considering turning it over to the police. If her fingerprints are on it... Well, then I guess he has the option of filing charges against her for stalking, and from everything else I know, there's a whole hotel of staff who would testify on his behalf about what she's been doing."

"Good lord," Michael said.

"That's not all," Liz said. "The manager has changed things without approval and has changed vendors. We're still paying the same price for everything, but I'm questioning the reasons for why he took it upon himself to switch. Dad had good working relationships with all of them. And that's not all. Beaumont and I had a meeting this afternoon and wound up in a row. I have special food and wine and some specific decor I needed to order for an upcoming event. I was given a very generous budget from the host for arranging everything to her request, and Beaumont told me he'd do the ordering. I challenged that and won the argument, but he was furious. I feel like something's going on and I can't see it. I'm going to call Dad in the morning. He needs to know this. It's still his hotel, but the man he hired to run it is sketchy. I feel it."

"Ah, honey, what a mess. I'm so sorry," Michael said. "And yes, I agree with you. Ray needs to know. This may be the tipping point for your dad."

"What do you mean?" Liz asked.

"Ray's well-being is more important than that hotel, and after this health scare, he may be thinking about selling it."

"I've thought the same, but I wouldn't ask," she said.

"You don't have to. Ray will decide what's best for him and for the hotel. You'll call him in the morning, and I promise you, Ray Caldwell will have a solution for your problem, because that's the kind of man he is."

Chapter 4

UNAWARE OF THE ONGOING DRAMA AT HIS HOTEL, Ray Caldwell was at breakfast with his wife, Patricia, when his cell phone rang.

Still on guard about Ray's well-being, Patricia frowned. "Let it go to voicemail, dear. Eat your breakfast."

But Ray had already seen caller ID. "It's Liz," he said, then put his food aside to answer. "Good morning, darling! What a wonderful way to begin my day. It's cold and blustery here. What's happening in Jubilee?"

"It's been snowing a bit off and on, but today looks clear. It's so good to hear your voice, Dad. Is Mom there, too?"

"Yes, she is. I'll put you on speaker."

Liz sighed. Her mom was going to be angry with her for calling, but there was no help for it.

"Hi, Mom! Love you!" Liz said.

"We love you back," Patricia said. "Are you two going to talk business?"

Liz laughed. "Yes, please."

"Then I'll leave you to it. Ray, you can eat while you

two are talking. Skipping meals will not serve you," she said.

"Yes, ma'am," Ray said, and blew her a kiss as she left the room.

"Take it off speaker, Dad," Liz said.

Ray frowned as he followed her instructions. "What's wrong?"

"Nearly everything, and it's escalating," Liz said, and then began to fill him in on everything she knew, what had been reported to her, and finished it off with Brendan's email. "I don't know what to do about this. I know my part of the hotel business, but I have no skills in hotel management. I'm so sorry to be bothering you about this, but Michael gave me some advice I thought it best to follow. He reminded me what a smart busi-nessman you are, and that whatever needed to be done, you would have the answers for it."

Ray sighed. "Well, I appreciate my son-in-law's faith in me, and I am so sorry that any part of this burden has fallen on you. I have an idea. If it pans out, I'll call you later today, okay? Just leave this to me. Don't tell anyone we've spoken. I don't want to alert Beaumont or his daughter to that fact. And you're right. Something is very off. I would never agree to changing vendors or wholesalers, and there was no need to even do so. Sounds like he's giving business to his buddies, but I'm wondering what he's getting out of that. I don't know what's going on, but we're going to find out. For now, you go and have yourself a good day."

"Will do, Dad, and thank you. Michael was right. You rock."

Liz breathed a sigh of relief as she disconnected.

But Ray was frowning when the call ended. He needed to get to his office, but if he wanted any peace today, he had to finish breakfast first. He picked up his fork, wrinkled his nose at the vegan sausage, and continued his meal.

———

Harley Banks had been home for weeks. The snowfall that had welcomed her home was over, but nothing was melting. It was still there, just slushy and dirtier—a cold reminder of winter in Chicago.

She'd passed her time by working out in the gym in her apartment complex and swimming laps in the heated pool. When it got too confining inside, she walked down the block to the sports bar on the corner, ordered a beer and cheese nachos smothered in jalapeños, then picked a game to watch on the array of TVs hanging on the walls as she ate. She knew a few regulars but didn't interact with them beyond a little friendly hazing and a game of darts now and then. She wasn't looking for a relationship, and if she had been, she would not have gone to a sports bar to find it.

She'd awakened this morning to a fairly empty refrigerator and decided it was time to put in a grocery order for delivery. She had the list at her elbow as she opened the site on her laptop and glanced down at the first item on her list—which happened to be spray cheese that came out in cute swirls that she put on her crackers—thinking how horrified her mother would be to know she liked and ate such plebian foods. But before she could type it into the search bar, her cell phone rang. She glanced at caller ID, didn't recognize the name or number, which was normal in her line of work, and answered.

"Harley Banks."

"Miss Banks, my name is Ray Caldwell. Do you have a few moments to speak with me? It is business-related."

"Of course."

"Thank you. You were recommended to me by Wilhem Crossley. He's a business acquaintance and, as I understand, a man you recently worked for. He speaks highly of you, by the way."

"Yes, I've done work for him. How can I help you?" Harley asked.

"I'm a real estate developer and hotelier, but due to some health issues I've been having, I had to install a manager at the location where I'd been living and working, and I've just received word that there are grave issues arising that needs immediate attention. My problem is, I don't know what's happening to cause them, and I'm suspicious of the financial end of it, too. Are you available?"

"Is this hotel in the States or overseas?" Harley asked.

"In Kentucky, at a popular tourist attraction in a mountain town called Jubilee."

"I've heard of it," Harley said.

"Excellent. So, you can imagine the setup on-site. My hotel is called the Serenity Inn. My daughter, Liz, is the event coordinator there, but what's going on is beyond her ability to cope."

"Tell me what's happening," Harley said.

Ray began to explain, in depth, what was happening and what he needed to know, and then added, "I was given to understand that you are also capable of corporate auditing, as well as investigating corporate crime, is this correct?"

"Yes, sir. I am a licensed CPA specializing in corporate audits, and my private investigator's license avails me of other skills when needed."

"Are you available now?" Ray asked.

"Yes. I can leave as soon as tomorrow, if need be," she said.

"Perfect," Ray said. "What kind of fee do you need to begin, and how do you bill for your work? Money is no object, but I want to make sure you are compensated as needed before you arrive."

Harley gave him the numbers and an account to which payments to her were to be made.

"Perfect," Ray said. "I'll have the upfront fee in your account as soon as we hang up. My daughter, Liz, will simply alert the staff that I have hired someone to do an audit. It won't be a surprise to anyone because of my recent health issues. I'm considering selling the hotel anyway and would need this for prospective buyers.

That will cover the reason for your presence at the hotel and give you access to every aspect of the business. If there's anything illegal happening, I need to know. And if it's just a really bad manager, I need to know that, too. Your suite, food, and hotel amenities will be comped. You will have a computer set up in your suite giving you access to every aspect of the hotel business, and you can work from there. I also want to know if the food quality and service is lacking. Those are details, but my main concern is the money angle. I don't like that the manager has changed vendors and wholesalers. That smacks of a control he was not given."

"Understood," Harley said. "As for arriving there, what kind of travel is recommended?"

"The nearest airport is in Bowling Green. You'd have to rent a car and drive over Pope Mountain to get there, but helicopter charters come and go in Jubilee regularly. There are three different music venues there as well as the other tourist attractions, so strangers come and go by the hundreds, even in winter. If you'd prefer to fly in, I'll send you by chopper, and you can rent a car in Jubilee to get around."

"Then let's do the chopper," Harley said. "Tomorrow or the day after if need be. I'm in Chicago. Just give me details as to where to hook up with a chopper service here. I'll rent the car myself in Jubilee and add the charges to your final bill."

"Done," Ray said. "I'll text you with details as soon as I get the charter scheduled. Oh…one other thing. My head pastry chef is a man named Brendan Pope. He's on the verge of pressing charges against Justine Beaumont, the manager's daughter, for sexual harassment and stalking. I don't want to lose that man. He's a star at his job, and he's local to the area and highly popular. If you get in a tight spot, you can count on him. He has two brothers who are officers with the Jubilee police force, and a cousin, Cameron, who is ex-special forces. And Cameron's wife, my niece, is ex-FBI. Pope Mountain towers over the town of Jubilee, and the people who live on that mountain are some of the best people you will ever meet."

Harley was surprised by the high level of government security clearance he'd mentioned and the chef's situation. "Sexual harassment is a common demon of a workforce, but I don't think I've ever encountered it in reverse. A man being the target, I mean."

Ray sighed. "Well, men in the Pope family have a habit of being born larger than life and shockingly handsome. As a man, I will admit I'm a bit envious of such amazing DNA." And then he laughed. "When you meet him, you'll see what I mean. But they don't mess around. Their reputations are spotless, and their word is gold. Just remember that."

"Yes, sir," Harley said. "I'll go ahead and pack, and wait for further information."

"It's cold there. Pack for warmth," Ray added.

"Duly noted," she said, and disconnected, then glanced at her shopping list and closed her laptop. No need ordering in a fresh supply of food when she was going to be leaving again, so she was back to DoorDash until she left. But she was going to need clean clothes, and went to start a load of laundry.

———————

Ollie Prine didn't have the skills to hack into airline passenger lists or rental car sites to try and find this Harley Banks, but all he knew was she'd probably flown out of Philadelphia, rather than drive. There was very little information about her online, with no website, no social media presence, and no information as to where she lived. He knew more about her parents than he did about her. The only photos he found were of her as a young girl, always standing between her parents at some uppity social function.

He was surprised to learn her father was Jason Banks, a NASA scientist, and her mother, Judith, a well-known playwright and screenwriter. Harley had a master's degree in math and a CPA license, but she didn't have an office. She didn't own property or a car. He'd tried to get a background check and gotten blocked. That surprised him. Whatever else she did, she didn't advertise it. If he hadn't seen her with his own eyes, he would have thought she was a ghost.

And then out of the blue, Berlin called him.

"Update me," he said shortly.

Ollie gave him the rundown about all of the roadblocks.

"I have something that might help," Berlin said. "She's based in Chicago. I don't have an address. Just a phone number, but don't just call her up like a dumbass. Be smart. Figure out a way to use that number to find her. Got a pen and paper?"

"Hang on a sec and I'll put it in my phone," Ollie said.

"What kind of an enforcer are you? You do not want any record of a connection to her."

"I'm the kind who'll off his mother for the right money," Ollie snapped.

"Write this down," Berlin said, and read off a phone number. "Did you get it?"

"Yes, I—" Before Ollie could finish, the line went dead. "Asshole," he muttered, added the number to his phone anyway, then proceeded to book himself a one-way flight to Chicago, made a hotel reservation, and went to pack.

———

Ray spent the rest of the morning getting Harley Banks's travel arrangements made. He'd chartered a chopper for the day after tomorrow, sent a text back to Harley with the travel information, and ended with a long phone call to his daughter, Liz, to update her on what he was doing.

As soon as she answered, he began filling her in.

"Liz, this is what's happening, and what I need from

you. Notify Larry Beaumont I've hired a woman named Harley Banks to do an audit of the hotel in preparation to put it up for sale. It's common practice and he'll think nothing of it. Make sure one of the nicer suites is made available for her while she's on-site. Have a computer from our offices installed in her room with an all-access password that will get her into any account she needs to see, and you register her at the front desk before she arrives, which will be the day after tomorrow. The pilot will notify you about twenty minutes before they land so you can have a car waiting at the heliport to pick her up. She will be accessing every aspect of the hotel, from the purchasing department to housekeeping, guest amenities, and dining, and interviewing any staff members she deems necessary."

"Are you really planning on selling?" Liz asked.

"Your mother has been pushing the issue ever since my heart surgery, and I do have to accept the reality of my situation, but I hadn't thought seriously of it until now. If all of this trouble is happening without me on-site, I don't want the hotel to go downhill, and it's a good cover for Harley Banks's arrival. You can reassure Beaumont that his presence is appreciated and ask him to assist her with any requests she might make of him. If he's up to something and he panics and starts cleaning up and hiding what he's been doing, we might never find out what it was. And, as for the daughter's behavior, I'll message Brendan myself. I don't want him to feel threatened or pressured in any way, and I also don't want to lose him."

"Understood," Liz said. "I love you, Daddy. Say hi to Mom for me. I miss you both so much."

"We miss you, too," Ray said. "Our best to Michael."

When the call ended, Liz began implementing her father's instructions, and Ray looked up Brendan's phone number in his contacts and sent him a text.

Brendan, I've been made aware of ongoing problems at the hotel and your problems with Justine Beaumont. Rest assured this is being dealt with. However, if anything new occurs or the stalking continues, let me know. This is also confidential info, but I want you to know I've hired a corporate auditor/private investigator to look into the hotel finances. Her name is Harley Banks. To the staff, she will simply be an auditor preparing the paperwork for putting the hotel up for sale. I gave her your name in case she needs on-site assistance. I would appreciate any help you can give her. Since my health problems, I'm not ruling out the need to sell, but that's all in the future. Right now, I'm trying to stop a leak in the system before it becomes a flood. I don't want to lose you. You are a very valuable member of my staff and a well-loved member of my extended family.
Ray.

Brendan was finishing up for the day when he heard his phone signal a text, but he was in the middle of prepping for tomorrow and let it go, then forgot about it. He'd driven his car to work because he needed groceries before he went home and was on his way to the supermarket when he remembered the text. As soon as he parked, he pulled it up and read it.

He was relieved that Ray Caldwell had been made aware of the trouble and grateful for the reassurance that he wasn't being held responsible for someone else's actions. It wasn't the first time he'd wondered if Ray would keep the hotel.

Now it appeared a lot of it hinged on what they found out about the current management. He wondered about the auditor, and then shrugged it off. She wasn't there to police Justine Beaumont. It was her father who was going to be under scrutiny, whether he liked it or not.

He got out and was walking across the parking lot toward the store when he felt a hand on his back, turned around, then smiled. It was Amalie.

"Amalie! How's it going, Sister?"

Being called anybody's sister, when she'd grown up without siblings or even knowing who her parents were, was a constant delight. Amalie loved being Sean Pope's wife, and his mother and brothers were the icing on the cake.

"All good," Amalie said. "Up to my eyeballs in tax returns already. I was getting ready to leave when I saw you get out. I just wanted to say how good it was to have supper with you the other night. We don't see you as much as we'd like."

"Gotta keep the people fed," he said.

"Understood. But we had a fun time with Ava when you brought her up. She wound up spending the night and sleeping with Shirley, but you probably guessed that would happen."

"Not the least bit surprised," Brendan said. "Mom is our lifesaver for every family emergency and every family drama we've ever had."

"She's a treasure, for sure," Amalie said, and then glanced at the time. "It's getting late. I don't want Sean to worry, so I'd better scoot." She gave Brendan's hand a quick squeeze goodbye, and then staggered but didn't turn loose.

Brendan watched her eyes lose focus, then close and waited, still holding her hand, still wondering what she would say. The whole family knew and accepted that Amalie had the "sight."

Then she began to speak. "Someone's coming who's going to need your help. Don't shy away from what happens between you. It's meant to be," she said, and then opened her eyes and looked up. "Gotta go. Sean's waiting," she said, and walked off as if none of that had just happened.

"Lord," he muttered, and then regained his composure and went into the store.

That night as Brendan was getting ready for bed, he thought of Amalie's prediction and couldn't help but wonder who was coming and how she would play into his life. Maybe it was the auditor, or not. Only time would tell.

But Ray's text had confirmed his decision to turn over the threatening message he had found on his door. He wanted all of this on record, should Justine decide to escalate some stupid kind of revenge. And just to be on the safe side, he sent his brother Sean a text.

I need a security camera set up at my place. If you're not too busy, could you do it tomorrow? It's my day off. I have a stalker at work and have already received one threatening note on my door, but I can't prove she left it there.

Within a minute, Sean answered.

What the hell, Brendan? Who is it? And yes, I'll be there first thing tomorrow! Have you told the police? If not, get your ass down to the station with that note and make a report. It's protection. And who's your stalker?

Brendan sighed. This was the push he needed.

The new hotel manager's daughter, Justine
Beaumont. The one I mentioned to you the other
day. I swear to God, something is wrong with her.
All of her behavior is almost manic, and I've turned
her down so many times in the past five months
that she's out for revenge. She even pulled a knife
on me about a month ago. She's nuts, and that's
all I'm going to say about it.

Sean fired back one last text.

If they're not already on, go turn on your outside
lights. Get to the station early tomorrow. Talk to
Aaron and Wiley before they go out on patrol.
Give them your statement and turn in the note.
Maybe they can get prints off of it. And I'll be at
your house by 8:00 a.m. I swear to God, I thought
Wiley's crazy exes were bad, but this is over the
top. Don't worry. We've got your back.

Brendan's shoulders slumped in relief.

He set the alarm on his phone, then put it on the
charger and crawled into bed. Just as he was falling
asleep, Amalie's warning slid through his mind.

*Someone's coming. She's going to need your help. Don't
shy away. It's meant to be.*

And then he slept.

————

It was a quarter to eight the next morning when Brendan Pope walked into the Jubilee Police Department. As always, Sergeant Winter was at the front desk. He looked up and grinned when he saw who was coming in.

"Morning, Brendan."

"Morning, Sarge. I need to speak to my brothers. I'm here to file a complaint."

"They're just finishing up roll call. I'll let Chief Warren know. Have a seat," Winters said.

Brendan walked back to the row of chairs lined up against the wall and sat down. Less than five minutes later, both of his brothers came charging up the hall like the front line of the Green Bay Packers. Aaron reached him first, but Wiley was right behind him.

"What's wrong? You're filing a complaint? Against whom?" Aaron asked.

Wiley followed up with his own question. "Are you okay?"

"I'm fine. Just being hassled."

Aaron grabbed him by the arm. "This way. We'll talk in private," he said, and took Brendan to an empty interrogation room, sat him down, and pulled up chairs around the table.

"Talk to us," Wiley said. He turned on the recorder and started the interview by introducing himself and Wiley, and then Brendan introduced himself as the complainant.

"Okay, Brendan, tell us why you're here, and who you're filing a complaint against," Aaron said.

Brendan took a deep breath. He'd kept this to himself for so long that it was going to feel weird even talking about it.

"I'm here because I've been stalked and harassed for the past five months by Justine Beaumont, the daughter of Larry Beaumont, who is the manager at the Serenity Inn where I'm employed."

He went into detail about everything that had happened, including the knife attack, and then got to the end of the story by pulling out the plastic bag with the note.

"When I came home from work, this unsigned note was on my front door. The words read: 'I'll make you sorry you were ever born.' It was taped to my front door. I haven't touched it. I removed it with tweezers and put it in this plastic bag, debating with myself as to what to do, but this situation feels like it's escalating. I'm having security cameras installed in case this happens again. I hope you can retrieve prints from the note that will prove who sent it. But if not, at least this report will be on file."

"Do you want to press charges?" Wiley asked.

"It depends whether you find her prints on the note or not," he said.

Aaron picked up the plastic bag. "We'll log this into evidence and send it to the lab. One way or the other, you will be notified of the results, and you can decide what you want to do after that. Is that satisfaction enough for you now?" he asked.

"Yes," Brendan said.

"Interview terminated at 08:20 a.m. Thursday, February 20th," Aaron said, and turned off the recorder.

"I know this wasn't easy for you, but you did the right thing," Wiley said.

"Why didn't you say something sooner?" Aaron asked. "I mean...five months of that had to be crazy."

Brendan shrugged. "Because I'm a grown-ass man and admitting all that's happening is a bit embarrassing. I've been hit on countless times in my life. We all have, and you know it. It was never a big deal, and never in a threatening manner. Never to this extent."

Aaron nodded. "Understood."

Wiley poked his little brother's shoulder, trying to lighten up the moment. "If you'd been born ugly, you wouldn't have these problems."

"Famous last words from the brother who had two women on his ass who came close to ruining everything with Linette," Brendan said.

Wiley grinned. "Yeah, there was that."

"I'm going to get this statement typed up," Aaron said, and walked out.

Wiley stayed behind. "And I never got to thank you for getting Ava up to Mom's house the night of the wreck."

Brendan smiled. "It was my pleasure. She's the funniest, smartest little thing, and she quotes Mikey Pope every other sentence."

Wiley sighed. "Yeah. We know. We get a nightly dose

of it, and she is smart. Don't know where she got it. God knows Corina didn't have a brain in her head, and whatever Clyde's mental capacity was, he'd long since soaked and fried it with booze and drugs."

"She's spent the first five years of her life observing everything because nobody told her anything. She took all of it in, and sorted and filed it into that little brain of hers until we came along and gave her permission to bloom. That's what love does," Brendan said.

Wiley was speechless. Brendan never had a lot to say in family gatherings, but when he did, it always mattered. It humbled him enough that it took him a few moments to recover. "Well, however it happened, I'm grateful for her presence in our lives."

"Me too," Brendan said. Then his phone buzzed. He glanced down at the message that appeared. "Sean is at my house. As soon as I sign my complaint, I'm heading home. I'll be set for security before the day is over."

———

Justine Beaumont was holed up in the penthouse, scrolling through social media sites, destroying her fifteen months of sobriety by drinking cola liberally laced with whiskey, and eating the peanut butter and jelly sandwich she was having for lunch. It wasn't her food of choice, but it was all there was in the penthouse kitchen, and she would die before she'd ever order food from room service again. She had installed the local delivery-service app on her phone and was already planning to order her food from the local eateries, have it delivered to the concierge at the hotel, and make them bring it up.

Her father had the audacity to try to talk to her again last night, but she wasn't having it. She was still furious with him and had locked herself in her room. When he came up for the night and knocked on her door, she didn't respond, so he sent her a text, telling her they needed to talk about ground rules that had to be obeyed if she were to stay with him here.

Her answer was brief and to the point. Go to hell. Then she turned up the sound on the TV and left it on blast all night just to ensure he got no sleep at all, unaware that he wasn't taking this lying down.

Larry went to his suite and called his ex-wife, Karen. The call rang and rang until he thought it was going to go to voicemail, then suddenly she picked up.

"Dammit, somebody better be dead for you to call me at this time of night," she snapped.

Larry didn't mince words. "I'm sending Justine back to Dallas. You can deal with her, or not. But I'm finished. She's caused so much trouble for me at this job that half the hotel staff are about to walk off the job. One employee is verging on filing sexual harassment charges against her. I'm not asking your advice.

I'm just giving you a heads-up about what's heading your way."

"She's not living with me!" Karen shrieked.

"Then she's on the fucking streets. After all the shit she's caused here, I have no doubt she'd make a good hooker."

Karen gasped. "How dare you say that about your own daughter?"

"She's your daughter, too, in more ways than one. We're no longer married because you couldn't keep your pants on around a man, and she can't keep her hands off them. She even took a knife to one of the employees. I'm sending her back to Dallas. What she does after that is on her."

Karen was screaming, "Larry, don't you dare—" when he disconnected, then went to take a shower, while his ex-wife had a meltdown of her own because she knew something about their daughter that neither Larry or even Justine was aware of.

The last time they'd sent her to rehab, the psychiatrist on staff had asked for permission to run some psychological tests on Justine. Karen agreed without a thought, but the diagnosis she got later blew her mind. It explained so much and, at the same time, was as good as a death sentence to every dream she'd harbored for their child.

According to the tests, which they'd run twice, their daughter ticked off every aspect of a narcissistic psychopath. She had no reactions to other people's pain or tragedies. Showed no emotion to anything that did not directly involve her, and when disciplined at the center, or had privileges taken away for infractions, she went after the people who delivered those decisions. She'd cut one doctor with a knife, and locked one of the cooks in a freezer for refusing to give her second helpings, and showed no remorse for what she'd done.

That was when Karen walked out. She turned her back on her husband and her daughter, and knew it was selfish and brutal, but she knew it was also the only thing she could do to keep from becoming her daughter's next victim, because it had been Karen who'd driven Justine to rehab, and it was Justine who was cursing her name as she walked out.

⸻

Larry's alarm went off at 6:00 a.m. He was up, dressed, and having breakfast in the dining room by seven. Usually, he ate and left without paying any attention to the staff, but after all that had occurred yesterday, he could tell they were uneasy at his presence, so he went out of his way to thank them for a coffee refill and praised the light-as-air biscuits with his meal.

He made a point of visiting every shop in the hotel, commenting positively on their displays, and then did a walk-through in the spa and gym area, speaking to attendants to make sure they had everything they needed. It was something he should have been doing regularly, but he'd taken the Serenity Inn for granted, assuming a well-oiled machine ran itself. And it had, until his daughter threw sand in the gears.

He stopped by Liz Devon's office and knocked, this time waiting for approval to enter, and then opened the door.

"Got a minute?" he asked.

"Absolutely," Liz said. "Come in, come in. There's something I need to tell you as well. I was just waiting for you to get in your office."

Larry sat down, this time without the attitude. "I want to apologize. I overstepped myself about your new event. I know better. Truth is, I let personal problems interfere with my job. It won't happen again."

Liz breathed a sigh of relief. "No problem. We've all been there. So, I got a call from Dad. I think Mom is guiding this decision, but it's probably for his own good. He's thinking of putting the hotel up for sale and has gone into preparatory mode. As you know, businesses like this always require an up-to-date profit-and-loss statement, and so he's sending a CPA to the hotel to do our annual audit, instead of waiting for year-end like we always do. He wanted me to reassure you that this in no way affects your job here. This is all still up in the air, but he wants to be ready, just in case."

"Ahhh, I wondered how his health was faring. I'm sure this wasn't an easy decision for him," Larry said.

Liz shrugged. "I'm sure it wasn't, but this hotel is only a small part of Dad's holdings, and he needs to slow down, for sure. Oh…he's comping a suite for the CPA. Her name is Harley Banks. The comps include meals and hotel services, so she'll work from inside the suite. She'll have full access to the hotel computer system, but in view only. She won't be interfering in any way with daily entries, etc. She'll just be getting the data she needs to do the audit. But since you have nothing to do with the intake of income or payout to vendors, none of that will affect you."

Larry nodded. "Right, but I'll always be available to answer any questions for her, should the need arise."

"Perfect," Liz said, and smiled.

He slapped his legs and then stood. "Well then, if that's it, I'll let you get back to work. Have a good day."

"You, too," Liz said, and then watched as he left her office. *Mission accomplished*, she thought, and went back to work.

Larry wasn't concerned about the audit. Everything ordered was paid for. Every bank statement was balanced. He was in the clear.

Chapter 5

JUSTINE WAS STILL DAWDLING THROUGH HER MAKE-shift lunch and booze, and wondering what Brendan "Hotshot" Pope thought when he found the note she'd left on his door. In her mind, she was imagining him worried, or maybe even scared. But the biggest error in that was assuming he would react the way she might react, should the situation be reversed. She'd threatened men before and been rewarded for it. What she didn't yet realize was that threatening any Pope was a dangerous thing to do. It meant threatening the whole family, something that should not be taken lightly.

She pulled up a TikTok reel and watched it three times, laughing hysterically and already buzzed as she drank the last of her spiked cola. After a few minutes, she tired of social media, threw her phone down on the sofa, carried what was left of her sandwich to the kitchen and dumped it in the garbage, poured another shot of whisky in her glass and chugged it like medicine. The liquor burned all the way down, but she felt good. All warm and just the tiniest bit fuzzy. Fuzzy enough to make another rash decision as she headed for her room to change.

She came out a short while later dressed in black Lycra pants that clung to every crevice of her ass, a pink clingy sweater, and a white fur jacket and boots. After a swipe of her reddest lipstick, and leaving her long blond hair in a long, messy mane, she was good to go. She was itching to party and whatever came with it. There was a whole town full of strangers she didn't know and would never see again. If she was lucky, she'd get laid. She didn't care where it happened, whether in the back seat of a car on a lonely road, or wherever the dude was staying.

But she needed transportation to get where she wanted to go, and went looking for her father's car keys. She found them on top of his dresser, left the hotel without leaving a note or a text to let him know where she was going, and headed for Trapper's Bar and Grill on the strip. The parking lot at the bar was only half-full. A little early for the lunchtime crowd to begin arriving, but never too early for a drink at the bar. She parked, got out, and walked into the place like she owned it.

———

Louis Glass, the bartender at Trapper's Bar and Grill, was drawing a beer for a customer at the bar when he saw the woman walk in. He knew the moment he saw her she was going to be trouble, because she paused a few steps inside the entrance, scanning the room like a buzzard looking for roadkill, and then headed for the bar. When she chose the only empty stool between three men to her right, and two to her left, she'd marked herself as product. They'd either look, or they'd buy. It didn't matter to her as long as she got noticed.

Then she shrugged out of her fur jacket and draped it across the back of the barstool, making the lack of a bra under the pink sweater immediately obvious to the five men she'd surrounded herself with.

"Be right with you, ma'am," Louis said.

Justine tossed her head and flashed a big smile. "Take your time. I'm not going anywhere," she drawled.

One of the men on her left leaned toward her.

"Buy you a drink, sugar?" he asked.

Justine shrugged. "Sure, why not? Whiskey. Neat."

Louis heard her and frowned. He'd been a bartender long enough to know this one came to drown something. She was either mad as hell at someone, or she'd been let down in some way, and he would have put his money on anger. Unaware she was already riding an alcohol high, he made a mental note to keep track of her drinks.

―――――――――

Oblivious to the bartender's hawk-eye attention to her drinks, Justine launched into her Dallas barhopping behavior and turned into the life of the party.

But the man who'd bought her first drink soon figured out she was more than he wanted to deal with, paid his bar tab, and left while she was downing shots with a guy who played backup guitar at one of the music venues.

That man two-stepped her around the little dance floor until she was dizzy, at which point she excused herself, claiming she needed to powder her nose, and staggered off to the ladies' room, while diners began coming in for lunch.

By the time Justine returned, business was booming. Tables and booths were filling up. Background music was all fiddles and guitars, but muted enough for private conversations among the diners. Servers were hustling between the kitchen and the tables, taking orders, delivering orders, and refilling drink glasses.

It was a typical day at the Bar and Grill until Justine came back, only to find her guitar man gone. She giggled, then shouted out as she slapped the bar for attention.

"Hey! Bartender! Where'd the guy go I was dancin' with?"

Louis frowned. Her laughter was shrill and forced and she was slurring her words.

"He probably left to get ready for the afternoon show," Louis said.

"Wha'ever," Justine mumbled. "I need a drink."

Louis shook his head. "I'm sorry, miss, but you're over your limit. How about a cup of coffee instead?"

The smile slid off Justine's face. "I don' wanna cup a' coffee. I want a drink, dammit!"

Louis shook his head. "Sorry, but I can't do that."

Justine started cursing, and the room went quiet.

Everyone was staring at the woman at the bar.

Mike, the bouncer, was already at her elbow to escort her out when Louis shook his head. "She's too drunk to drive," he said, and reached for the phone.

The moment the bartender turned his back, Justine grabbed a bottle of beer from a man at the bar and threw it at the back of Louis's head. It shattered, cutting his head, leaving glass embedded in his hair and scalp, and spilling beer all over the back of his shirt.

The pain was abrupt and unexpected, but Louis didn't hesitate as he called the police. The dispatcher answered.

"Jubilee Police. What is your emergency?"

"This is Louis Glass at Trapper's Bar and Grill. I have a drunk and disorderly I need picked up, and make it quick," he said, then disconnected.

Mike the bouncer had her in a light restraining hold when all of a sudden, she twisted out of his grasp, then turned and clawed the sides of his face with her nails, and made a run for the door. But the floor was tilting, and the room was beginning to spin.

Instead of moving forward, she went sideways, fell across a table full of diners, knocked two of them out of their chairs, and upset the food. The meal they'd been

eating was on the floor, and both women who'd fallen
out of their chairs were crying. One woman was screaming about the pain in her arm, another was holding on to
her side and crying.

Justine was in the act of trying to escape when she
slipped in a puddle of ketchup and sat down on a basket
of french fries.

"Shit," Louis muttered, and turned around and made
a second call for an ambulance.

The dispatcher sent out the call, and as luck would
have it, Officers Pope and Leedy were in the act of passing the bar and grill when the call went out.

Wiley Pope hit the lights and siren, made a quick
U-turn, and pulled into the parking lot as Doug Leedy
was calling in their response. They began hearing
screams inside the bar the moment they got out of the
cruiser, and took off running.

But once inside, it was hard to figure out where to
look first—at all the blood on the bouncer's face, the
people in the floor, a half-dozen other diners standing
around them and food all over the place, or Louis, who
was coming toward them holding a bloody bar towel on
the back of his head.

"What the hell happened here?" Wiley said.

Louis pointed to the woman in black Lycra who was
sitting in the floor.

"She happened. I quit serving her drinks. She had a
fit, threw a beer bottle at the back of my head, clawed
Mark's face to shreds, and made a run for the door, then

fell into the table of diners before we could catch her. I've already called for an ambulance, but not for her. The women she knocked out of their chairs are injured. The drunk blond in the floor is the only one of all of us who isn't injured. That red stuff all over her face and hands isn't blood, it's ketchup. She slipped in it and sat down in a basket of fries."

Wiley blinked. "Do you know who she is?"

Louis shrugged. "She introduced herself to every man at the bar as Justine Beaumont. She ran up a bar tab, and I will be pressing charges for assault on me and my employee, for personal injury of my customers, and for destruction of property and the unpaid bar tab. Can't speak for the ones she injured, whether they will sue her for personal damages."

A slow grin spread across Wiley's face. "Justine Beaumont? The hell you say. Hey, Doug, since that's ketchup and not blood, we don't have to wait for the EMTs before we move her. Help me get her up and out of here before she does any more damage."

"I'll cuff her, then you get her out of the fries," Doug said.

Aaron Pope was entering the bar with a trio of other officers, with the EMTs right behind them. When Aaron saw his brother and partner in the thick of it, trying to get a drunk cuffed and up off the floor, he headed toward them.

Justine was screaming and crying, claiming someone had pushed her and she didn't deserve this, when Wiley stepped into her line of vision. All she saw was a familiar face and started begging.

"Brendan! Help me. I'm sorry. Help me!"

And then Aaron appeared, and she groaned. "I don't feel so good. I'm seeing double," she mumbled.

Now that she was cuffed, Wiley pulled her upright. "I'm not Brendan. And you're not seeing double. We're his brothers, and you're going to jail for assault, drunk and disorderly, and destruction of property."

"Noooooo," Justine wailed. "Daddy will kill me."

"I wouldn't blame him," Wiley muttered as he and Doug escorted her out of the bar and transported her to booking, leaving Aaron and the other officers to police the area as the medics transported the injured women.

After that, one of the waiters took over behind the bar, while staff began cleaning up the area.

Waylon Parker, the bar manager, had been in the bank when he got the call. He arrived on the scene and began apologizing profusely to the diners, then comped dessert for everyone on the premises.

Mike, the bouncer, drove himself and Louis to ER for treatment, and chaos in Trapper's Bar and Grill finally came to an end.

But not for Justine. Her troubles were just beginning. She was booked into jail pending her arraignment and was still begging for mercy when they closed the cell doors. At that point, her tears dried up, and she shifted to curses and threats, until she realized there was no one around to hear her, then flopped down on the bunk and passed out.

———

Liz Devon was in the storeroom checking out the recent arrival of part of the shipment for Josie Fallin's event when one of her staff came in running, wide-eyed and breathless.

"You will *not* believe what just happened," he said. "Jezebel Justine just got herself arrested in Trapper's Bar and Grill!"

Liz gasped. "What in the world did she do? How do you know?"

"My wife is a waitress there, remember? She said Justine was drunk. Louis wouldn't serve her any more liquor. Tried to offer her coffee. She started raising hell. He went to call the police and she threw a beer bottle at the back of his head. He's bleeding, and she turns on the bouncer, scratches his face into bloody rows, and tries to make a run for it. But she's so drunk that she staggers and falls onto a table of diners, knocks two women out of their seats. They're both injured, and then she's still trying to get away, slips in spilled ketchup and sits down in a basket of fries. I kid you not."

"Oh my God!" Liz mumbled. "Does Larry know?"

He shrugged. "I'm not gonna tell him, that's for sure. Oh…and here's the irony. When Wiley Pope and his partner arrested her, she thought Wiley was Brendan."

Liz was in shock. "This is a mess, and it could affect the hotel's reputation. Like it or not, Larry has to know. Just lock the storeroom up for me. I'll come back later to finish inventory."

"Yes, ma'am," he said.

Liz grabbed her clipboard and bolted, calling Larry's office cell as she went.

———————

It was just after lunch when Larry went to the penthouse to check on Justine. But she was nowhere to be found and his car keys were missing. He tried calling her, but it kept going to voicemail. He was going down in the elevator, cursing beneath his breath, when his phone rang. He answered without bothering to look at caller ID, hoping it was her, but it was Liz.

"Larry, it's Liz. Have you spoken to Justine recently?"

His gut knotted. "No. Why?"

She sighed. "We have a situation. She got drunk in Trapper's Bar and Grill, and to make a long, ugly story short, she assaulted the bartender and the bouncer and left them bleeding, fell into a table of diners, injured two women seated there, broke furniture, and was booked into jail. I have no idea how many charges will be filed against her, but this doesn't just affect you and her. A scene like this affects this hotel's reputation, as well, once it gets out who she is and where she lives. We're going to suffer repercussions. You need to get a lawyer down there ASAP and deal with this."

"Oh my God," he muttered, and broke out in a cold sweat. "One more day, and I would have had her on a plane to Dallas. Do you have to tell Ray?"

"Of course, I have to tell him. This hotel is his business, not yours," Liz said, and disconnected.

"Well, that explains why she isn't answering her phone and where my car is," Larry muttered. He rode the elevator down to the lobby, went to the concierge desk and asked for the shuttle van to be brought around, and had the driver drop him off at the police station.

He entered the lobby area, walked up to the desk, and introduced himself.

"I'm Larry Beaumont. I believe my daughter, Justine Beaumont, was recently arrested. Is she in jail?"

Sergeant Winter checked the computer. "Yes, she is."

Larry sighed. "She has the keys to my car in her personal effects. She took the car without my knowledge or permission, and I wonder if I might retrieve them, please?"

"Have a seat," Winter said, and then called the chief's office.

Chief Sonny Warren was talking to Wiley and Doug when his desk phone rang. "Just a sec," he said, and answered. "What's up, Walter?"

"Justine Beaumont's father is in the lobby. He says his daughter took his car without his knowledge and is wondering if he might have his car keys back."

Sonny glanced up at Doug and Wiley. "Bring him back to my office. We need to have a conversation."

"Yes, sir," Walter said. "I'll walk him back myself."

Sonny hung up. "Justine Beaumont's father came looking for his car keys. Didn't ask a damn thing about his daughter's welfare. I wonder how many times he's had to do this before."

"She has some priors, but they're minor compared to this," Doug said.

"Was there a set of car keys on her when she was booked into jail?" Sonny asked.

"Yes, sir," Doug said.

"I need you to go get them. The car belongs to her father. We haven't towed it yet, have we?" Sonny asked.

"No, sir. It's still in the parking lot at Trapper's. Do I need to notify the tow service?" Wiley asked.

"No, her father can retrieve it without issue. It's not part of her arrest. What I want *you* to do is compare the fingerprints on the note your brother brought in against the prints we just took off Miss Beaumont. If they match, please call me to let me know."

Wiley stood. "On it, sir," he replied, and was walking out of the office when Walter and Larry walked in.

Larry paused, staring at Wiley in disbelief. "Brendan?"

"Brother," Wiley said, and kept walking.

Larry was stunned. "The resemblance is remarkable," he muttered.

"Brendan has three older brothers. They all look alike," Walter said, then introduced him. "Chief, this is

Mr. Beaumont," Walter said, and closed the door behind him as he left.

Sonny eyed the man, thinking he looked soft and spent too much time behind a desk, and then shrugged it off. These days, the same could be said of him.

"Take a seat, Mr. Beaumont. Your daughter is in a lot of trouble."

Larry's face was already flushed from embarrassment. "My daughter has been nothing but trouble since the day she started first grade. But she's no longer a child. She's twenty-four years old, and whatever she's done is on her. All I want are the keys to my car that she took without asking."

"I sent one of my men to get them. Do you want to talk to her?" Sonny asked.

"No, sir, I do not. As for lawyers, she can get a court-appointed one, just like every other indigent. She has never worked a day in her indulged life. She didn't want my advice, ever, and only wanted my help when she was in trouble. And that's not happening. Not this time."

There was a knock at the door, and then Doug popped in and laid the keys on Sonny's desk, and walked out again. Before Sonny could pick them up, his phone rang. It was Wiley.

"Yes?"

"Perfect match, sir," Wiley said.

"Thank you," Sonny said, and hung up.

"That was one of my officers. It appears that your daughter's prints match the ones found on a note that was turned in to us when Brendan Pope reported a threatening note left on his front door. It will now be up to him as to whether or not he files charges for sexual harassment and stalking."

Larry moaned beneath his breath. "When did this happen?"

"Previous to today is all you need to know," Sonny said. "You have your keys. You don't wish to speak with your daughter. Do you intend to post bail after her arraignment?"

"Hell no," Larry said.

Chief Warren nodded. "We will notify her about her rights to a court-appointed lawyer. Right now, she's passed out drunk in a holding cell. If you will please follow me, I'll walk you out," Sonny said, and dropped the keys in Larry's hands, then exited his office with Larry scurrying behind him to keep up. When they reached the front entrance, he paused.

"Which direction do I go from here to get to Trapper's Bar and Grill?"

Sonny pointed. "Take a left as you leave and start walking. It's on the strip. You can't miss it."

"Thank you," Larry said, and glanced up.

Clouds were moving across the sun. He should have worn his overcoat, but he was so rarely outside of the hotel that he forgot it was still winter. He began walking at a rapid pace to keep warm, only to realize he was out of shape and soon out of breath. When he finally reached the parking lot, it didn't take long for him to spot his car.

As soon as he got in, he breathed a sigh of relief that he was in out of the cold and then headed back to the hotel. And all the while he was driving, he kept wishing he could just drive out of Jubilee and never look back.

Instead, he called his wife.

Karen answered on the second ring. "What?"

"Your daughter is in jail for drunk and disorderly, assault, destruction of private property, injuring two diners in a local bar and grill, and on a separate charge to that incident, a report was filed on her a few days ago for stalking and leaving a threatening note on the person's front door."

Karen gasped. "Oh my God, what did you do to cause all that?"

"Me? What did *we* do would be the better question. I know she needed consequences for every misdeed she ever committed and never got them. I know you personally bought her out of shoplifting charges and slept with somebody to make the DUI go away."

"How did you know about—" Karen cried, and then realized she'd just admitted to cheating on him and changed the subject. "What are you going to do?"

"Nothing. Absolutely nothing. I'm probably going to lose my job because of her. To hell with her. To hell with you. I'm sorry I ever met you. I'm sorry she was ever born," he said, then disconnected and drove back to the hotel.

Karen was in hysterics. She kept calling and calling,

but he didn't pick up, and Justine was still passed out, unaware that she'd just been abandoned to her fate.

———

Wiley sent Brendan a text.

> Your nemesis is in jail for wrecking Trapper's Bar
> and Grill. Call me.

But Brendan was decorating a special-order cake for a birthday celebration scheduled for this evening and focused on finishing it. The daughter of one of the families staying at the hotel was turning sixteen, and her birthday wish had been a trip to Jubilee to see Josie Fallin in concert. He was going out of his way to make it everything they'd asked for. Creating joy for people from things he baked was why he'd chosen this career.

He had his phone set on vibrate and was so focused on making the icing on top of the cake look like snow-drifts, and blowing gold dust onto the peaks, that he didn't even notice an incoming text.

It wasn't until he'd finished and put the cake into the cooler to set that he stopped to check his messages. When he saw the one from Wiley, a sense of relief washed over him. Justine Beaumont had way too many problems to be chasing him anymore.

Karma.

He slipped the phone back in his pocket and

returned to his workstation. Anthony, his sous-chef, was already cleaning up the area and cleaning Brendan's equipment, taking care to put it back in the places he kept it.

"Good job," Brendan said as he walked past the area.

"Thank you, Chef," Anthony said.

"I'm going to take a quick break. Has that last batch of dough proofed yet?" Brendan asked.

"Another fifteen minutes to go, Chef."

"I'll be back before then and we'll get the rolls worked up and in the oven. Last batch of the day can't come too soon, right?"

The young man grinned. "Yes, Chef."

Brendan took off his chef's cap, stepped out of the kitchens, rode the staff elevator down to the back entrance, and walked out of the building. The cold air against his skin was welcome as he pulled out his phone and returned Wiley's call. The phone rang twice and then Wiley answered.

"I take it you read my text," he drawled.

"What the hell?" Brendan asked, and Wiley told him.

"What I need to know from you is, now that you know for sure that Justine Beaumont left that note on your door, do you want to press charges?" he asked.

Brendan didn't hesitate. "I think, considering the big mess she's already in, I'm gonna let it ride."

"Your call, Brother. I'll make the report and leave the complaint pending," Wiley said.

"Thanks for your trouble," Brendan said.

Wiley chuckled. "Not trouble. Just part of the job," he said. "Take care. Talk to you soon."

They ended the call and Brendan went back to work. By the time his day was coming to an end, the last batch of rolls were out of the oven. The dessert carts were full for the evening rush, and one sparkly-as-snow birthday cake was waiting for him to deliver to the girl who had turned sweet sixteen.

He stayed at the hotel past his quitting time so he could personally present the cake. Once it was time, they lit the silver sparkler candles on the cake, causing a stir of excitement among the diners as the elaborate cake was being wheeled through the dining room toward a table for twelve.

The birthday girl was a cute little redhead, wearing a very grown-up party dress and heels. When she saw the cake, she began laughing and pointing and clapping her hands, and when Brendan stopped at their table, he spoke first to the father.

"Sir, if I may?" Brendan asked, and took the girl's hand.

Her father was beaming and nodded.

"For you, pretty girl, your sparkly-as-snow cake," Brendan said, and kissed the back of her hand. "Enjoy your special day. My sous-chef will remove the sparklers and serve the cake after you've made your wish."

Then he nodded at the family before heading back to the kitchen, oblivious to the admiring looks he was getting from other diners.

Something banged just outside the door to the cellblock, startling Justine awake. Her head was throbbing,
her belly rolling, and even before she opened her eyes,
she smelled a faint scent of urine.

What the hell? Did I pee the bed?

And then she opened her eyes, saw the bars on the
cell, and remembered.

"Oh shit," she muttered, then began shouting and
calling out for the jailer.

The jailer heard her, but instead of responding, he
picked up the phone and called the chief.

Sonny Warren was in the middle of writing up a
report when the call came through. He answered without taking his eyes off the screen.

"Chief Warren speaking."

"Chief, it's me, Randy. You told me to let you know
when Justine Beaumont woke up. She's awake and
shouting."

"Thanks, Randy. I'll be right there," Sonny said, hung
up the phone, and hit Save on his report, then left his
office.

He walked through the building, winding his way
toward the cellblock in the back. Before he was even
halfway there, he could hear her, and was thinking she
was going to have way more to shout about after their
talk. When he got to the jailer's desk just outside the
cellblock, Randy looked up.

"You want me to go in with you, Chief?" Randy asked.

"Are the security cameras working?" Sonny asked.

"Yes, sir," Randy said.

"Then we're good here," Sonny said, knowing they would be his backup if he was ever accused of impropriety. He opened the door to the cell block and walked in.

Justine was right in the middle of a hissy fit when she saw a cop walk in. "It's about fucking time!" she cried, wiping tears from her face. "I should report you to the chief of police!"

"I'm the police chief. Chief Warren. You've had your rights read to you. You are being charged with drunk and disorderly, two accounts of assault, property damage, and bodily injury to two women who were eating there. One has a broken arm. The other, cracked ribs. Your father has already reclaimed the keys to his car and has advised that he will not be calling a lawyer on your behalf."

Justine was already reeling from the reality of her situation when she heard those last words. She let out a scream of despair that would have put a howling wolf to shame.

"He can't do that!" she wailed.

"Oh, yes, ma'am. He can and did. You are not a child, you are a twenty-four-year-old adult woman, and in the eyes of the law, he does not owe you shelter or support. You can call a lawyer for yourself, or a court-ordered attorney will be furnished for you. You will be arraigned sometime within the next twenty-four hours, and I assume bail will be set. You also need to know your father has no intention of putting up bail money. I'm allowing you a phone call. Think carefully who that might be before you waste it begging for something you're not going to get."

All the while the chief had been talking, Justine had been backing up all the way to the farthest wall of the cell, as if trying to get away from the truth of her situation. She was pale and shaking, and her stomach was rolling. All of a sudden, she dropped to her knees, wrapped her arms around the toilet bowl, and threw up until she was gasping for breath. When there was nothing left to come up, she dragged herself to the bunk and sat staring at the floor, unaware the police chief was still there.

"Do you want to make a call?" he asked.

She jerked, startled at the sound of his voice. "Mama. I want to call my mama," she whispered.

"Do you know her number?" Sonny asked.

Justine nodded.

"Wait here," Sonny said, and went to get Randy. "I'm giving her time to make her phone call. Bring the cuffs," he said.

Randy opened the cell, cuffed her, and then he and the chief escorted her to a phone and gave her a little space to make the call.

Justine was shaking. "Don't I get any privacy?" she asked.

"The only privacy you have left in this situation is what passes between you and your lawyer," Sonny said.

Justine's hands were trembling as she made the call to her mother, praying as she counted the unanswered rings and scared it was going to go to voicemail. Then just at the last moment, the call picked up.

"Hello."

Justine started crying. "Mama…Mommy…I am in so much trouble and I'm so sorry. Daddy has washed his hands of me. Will you help?"

Karen sighed. "I know. He called me. What do you need?"

"I will be arraigned sometime within the next twenty-four hours and bail will be set. But there's no one to put up bail money, and I don't know how much it will be. Will you come? I won't be allowed to leave Jubilee until this is over, and I'm pretty sure Daddy won't let me back in the penthouse, either. I don't know what to do." Then she broke down sobbing.

Karen succumbed to resignation. She'd run out on Justine once. She couldn't live with herself if she did it again.

"Yes, I'll come, and I'll find a bondsman to post your bail. We'll figure the rest out after I'm there, and I'll talk to your father. We'll figure something out."

"Thank you, Mama. I'm so sorry. I'm so, so sorry," Justine said.

"I know you're sorry you're in jail," Karen said. "But

I wonder how sorry you are about what you've done to other people. I'll see you soon," Karen said.

"I love you, Mama," Justine said, but her mother had already disconnected. "Bitch," she muttered, and went quietly back to the cell, then lay back down on the bunk and turned her face to the wall.

Chapter 6

OLLIE PRINE ARRIVED IN CHICAGO, CAUGHT A CAB to his hotel, and was trying to remember the name of the guy he'd done time with who lived here. If he could find him, Harley Banks might be high-profile enough in the city for someone to know where she lived. His name was something like Shultz, or Shulter. He'd remember it in a bit when he quit thinking about it. That's how names always came to him. When he let go of worrying about it.

―――――――

Harley Banks was already packed for her flight tomorrow and was in the living room with her feet up, balancing her laptop as her fingers flew across the keyboard. She was doing what she always did before beginning a new case—getting background on the people she would be working with.

She already had notes on Ray and his family and was running a background check on Larry Beaumont and his daughter, Justine.

She now knew Larry's daughter had been kicked out and failed out of two different colleges. She had been arrested for shoplifting and picked up on one DUI that was dismissed. Both criminal offenses were in Dallas, Texas, and she had no work history, but she did have a record of rehab stints for alcohol abuse. Harley was still running checks when an update appeared on Justine's police record. She'd just been booked into jail in Jubilee, Kentucky, on various charges, all stemming from drunk and disorderly.

"What a mess," Harley mumbled, but she found nothing of note on Larry Beaumont. His credit rating was decent, and he paid alimony to his ex-wife every month without fault.

The last person on Harley's list was Brendan Pope. She started by running a standard background check, and got a surprise when she learned he'd changed his last name from Wallace to Pope just after he graduated high school, as had his mother and three brothers, just before they moved residence to Jubilee. She'd never run across a situation like this before and was extremely curious as to why this happened until she ran a check on Clyde Wallace, the man listed as the father on the birth certificates.

"Holy shit," Harley muttered. "His father is a lifer. He nearly beat his wife to death, then killed two random people afterward in a drug-induced spree."

She kept running searches and found a couple of blurry photos of Brendan during his years at the

Culinary Institute of America. She had a list of the places he'd worked in later, most of which were upscale places in New York City, many of which she was famil-iar with.

By the time she'd finished his background check, other than a couple of speeding tickets for riding a motorcycle too fast when he was still in his teens, he was clean as a whistle. But it was seeing his DMV photo that had taken her aback. Traditionally, those photos were supposed to be a joke. His picture looked like a Hollywood headshot. Ray was right. He was a hand-some man.

━━━━━

The same night Harley Banks was running Brendan's background check, he was driving home on autopilot. He didn't remember anything but the glare of head-lights and the noise of Jubilee at night until he turned down the street where he lived. At that point, he began slowing down and then pulled up into the driveway. Remembering the note from before, he glanced toward his front porch, eyeing the security cameras and the motion-detector light that came on at his arrival, but nothing had been disturbed, probably because his stalker was in jail.

Satisfied that his security was in place, he pressed the remote and sat waiting for the garage door to go up, then drove in and closed the door behind him.

Walking into a dark and silent house was never welcoming, but it was his life. It was just the loneliness that got to him.

Sean had Amalie.

Aaron had Dani.

Wiley had Linette and Ava.

He had a stalker named Justine.

He felt like he'd fallen down a rabbit hole and couldn't see daylight anymore. Nobody knew he felt this way, which made it even worse.

As a kid, he'd always told his troubles to his mom, or his older brothers, but he'd long since aged out of that privilege. And if he said anything now, it would only turn the family into matchmakers who'd start setting him up.

He went through the house, turning on lights as he went, kicked off his shoes, traded jeans for sweatpants and a sweatshirt, and turned up the heat as he went back to the kitchen.

Three scrambled eggs and two pieces of toast later, his last meal of the day was over, and he couldn't sit still. He needed to outrun the ghosts from his past or he'd never sleep. It was cold and dark, but the roads were clear and dry, and they were calling.

Within minutes, he was in the garage in his biker gear, rolling out the Harley. He mounted as the garage door was going down behind him. The rumble of the engine was fine music to his ears. It was purring like a contented lion as he rode out of his neighborhood.

Once he reached the highway, he turned west through Jubilee. As soon as he hit the blacktop road leading up the mountain, he accelerated, riding the Harley like a runaway rocket. The modified LED headlight cut through the dark like a knife, while the roar of the engine blasted through the quiet of Pope Mountain.

He was headed for the top.

———

Cameron Pope was on the back porch with Ghost, listening to the night sounds on the mountain and watching as the old dog investigated the perimeter of their world, sniffing at all of the fence posts and under the branches of leafless bushes as diligently as he'd sniffed out bombs for Cameron and his men in Iraq.

In the distance, Cameron could hear someone coming up the mountain, but it didn't sound like a car or a truck, and whatever it was, it was coming closer. When it finally flew past, he realized it was a motorcycle.

Ghost was at his side now, intent on protecting if the need arose, but the roaring monster was already gone. Cameron laid a hand on the old dog's head.

"It's okay, boy. It's just Brendan, still trying to break the sound barrier with that Harley. Still trying to outrun his ghosts."

———

Brendan rode all the way up to the mountain's peak and then stopped and shut off the engine, toed down the kickstand, then sat astraddle the bike in the dark.

A three-quarter moon was hanging over his head, and he could hear the faint roar of Big Falls off to the north. Pope Mountain was only one peak in the chain of the Cumberland Mountains, but it was theirs…the Popes, the Cauleys, and the Glass families. But for the paved road beneath his feet, it was the same as it had been when the Chickasaw were here, and then the trappers that brought the first Pope to this place.

As he sat, a deer walked out of the woods, crossed the road in front of him, and leaped a ditch only to disappear into the trees on the opposite side. The fact that it did not fear him was surprising.

"Thank you for the honor," he said, then glanced at the time. It was after midnight. He was already looking at no more than four hours of sleep before he had to get up for work, but the ride had been worth it.

He put his helmet back on, toed up the kickstand, and started the engine. The rumble turned to a roar as he started back down the mountain, but not as fast, nor as desperate as he'd been going up.

———

The wind was whipping the treetops up on the mountain. It was bitterly cold, but Shirley Pope's house was snug and warm. Central heat was humming, and there was a big log burning in the massive fireplace.

Sean had been in Bowling Green most of the day fixing a glitch in the computer system of a bank, and Amalie had clients in and out of her CPA office all day. They were both happy to be home.

Shirley had abandoned them after supper for a bubble bath, leaving Sean and Amalie in the living room by the fire, watching TV.

Amalie shivered. "The wind isn't blowing, it's shrieking. Trouble is coming, but I already warned Brendan when I saw him the other day."

Sean stilled. "Warned him about what trouble? What did you see?"

"A woman comes. She will need his help. And she will matter in his life. Beyond that, I don't know."

Sean sighed. "Well, whatever it is, we won't let him face it alone."

Amalie scooted up beside him, then turned to face him and reached for his hands. "I have something to tell you. I wasn't keeping a secret. I was just waiting to make sure before I spoke it."

Sean curled his fingers around her hands. "Okay... I'm listening."

"We're going to have babies."

Sean's eyes widened, and then he was laughing and hugging her. "Oh my God, darlin'...that's the most wonderful news ever! I'm going to be a father! You're going to be a... No, wait, you are already a mother. You're growing our baby."

Amalie was laughing with him because he still hadn't connected all the dots.

"Not a baby, Sean. Babies, as in twins. We're having two."

His eyes widened. "Oh wow! How did we manage that?"

Amalie smiled. "I would assume the usual way, with gusto."

He brushed a soft kiss across her lips. "You are my heart…my love…my forever woman. What a gift you have given me." And then the questions began. "How far along are you?"

"Twelve weeks. I asked for an ultrasound because I had a vision that there were two, and I wanted to be sure it was real and not just a dream."

"Are we telling everyone now or…?" Sean asked.

"Mom is making dinner for everyone Sunday. Why don't we make the announcement then?" Amalie said, and then sighed. "We can tell Dad together via Zoom whenever we can get him still long enough to make time."

"Your dad loves you to distraction. He'll always make time for you," Sean said, and ran his finger along the side of her jaw where the burn scars were, then eyed the white streak in her hair that had appeared after the wreck that nearly killed her. "Wolfgang Outen is going to dote on being a grandfather, just like he treasured finding out that you existed."

Amalie shivered. "I know. It's just all so new and a

little bit scary. I want to be the best mommy ever, but I never had one, so I'm a little afraid I won't know how."

Sean cupped her face. "Baby...you're so full of love that it's going to overwhelm you when they lay them in your arms. And you have me, and Mom, and a whole family of brothers and sisters-in-law who are going to fuss over who gets to hold them, and I'll be right beside you all the way. We're going to be fine. What's going to be hard is keeping this little secret until Sunday."

The wind was still shrieking, but Amalie didn't hear it anymore. She was too full of joy and laughter to let it in.

———

Harley Banks's flight in the Sikorsky X2 from Chicago to Jubilee took less than two hours. She'd flown in helicopters before, but never this distance or this fast. Flying over the Cumberland Mountains, some of which were snowcapped and dense with forest in winter mode, was a reminder that she was heading into unfamiliar territory. She was used to snow, but not on mountains. The corporate world she worked within was in hugely populated areas, but she felt drawn to the new experience. All of a sudden, the chopper dipped and swooped down the slope of the mountain, giving her the first glimpse of the town below.

It was smaller than she'd expected of a tourist attraction. Insulated from the outside world by the surrounding mountains, but definitely not isolated. She was surprised to see so much activity at this time of year, especially since Jubilee did not cater its tourism to winter sports. Her musings ended when the chopper set down.

"Your ride is on the way, Miss Banks, but it's thirty-three degrees this morning, so we'll just wait here until it arrives," the pilot said.

"Right," Harley said as she unbuckled her seat belt.

A couple of minutes later, a sleek black car pulled up, and young man in a hooded parka got out on the run. The pilot helped her down from the chopper, and Harley was immediately facing the cold and the rotor wash all at the same time. She zipped the front of her coat up all the way to her chin and started walking.

"Welcome to Jubilee, Ms. Banks. I'm Kevin with the hotel concierge. I'll get your luggage. Just follow me."

The pilot was right. It was cold—Chicago cold. She followed the concierge to the car and was soon seated in the back seat of a very warm and comfortable Lexus.

Ray Caldwell is class all the way, she thought as she ran her hand across the luxurious leather, then caught a glimpse of her reflection in the window and sighed. On a good day, her curls were unruly, but right now her hair was in chaos. She hastily finger-combed it back into place as Kevin jumped into the driver's seat.

"All set, ma'am?" he asked.

"Yes, thank you," Harley said, then sat back and enjoyed the brief ride from the heliport to the Serenity Inn.

Liz Devon was waiting just inside the entrance, but when she saw the woman getting out of the car, she couldn't help but stare. She'd been imagining all morning what a corporate PI with an accounting degree might look like, but a runway model had never entered her mind.

Harley Banks was stunning. A slim angular face with cheekbones to die for, almond-shaped eyes beneath black, perfectly arched brows, and full lips completely devoid of color, with thick tumbling curls so black they looked blue.

The moment she entered the lobby, Liz stepped forward.

"Ms. Banks, I'm Liz Devon, Ray Caldwell's daughter and the event coordinator for the hotel. I've already checked you in. Your suite is ready and waiting. Kevin will take your bags to your room. You're on the eighth floor. Our main dining area is on the tenth floor. The views from your room and our dining area are spectacular."

"Wonderful," Harley said as she fell into step beside her.

"How was your flight?" Liz asked as they headed for the elevators.

Harley arched a brow. "Fast."

Liz smiled. "Let me guess. Dad chartered a Sikorsky. He loves to travel in those."

"That he did," Harley said. "I have to admit, the location of Jubilee as a tourist attraction is surprising, actually quite unusual. I would have thought there would be more tourist features farther up the mountain. I noticed as I was researching the place that hiking up there is not an option, either."

"This place was settled by a Scottish trapper in the early 1800s. He settled here and built a little cabin that became a trading post for furs. Took a Chickasaw woman for a wife, and as the years passed, a little community grew. They named it Jubilee. The people who live on Pope Mountain are all descendants of three original families: Pope, Glass, and Cauley. They work in Jubilee and help foster the tourist industry, but they treasure and protect their privacy, too, and the mountain is off-limits to tourists. The town itself is owned by a corporation that controls the growth of Jubilee, because enlarging it would also mean destroying its natural beauty. And controlling it in this way actually makes sense. Our head pastry chef is Brendan Pope. We were really fortunate to bring him in. He's classically trained and has quite a following. He's a really nice guy. You'll meet him and all the rest of the staff soon enough."

Harley was listening without comment, absorbing everything around her. The little gift shops, a jewelry shop, the small coffee shop off the lobby, a café-style restaurant for casual dining, a barber/beauty shop, and signs directing to the gym, the indoor pool, and a spa.

It had all of the amenities, but she was curious about the rooms.

Their conversation ended when they got on the elevator with some other guests, and when they finally reached the eighth floor, they exited.

"It's just down the hall to your right. Room 800." Liz swiped the key card, then opened the door and stepped inside to let Harley enter.

Her bags were already on the bed in the adjoining room. The curtains had been pulled away from the sliders leading out to a small balcony, and the view of Pope Mountain was right before her. There was a coffee bar and mini-fridge, a living area with a big-screen TV and comfortable-looking furniture, and they'd set up a whole workspace against one wall, with a hotel computer and a printer/scanner so she could access all she needed.

Harley was impressed. "This is comparable to any of the finer hotels I've ever been in. Your father knows his stuff."

Liz nodded. "He's been in real estate and hotels all of my life." She pulled a small notebook from her pocket and handed it to Harley. "This is the log-on info you'll need, along with a password already preset for you. There's also a list of every link connected to the hotel, including banking. Our bank has been notified that an audit will be happening, and you have view-only approval to access whatever information you need to see there. If there's anything we've missed, just call me. Oh…beside your room being comped, you have free rein to eat wherever you wish here in the hotel, or use room service. Just sign your room number to the bills and they'll be covered by the hotel, too. Enjoy the gym, pool, and spa as well, and don't hesitate to try out the main dining room at your pleasure. Try some of Brendan Pope's breads and desserts, as well as the food of Chef Randolph, our chef de cuisine."

"What about Larry Beaumont, the hotel manager, and his daughter, Justine?" Harley asked.

Liz rolled her eyes. "Ask Beaumont anything you need to know, but he gets no information about you other than you're here to audit, and I'm your contact. As of yesterday, his daughter, Justine, was jailed on numerous charges, including drunk and disorderly and assault, and Larry isn't forthcoming with what's happening. Personally, I'm just hoping her behavior doesn't fall back on the hotel, since this is where she was living when all this happened."

Harley didn't let on that she already knew. "You have a plate full here, don't you?"

Liz's shoulders slumped. "You have no idea. Now, I'll let you get settled. This is my card with contact information when I'm not on-site. Otherwise, I'll likely be on the premises during the day. I hope you are comfortable here."

"Thank you," Harley said. "I'm sure I will be."

Liz let herself out, and Harley turned the dead bolt

and fastened the security chain for added security, then turned around and looked at the luggage on the bed.

"Here we go again," she said, and began unpacking.

———————

Except for a court-appointed lawyer who mumbled when he spoke, Justine Beaumont suffered through her court appearance alone. Her father didn't show. Her mother had promised to be there but wasn't. She didn't know if her mother would appear to make bail, and she didn't want to hang around Jubilee any longer than she had to. But she balked when she found out that if she pled not guilty, a court date would be set which could take months, and she couldn't leave town. If she pled guilty, the lawyer said she would likely be charged for all the damages she had to pay for, and they'd have to take a chance on the judge not handing down jail time to go with it.

It was a knee-jerk decision, but when the moment came, and Justine was asked by the court how she pled, she turned on the tears, slumped her shoulders, and spoke in a faint, shaky voice. "Guilty, Your Honor. I got drunk and I am horribly ashamed that I hurt others in the process. All I can say is, I will never take another drink as long as I live." Then she stood there trembling while quiet tears rolled down her pretty little face.

Her juvenile records were sealed. She didn't have any speeding tickets or priors, and the rehab visits had all been voluntary, so the court had no records, and the judge had a backlog of cases waiting.

"Do we have a firm amount of the cost of damages?" he asked.

The lawyer nodded. "Yes, Your Honor," he said, and handed the paper to the bailiff to pass on to the judge.

The judge scanned the lists, which also included medical treatment for the injured men and women, and then looked up.

"Miss Beaumont, this list of damages in no way absolves you of any personal charges the injured people may choose to sue you for. Do you understand that?"

Justine choked on a sob. "Yes, Your Honor."

"The actual damages you incurred are for broken glassware and spilled liquor, and an unpaid bar tab, plus fines for all that you were charged with. The assault charge came as a result of your inebriation, and not an actual, intentional assault, so I am voiding that. The total damage, which includes the medical treatment for the four people who were injured and the fines from your charges, comes to six thousand, five hundred and seventy-five dollars. Once you have satisfied that amount to the court, the case will be closed. You will be remanded to the local jail until such monies have been collected."

Justine groaned, then flinched at the sound of the gavel. A policeman put her back in handcuffs and took her back to the jail.

She knew she'd dodged a huge bullet, but coming back to the jail only fueled her anger. All she felt was abandonment. She still refused to accept that all of this was the end result of choices she made.

When Randy, the jailer, shut the cell doors behind her, she turned around, threw back her head, and screamed. She stopped to take a breath, eyeing his reaction. There was none. And when he calmly walked out of the cell area and shut the door, she sank down on the bunk in total defeat.

She had no parents. No money. And the chances of getting out of here were slim to none without them. She didn't know what was going to happen next, but she would die in here before she'd ask either of them for help again.

Karen Beaumont arrived in Jubilee just after 2:00 p.m., googled the address of the Jubilee PD, and drove until she found the station. She dreaded this as much as she'd dreaded childbirth, but she parked, then entered the building and approached the front desk.

"I'm here about Justine Beaumont's arraignment. Can you tell me when and where it's being held?" she asked.

"That's already happened," Sergeant Winter told her. "She pled guilty."

Karen gasped. "She what?"

"She pled guilty, but she won't be released until the damages have all been paid."

"What are the damages?" Karen asked.

Winter pulled up her file on his computer. "Six thousand, five hundred and seventy-five dollars. No checks. No credit cards. Cash money, only."

The blood drained from Karen's face. She felt faint, in a panic as to what would happen to her daughter in jail if she didn't get out, because she didn't have that kind of ready money.

"Thank you," she mumbled, and went back to her car, laid her head on the steering wheel, and burst into tears. After she'd cried herself out, she started driving toward the hotel where Larry worked.

———

Larry stomped into his office, slamming the door shut behind him, and then dropped into his chair. He just found out the auditor was already on-site and in her suite. He wanted to be pissed that he hadn't been notified and that he wasn't the one to meet her, but he knew better. This was all about Ray getting ready to sell, and the logical go-between for that would be Ray's daughter, Liz.

Still, he felt it only proper that he introduce himself, but to do that, he first had to find out what room she was in. He was about to call Liz when his cell phone rang. When he saw who it was, he thought about letting it go to voicemail, but knew she'd never stop calling, so he decided to get it over with and picked up.

"Why are you calling me? I said all I ever cared to say to you yesterday."

Karen frowned. She wanted to argue, but she needed his compliance. "Too bad. We have a child together."

"No. We don't have a child anymore. Just a grown-ass troublemaker who shares our DNA. What do you want? I'm busy."

Karen's heart skipped a beat. This was the maddest she had ever known Larry to be, and something told her it wasn't going to get better, but she had to try.

"I'm in Jubilee," Karen said.

"Peachy. Kindly do not register at this hotel. I don't want you or her under this roof."

"Larry, don't be this way. I came to bail Justine out of jail, only to find out she pled guilty at her arraignment and somehow managed to skip being sentenced to jail time, but she has to pay all the fines and damages before they'll release her. It's six thousand, five hundred and seventy-five dollars, or she just rots in jail."

Larry lost it. "Did it ever occur to you that might be where she belongs?"

"Larry! Don't!" Karen wailed.

He could hear the fear and tears in her voice. He wanted to hate both of them. He was so sick of their drama.

Karen was desperate. "I don't have that kind of money. I can't use a credit card, although I have one paid off that would work. If you'll come up with the cash to get her out, you can skip the next three months of my alimony. It would come to about the same amount."

He frowned. "I don't trust you. You have to put that in writing first, so you can't haul me back to court and claim I'm not paying you."

"I will! I promise!" Karen said. "You write it, and I'll sign it the moment you hand me the cash. You might be ready to abandon her, but I can't."

Larry snorted. "Oh, please. You abandoned her four years ago after you dumped her off at rehab. Why do you think she's been living with me?"

Silence.

"Well?" Larry asked.

"Yes. Fine. You're right," Karen snapped. "And when I get her out of jail, I'm taking her back to Dallas with me. We'll figure something out, and you'll resume my alimony payments in a timely fashion?"

He sighed. "Yes."

"I'll need to go to the penthouse to pack her clothes," Karen said.

"No. You don't need to do anything but get the hell out of town. Her clothes are already packed and down in storage behind the front desk. I'm going to have to go down to the bank to get the cash. I'll meet you outside the hotel in an hour, with her luggage. And then I swear to God, if either one of you ever calls me again, it better be to tell me someone died…preferably you or her."

He hung up in her ear.

Karen gasped, and then shivered. She'd never been afraid of Larry before, but she was now.

Larry's thoughts were spinning. He had plenty of money in his special Dallas account, but he'd never had a need to withdraw any of it until now. He ran upstairs to the penthouse to his personal laptop and logged into his banking.

A couple of clicks and he transferred seven thousand dollars from the special account into his personal account here in Jubilee. He waited until he saw the money deposited in that account, then headed downtown, hurried into the bank, wrote a check for the exact amount of cash needed to pay for the damages, and drove back to the hotel. He had fifteen minutes to spare when he raced back inside, retrieved the luggage with Justine's clothes, and had them taken outside.

The day was cold but clear, and the fresh air in his face felt like a cleanser in more ways than one. He was getting rid of two problems in one blow today. Within a short time, both the women in his life would be on their way back to Dallas. The trouble Justine had caused at the hotel would be behind him, and his life could finally settle into a normal routine.

———————

Karen had been parked in the hotel parking lot, making reservations while she waited out the hour, planning where they'd stay overnight on their drive back to

Dallas. She had visions of them hanging out together, doing mother-daughter stuff, whatever that was. She'd never done it before, but better late than never.

She'd seen Larry drive away, and she'd seen him come back. She was watching when the bellhop brought out three suitcases, with Larry walking out behind him, and took that as her signal. She started the car and headed for the front entrance, then pulled in and popped the trunk before getting out.

Larry didn't even look at her. He just pulled a paper out of his pocket and handed her a pen. She signed her name and held out her hand. He put an envelope in her palm and loaded the suitcases without saying a word, then turned his back on her and went inside.

Karen closed the trunk, got back in her car, and headed to the jail.

Chapter 7

Justine had begged a towel, washcloth, and a bar of soap from Randy the jailer, and after an okay from the chief, Randy handed them to her through the bars. But when she tossed it all on the bunk and started stripping, he made a run for it. He didn't want to be caught on camera with a naked woman behind the bars, especially one this crazy. He went back to his desk, and as soon as he confirmed she was intending to wash up in the little sink beside the toilet, he looked away.

She craved the luxury of a nice hot shower, but she was going to happily settle for just feeling clean again, even if she had to put dirty clothes back on. The soap was abrasive and smelled like pine trees. The cell was a little too chilly for this, but she didn't care. She was barefoot and bare-assed to the world when she got her washcloth wet and soaped it before then started scrubbing and rinsing—first her face, scrubbing off every ounce of old makeup, and then scrubbing her way down, until the last thing she washed were her feet. She wiped what she could of the ketchup off her pants, then tossed the wet washcloth in the sink and started drying.

Her pants were still damp as she put them back on, then finished dressing and sat down.

Later, Randy brought her a food tray—a cold sandwich, a bag of chips, and a bottle of water—and left without meeting her gaze.

She thought of all the fine food she'd had from room service, as well as the fine food she'd rejected, then sat down and ate without tasting, refusing to cry. Refusing to feel sorry for herself. Instead, letting all of that fuel her rage. Justine accepted that she'd never finished what she started, but all that was about to change. Before she died, she would make her parents pay—and maybe she'd add Brendan Pope to that list. If he hadn't been so mean, none of this would have ever happened.

Hours later, she was on her bunk, lying on her back and watching the second hand sweep around the face of the clock on the wall across from her cell. She'd watched every minute pass for the last five hours while playing out payback scenarios in her head, when she heard the jailer's keys jingling.

She sat up as the door opened. The jailer and the police chief walked in. She watched them approach without moving. Staying silent. Waiting to find out what kind of hole they were going to drop her in when the jailer unlocked her cell. Suddenly, the chief was standing between her and freedom.

"Your mother is here," he said. "The fines and cost of damage you incurred have been paid. It does not prevent anyone you injured from suing you personally, but in the eyes of the law, you are free to go."

Justine was shocked. Her mother had come through! She swung her legs off the bunk and stood, then walked beside the chief all the way to the lobby without speaking. They stopped at the front desk, watching as the desk sergeant returned her personal belongings.

She went through her purse, checking the contents. Makeup, a couple of condom packets, a maxed-out credit card, and no cash. She opened the big paper bag they'd given her and pulled out the white faux fur jacket she'd taken off in the bar, then put it back on and signed the receipt sheet.

"Is that it?" she asked.

Chief Warren nodded. "Yes, ma'am. That is all."

Justine slung her purse over her shoulder and walked out into the cold mountain air.

The moment Karen saw Justine exit the station, she started crying, jumped out of the car, and opened her arms to hug her. Justine stood within her mother's embrace without responding.

"Oh, honey! Bless your heart! It's cold out here. Let's get into the car where it's warm," she said.

Justine slid into the passenger seat and went into attack mode, pitching her voice to something between a pitiful whine and unforgivable accusation.

"You both left me in jail. You didn't show up for court. I thought you didn't have the money," Justine said.

Karen blinked as her empathy faded.

"Where the hell is my 'Thank you, Mommy'? It takes a hell of a long time to drive from Dallas to here. You're the one who was bawling and begging when you called, telling me you didn't know when you'd be arraigned, which means neither did I. I got here as fast as I could...and you're right. I didn't have the money to pay for this ridiculous mess you made. But your father did, and I just traded three months of my alimony...the money I live on...so that your father would give it all to me now in one lump sum. I just got you out of jail with my rent and food money, you ungrateful little bitch."

Justine shrugged, quickly reassessing her attitude. She didn't want to be kicked out of both parents' homes.

"Sorry. I'm going to have PTSD from that jail."

"It won't compare to the PTSD you have given your father and me for the last ten years. Stop making everyone else at fault. You're the one who's responsible. And as usual, you're also not the one paying to fix it."

Karen started the car and began backing up, and then as soon as she could, made a turn and headed toward the highway.

"Wait! Where are we going?" Justine asked.

"Dallas," Karen said.

"I need my things! All my clothes!" Justine cried.

"They're in the trunk. Your father had them packed and waiting at the front desk. He is so done with you... with the both of us," Karen said.

Justine glanced at her mother, saw the tears on her

cheeks, and then looked away. It was going to be a long trip home, but at least she was getting out of this hill-billy town, once and for all.

———

Harley Banks had unpacked and was in the bathroom trying to do something with her hair. After she was sat-isfied most of the wild curls had been tamed, she peeled the wrapper from a fresh bar of soap and washed up, then opened the little bottle of hand lotion and rubbed some into her skin. It didn't have much of a scent, but it served its purpose.

After that, she went straight to the computer, logged on with her new password, and made a quick check of all of the links on the site, then logged back out again. She needed to see the hotel in its entirety and what it had to offer before she began digging into the business side.

She reached for the hotel brochure, absently scan-ning the listed amenities, then studying the little map to locate the gym, hair salon, coffee bar, and gift shop, then how to get to the main dining area of the hotel.

One of the photos on the brochure was of a bath-room with luxurious amenities, even a close-up of the cute little woven basket containing extra soaps, small bottles of shampoo and hand lotion.

Harley glanced at it, and then paused and looked at it again. All of the comped toiletries in the photo had the distinctive Serenity Inn logo—pine trees and the image of a mountain on the label.

Frowning, she carried the brochure into the bathroom. The same little basket was on the counter, but instead of what was in the photo, there were just white plastic bottles for lotions, and shampoos, plain wrappers for the soaps. No fancy labels. No special scents. Just labels with the words *shampoo* and *lotion* and *soap*.

She made a mental note to check the vendors Ray used against the vendors supplying the hotel since Larry's arrival, and then glanced at the time. It was getting close to noon, and she was starving.

She never ate when she flew because it made her sick, so food was the first thing on her mind. It was too cold to play tourist and walk down to the strip, and she didn't want room service. Tomorrow she'd rent a car, but not today. It was too cold to sightsee, and she wanted a feel for the hotel, and maybe to catch a glimpse of Brendan Pope.

Still wearing black leather pants and black boots, and the thick, white cable-knit sweater she'd traveled in, she pocketed her key card, dropped her cell phone in a small shoulder bag, and left her room, pausing a moment in the hall to reorient herself toward the elevators, and wound up waiting a couple of minutes at the elevators for a car to arrive.

The car was nearly full when it stopped. "Room for one more?" she asked, and the residents quickly shifted to make room for her.

Men gawked. Women glared. She ignored it all. Business as usual.

Everyone in the elevator exited at the same time, obviously all of them heading into the dining room for lunch. She joined the waiting line to be seated, and when it became her turn, the hostess grabbed a menu.

"Table for one, please. Preferably against a wall or in a corner," Harley said.

The hostess nodded. "This way, please," she said and seated her at a small table for two in the corner against a wall, giving her a grand view of the town below. "Your waiter will be right with you. Enjoy your lunch," the hostess said, and hurried back to her station.

Harley leaned back and relaxed. She was here. The job was ahead of her, and she had all the confidence in herself that she knew how to do it. She opened the menu and began scanning the selections, trying to decide what to order. But whatever she ordered, she was saving room for dessert. She was curious about the man in Justine Beaumont's headlights and wanted to see what all the fuss was about. What better way than to sample his wares?

A few minutes later, her waiter arrived. He was a wiry young man, barely out of his teens, with sandy hair and a friendly face. He went momentarily mute as Harley looked up and smiled.

"Uh…" Then he remembered his job. "I'm Lee. I'll be your server today. Can I get you something to drink?"

"Coke on ice," Harley said.

He nodded. "Are you ready to order, or do you need a few minutes?"

"I'm ready. I'll have a bowl of potato soup and the jalapeño corn bread."

"Yes, miss. Good choice on a cold day like today. Maybe an appetizer to start you off?"

"No thanks," she said, and smiled at him again as she handed him the menu.

Still a little dumbstruck by her beauty, Lee nodded and scurried back to the waiters' station, entered the order on the computer, and then went to get her drink, then hurried back to her table with the Coke on ice. A server followed, pushing the bread cart, and left a miniature loaf of herb bread served on a small wooden cutting board, along with a ramekin of whipped butter.

"Enjoy. Your food will be out soon," Lee said, and left Harley sampling the savory bread.

The moment he walked into the kitchen, he whistled between his teeth. "I just saw the most beautiful woman. Damn, y'all, she's sitting alone at the back table by the windows. Blackest curls surrounding that gorgeous face... There are no words," he said, then picked up an order and headed out to deliver it.

When a few members of the staff started to peek out the door, Chef Randolph waved a knife in the air. "I don't care if she's sitting there naked. Get back to your stations," he roared.

Brendan chuckled beneath his breath as he added a

single pink buttercream rose onto the tiny cake he had waiting and looked around for his sous-chef.

"Anthony, bring the mini-cart. We have a couple celebrating their fiftieth anniversary. We don't want to keep them waiting."

He placed the little cake on the cart, added the ice bucket with the demi-bottle of champagne, and headed for the dining room.

"Get the door," he ordered, and Anthony ran ahead to push it open, then followed along to serve as sommelier when the cake was served.

Brendan knew the couple was at table twenty, but once he saw them, they would have been impossible to miss. A tiny little woman with snow-white hair, sitting beside a thin man with stooped shoulders and a snow-white mustache. He had a frizzy halo of white hair that rested just above his ears, and they were talking head-to-head and holding hands.

Brendan knew their names were Joe and Neelie, and when he reached their table, the look between them put a lump in his throat. He wanted that. A love and a woman who loved him enough to stay the course. Then they saw him, and the little woman clapped her hands.

"Oh, Joe! Look what they brought!"

Brendan set the little cake in the middle of their table.

"Happy Anniversary, Joe and Neelie. From all of us at the Serenity Inn, wishing you another fifty more!"

"I had pink roses in my bridal bouquet!" Neelie cried.

"A little bird told me," Brendan said, then nodded at Anthony, who promptly set two champagne flutes at their places and did the honors. The pop of the champagne cork was heard across the dining room as Anthony began filling each flute with the bubbly wine. The waitstaff, who'd been cued to participate, moved to the celebratory table and cheered in unison—

"Happy fiftieth anniversary, Joe and Neelie!"

The diners joined in by cheering and clapping as the elderly couple toasted each other and took their first sips of champagne.

Then Brendan picked up the cake knife and handed it to Joe. "I believe you two have done this before," he said.

Neelie was giggling as Joe took the knife.

"We do this together," Joe whispered.

Neelie laid her hand over his, and together they pushed the knife down through the cake all the way to the plate.

"Allow me," Brendan said, and sliced a piece of cake for each of them. "With our best wishes," he said, and as he was turning around, purposefully looked in the corner of the room, to the woman sitting alone at a table for two, and realized she was looking at him.

Their gazes locked, and time stopped.

Lee the waiter wasn't wrong. She was stunning. But she was looking at him with an intensity that strangers didn't evoke. Did he know her? Or the better question might be, how did she know him? It took every ounce

BAD SEED   149

of restraint he had to turn around and walk away when all he wanted was to hear her voice.

━━━━━

Harley was still shaking from the look that passed between them.

Brendan Pope's picture at the DMV did not do him justice. He was stunning—and tall, so tall—with a massive build to go with it. Broad chest and shoulders. Long, muscular legs. A true giant in the room, and he'd just treated that darling little couple with quiet dignity. No wonder Justine Beaumont had lost her mind over this man.

At that moment, her waiter came back with her food and brought her a refill of her Coke on ice while trying not to stare.

"Will there be anything else?" Lee asked.

Harley nodded. "I'll be wanting dessert."

"Yes, ma'am, I'll bring the dessert menu shortly," he said.

"No, just ask the pastry chef to choose something for me," she said.

A bit taken aback, Lee nodded. "Yes, ma'am," he said, hurried back to the kitchen, and straight to Brendan's workstation.

"Chef, the lady at Table 12 will be wanting dessert in a while. She asked if you would mind choosing something for her."

The hair crawled on the back of Brendan's neck. He went still, and then nodded. "I don't mind."

"Let me know when it's ready and I'll serve it," Lee said.

"No need. You let me know when she's ready and I'll deliver it."

"Yes, Chef," Lee said, and hustled back to deliver another order.

Brendan went to the cooler with a dessert plate, eyed the trays of ready desserts, chose a strawberry napoleon one from the trays, and then left it on the plate awaiting delivery, and went back to work.

Pans of herb bread were coming out of the ovens, more were going in, and he didn't have time to let his thoughts wander.

But at the other end of the kitchen area, Chef Randolph was vocally objecting to the cuts of meat his sous-chef just brought from the cooler.

"What is this?" he yelled. "These aren't porterhouse cuts!"

"That's what was delivered, and the boxes are clearly marked," the sous-chef said. "Maybe it was a packing error. I'll look again."

Randolph frowned. "You take over the grill. I need to see this for myself!" he said, and stormed off.

It didn't take long for him to see that his sous-chef was correct. The delivery was clearly marked, but the meat inside was not what they'd ordered. The cut was similar, but it was from a lesser quality of meat.

He began looking through the rest of what they had on hand, and then stormed out. This wasn't the first time this had happened, and he was fed up. He went back to work, but when this shift was over, he was going over the manager's head and straight to the boss's daughter about the poor quality of meat being ordered. It wasn't what he requested, and this wasn't up to Randolph's standards.

While Brendan was working, he got a text from Liz.

Dad's auditor, Harley Banks, is on-site. She's been given free rein through the hotel. Oh...just a heads-up. She's stunning.

Maybe that's why the woman was staring at me. She already knows who I am and what I look like. I misread the whole thing. Or did I?

Now he was anxiously awaiting the signal from Lee to deliver her dessert, and when it came, he dropped what he was doing, took the plated dessert from the cooler, and placed it on a tray.

"Anthony, watch the timer on the breads," he said, and walked into the dining room with the woman's dessert.

———

Harley was reading a text from Ray Caldwell when she sensed someone standing beside her. It was Brendan

Pope, and she hadn't even heard him coming. Yet here he was, and it appeared she'd underestimated him. He didn't just choose a dessert; he was delivering it. He'd not only read her play, but he'd also called her bluff. Maybe she'd unleashed something she didn't know how to handle.

"Your dessert, ma'am. A strawberry napoleon. Enjoy."

Harley smiled, and then stood and held out her hand. As tall as she was, she was still looking up when she spoke.

"I'm Harley Banks, and you surprised me, Chef Pope. I didn't hear you approach."

"Brendan," he said. "It's a pleasure to meet you. Ray told me you were coming. He also asked me to watch out for you if the need arose."

"Really?" Harley said.

"Yes, ma'am." He pulled a card from his pocket and laid it on the table. "My personal cell number, just in case."

"Nobody calls me 'ma'am.' Just Harley, okay? When you get time, would you mind coming to my suite after you clock out? I need to pick your brain a bit. I promise it won't take long."

"Yes, ma'am. Happy to help," he said, and left her standing.

Harley watched him walk away, thinking how remarkable that a man that big could move with such grace. *Why do I feel like I've just been sideswiped?* She plopped back into her chair, eyed her dessert, and then picked up her fork.

"Taste test," she muttered, and poked the fork into the light-as-air puff-pastry sheets, down through the vanilla pastry cream and thinly sliced strawberries, all the way to the plate, then scooped up the bite and popped it in her mouth. "Oh my God," she muttered, and rolled her eyes, savoring the crisp and smooth and fruity all on her tongue.

Lee the waiter appeared with a coffee, smiled as he set it down, and disappeared.

"I could get used to this," Harley said, and didn't look up until she'd eaten every bite.

While she was downing dessert, Brendan was sliding fresh bread onto cooling racks, and pretended meeting her was no bigger a deal than meeting any dinner guest, but that would have been a lie. And, he was going to have to face her again tonight after work.

Harley Banks might just be the most beautiful woman he'd ever seen, but he was so used to dodging Justine that he was still in stealth mode.

He hadn't forgotten Amalie's warning. If he was to believe it, then he had to accept that sometime during her stay, Harley Banks was going to need him, and that she would matter in his life, and not to push her away.

Alex Fallin, the young man Brendan had pulled from the roof of the overturned bus, was healing nicely, and his sister, Josie, had finally quit crying every time she looked at him, thank God. At first, she'd scared him, making him think she knew something about his injury that he did not, and he had begun to wonder if he was going to die.

He'd traded the hospital bed for a bed in her touring bus and spent his time watching TV and sleeping and eating when Josie popped in to check on him throughout the day. Every time she came back to the bus, she would talk about the man who'd saved his life. Then this morning, Josie walked in with a cinnamon roll and plopped it down on his table and started talking.

"I brought you something good. It's a cinnamon roll from a place downtown called Granny Annie's Bakery. They are so good. And the coolest thing! I found out that the woman who runs the bakery is Brendan Pope's aunt. I told her how he saved you."

"Nice," Alex said, and took a bite, chewed, and swallowed. "Oh man, you were right! This is amazing!"

Josie's phone was buzzing, but she was ignoring it. She just kept looking at her brother. He was eight years younger, but after their parents divorced, they both stayed with their dad. It had been the saving grace for both of them.

After Josie became famous, her mother tried to come back into her life, but Josie didn't buckle. And then last year their father died. Alex graduated college in December and was coming to live with Josie while he began job hunting. Then this happened. Josie was so grateful she hadn't lost him, too, that for the first couple of days, all she'd done was look at him and cry about what might have been. But that fear had finally passed, and watching Alex plow through the sweet roll made her happy.

"Guess what else I found out about Brendan Pope. He's the head pastry chef at the Serenity Inn. That's where I'm hosting a fan-club event in a few days," she said.

Alex glanced up. "I think I remember him mentioning something about working there, but I was kind of out of it. So, he bakes stuff?"

"Apparently that skill runs in the family," Josie said, pointing to the cinnamon roll. "I talked to your doctor. I can get some crutches for you now. I'll do it today, but you still have to keep weight off your leg until your staples are removed."

Alex nodded as he licked the sugar off his thumb and finger. "I'm really sorry all this happened. I wanted to spend some time with you, and now you're having to take care of me."

Josie patted his foot.

"Sugar, I've been taking care of you since you learned to walk. I miss you. Being on the road gets lonesome. I'm so damn grateful you didn't die in that wreck."

He grinned. "Me too."

Harley changed from her travel clothes into an old pair of jeans and a nondescript sweatshirt, swapped running shoes for the boots she'd been wearing, and spent a couple of hours at the computer, setting up a spreadsheet for the audit.

Once she was satisfied with the start she'd made, she pocketed her key card and left her room to find the manager's office and introduce herself to Larry Beaumont. She'd learned a long time ago that, in her line of work, presenting herself as harmless made everything better. She already knew the office was on the fourth floor and took the stairs down four flights instead of waiting for an elevator.

It was simple enough to locate the office from the sign on the door, and she promptly knocked, then waited for permission to enter.

Larry was at the window in his office overlooking the back side of the hotel. From where he was standing, he could see the whole of Pope Mountain, part of the creek and the swiftly flowing water that came down from some spring up above, and the back end of a parking lot for one of the music venues. Sometimes when he looked at the scene, he felt the mountain's majesty. Other times, he felt a threat from its presence, as if it was barring him from getting too close. Today, he felt hemmed in, which had nothing to do with his location and everything to do with his family.

He wanted a drink. But he was on the job. Then someone knocked. He jumped from the unexpected sound and then turned.

"Come in," he said.

The door opened to a woman so stunning that he forgot to breathe.

"Mr. Beaumont?"

"Yes?"

"I'm Harley Banks, the auditor Mr. Caldwell sent. I wanted to introduce myself."

Larry smiled. "Yes, of course! Come in! Take a seat."

Harley closed the door behind her as she entered, then sat. It was hard to pull off being the numbers nerd when she wore this face and hair, but she'd become adept at not calling more attention to herself than necessary.

"How was your trip?" Larry asked.

Harley noticed he was still standing. A very male move in trying to assert authority.

"It was fine. My suite is quite comfortable and roomy enough for me to work in. It's much appreciated. Thank you," she said.

"You're most welcome! Good to know it suits. I like to make sure our guests always have everything they need. It's quite cold here this time of year, so do let me know if you're not comfortable."

Harley already knew Ray had ordered it all, but

Larry appeared to be taking full credit. However, trying to look like a big shot was not a crime.

"It is cold here, but I'm from Chicago. I left several feet of dirty slush and snow behind me, and more predicted, but Jubilee wears her winter coat well."

Larry blinked. *She's beautiful, obviously intelligent or she wouldn't be an auditor, and she speaks like a poet. I wonder if she has a significant other?* Then he realized she was still talking and tuned back in.

"Necessary now and then for me to view parts of the hotel that are off-limits to guests, although I'm certain you already know that. Just know that I won't get in the way of anything. I'm just auditing, not redecorating," she said, and then laughed.

The sound went all the way to Larry's toes as he laughed along with her. Then to his dismay, she was on her feet and in the act of leaving.

"Thank you for letting me disturb a bit of your day. I'll be on my way now. I'm taking a little tour of the shops and guest amenities. I rented a car that will be delivered here sometime tomorrow. Other than that, I think we're good for now."

Larry hurried to open the door for her and, as she walked past him, realized she was taller than he was. He watched her walking away before he shut the door and then went to the bottom drawer of his desk, pulled out a bottle of whiskey and a shot glass, and poured himself a drink. He tossed it back in one gulp, then rode out the fire and heat as he swallowed, before returning the bottle to the drawer.

"That is one fine woman," he muttered, and went back to work.

Satisfied that hand had played out as she intended, Harley took an escalator downstairs to the lobby and began wandering through the shops, eyeing what was for sale, and noting how the shop clerks interacted with the guests, then took the elevator down to the pool area. Rising vapor from the water was visible from where she was standing, which told her the pool was heated.

She found the spa area and stopped in to visit a bit and pick up a brochure.

"Welcome to the Serenity Inn. I'm Tori. Are you here to book an appointment?" the receptionist asked.

Harley shrugged. "Maybe later. I'm going to be here for a while. I'll check my schedule and get with you later," Harley said, and left the spa.

She was back up on the ground floor and walking through the lobby when she saw a police car come to a quick stop at the front entrance. Curious, she paused to watch, and as they got out, she did a double take. The tall one with black hair could have been Brendan Pope's twin. Then she remembered he was one of four brothers, two of whom were officers with the Jubilee police force.

Both officers came hurrying inside in long, hasty strides as two security guards from Hotel Security came out of a room with a fortysomething woman in restraints and handed her over to the officers.

One guard quickly read off her particulars.

"Virginia Taylor. Age forty-seven. Caught in the act of picking a man's pocket in the bar. When searched, we found a purse full of wallets belonging to some of our guests."

Virginia had been crying. Her mascara was smeared and there was lipstick on her teeth, likely from biting her lip as she was doing when they handed her over.

"This has all been a misunderstanding. I think some teenagers planted that in my purse while I was at the bar," she wailed.

The moment that excuse came out of Virginia's mouth, Harley saw the Brendan look-alike frown as he pulled out his handcuffs.

"Well, Virginia, you didn't think that story through. Teenagers aren't allowed in the hotel bar. Please stand still," he said, and read her the Miranda rights, but when he went to cuff her, she let out a wail.

"You're hurting me. I have witnesses," she whined.

He looked up, eyed the gathering crowd, and snapped on the second cuff. "I'm not hurting you. You're hurting yourself. I asked you to stand still and you chose to ignore the order. And yes, there are people witnessing your arrest for pickpocketing."

"I have rights. What's your name and badge number?" she shouted.

Without missing a beat, he rattled off the info.

"Officer Wiley Pope…spelled like the one in Rome…related to half the population of Jubilee. Badge number ten, as in the number after nine, but the one before eleven." And then he slipped his hand beneath one elbow while his partner took the other, and they walked her out of the hotel to the tune of continuing verbal complaints.

It was all Harley could do not to laugh. She didn't know about the rest of Brendan's brothers, but on the job, this one was unflappable. She was still smiling as she headed back to her room.

Chapter 8

OLLIE PRINE HAD EXHAUSTED ALL OF HIS CHICAGO contacts and online searches. He had finally remembered the man's name he'd known from prison. It was Schyler, and he was dead.

He was toying with the idea of ignoring Berlin's orders and just calling the number with some cocked-up lie, when it occurred to him to check food delivery services. He didn't have the hacking skills for that, but he knew someone who did. He pulled up the contact list on his cell phone and then made a call. To his dismay, it rang and rang with no answer. Just as he was about to leave a message, he heard a high-pitched whiny voice.

"Hello?"

"Hi, is Rosey there?"

"She's dead. Who is this?"

"Ah, man, I'm sorry to hear this. Is this Thor Kowalski all grown up? it's me, Ollie Prine."

"What do you want?" Thor asked.

"Don't be like that," Ollie said. "We've known each other for years."

"Yeah, you *knew* my mother, in the biblical sense,

but I was just the kid on the other side of the locked door who was listening to you screw her. So, again, what do you want?"

"Are you still all computer techy?" Ollie asked.

"I'm a gamer, and a hacker when I wanna be. What's it to you?" Thor asked.

"Awesome. Want to make a couple of hundred bucks?" Ollie asked.

"To do what?" Thor asked.

"I have a name and a phone number, but I need the address to go with it. I was thinking of finding this person through food delivery services. I mean, everyone uses them these days, so their name and address should be in the system. All you have to do is check the customer lists for food delivery in Chicago and find the address."

"Why do you want her address?" Thor asked.

"None of your business," Ollie said.

"Are you gonna kill her?"

"Ask me a question like that again, and you'll be first," Ollie said.

"A thousand dollars, and what's the name and number?"

"What the fuck!" Ollie shouted.

"Take it or leave it," Thor said.

"Fine, all right! Fine! But you don't get a penny until you tell me you have the name and address."

"What if there are several people with the same name? How will I know which is the one you want?" Thor asked.

"Well, they won't have the same phone number, though, will they?" Ollie snapped. "It will be an upscale address, and it's a woman named Harley Banks. I'll text you the number."

"If I do find it, I will let you know, and at that time, you will Venmo the money, and then I'll give you the info."

"No way! I'm calling the—"

The line went dead. Ollie cursed and made the call again.

Thor picked up, but said nothing.

"Fine, it's a deal," Ollie said.

"I'll be in touch," Thor said, and hung up again.

"Little prick," Ollie muttered, but if it got the results he needed, the thousand dollars would be a bargain.

He stretched out on the bed, laid the phone beside his pillow, and upped the volume on the cartoon channel he'd been watching. He'd grown up on Looney Tunes, and when he was frustrated at life in general, he always returned to the days when life consisted of peanut butter and jelly sandwiches and Bugs Bunny and Elmer Fudd.

———

Harley ordered room service at dinner—nothing fancy, just soup and a sandwich, but when the order arrived, there was also a small chocolate tartlet on the tray, topped off by a perfect swirl of whipped cream with three raspberries and a mint leaf strategically placed against the tart.

Brendan!

She wasn't going to second-guess the reason, because it was basically chocolate pie, and she never said no to pie. She was wishing for something to read while she ate, but there weren't any books in the suite, and she hadn't thought to bring any with her, so she turned on the TV, and caught up on national news as she ate.

It was cold outside, but she had already settled into the snug comfort of the room, finishing up the last of the soup, when she got a call. The moment Harley saw caller ID, she sighed. *What now?*

"Hi, Mom."

"Hello, darling, where are you?" Judith asked.

"Out of town on a case. Why?"

"I just wanted to let you know I'm flying to the villa tomorrow. It's not prime weather in the south of France, but it's far better than where I am. I'm sick of this nasty weather here. Your father is in DC at NASA headquarters at the moment, but will be going down to Houston in a couple of days and working at the NASA facility there for an extended period of time. I have no wish to winter alone in New York City. I was calling to see if you wanted to go with me, but I guess since you're already working again, that's out."

The pitiful tone of her mother's voice made Harley feel guilty, but such was life.

"You're right. I can't possibly go with you, and we both know you're going to have a good time. You always do. You have your little squad of buddies there. I should probably be telling you to behave yourself."

Judith giggled. "Oh…I know. I just hate traveling alone."

"I do it all the time, Mom. You'll read and sleep your way there anyway. Travel safe. Thanks for letting me know where you'll be."

"If anything comes up and you need us, you can always call your father."

"Right. Will do," Harley said, knowing she would never ask that man for help.

The call ended. Harley put her phone aside, upped the volume on the show she was watching, and reached for the plate with the little chocolate tart, forked a raspberry, swiped it through the whipped cream, and then forked off a piece of the tart and popped the whole bite in her mouth. The chocolate was smooth as silk. The whipped cream was to die for, the raspberry a perfect accompaniment, and the tart crust had a most delightful flaky, buttery crunch.

She ate the rest of it in three bites and was sorry when it was gone.

But the treat had been both delicious and unexpected, and she'd been raised with proper manners, so she picked up her phone, scrolled through her contacts until she came to the number Brendan had given her, and sent him a text.

Thank you for dessert. Your baking skills are
amazing. I am in awe. I burn canned biscuits.

She hit Send before she could change her mind, and
then set the food tray out in the hall for staff to pick up,
grabbed a sweater from the back of the sofa, and walked
out onto the balcony.

The moon hanging in the sky was backed by an explo-
sion of starlight above the majestic mountain. In the dark,
Pope Mountain was nothing but a looming pyramid, hiding
all the people up there within the density of the forest.

She couldn't imagine what it would be like to be
rooted in one place. Did the people here know what the
rest of the world was like, or did they even care? It made
her wonder what it would be like to be so happy, so
soul-satisfied that you would never want to leave. She
couldn't imagine it. But the longer she stood, the more
evident it became to her that she felt this way because
she'd never met anyone special enough who wanted her
as much as she wanted him.

She took a deep breath, inhaling the cold night air,
and as she stood, felt something cold touch her cheek,
like a butterfly kiss. She looked up in surprise to see tiny
snowflakes swirling aimlessly in the air and shivered as if
a ghost had just passed by. The feeling was so unsettling
that she went back into her room, locking the sliders
behind her, then closing the drapes.

As she was turning around, she heard her phone
signal a text and saw it was from Brendan.

You're welcome. I'm getting off work now. Do
you still want to speak to me? If so, I need a room
number.

Harley quickly responded.

Yes, please. Room 800. See you soon.

———————————

Brendan's pulse kicked. He didn't know how this was
going to go, but he liked her sense of humor and had
laughed at the "burned canned biscuits" remark. Bottom
line—he wanted to see her again. He grabbed his coat
from the employee lounge and took the staff elevator up
to the eighth floor, got out, and started up the hall. When
he reached the right door, he knocked twice and waited.

Seconds later, the door swung inward, and she was
standing before him in her sock feet, devoid of makeup,
hair in a tumble, wearing faded pants, an old sweatshirt,
and a smile sweet enough to break a heart.

*Chill, Pope. She's not Justine, and you're a grown-ass
man. That smile is real, not fake, and you already know
she's more than a pretty face.*

"Brendan, thank you for this! Just toss your coat on
the back of that chair and come sit. I'm sure you've been
on your feet all day."

Brendan's thoughts were in free fall as he followed
her to the sofa.

"Can I get you something to drink? Have you had your dinner?" she asked.

"I'm fine," he said.

Harley sat down at the far end of the sofa, picked up a pad and pen from the coffee table, then turned to face him and crossed her legs to make a lap.

"Please forgive me for intruding on your time. I've been given permission to visit every aspect of the hotel during the audit because Mr. Caldwell wanted a full report, but I don't feel comfortable stomping into the kitchens of a hotel this size and quizzing people when they're trying to work. I was hoping I could ask you and save the interference. Is that okay with you?"

Her eyes are blue-green—like she came from the sea.

"Brendan?"

He blinked. "Oh, sorry... I was just thinking about what you said. Ray is family. I'll do anything to help."

This was news to Harley. "Family?"

And for the first time, he began to relax. "Well, mountain-style family. Ray's niece, Rusty Caldwell, was an undercover FBI agent before she married my cousin Cameron Pope. He was with Army Special Forces during his tours of duty. Rusty and Liz Devon are first cousins. Their dads were brothers. So, now, despite the lack of blood connection, Ray Caldwell's people are now our people, too."

His smile left a knot in Harley's stomach. *Men shouldn't be this...this...perfect.*

"Are there a lot of you?" she asked.

He laughed, and the knot in her belly tightened.

"A mountain full. A valley full. It was a Pope who first came to the valley where Jubilee now exists. His name was Brendan Pope. I'm named for him. He was a trapper. A giant of a man from Scotland, who took a tiny little Chickasaw woman named Cries A Lot for a wife. Then he started a trading post that became a settlement that became a town called Jubilee, and all of the ensuing generations chose the mountain over the valley for their homes. Their original land grants still remain in their families. There have been Popes here since the early 1800s. The first Brendan is why we're all so big and tall, and Cries A Lot is where our dark eyes and black hair came from."

Harley's lips had parted in disbelief, and she'd forgotten to shut them. She was so caught up in the story that she'd forgotten why he was here.

"That's the most amazing story I've ever heard," she said.

"That's not the half of it," he said. "Their lives together came to a tragic end when Cries A Lot, who he called Meg, went up Pope Mountain one day to pick berries and never came home. They searched for her for days. Didn't know what happened, and for the next century and a half, she was lost—until we stumbled upon the journal Brendan had kept. It's now in the Library of Congress in DC, but we hadn't known about Meg going missing until we read the journal. The tragedy took us all by surprise, and ultimately fueled an all-family search.

"We knew from the journal where she'd been before she disappeared, because they found her berry basket and berries spilled all over the ground around Big Falls. So, we began a search, using modern technology like drones with cameras that map topography and GPS that maps what's beneath the ground. I was up in the woods south of Big Falls with my brother Sean and some other searchers. One second, I was talking to Sean, and then I took a step and disappeared straight down into a hole. Scared Sean out of his mind, and the broken boards ripped gashes in my back and side on the way down."

Harley gasped. "Where did you fall?"

"Into what had once been a cellar below a settler's cabin. The cabin had had long since disappeared, and the floor above the cellar had finally rotted through just where I stepped. But I fell at the feet of the woman we'd been searching for. And there she was..." Brendan stopped, took a deep breath, and then looked away for a moment, gathering himself and his emotions. "There she was, or what was left of her... A tiny skeleton, lying on her side with her hands clasped in prayer." He looked up, straight into Harley's eyes, then shook his head. "It changed me. Me finding her seemed like a prophecy fulfilled. Meg's Brendan had never stopped searching the mountain, but died without finding her. Then here I come, nearly two hundred years later—a sixth generation grandson with the same name, and I found her."

Tears were rolling down Harley's face. "Oh my God.

Did you ever find out what happened? How she got down there?"

"Yes. It's a really long story, but I'll give you the quick version. It was during the Civil War. A group of Rebel soldiers came through Jubilee pulling a wagon. Rumor had it the wagon was carrying gold to fund the war. But when Brendan and his friends went looking for Meg, they found the wagon broken down on the roadway. We surmise the soldiers panicked. They couldn't leave their treasure unguarded, and the wagon was of no use. They carried the treasure into the woods to hide, planning to come back for it, came upon Meg picking berries, and abducted her so she couldn't tell where they put it. They trailed the tracks of the soldiers, thinking maybe they'd carried Meg off, but miles later, found the men all dead from some skirmish and no sign of Meg. So now the treasure and Meg were lost to time. The really tragic part of that is that we think she was still alive when they dropped her into the cellar with their treasure."

Harley gasped. "How could you know that?"

"Because when I found the bones, they were in a posed position. I could almost see her as she'd been… as if she'd curled up on her side to pray and fell asleep. Only she never woke up. No way would the soldiers drop her down there and then arrange her body."

"Was the treasure still there?" Harley asked.

Brendan nodded. "Only it wasn't treasure after all. No gold. Just paper. She was killed for a trunk full of Confederate money."

The horror of it all was on her face. "Oh, Brendan! No!"

"Yeah," Brendan said. "I'll take that drink now, if the offer's still good."

Harley leaped to her feet and ran to the mini-fridge. "Wine. Longneck beer. Cans of soda. Bottles of water. Name your poison."

"Dr Pepper. I don't drink and drive," he said.

She handed him the cold can and returned to her seat. "Speaking of your brothers, Wiley came to the hotel today with another officer to pick up a woman who'd been caught picking pockets. He's something else, isn't he?"

Brendan grinned. "You could say that. Aaron is the oldest, then Sean, then Wiley, then me."

"Are all of you tall?"

"I'm the tallest in the family by a couple of inches, but family gatherings are like being in the Land of the Giants. If you're here long enough, maybe you'll get to meet them one day. Now, sorry for the history lesson. How can I help you?"

"Right," Harley mumbled, picked up her pad and pen again. "Since you spend your working hours in the kitchen of the main dining area, is there anything about it that has changed since the manager was put in place…like changing vendors or the ordering of products? Anything like that?"

Brendan took a sip of his drink, thinking back. "I know Chef Randolph has complained that the meat he's receiving is of a lesser quality than what we've offered before, and he raised hell just today about the quality of cuts on porterhouse steaks that he'd ordered."

"What about your side of the kitchen? The baking area?"

"The dairy I use is not what we used to get. Other than that, the bakery is not directly affected. I still have the kinds of flour I need. Eggs are eggs. Sugar is sugar. We came close to a staff walkout because of Beaumont's daughter, Justine, but she's out of the picture now."

"Really? How so?" Harley asked.

"I was told her mother paid off the damages she caused at a local bar and took her back to Dallas with her. That's all I know, and I only know that because of my brother."

"What do you think of Larry Beaumont?" she asked.

"I know nothing about how he's doing his job, but I don't like him personally. No, that's the wrong word. I don't trust him," Brendan said.

Harley glanced up. "Why not?"

He shrugged. "Instinct. Gut feeling," he said, and downed the rest of his drink.

"Understood," she said. "I'm not going to keep you any longer. Thank you so much for tonight, and for the surprise tart, and most of all, for the story. I hope you know how blessed you are to have a history like that. And family who stand behind what you do."

As Brendan stood, he immediately flashed on Clyde Wallace, the father they'd disavowed.

"We have our mother to thank for that."

"She sounds special," Harley said, and thought of the father in prison, but said nothing. If he wanted her to know about all that, he would tell her. Otherwise, it was her secret to keep. "I'll walk you to the door," she said, then opened it and stepped aside to let him pass.

Brendan was halfway out the door when he paused on the threshold and looked back. There was a long, silent moment between them, each searching the other's face for something more than the words they'd spoken. And then he took a deep breath.

"You know how to reach me. Sleep well," he said, and left.

She stood in the doorway, watching the swing of his shoulders and long stride as he walked away, then shivered, remembering what he said about being the end of a prophecy and wishing someone like him was a part of her future.

Hours later, and long after she'd gone to bed, she dreamed of a snake coming out of the shadows and coiling around her like a noose, then of a wolf standing beside her and the snake dead at her feet, and woke up in a cold sweat.

———

Brendan drove home in silence, went through the usual motions afterward, but was too keyed up to sleep. He kept prowling through the house, digging through the pantry for cookies, downing a longneck bottle of beer in front of the gas fireplace while the wind rattled the screens in his windows, and sifting through unanswered emails.

The feeling he had was unsettling, but he couldn't pinpoint what had caused it. It felt like he knew some-one had planted a bomb with a timer, but no one knew where it was or when it might go off.

Instinct told him Harley Banks's arrival was at the center of it. But was it just how she affected him, or how what she was doing affected the hotel? One thing he knew for certain: she was already under his skin. He just had to be careful not to let her into his heart. He didn't want a hit-and-miss lover. He wanted a forever woman or nothing at all.

———

The next morning, Harley ordered breakfast from room service and was sifting through the hotel links and adding figures to her spreadsheet when it arrived. She'd ordered a simple meal. Scrambled eggs, bacon, and biscuits.

"Good morning, Miss Banks. Shall I put this on your table?"

"Yes, please," Harley said, and waited at the door, then turned the dead bolt after the man left.

She removed the cloche from her plate and the napkin from her breadbasket, she reached for the butter, slathering some on the biscuits while they were still warm. She thought of the bowl of cold milk and cereal she would have fixed for herself at home and dug in. The food was good, but the biscuits were sublime.

"If that man makes love to a woman the way he handles flour, butter, and sugar, someone's gonna die happy," she mumbled, and took another bite.

As soon as she finished breakfast, she went straight to the computer and started with the purchasing department and went back a year, beginning six months before Ray Caldwell's health scare, and began to enter figures on three separate spreadsheets. One tracking the time Ray was there. One after Beaumont's arrival, and then another spreadsheet for the audit.

The quantities ordered from month to month varied with regard to the numbers of guests at any given time. The cost of products was the same under both time-lines. The payments going out to vendors matched the invoices for both Caldwell and Beaumont. The only difference was the lower quality of products.

It was slow, tedious work, like looking through cracks trying to see a panorama. She'd been at it for hours when she received a message from the front desk that her rental car had been delivered and she needed to come sign for it, so she pocketed the key card and her phone, then grabbed her wallet in case she needed to verify her identity, and left the room.

Once she reached the lobby, she saw a tall, skinny man with black hair standing near the front desk. His back was to the lobby, but the jacket he was wearing had a big Jubilee Car Rental logo across the back.

"Hi, I'm Harley Banks. I believe you're waiting for me," she said.

The young man turned, then smiled. "Yes, ma'am. You requested an SUV. It's the black Chevrolet Equinox in the front row there," he said, and pointed to indicate which direction.

Harley looked out the front windows. "Yes, I see it, thanks."

He produced a clipboard with a rental contract. "If you'll just sign this, we'll be good to go, and you did request our insurance policy as well. Is that correct?"

"Yes. Where do I sign?"

He pointed. "Here and here."

After she signed, he gave her the bottom copy and handed her the keys. "The tank is full. If you have any problems, our number is on your contract. Is there anything else I can do for you?"

"I'm curious. You resemble someone I know. By any chance, are you related to the Pope family in any way?" she asked.

His polite smile turned into a full-fledged grin. "Yes, ma'am. I'm Liam Cauley. My granny is a Pope. She runs Granny Annie's Bakery downtown. My mom works there, too. Granny makes the best sweets ever...except for maybe my cousin Brendan. He's the head pastry chef here. His stuff's right up there with Granny's. If you go to her bakery, tell her Liam sent you."

Harley smiled. "Thank you, I will." Then instead of walking away, she stood, eyeing Liam's long, lanky stride as he exited the hotel and got into a pickup truck idling in the driveway.

Definitely got the DNA, she thought.

She went back up to her room, dropped off the keys and paperwork, and then headed to the dining room above.

The noon rush had come and gone, but there were still diners scattered about. Harley chose the same table as before. When she was eating alone, having a wall at her back was a safety quirk of hers, and the view from that area was spectacular. She was scanning the menu when her waitress appeared and took her drink order. By the time the girl returned, Harley had made up her mind.

"I'd like a chicken Caesar salad, some savory herb bread, and a refill of this tea when you bring my food."

"The herb bread is complimentary," the waitress said. "A fresh batch is just coming out of the oven."

"Fabulous," Harley said. As the waitress walked away, Harley caught a glimpse of her reflection and rolled her eyes. "Damn hair," she muttered, and finger-combed the unruly curls.

A couple of minutes later her bread arrived hot from the oven and with a ramekin of butter. Her first bite was as good as she remembered. *Food for the gods,* she thought, and was on her second hunk of bread and butter when her salad was delivered.

"Enjoy," the waitress said as she refilled the tea in Harley's glass and then hurried away.

Harley read through her emails as she ate, responded to two different requests for her services, informing them she was unavailable at this time. She had an email from her mother, informing her that she was at the villa and that Harley's father was en route to Houston, and a strange email from Wilhem Crossley, asking her to check in with him. He needed to know if she was okay.

She paused, frowning as she reread the message and sent a one-word response.

YES.

But the actual wording of it bothered her. She'd never had a client follow up like this, and it made her wonder why. The only loose end to that whole case had been never finding out who'd been running that scam, but she'd considered that a job for the police and never gave it a second thought. Until now.

She'd already decided to call him when she got back to her room, and finished her lunch. She was waiting for the waitress to bring her the check, and when she arrived, she gave Harley a small box as well.

"From Chef Pope. For your sweet tooth," she said.

Instant delight shifted her concern about the strange message.

Harley smiled. "Me and my sweet tooth thank him," she said as she signed the check to her room.

The waitress giggled. "I'll tell him."

Harley tried to guess what was in the box all the way back to her room, but whatever it was, she smelled cinnamon, and the bottom of the box felt warm. Two men were in the elevator when she got on, and out of habit, she moved to the back of the car so she could keep an eye on them. Once she exited the elevator, she kept glancing over her shoulder to make sure she was still alone, and by the time she got back to her room, her heart was pounding.

She was beginning to be concerned. There were too many unanswered questions going on at once. The unknown boss behind the trafficking ring. The mystery she was trying to solve for Ray Caldwell, and the mystery of what was in this little box.

As soon as she reached the countertop of the minibar, she opened it, then gasped. A huge, soft, golden-brown cinnamon roll was inside, drizzled with white icing and oozing layers of butter, sugar, and cinnamon from within the rolls. Without hesitation, she tore off a piece with her fingers and popped it in her mouth.

Sex in a box. Right up there with orgasms.

She ate half of it, then made herself stop, saving the rest for later.

She licked the sugar from her fingers and pulled up Crossley's text, read it again, then called him. The phone rang twice and then Wilhem answered.

"I knew you'd call back," he said.

"Why?" Harley asked.

"Because my message was a bit cryptic, and you're nobody's dummy."

She took a deep breath. "What's happened?"

"Maury Paget, the accountant who agreed to testify, is dead. They found him in his jail cell. He'd been strangled. The federal agent who was in charge of the case is dead. He was stuck in traffic when someone on a motorcycle rode past his car window and shot him in the head. And last night, the warehouse where it all happened burned to the ground."

Harley was in shock. She didn't realize she was holding her breath until she felt the room begin to spin.

"Oh my God."

"If you're home, find a place to disappear. It's common knowledge that you're the one who found out what was happening. I don't think you're safe. If you're on a job somewhere else, be careful. Don't take calls from numbers you don't know. They may already be trying to find you."

"Thanks for the heads-up. Right now, I'm in a secure location… I think. Do you have any idea who's behind this?"

Wilhem sighed. "My guess is that it's likely the one who got away…the one we couldn't identify. Just be careful."

The line went dead.

Harley dropped the phone and covered her face. She didn't know what to do. Stay here and possibly put other people in danger, or make a run for it and then look over her shoulder for the rest of her life—however long that might be.

This was a waking nightmare. She needed to talk to someone, but not Ray Caldwell. All this would do was stress him further. And if she left, whoever was killing off the people responsible for bringing down the gang wouldn't hesitate to kill someone here just for information as to where she'd gone.

She thought of Brendan. Ray told her to go to him for help. She knew Brendan's brothers were with the police, but was a town this size equipped for a hit man?

She sent him a text.

> Something has come up, and I need to pick your brain. I promise I won't make this a habit, but I need some serious advice. Do you have time to stop by again after you get off work?

The waitress had just delivered Harley's message to Brendan, thanking him for the dessert, and he was smiling and remembering the urge he'd had to bury his fingers in all those black curls and kiss her senseless as he was leaving her room last night. He still didn't know where all this was going, but he wasn't afraid to find out.

Then his phone signaled a text. It was from Harley. He was expecting another thank-you, but it was something else, and even as he was reading it, the hair crawled on the back of his neck. Every instinct he had was telling him this was serious.

See you around 6:00 p.m. if I'm not delayed.

Chapter 9

HARLEY SET ASIDE THE AUDIT FOR RAY AND LOGGED into her personal laptop to the files pertaining to the Crossley case, and began reading through it again, wondering if enough time had passed that she'd spot something she'd missed.

About four hours in, she was looking at the paperwork with Wilhem's forged signature. After finding out the accountant was a major link in hiding money, they had assumed he'd done it, but he'd never had a chance to make a full statement because his lawyer had been waiting to see what deal he could make for Paget's testimony.

Harley's mind was racing. Who else would have been close enough within the organization to have had immediate access to Wilhem's business? She shoved the laptop back in disgust and got up, muttering to herself as she opened the sliders to the freezing air. The cold felt good on her heated face, and standing in the dark gave her a false sensation of security. But within seconds, she realized how vulnerable she was, silhouetted against the light behind her, and hurried back inside, locked the sliders, and pulled the drapes over them.

All it would take was a sniper with a zoom scope on a high-velocity rifle, and she'd drop, just like the others. The worst-case scenario to her occupation was really happening.

Why did I assume the feds would dig further? I gave them the whole setup. I gave them the location and access to the gang. They freed the women and children who'd been kidnapped. It was a feather in someone's cap. Maybe they didn't want to dig any further, or maybe they were still investigating and that's why the agent was murdered. And now here we are… God! I knew better!

Frustration gave way to fear, and fear to tears. When the knock sounded at her door, she jumped a foot, and then remembered she had asked Brendan to come by. Now she was worrying about even mentioning it and getting him involved, then rolled her eyes. She'd already involved everyone by coming here. She swiped the tears from her cheeks, peered through the peephole, then opened the door.

Before she could say a word, Brendan saw she'd been crying and didn't wait to be invited inside. He walked in, kicked the door shut behind him, and then gently grasped her shoulders.

"What's wrong?"

It was the set of his jaw and the flash of fire in his eyes that set her course.

"I think there's a hit man on my tail."

A blood rush of shock, then anger rolled through him. He took her hand led her to the sofa. "Sit. Talk."

She nodded, took a shaky breath, and spilled the whole story, right down to the text she'd just received from Wilhem Crossley.

"I've been debating with myself all afternoon as to whether I stay here and unintentionally cause someone else to come to harm, or leave and have the hit man wind up here and start killing people in an effort to find out where I went. This is a nightmare," she said, and in frustration, shoved her fingers through her hair.

"You don't run," Brendan said. "Whatever is coming needs to end here."

"That's my first instinct, too, but I need to let the police here know the possibilities. I don't know if they're equipped to deal with something like this."

"They took down their own human trafficking ring a few years back. They've solved murders. Solved a theft that originated from the Library of Congress in DC. Caught murderers who trailed their victims to this place. Do you remember when Wolfgang Outen supposedly died in a chopper crash?"

She nodded.

"That crash happened here. And to make a long story short, a daughter Wolfgang never knew he had was living here. During that long, complicated investigation, the Jubilee police, including my brothers, were assisting the FBI and the FAA. My brother Sean took a bullet meant for Wolfgang's daughter and nearly died."

"Okay, I'm convinced," Harley said. "Does his daughter still live here?"

"Yes, she's a CPA. She has an office downtown next to the bank, but she lives up on the mountain with my mom."

"Really? Why?"

"Because Sean married her. They were already planning the wedding when she found out she had a father. Getting shot didn't change a thing."

Harley sighed. "I am scared to death of something happening to you because of me, but I don't think I have any other options here."

"Will you let me help you?" he asked.

She was still locked into his steadfast gaze when he held out his hand. Without saying a word, she grasped it.

"I'll talk to both brothers tonight. They'll talk to Chief Warren, and then they'll likely need to talk to you. But I'm guessing the fewer people who even know you're here, the better, so I'll see if they're willing to come to you."

Harley curled her fingers around his. "Thank you."

He nodded. "Order everything from room service. Don't leave your room until we work out some kind of guard situation."

"This is crazy. I don't even know who to guard against."

"We'll figure it out," Brendan said. "I'll talk to Cameron. His wife, Rusty, was an undercover agent for the FBI. Even though she quit the force after they got married, she might still have some contacts."

"Jubilee is a deceitful little place. It looks so picturesque and innocent," she said.

"There is no innocence left in this world," Brendan muttered. "Popes don't run from trouble, and we take care of our own. Have you eaten anything?"

"No, I don't think I can't face—"

"Give me a sec," he said, took out his phone and sent a text. "Now, last night I gave you a Cliffs Notes version of the origin of my people. It's your turn. Tell me about your family."

"You don't want—"

He put a finger over her lips. "Oh, but I do."

She scooted back to the corner of the sofa and, like last night, turned to face him, curled her legs up under her, and started talking.

"I am an only child and a huge disappointment to my parents. I was born with this face, which pleased my mother, and born with my father's intelligence, which pleased him to no end. But when I began to follow my own path instead of what they wanted of me, they let me know how I was wasting my life, and their continued dismay exists to this day."

"Who are they? Where do they live?" Brendan asked.

"Jason Banks, NASA scientist. At present in Houston, working on another 'secret' something or other. Judith Henry Banks, well-known American playwright and screenwriter. They live in New York City, also in an apartment in Houston, sometimes in a villa in the south of France, and at the vineyard they own in Calabria, Italy. At the present, Mother is at the villa. She belittles my work because it's so ugly and constantly reminds me how the work demeans me, because I'm basically digging criminals out of their hiding places."

"At the risk of criticizing people I don't know, I'd say your parents are very shortsighted. My mother, Shirley, on the other hand, was, and still is, our biggest cheerleader. Actually, it's our mother who is the Pope. My father's name is Clyde Wallace. He was a drug user and a drunk who beat the hell out of all of us from the day we could walk and nearly killed our mother. He's doing life for murdering two people while he was high. We changed our last name to Mom's maiden name to get away from the shame of him. Mom inherited her family home after her mother passed away. We came home to the mountain. It saved us all."

He paused, suddenly lost in the past.

Harley had been watching the expressions changing on his face and hearing the tone of his voice shift in and out of anger. They were barely past the total-stranger stage, but every time she saw him, he pulled her deeper into a world she barely understood. Then all of a sudden, he looked up, as if remembering where he was, and turned to face her.

"We all have shit to deal with in life. The lucky ones are people like us, who have found our calling. Your job is an invaluable tool. All I do is fill people's bellies, but at the same time, I'm giving them a piece of me. I share my skills with the world, just as you do. But the last few months with Ray gone have been hell here, and I was thinking of quitting to get away from the chaos. I'm really glad now that I did not."

Harley sighed. *He did it! He told me. It couldn't have been easy for him to admit all that, but he never blinked, never wavered, never apologized, because he had nothing to apologize for. God, please don't let me get killed. I want to know this man.*

"I'm glad you didn't quit, too," she said, but before she could say more, there was a knock at the door.

"I'll get that. It should be supper," he said, and unfolded himself from the sofa and headed for the door, checked the peephole, and then opened the door.

Aaron walked in carrying two bags from Granny's Country Kitchen.

Harley saw the man, then the face, and was on her feet in seconds. There was no mistaking who it was. *Another brother!*

Brendan escorted him in, talking as they walked. "Aaron, come meet Harley. Harley, this is my oldest brother, Aaron Pope. Aaron, this is Harley Banks. Ray hired her to audit the hotel. He's thinking of selling."

Aaron was all smiles as he handed Brendan the bags and went straight to Harley with his hand outstretched. "It's a pleasure."

Brendan put the bags on the table. "I also told him you have a problem you need to discuss with the police."

"We're always happy to assist in any way we can. What would be the nature of your problem?" Aaron asked.

"I'm pretty sure someone from the last case I just worked has sent a hit man to take me out. I got a warning today from the last man I worked for. Two people related to the crime I uncovered are dead. One was an informant, the other a federal agent who worked the case of criminal activities I uncovered in my job, and the warehouse where the crimes took place burned down today."

Aaron's eyebrows rose slightly, but that was the only indication he gave of the surprise. "You must be some kind of special CPA."

"I also have a PI license and specialize in rooting out corporate crime, but that's for us to know and no one else to find out. Okay?"

"Understood. Okay…so I'm going to leave you two to your dinner. BJ, I'll talk to the chief tomorrow morning first thing and fill Wiley in as well, because…family."

Brendan pulled a pair of twenties from his wallet and handed them to Aaron. "Thanks for the delivery."

"Keep your money," Aaron said. "This is on me."

"Nope. I might want you to do this again sometime," Brendan said.

Aaron grinned. "When they were passing out subtlety, you thought they said soup and were waiting in line for seconds," he said, but he took the money, then gave Brendan a quick hug. "You be careful. And you take good care of Miss Harley. She reminds me of Mama when she was young. All spit and fire and stood her ground regardless. You wouldn't remember her that way."

Brendan nodded. "Thanks again, Aaron."

"Follow me out. Turn the dead bolt after I leave," Aaron said.

Harley had never in her life felt tiny until these two men walked into her space. She couldn't imagine what it would be like to have people like this at her back, and after knowing all she did about this family, she silently accepted being compared to their mother in any way as a compliment.

Then Brendan came back and began taking out all of the to-go boxes from the bags, and Harley followed, opening cartons he handed her, licking gravy off her finger, and watching the way his eyebrows knit as he eyed the preparation and wondered if he was thinking he would have done it different, or better.

Then he caught her staring, winked, and handed her a fork.

Harley grinned. "Curiosity killed the cat, didn't it? So, meow, and all that. He called you, BJ. What's that stand for?" she asked.

He laughed. Her sense of humor was delightful. "Brendan James, but the family has always called me BJ."

"I see we're having fried chicken, mashed potatoes and gravy, some kind of casserole, and corn bread. Looks good. Smells even better," she said.

"It's sweet corn casserole with onions and red and green bell peppers. City girl, meet country boy. Dinner is served."

She pulled out a chair and sat. "Why the change from BJ to Brendan?"

He was at the end of the table. More room for long legs. He pulled out a handful of paper napkins and handed half of them to her.

"You're gonna need these, and don't you dare try to eat fried chicken with a fork. Use your fingers. As for the name change, I'm Brendan at work, but growing up at home, the only times I heard Brendan James come out of my mom's mouth was for leaving wet towels all over the bathroom floor. I have since evolved."

She laughed. "Brendan fits you. I'll stick with that," she said, then picked up a piece of chicken and took a bite. It tasted good. Maybe it was the company she had, she thought, and kept eating.

Her laugh went straight to Brendan's heart. He wanted to hear it again, but he'd settle for fried chicken. He was starving.

They ate and talked and traded stories about their jobs, then it morphed to personal questions.

"Ever been married?" he asked.

Harley shook her head. "Not even close. A couple of relationships in college. The nature of my work does not encourage relationships. What about you?"

"No engagements. No marriage. Dated some when I was in high school, but then Clyde ended all that, and after I went to the Culinary Institute in New York to study, there was no time for anything but work and more work. I want what my brothers have. A forever wife who will love Jubilee and Pope Mountain as much as the rest of us do. I've lived in cities and traveled some in Europe, working my way through other restaurants, and what I learned I brought home.

"I was working in big restaurants in New York, and for a while it was exciting, but it got really old spending holidays alone, feeding other people who were celebrating, then going to a twelve-by-twelve-foot apartment and trying to sleep with a feuding couple across the hall, a family with a dog to the left, and a violinist in the apartment to the right of me who was constantly practicing. Coming back to Pope Mountain was inevitable. Family means everything to us."

Harley heard the loneliness and knew exactly what he meant about going home alone. Even after all these years, laughing alone at something on TV made her feel even lonelier. Holidays were depressing. No social circle meant no hosting game nights or dinner parties.

Some days she just wished for a simple hug. A human touch. Someone who cared if she slammed a door on her finger. Someone to curl up against in bed on a cold Chicago night.

She listened to the rumble of his voice in silence. It was deep and a little raspy, and she thought about what it would be like to love someone this rooted to where he lived. He'd already seen the world in which she'd grown up and rejected it. She wondered if she'd ever fit into a world like this.

Meeting Brendan Pope had been a game changer. She'd never considered changing her lifestyle until now, and he might never see her beyond being another woman causing trouble in his life. But she wanted him to. She didn't know how to say, "Let that forever woman be me," to a man she barely knew, so she changed the subject.

"I always wished for siblings and envied people with big families. You know, the generational holiday get-togethers with grandparents, aunts, uncles, siblings, and all kinds of nieces and nephews. Do any of your brothers have children?" she asked.

"Our family gatherings are huge. When it's an all-mountain gathering, we have it at the Church in the Wildwood. It's near the top of Pope Mountain. My brothers don't have children, but my cousin Cameron does, and my brother Wiley is raising our little half-sister, Ava. We didn't even know she existed until one of Clyde's old girlfriends showed up and basically gave her away to us. She was a tiny, undernourished five-year-old who was afraid of almost everything and thought if she stayed still enough, she could make herself disappear. Something clicked between her and Wiley, and long story short, we're all her brothers, but Wiley became her legal guardian. She wanted to call him Daddy, but they settled for Bubba. He is her world. Mom fell in love with her. Ava calls her Grandma, so she already has one grandchild. It's not by blood, but of the heart."

"That's so special," Harley said, thinking of the children who'd been rescued from the trafficking ring she'd exposed. "I think Ava had a guardian angel. Most children don't escape that kind of life. Children were some of the hostages who were rescued in my last case. God only knows how much money my meddling cost someone, and it's likely why someone wants me dead. Payback."

Brendan reached out and covered her hand with his. Harley looked up.

"I won't let that happen," he said.

"Neither will I if I see him coming. Beyond the fact that I own a gun and have a license to carry, I can't protect myself if my enemy has no face."

Brendan gave her hand a gentle squeeze. "I've got your back. Just remember that. Are you afraid to be here tonight on your own?"

"No. Dead bolt. Safety chain. Eighth floor. Big-ass gun."

He threw back his head and laughed, and laughed. "God, woman, you sound like a Pope. Takes no guff. Also takes no prisoners."

Harley grinned. Her family didn't approve of her. And they'd hate this whole lifestyle. But it was growing on her, and so was he. She got up and started gathering up their trash, and with his help, soon had everything bagged and cleaned when he got ready to leave.

"I'll dump the trash on my way down," he said as he was putting on his coat. "Aaron will talk to Wiley and to

Chief Warren tomorrow. They'll get in touch with you, so you just do your thing. Focus on what you came here to do and trust us to keep you safe."

She nodded. "I won't go anywhere, but I am going to figure out who wants me dead."

———————

Karen Beaumont did not regret paying off Justine's debt to get her out of jail, but without the ensuing three months of alimony, they would be skimping to get by. However, skimping was not part of Justine's world, and she was about to burst the bubble of her mama's sense of self-sacrifice.

Justine was happy to be in Dallas. Even if she was back under the same roof as her mother, it was better than Jubilee.

It was their third day back, and after 10:00 a.m. before she got out of bed. When she went to shower, she discovered her favorite shampoo bottle was empty. She gave it a toss in the trash and went to look for her mother, then found her in the utility room, putting wet clothes into the dryer.

"Mom, I need to borrow your car. I'm out of my shampoo," Justine said.

"You'll have to use my shampoo. It's on a shelf in my shower. Help yourself," Karen said.

Justine stared. "I don't use that kind. I want my kind. It makes my hair silkier."

"Your kind costs over twenty dollars a bottle. Do you have money?" Karen asked.

Justine frowned. "You know I don't. Daddy cut off my allowance!"

"And my alimony has been cut off for the next three months because of you, so there's nothing for extras. I'm going to start back as a hostess at the steak house I used to work at. We'll be lucky to get the rent and bills paid," she said. "Besides, aren't you a little embarrassed to assume that at your age, you're still due an allowance?"

"Don't you start!" Justine whined. "You sound just like Dad."

Karen rolled her eyes, hit the Start button on the dryer, and started to walk past her, when Justine grabbed her by the arm and yanked her around.

"Don't you dare walk away from me when I'm talking to you!" she hissed.

Karen froze, so shocked by the assault that there was a moment when she was actually afraid. And then her eyes narrowed. She looked down at the hand gripping her arm, and then back up at Justine.

"Take your hand off me," Karen said.

Justine glared.

"NOW!" Karen screamed.

Justine stumbled backward, tripped on an empty laundry basket, and then fell into it.

"You pushed me!" Justine shrieked.

"I never touched you and you know it, but next time I will," Karen muttered. "I'm not the easy touch your father was." Then she bent down, until her face was only inches away from her daughter's, and the tone of her voice shifted from bored to menacing so fast Justine forgot to breathe. "I was mean and badass before you were even a thought in the universe, and I will put you out of my house in two seconds flat if you *ever* act like this again. Do. We. Understand. Each. Other?"

Justine nodded.

Karen started to walk off and then stopped and turned. "Get out of my laundry basket before you break it," she snapped, and strode out of the room with her chin up and her hands curled into fists.

Justine got up, went to get her mother's shampoo, and disappeared into her room. Her heart was pounding, and she was slightly sick to her stomach. She'd seen this side of her mother, but it had always been directed at her father, never toward her. Until now.

She had to rethink her situation. She needed money to get away from here, but even if she had it, she had nowhere to go. The obvious answer to her future was out there. She just had to figure out how to find it.

───────

Ollie Prine had been in Chicago far longer than he'd planned, and now he was waiting on a scrawny, pencil-neck twenty-year-old for answers. It was driving him crazy. He hadn't heard from Thor in almost thirty-six hours and was beginning to think this was going to be a bust when the kid finally called.

Ollie answered on the first ring.

"Yeah? Did you get it?"

"Yes. She's living in an apartment in the South Loop. High-end living. One thousand now, and then I will send you the info. I'll text you my Venmo addy."

Before Ollie could say a word, Thor disconnected.

Ollie ended the call and waited. The text came a minute later. Ollie immediately complied, hit Send, and then waited again, knowing Thor wouldn't respond until he'd received the money and banked it, but Ollie's relief was at an all-time high.

A few minutes later he got the text with the info, grabbed his coat and the package he'd already prepared, and headed out the door to make a delivery. He'd rented a car and had all the technology to make himself look like a delivery man, including the label scanner that required a signature to accept. He had the address and the apartment number. His only drawback might be if there was security in the lobby, but he'd deal with that if it happened.

If he couldn't gain access to her apartment, he'd be on a stakeout again, waiting for her to leave the building. He hurried to the parking garage to get his car, entered the address in his GPS, and was soon on the way to pay a visit to Harley Banks.

Ollie felt good about this as he wound his way through the Chicago streets. He wanted this over with, and even more, he intended to end his association with Berlin when this job was done. A warmer climate was calling. He could almost hear it.

Thirty minutes later, he arrived at the location, parked in an area marked Delivery, patted the shoulder holster inside his coat to make sure the gun was still secure, checked to see if his cap was on straight, and then exited the car.

The building was imposing. The lobby was opulent. And the information desk in the center of the room was manned by an armed guard, which may or may not put a kink in his plan. He approached the desk, glanced at the name on the package, then looked up at the guard.

"Special delivery for Harley Banks."

"You can leave it with me. I'll see that she gets it," the guard said.

"She has to sign for it," Ollie said.

The guard shook his head. "Sorry, but she's away on business. We're authorized to sign packages for her in such cases."

Ollie stifled a groan. *Not again!* "Then do you have a forwarding address?"

"No. Sorry," the guard said.

Ollie shrugged and walked out, got in the car, and began pounding his fists on the steering wheel until the knuckles were red, then called Berlin. It went to voicemail.

It's me. Harley Banks's apartment IS in Chicago,

*but she's not there. She's a damn ghost. I'm not
a hacker. I can't check travel schedules. I don't
know where she's gone, and I'm coming back to
Philly to await new orders.*

Ollie went back to his motel room, bought a ticket
for the next flight to Philadelphia, then packed and
checked out. The flight left in a few hours, but he was
going to the airport now. At least he could walk around
without freezing, get some food to eat, and wait there.

———————

By the time Berlin heard the message, Ollie was already
in the air. Berlin knew he could just let it go. Paget's
death was blamed on an inmate and already forgotten,
and the feds were sifting through eighteen years' worth
of criminals the dead agent had helped put away. He
reasoned that they couldn't find someone they didn't
even know existed. But it rankled. He'd been bested by
a woman. A really smart woman. And that didn't feel
safe.

Chapter 10

THE FIRE AT THE WAREHOUSE HAD TAKEN THE FIGHT out of Wilhem Crossley. After the raid, he'd mistakenly assumed it was over. Then the murders and the fire happened, and he began to wonder if it was a warning to him that he'd be next—or even worse, that his son might become a target.

After calling Harley Banks to warn her of his fears, he called his lawyer into the office to update his will and to make certain provisions in case he was unable to make decisions for himself, and then he canceled all of his appointments and went home.

Tip saw his father leaving the building, but instead of calling his dad, he called his secretary.

"Frieda, I just saw Dad getting into his car. Is he okay? Did he say where he was going?"

"Once his lawyer left, he said he was going home for the day," Frieda said.

Tip frowned. "He met with the lawyer?"

"Yes, sir."

"Okay, thanks. I think I'm going to run by the house to check on him. He's been depressed about the warehouse fire. Thanks for the info," he said, and headed home. He found his father in the library, sitting before the fire with a glass of whiskey on the table near his elbow.

"Dad! Are you all right?"

Wilhem turned, frowning. "Tip! What are you doing home?"

"I came to check on you. What's wrong—and don't tell me nothing, because I know better. Talk to me. I'm not just your son. I'm also your partner. If there's trouble, I need to know about it, too."

Wilhem's hand was trembling as he reached for the glass of whiskey, took a sip, and then set it aside and leaned back, staring through the mullioned panes of the french doors leading out onto the patio.

"See that pair of cardinals at the feeders?" Wilhem asked, pointing.

Tip walked past Wilhem and gazed out onto the snow-covered lawn.

"Yes, I see them. What about them?" he asked.

"Now look over to the far left, there...under the holly bush. See the feathers in the snow?"

"Yes, looks like a hawk or some predator killed a bird. So what? Survival of the fittest, and all that," Tip muttered.

Wilhem grunted. "Yes, and the animal world and the human world aren't so different. We're all going along, minding our own business, doing what we do every day, and we forget that life can end in the blink of an eye. We think we have everything under control, and we're being honest and fair, and we forget to look behind us. Or above us, as the case may be for the bird. That's what happened to us. While we weren't looking, someone took advantage of our business, betrayed our trust, and then killed to hide their deeds. I can't fight what I can't see," Wilhem said. "I think burning the warehouse was a warning. A kind of retribution for messing up someone's dirty little nest. I'm afraid they'll hurt you. I'm afraid that auditor I hired to do a simple job might be in danger because of her association with me."

Tip sat down on the ottoman at his father's feet. "I'm here, Dad. I can take care of myself, and I'll hire guards for you. I'll even call the auditor myself and warn her to be careful. Is her number in your phone? Give it to me. I'll call her now while we're here together."

"I already called her," Wilhem muttered.

Tip sighed. "Again, I remind you we're partners here. I need to be kept up to date with what you're doing. So, what did she say? Was she worried? We can hire some security for her at her apartment."

"She's not at her apartment. She's already on another job."

"Then where is she? We'll get security on-site for her. I don't want you fretting."

The cardinals had flown off and Wilhem was staring at the bird feathers scattered on the snow. "All I know is she's not at home."

Tip knew his father's health was fragile. He feared this would trigger a heart attack. "Then give me her number and I'll check in with her to make sure she's doing okay so you can quit worrying. I think the arson investigator is due tomorrow. I plan to be on-site at the warehouse to see what he has to say. Oh…what was her name again…Harlow Banks?"

"Harley. Harley Banks," Wilhem said, then pulled her number up on his phone and Tip added it to his contact list. "I think I'm going to go up and lie down for a bit," he said, picked up his drink, and walked out.

Tip watched him leave, frowning at the sight. He'd never thought about his dad getting old. But it was as if he'd aged ten years overnight. What a mess. What a miserable mess.

───────

Harley's sleep was restless, and she was grateful when the sun finally came up over the mountain. She dressed, made a pot of coffee, and snagged a protein bar from the mini-fridge before returning to her spreadsheets.

It was just after 8:30 a.m. when the phone in her room rang.

"Hello?"

"It's me," Brendan said. "You haven't called room service for breakfast, so I'm checking on you."

Harley was unaccustomed to having anyone for backup and was touched by his concern.

"Whoa. You really meant it when you said you'd help, didn't you?"

"I always mean what I say. I just don't always say what I'm thinking. So, what sounds good? Hot oatmeal with brown sugar and peaches, pancakes and bacon, or a ham and cheese omelet with fresh croissants?"

"Yes," she said.

He chuckled. "Pick one."

"You had me at omelet and croissants," she said.

There was a long moment of silence, and she thought they'd been disconnected. "Brendan, are you there?"

"Yes, ma'am, just absorbing the fact that the way to your heart might be through your stomach," he said.

Now she was silent.

"Sorry if that was out of order. I'll turn in that order for you. Coffee and juice?" he asked.

"Yes, please, and I am not offended by anything you've said."

She heard a soft sigh. "Good. That would never be my intent. The police will be contacting you today. If it's okay, I'll stop by this evening before I leave work."

"It's very okay. Considering the tedium of my job, you are becoming the highlight of my day. See you later."

"Absolutely," Brendan said. *I am the highlight of her day, and she's becoming the woman of my dreams...and in them, too. What the hell am I going to do when she leaves?*

Then he shook off the worry, wrote down the order, and turned it in to room service.

A short while later, there was a knock at Harley's door, and then a voice, "Room service."

She recognized the waiter with the food cart and let him in, and as soon as he was gone, she sat down and ate her way through the best breakfast she'd had in years.

Hours later, she was working on the last six months of data from the hotel purchasing department when she got a call from the front desk.

"Miss Banks, there are three policemen here to see you. May I send them up?"

"Yes," Harley said, then quickly hit Save on what she'd been working on and made a run for the bathroom to check the condition of her hair.

Some women put on makeup before the arrival of guests. Some changed clothes to present their best appearances. Harley just needed to make sure her hair didn't look like she'd stuck her finger in a light socket. Brushing and combing hair like hers never happened, but she could work wonders with her fingers and a hair pick, and after washing a smear of ink from her cheek, she went back to the living room.

Moments later, there was a knock at the door.

After a quick look through the peephole, she opened the door. Aaron and Wiley Pope were flanking a fit, middle-aged man in uniform with a Harrison Ford squint and a serious set to his jaw. He immediately flashed his ID.

"Police Chief Sonny Warren, and Officers Wiley and Aaron Pope. May we come in?"

"Yes, of course," Harley said, and stepped aside for them to enter, then led them into the living area.

She chose the chair next to the sofa, then gestured for them to sit. They moved in unison, removing their hats, and as they sank into the cushions, Harley read their body language.

Aaron flashed a quick smile. Wiley was already sizing her up, and the police chief was obviously curious and leaning slightly forward. She quickly opened the conversation.

"Thank you for coming. As you know, I find myself in a precarious situation, and will be grateful for any help or advice you might give me."

"I know what Brendan told his brothers, but I want to hear all of it from you," Sonny said.

"Right," she said, and began explaining her previous job and what she'd uncovered, and the ensuing raid on the warehouse, all the way to the phone call with Wilhem Crossley and her concern as to whether to stay or go.

"Do you have any idea who's behind this?" Sonny asked.

Harley shrugged. "I assume, the boss behind the trafficking ring. I never did uncover a name and the only money trail I found went from Wilhem Crossley's business to shell companies in foreign countries. There was no direct paper trail from the warehouse back to Wilhem. And now the accountant who was juggling numbers is deceased."

"What are the feds doing about this?" Sonny asked.

"I have no idea. I was debriefed for several hours, turned over all my notes to the federal agent in charge of the case, and assumed they would follow up."

"And that's the federal agent who was murdered," Sonny said.

"Yes, sir."

"My guess is that's what got him killed," Sonny said. "I know when one of our own goes down, we comb heaven and earth to get justice, and sometimes things get lost in the shuffle. That case will wind up on some-one else's desk, and they may or may not view it as a priority since the gang was arrested, the hostages freed, and the warehouse torched. They'll be focus-ing on finding the shooter. I'll make some calls to see where they stand with it, but if I do, and if there's a mole in their unit who's been looking the other way, my call could send a signal to the hit man as to where you are."

Harley's eyes welled, but she was furious. "Don't anybody freak. I'm not about to go all weepy here. I cry when I'm mad," she muttered.

Aaron smiled. "That's way better than what Wiley does when he's mad."

"That's not fair. I don't hurt people," Wiley said.

"No, but you can yank a knot in someone's attitude faster than any other officer on my force," Sonny said, and then they all laughed, including Harley.

"I understand the reference. I recently had the

privilege of witnessing one of Wiley's most impressive arrests," she said.

Wiley sat up a little straighter. "You did?"

"I did, to the chagrin of a pickpocket named Virginia, who demanded your name and badge number." Then she rattled it off in the same clipped tone that he'd used. "'Officer Wiley Pope…spelled like the one in Rome… related to half the population of Jubilee. Badge number ten, as in the number after nine, but the one before eleven.'"

Both Aaron and the chief burst out laughing.

Wiley grinned, completely unashamed.

The laughter shifted Harley's tears. "Okay, my mad is dissipating. And I'm not one to run or hide. I asked for your help and I'm not about to start telling you how to do it. Make the call. I'm not leaving this room until I finish the job I came to do, and then when I do leave, I will shout to the rooftops where I go next. At least that will eliminate the danger afterward to anyone here."

"Do you want a guard?" Sonny asked.

She shook her head. "Putting a guard on the door outside this room will advertise my location. I'll just work fast and hope for the best."

"You have Brendan," Aaron said. "He's already on your side and as faithful as the day is long. Trust him. We all know he's the best of us."

"Just don't tell him we said so," Wiley added.

"I wish I had a family like yours," Harley said.

"There's always room for one more," Aaron said.

Harley saw them out and locked herself back in, but Aaron's words were still ringing in her ears.

She went back to work, only to be disturbed a short while later by the maid who came to clean, and then a member of the staff refilling the snack bar and mini-fridge. At that point, she stopped work and retreated to the sofa until they were finished.

But before she could get back to work, the house phone rang again. It was the manager, Larry Beaumont.

"Good afternoon, Harley, this is Larry. I just wanted to make sure you have everything you need, and that if you have any questions, don't hesitate to call me."

"All is well, and work is proceeding. The room is very comfortable, and the food and room service are superb," she said.

"Good to know, and remember, I'm available any time."

"Thank you," Harley said, and hung up.

His jovial tone and continued reminders that he expected her to need his input to do her job both aggravated her, as well as raised an inner alarm. In her experience, the ones who were too helpful were always trying to throw suspicion on someone else.

And now that he'd interrupted her workflow, she was curious enough to log onto the website of the wholesale vendor furnishing toiletries to the hotel. After locating the same products that Beaumont had been ordering, she clicked on the Chat With option. As soon as someone responded, she pretended to be the owner of several B and Bs and wanted to know in what quantities the toiletry products were sold and what the prices were.

A minute or so later, the answer popped up along with the question, *If the prices are suitable, are you ready to order? If so, I can send you a link.*

She was already stunned by the difference in costs and responded with an *I'm still checking other sources. Thank you for your information*, then left the website.

She went back to her spreadsheets and started putting in the numbers of quantities ordered by the hotel for the past six months, then used the cost from the website as what the invoices should have reflected, and started to smile. Bingo!

She began running a background check on the owner of the wholesale business, and then repeated the process for the meat wholesaler as well, and found that the discrepancy of his meat costs to other customers versus what he was charging the Serenity Inn was huge.

If she could find a link between them and Larry Beaumont, then she'd know he was getting some kind of kickback. She just needed to prove it. Right now, everything depended on what the background checks revealed, and that was all still in progress, so she returned to the spreadsheets. No matter what else she uncovered, Ray was still expecting the profit-and-loss statement and his audit.

It was well after 6:00 p.m. when she finally stopped for the day. Her eyes were tired. The numbers were beginning to blur, and her neck and shoulders were sore. She needed to make a massage appointment at the spa downstairs. But she was starving, and she hadn't heard a word from Brendan since this morning, and it bothered her that it mattered.

He's a heartbreaker, Harley. Mind how you go.

She picked up the room service menu, scanned the options, and then picked up the phone and gave them her order. Cheeseburger with fries. A Coke and a chocolate tart. Harley's version of health food. Her mother would be appalled.

Time passed, and with no word from Brendan, she assumed work had interfered and thought no more about it. Nearly an hour later, a knock at her door, and a voice. "Room service."

She peeked through the peephole and sighed. It was him.

He wheeled in the food cart, kicked the door shut behind him, and then paused. "I have invited myself to supper. Is that okay?"

Harley laughed. "Very okay," she said, and began clearing a spot at the far end of her table. As soon as the food was laid out, they sat, this time with the ease of old friends.

"Did you have to work late?" she asked.

Brendan was already chewing a fry and nodded as he swallowed.

"Somebody didn't show up for their shift, and we all had to pitch in to cover the lack. It wasn't bad. There have certainly been worse times. How was your day?" he asked. "Did my brothers show up?"

"Yes, and the police chief. He's very nice. He's going to make some calls to see where the feds are on the case, in the hopes they'll know something we don't. I pulled up my notes on that case, thinking since time has passed, I might see something I missed before, but I keep going in circles."

"Talk to me about it if you want. If it's not privileged information or anything, I'm a good sounding board."

Harley paused. "Really?"

"Absolutely, lady. I'm your man, remember?"

"Give me a sec," she said, took a quick bite of her burger, then bolted out of the chair and sprinted across the room. She was still chewing when she came back with her laptop and opened it.

"Okay, here goes. After it all went down, a man named Maury Paget was the only Crossley employee involved in the gang that I could identify. During questioning, he agreed to testify for a reduced sentence, but was killed in his cell. Obviously, to silence him from testifying."

"Right," Brendan said.

"And, I get why the federal agent was murdered. In the hopes that the case he was working would wind up in a slush pile. What I don't get is why I'm being targeted. I turned over everything I knew to the authorities. I wasn't a threat. I didn't have a horse in the race. I'm just a numbers woman."

Brendan had been eating while she was talking, but so far, he saw the logic in everything she said, until she questioned her part.

"So, what if it's not about the usual revenge, but simple payback for being bested by a female? It wouldn't be the first time a man's ego controlled his behavior," he said.

Her eyes narrowed. "Okay…I can see that, but the warehouse fire doesn't add up. Why burn down an insured warehouse and all the contents? That loss is going to yield millions of dollars in insurance benefits for Crossley Imports, which would benefit Wilhem Crossley, not punish him."

"Maybe that was just a random incident, completely unconnected to the raid," Brendan said.

"Maybe so," she said, but kept staring at the notes, scrolling down, then back up to check the timelines as she ate.

"So, what about this?" Brendan asked. "What if the fire wasn't about punishing Wilhem, but about recouping losses from what he lost that was being funneled into the trafficking ring?"

Harley nodded. "I've thought of that, but it doesn't ring true for the man I knew. Remember, he's the one who realized something was wrong within his company. He's the one who hired me to find out where his money was going. He's been dead honest with me from the start, and when he found out about the countless women being funneled through the warehouse, I thought he was going to pass out."

"Okay," Brendan said. "Then if it wasn't Wilhem who'd committed arson, who else benefits from the insurance payout?"

Her frown deepened. Her fingers were resting on the keyboard as she let that question sink in.

But Brendan kept up the questions. "Who else besides the old man would have had easy access to the warehouse and control of the purchasing department, other than this Paget guy who got arrested for it?"

"God! I can't imagine. I ran background checks on every employee who ever handled money at Crossley or had access to the financial department. I even ran one on Wilhem, but didn't tell him. Who did I miss during the three weeks I was there?" And then it hit her. She missed the man who wasn't there!

"Oh my God! It was right in my face! Why didn't I see it before?"

"See what?" Brendan asked.

"Tipton Crossley! Wilhem's son, heir, and co-owner. He wasn't there. I never met him. It never occurred to me, but he's the man who is taking over the business so Wilhem could retire. He already oversees the purchasing and accounting side of the company. The man who travels all over Europe and Asia, buying products to import to the United States. He could easily forge his father's signature on anything." Then she stopped herself. "No. No. This doesn't make sense. Why would he take such an ugly route into human trafficking? His father is rich. I saw Tip's salary and bonuses when I was auditing. He has no reason to commit this kind of crime. He wants for nothing."

Brendan looked past her shoulder to a painting hanging on the wall, then wadded up his napkin and tossed it into a nearby wastebasket like he was going for three points. It landed in the basket without hitting the rim.

"Sometimes, pretty lady, it's not about want, but the adrenaline rush of danger. For some people, no matter what they have, it's never enough."

Harley had seen that look in his eyes before and knew that, for a few moments, he'd been somewhere else.

"At this point, anything is possible, I guess. I know nothing about his lifestyle. What I do know is that opening this can of worms could backfire or bring the unnamed kingpin to justice, but if I follow this lead, I am going to need help. I do not have the clearance for deep diving in personal lives or hacking into bank accounts."

She was frustrated and worried, and trying to figure this out before someone killed her, and Brendan felt helpless. But when she closed the laptop and set it aside, it was as if she had the weight of the world on her shoulders, and he thought of Rusty.

"I don't know if she'd agree or not, but I can call Rusty Pope, the cousin who's ex-FBI. She may still have contacts who would help, and she may know some other agents who were part of busting up that gang… if you want me to."

She didn't hesitate. "Yes, I want you to. Explain what we've talked about, and if she's willing to give me some pointers or advice, I'll gladly take it. If she is, just ask her to give me a call."

"That much I can do. Now, back to your visit from the PD. Are they going to put a guard on your room?" he asked.

"I told them not to. All that would do is alert a hit man as to where I was. And on another note, I like your brothers. They're sweet and Wiley's funny."

"Yeah, he's a character for sure, but he is the guy who'll have your back faster than you can blink. He walked in on a bank robbery in progress a couple of years back. The perps were caught off guard, and by the time they knew he was there and fired at him, he stepped behind a pillar and put two on the floor. He fired off a shot at the last one, too, but took a bullet in the chest. It knocked him completely off his feet and would have killed him but for his bulletproof vest."

Harley was finishing her burger the whole time he was talking, completely caught up in the story.

"That's awful! Was he hurt bad?"

"Cracked rib, knocked the breath out of him. And his girlfriend, Linette, was one of the hostages. They'd already killed one of the bank executives before he got there. After the shooting, everyone who'd been on the floor gets up and starts running toward the door. He can't breathe, but he's trying to get up to stop them from leaving the scene, knowing the police will have to question everyone there. We're all tough. Wiley always says Clyde beat the mean out of all of us until the only thing left was the good our mama gave us." Then right in front of her, he snagged a french fry from her basket and ate it.

Harley laughed and, without thought, started to dab at a drop of ketchup at the corner of his lip with her napkin. He grabbed her wrist and dispatched the ketchup with one lick, then kissed the back of her wrist as an apology.

"I was savin' that for later," he said.

Harley burst out laughing. "You are a caution and a delight. I have never met a man like you."

"Is that a good thing or a bad thing?" he asked.

"Oh, it's a good thing, for sure. What else do you know how to do besides be your witty self, go fast on motorcycles, and bake like an angel?"

"I'm an open book," he said. "All you have to do is turn a page."

And just like that, the moment went from light to weighted with insinuations she could explore or ignore.

"I love to read," she said, and pointed at his ketchup ramekin. "I'm out of ketchup. Can I double-dip in yours?"

Brendan took a breath. Right now, he was thinking about everything they could do together besides share leftover ketchup. *Don't say it. Just don't the hell say it.* Instead, he set the ramekin beside her plate.

"Sure thing. My fries are gone. Help yourself."

They continued to eat, sometimes in mutual silence, sometimes popping up a new question, until they were down to dessert.

"I'm saving my tart for later," Harley said, and got up to put her tart in the fridge, then turned around just as Brendan ate his tart in two bites.

When he caught her smiling, he shrugged: "I have never been completely full in my entire life, so if there's food in front of me, I eat it."

"It's those long legs of yours," she said. "Impossible to fill up, I guess. And I cannot imagine how your mother kept four of you fed."

"Some days she didn't eat. We didn't know it at the time because we were just kids. Aaron figured it out when he got older. After that, we all refused to eat until she had food on her plate, too."

Harley's eyes welled. "Sometimes your stories make me cry. Other times, I have this overwhelming urge to hug away all your bad memories."

Brendan stood up and opened his arms.

"We're all huggers in my family. I would treasure one of yours."

Harley didn't hesitate. She walked into his embrace, laid her cheek on his chest, and wrapped her arms around him. It was like hugging a mountain of man and muscle, and she'd never felt so safe.

Her curls were right beneath Brendan's chin. They were as thick and soft as he'd imagined, and the moment she was in his arms, it felt familiar, like she'd been made to fit. He wanted to kiss her, but all she'd offered was a hug, and that was enough.

Then she turned loose and stepped back. "That felt exactly like I thought it would. And selfishly, I needed your hug more. Thank you."

Brendan ran the back of his finger down the side of her cheek.

"That which is given freely needs no thanks, but repeats are always welcome. You need to rest, so I'll take myself home."

They put all of their plates back on the food cart, and Brendan wheeled it out into the hall. "Lock yourself in, lady. I don't want anything to happen to you."

"Talk to you tomorrow?" she asked.

"Count on it," he said, and pulled the door shut after himself, then waited until he heard all the locks turn and the safety chain jingle before leaving.

Harley was still thinking about Brendan when she went to run her bath. She was hoping the jets in the Jacuzzi would help ease the muscles in her neck and shoulders, but the moment she stripped and felt the air on her skin, she shuddered.

What would it be like to make love to that man?

She sensed a fire within him he had yet to reveal. He'd already shown her who he was. A man rooted to the place of his ancestors, while she had no roots and no familial bond with her own parents, let alone any unknown ancestors. Instinct told her that he would take everything she was willing to give, and return it a thousandfold. But she doubted herself, and doubted her ability to find a place in this world of his.

———

Brendan was standing in the shower, letting the heat and force of the hot water pelt the muscles in his back and shoulders. He was tired from the day's work and aching with a want that might never be fulfilled. He didn't know how to make love to her and then let her go. He wanted her, but he was also falling in love. Then he reminded himself. The bigger issue here was keeping her alive.

———

Brendan was off to work before daylight. There was bread dough to start, and hungry people to feed, but his mind was still on the dream he'd had last night.

One moment he'd been dreaming about a fish market in New York City, when the dream morphed, and he was in the banquet room of the Serenity Inn, at Sean and Amalie's wedding reception, and the music changed from a two-step to a waltz, and Aunt Ella came out of the crowd, still wearing the blue dress she'd worn to Sean and Amalie's wedding and reached for him, putting both hands upon his shoulders.

Dance with me, Brendan. Just like we did before.

So, he took her in his arms, feeling the fragility of her tall, willowy body as they began waltzing around the dance floor. She was holding on to him for balance as they began, and he was taking care not to go too fast, when he realized that her snow-white hair was turning black, and the crown of braids she always wore was coming undone. They were moving faster now as he watched the thick, dark hair falling across her shoulders and down her back. He was seeing her skin lose all the wrinkles and her blue eyes sparkle with the burst of youth, and seeing her as who she'd been before the years left their marks on her face. And then all of a sudden, the music stopped, and the young Ella was still in his arms when she leaned forward and whispered in his ear.

My darling boy. Don't be like me and get left behind. Dare to love. Take the chance. She's worth it.

Her sorrow pierced him like an arrow to the heart, and then she was gone. He woke up with tears on his face and realized she'd just told him something no Pope living ever knew.

The reason why Ella Pope never married. She'd loved once, wholly, deeply, and for whatever reason, she hadn't seized the moment and lost him forever. Brendan didn't want that to be him, holding on to the fear of loss, rather than giving himself permission to dare fate. To take chances with love.

If there'd ever been love between Clyde Wallace and Shirley Pope, it was gone by the time he'd been born.

He knew how relationships were supposed to work, but it was the thought of falling in love with Harley and then losing her that was holding him back.

Ella came with a message, reminding him that if he did nothing, then she was already lost. So, when he pulled into the employee parking lot at the hotel, he was ready for this day and for whatever it took to keep her safe. After that, he was playing the hand as Harley dealt it and would make peace with the end result.

Chapter 11

HARLEY'S ROOM SERVICE ORDER FOR BREAKFAST arrived just after 7:00 a.m. An order of bacon, a trio of croissants, extra butter, honey, and a pot of coffee. When it arrived, she began removing the dishes from the tray. As she picked up the basket of croissants, she saw a note beneath it.

> Good morning, Sunshine. Text if you need me. I'll see you this evening. FYI—for your daily sugar fix—apple pies with cheddar cheese crusts coming out of the oven.

Sunshine. She smiled, and made a mental note. Apple pie definitely happening in her belly today. She ate while everything was still hot, put her tray back out in the hall, and sent him a text in return.

> Sweetest wake-up message ever. Apple pie it is!

Brendan heard his phone signal a text, went into the cooler to grab some more eggs, and read it while he was standing in the cold and thought about waking up beside her.

He'd already talked to Cameron last night about Harley's request to talk to Rusty and given them Harley's number. The rest was up to them, and he had more Dutch babies to make. He took a half-dozen blocks of unsalted butter from a shelf and went back to his station.

"Anthony, make sure the fruit is ready for the Dutch babies, and when you whip the cream, almond flavoring, not vanilla."

"Yes, Chef."

Then Brendan eyed the three other sous-chefs in the baking area and frowned.

"Rick, egg wash only…no herbs or salt sprinkles. George, go lightly with the dusting sugar. You're not powdering a baby's butt, okay?"

"Yes, Chef," they echoed.

"And you…little mermaid…yes, the dough needs punching down, but not like you're trying to cold-cock someone," Brendan cautioned.

Ariel Halsey liked the nickname Chef had given her, but she never wanted to disappoint him.

"Sorry, Chef. I know better," she said.

Brendan winked. "I know you do. So, who made you mad this morning?"

She blushed.

They all laughed, and the morning rolled on.

Harley's background checks on Beaumont's two new vendors were revealing. The owner of the wholesale house was Joe Ellis, Beaumont's cousin, and he knew the meat wholesaler, Louis Freid, from previous jobs he'd held.

That was the link she'd been looking for. The vendors were overcharging for their inferior products and getting away with it because the invoices reflected the same costs as from the companies Ray had been using.

Larry set all this up after his arrival and had to be getting kickbacks. But without his permission, which she was never going to get, she wouldn't be able to find a paper trail without a court order. She needed to let Ray know and see if he wanted to alert the authorities, so she sent him a detailed email regarding her findings and went back to work on his audit.

An hour or so later, Ray returned her message, informing her to say nothing to anyone else, that he would be dealing with the rest of this from his end, and to take her time with the audit. She was relieved she didn't have to get into the dirty side of this with Beaumont on her own. The last thing she needed was two angry men trying to end her earthly existence.

Harley's email had set a fire under Ray Caldwell. He was already on the phone with his lawyer, asking for advice about the best way to proceed. Hours later, he and his lawyer had a meeting with federal agents who dealt with corporate fraud. He filed charges against Larry Beaumont, gave the agents all of Harley's information, and left it in their hands. They're the ones who had the power to get into Larry Beaumont's bank records to see where his kickbacks were coming from and where he was banking the money.

Larry Beaumont's days of employment at the Serenity Inn were about to come to a swift and painful end.

———

It was nearing noon when Harley's cell phone rang. She marked her place on the spreadsheet, then saw caller ID, and froze.

"What the hell?"

She let it ring until it went to voicemail, then listened to the message afterward.

Miss Banks, This is Tip Crossley, Wilhem's son. I'm just now catching up on everything that's been happening while I was gone. I got your number from Dad, and I want to offer you private security until this is all straightened out. Let me know your location, and I'll get you some protection.

The hair was standing up on her arms, and her heart was pounding. This didn't feel like an offer of protection. It felt like a fishing expedition. The call unsettled her enough that even after she went back to work, she couldn't focus. The urge to run was huge, but she suspected that would be playing into their hands. Frustration was at an all-time high, and the more she thought about it, the angrier she became.

And just as that thought was born, her phone rang again, and this time when she saw caller ID, she answered.

"Hello, this is Harley."

"Nice to meet you, Harley. I'm Rusty Pope. You are in something of a mess, aren't you? Talk to me."

"You don't know how much I appreciate this," Harley said. "I don't know how much Brendan told you."

"It doesn't matter," Rusty said. "Start from your beginning. I'm just going to listen, and then we'll go from there."

Harley was too hyped up to stay still and began pacing the floor as she unloaded, beginning with why Wilhem Crossley had contacted her, to the phone call she'd just received from Tipton Crossley.

"And that's where I'm at," Harley said. "I either need to clear Tip Crossley's involvement or nail his ass to the wall."

"I've been taking notes. I can help," Rusty said. "I've been doing some consulting work with the agency again, so I'm back in the loop, so to speak. Give me a couple of days to see what I can find out, and if something new ensues, call me. The last case I worked before I retired was human trafficking happening right here in Jubilee. They were using the influx of single young women here on holidays as a shopping cart. We finally took down the cell operating out of here, but never found the source. It's impossible to eradicate this, but at the same time, it's imperative that we never stop trying."

"This is new for me," Harley said. "Most of my work involved white-collar crime within corporations. I've never been on a hit list before."

The slight edge of panic in Harley Banks's voice resonated personally with Rusty. She'd lived through many hairy incidents during her undercover work.

"I empathize, believe me," Rusty said. "Just pay attention to everything. If something feels off, then it probably is. Instinct is our self-preservation button. I'll be in touch."

Harley's sense of relief was huge as the call ended. Nothing was resolved yet, but now she had someone on her side who could help. The longer she was here, the more impressed she was by the tight-knit community on Pope Mountain. She'd only seen it from the air, but now she wanted to see it from the ground, to stand in a place where lives and secrets were sacred to the people who lived there.

Rusty went looking for Cameron and found him in the living room on the floor with their daughter, Ella, sitting up between his long legs; their son, Mikey, was building a Lego block tower for Ella to knock over; and Cameron's dog, Ghost, lay nearby, keeping an eye on his people.

"What a perfectly beautiful sight," she said, as she entered the room.

Cameron looked up at the daring redhead who'd long ago captured his heart and smiled.

"Yes, you are," he countered. "So can you help?"

She nodded. "You know what's a little weird about this?"

"What?" he asked.

She eyed Mikey, trying to figure out how to say what she wanted, without her little "big ears" sharing it all over Jubilee.

"That other trafficking thing we worked on, right before I retired… We lost the trail in the same city where Harley uncovered the new one."

Cameron stilled. "Big coincidence at the least," he finally said.

She nodded. "So, are you guys okay here for a bit? I need to make some calls."

"We're good," Cameron said, and at the same moment, Mikey threw up his hands and yelled.

"Your turn, Ella!"

Ella leaped to her feet and karate-kicked the tower block Mikey had just built.

Blocks went flying.

Startled, Ghost jumped up with a *woof* and then nosed the back of Cameron's neck, making sure all was well.

Cameron threw back his head and laughed.

"That's your mini-me," he said.

Rusty frowned. "Who taught her that?"

"I did, Mama," Mikey said. "I'm teachin' her self-offense."

"Obviously…and it's supposed to be defending, not offending… Lord," she muttered. "And he's your mini-me," she added, pointing to Mikey.

Cameron's laughter followed her back to their office, and moments later, she was typing out all of her notes from her phone conversation with Harley Banks and saving them in a file. As soon as she finished, she typed a detailed letter, attached the notes, and emailed it to Special Agent Jay Howard, the agent she used to work with, who was now part of a task force investigating human trafficking on the East Coast.

The ball was rolling. It remained to be seen if any of it would come undone.

───────────

Jay Howard knew Rusty Pope had resumed work with the Company. It was consulting only, but she was so good at research and spotting the holes in written testimonies that they were glad to have her back.

After he received the email and the attachments she'd sent, at first, he missed the point. Some PI named Harley Banks had been warned of a hit man on her trail because of a crime she'd uncovered during a corporate audit. But as he read further, realizing it was connected to the recent raid on the Crossley warehouse in Philadelphia and that Wilhem Crossley himself had been the one to warn her, he began to take notice. He began opening the attachments and reading the notes Harley made on the son, Tipton Crossley, and he was hooked. Tip Crossley was already a person of interest in the case, but they had nothing on him.

He sent a quick message to the rest of the team to meet in his office first thing tomorrow morning. That he had new information to share.

———

Ollie Prine was back in Philadelphia, sleeping in his own bed, doing his own laundry, and catching up on past-due bills. Without a warehouse to go to, and everybody in jail or on the lam, he didn't have anyone to hang out with. And, he was fairly confident after Paget was killed that nobody would have the guts to rat him out for missing the raid.

In his dreams, he wished Berlin would take a hike. He was tired of this hunt for some woman just for petty revenge. He couldn't walk out. Berlin would just have him killed. Ollie knew too much about all the wrong things.

Then the very next day, someone knocked on his door. He opened it to find a messenger standing on his doorstep. "Oliver Prine?" the kid asked.

Ollie nodded.

He handed Ollie a packet and held out an iPad. "Sign here, please," he said.

Ollie signed his name and the kid turned around and left.

Ollie went back inside and opened the packet.

Five thousand dollars in one-hundred-dollar bills labeled Travel Money. An address for a hotel in a town called Jubilee, Kentucky.

And a four-word demand: GET IT OVER WITH.

———————

Two days later, Harley was up before daylight, still working on the hotel audit and sick of this room. She was tired of her own company. Tired of hiding. Tired of this feeling of being hunted and not knowing her enemy's face. She had a pounding headache. Either too much coffee and no food this morning, or eye stress from staring at a computer screen for days, or a little of both.

She hadn't seen Brendan since the night before last. He'd worked a double shift last night and called to let her know he wouldn't come by because it would likely be after ten before the kitchen shut down, but that, too, put her in a snit, which made her realize she was getting attached.

Finally, she shut down her workstation, took a couple of painkillers, and lay down on the sofa to rest her eyes. Then her phone rang. One glance at the screen and she answered.

"Hello."

"Morning, Sunshine. What's happening in your world today? Need anything? It's my day off. I'm all yours if you need me."

If I need you? What about if I want you? But she didn't say it. "I'm being all pitiful today. I have a headache that's going to make me sick. It happens when I've been staring at a computer screen too long, and I want out of this room."

There was a moment of silence, and Harley thought he'd hung up.

"Brendan? Are you still there?"

"Yes. Just thinking. Have you ever ridden on a motorcycle?"

"Yes, but not steering. Just a passenger, why?"

"Put on some warm clothes, and boots if you brought some. Gloves if you brought some. I have an older biker jacket from my high school years, and yes, I'm one of those men who doesn't throw anything away. It should just about fit you. If you're game, I'll smuggle you out of the hotel through the staff entrance. Nobody will know who you are with the biker's helmet on, and with a little speed and some fresh air, we'll blow the cobwebs out of your pretty head."

She swung her legs off the side of the sofa. "Are you serious?"

"With you, always."

She shivered. "I'm game."

"Good. Get changed. I'll gas up the Harley and see you in about fifteen minutes."

Harley was already running down the hall to the bedroom to change clothes as he ended the call. She peeled down to underwear and was patting herself on the back for packing her old cowboy boots. She'd arrived in black leather pants, and she was going to escape in them, too. The warmest shirts she'd brought were sweatshirts she lounged in. She grabbed the one without holes. She wasn't wearing makeup, but she put some moisturizer on her face against the cold, grabbed her phone, her best leather gloves, the key card to her room, and her wallet, and went to the living room to wait.

Her heart was pounding, and her headache was already receding. This felt like a turning point. She was at a crossroads in her life, and she was choosing the road to him.

Then came the knock.

She checked to see who it was, and then opened the door, and there he stood. Shiny black helmet. Black leather pants and a silver studded jacket. Well-worn biker boots, carrying a leather jacket and another helmet. He flipped up the visor on his helmet and winked, then slipped inside.

The hair was standing up on the back of her neck, and all she could do was stare. The pastry chef had turned into the Terminator, and if she hadn't known who was beneath that helmet and black leather, she would have been running.

"Are you ready to do this?" he asked.

His voice pulled her off the ledge of panic. It was still the Brendan she knew. The one who'd hugged away the sadness she'd felt the other night.

"Jacket first," he said, and held it out. She slipped her arms into the sleeves as he pulled it up over her shoulders, then turned her around. "Inner pockets have zippers. Phone, key card, wallet in those and zip, then we'll fasten the front."

Harley was focused on instructions and missed the look in his eyes, which was just as well. He wasn't crossing any line, but he also wasn't going to hide the growing feelings. As soon as she buckled and zipped all the pockets, he handed her the helmet.

"These have linked communication features. Bluetooth. We can talk to each other over the built-in mics while we ride."

She slipped it on and then stood while he buckled the chin strap.

He gave her a pat on the shoulder and a thumbs-up. After a quick look out in the hall, they headed toward a staff elevator. She put her gloves on in the elevator and then they took the back way out of the hotel without a hitch.

The motorcycle was parked outside the door. It was huge like him, and decked out in black and silver like him, and she felt like Cinderella about to climb into the gilded carriage and ignored the fact that Cinderella's carriage had begun its life as a pumpkin. But this bike was no pumpkin. It was the real deal, and so was the man astride it.

All of a sudden, his voice was in her ear. "Behind me, Sunshine, and hang on."

She felt like giggling. She swung her leg over the bike, settled into the seat, and slid her arms around his waist. When the engine fired up, she felt that rumble all the way to her soul.

He toed up the kickstand and they were gone.

Brendan took all the backstreets to get them out of town, and once he reached the highway that led up the mountain, he gunned it. He heard her gasp and then laugh, and that's when he knew she was going to like this ride.

———

Barely a mile up the mountain, the last remnants of Harley's headache were gone. Riding with this man was like nothing she'd ever known. His size alone gave her a sense of safety—like she was flying, but sheltered by the wall of his body. And every time they passed a mailbox on the side of the road, that deep raspy voice of his was in her ear, calling off names of those who lived there and their relationship to him. It was a roll call of Pope Mountain, and for the first time in her life, she became aware of the continuity of a people to a place.

As they passed a mailbox with a red cardinal painted on the side, he said, "My mom, Shirley Pope, lives up that road. It's our homeplace."

Harley heard a gentleness in his voice as they flew past, and thought of her parents, living life but living it apart. Always apart. It was no wonder she had no sense of roots. And then the timbre of his voice rose.

"Look, Harley. To your right. A fox slipping through the underbrush."

"I see it!" she cried.

Brendan heard the delight in her voice.

Another mile up and her voice was in his ear. "How far up does this road go?" she asked.

"All the way to heaven," he said.

A lump rose in Harley's throat. And here she thought she'd have to die to get there.

Another fifteen minutes and she realized the slope was leveling off, and they were actually riding on level ground. He began slowing down, then turned north off the black-top, rolled down a gravel road, and came to a stop.

There was an old wooden sign at the edge of the parking lot. CHURCH IN THE WILDWOOD. The church looked like something out of a children's fairy tale. A pointed roof with a bell tower, a portico over the front door. Windows ran along the sides of the long, white single-story building, and massive trees stood all around the area, waiting to grow back their leaves as the weather warmed and provide welcome shade in the months to come.

Brendan dismounted, then helped her off and put their helmets in the seats.

She combed her fingers through her hair to shake out the curls, and then did a slow three-sixty-degree turn, taking in the sights.

"How's your headache?" he asked.

"You're just what the doctor ordered. It's gone. It's beautiful up here, and so peaceful," she said, then pointed to a little house farther back. "Who lives there?"

"Brother Farley, the preacher. He's old as the hills now, but that's his home, and he still manages to preach a Sunday sermon."

"Will he care if we're here?" she asked.

"No. The mountain and the church belong to all of us."

"Do tourists come here?" she asked.

"The mountain is off-limits to sightseers. We don't bring people up."

She turned and looked at him. "Then why am I here?"

"You're not just people."

Her heart skipped. "What am I then?"

"Maybe more than you should be, but nothing I can deny."

She saw want in his eyes, but she knew he wouldn't take what wasn't given, and she honored that in him.

"We're sure from two different worlds..."

"Depends where you're standing," he said. "Right now, we're in the same place, trying to figure out your next move. I know what I want, but I don't know your heart's desires. I only know you steal ketchup and love sweets. I know you're smarter than most, and you trigger every protective instinct I have, and I brought food. Are you hungry enough to sit in that little patch of sunshine on the front steps and eat with me? I brought chicken-salad sandwiches and apple hand pies."

"Lord. Here I was, fast-talking myself into whatever you were going to suggest next, but I did not expect it to be chicken-salad sandwiches and... What are hand pies?"

Brendan smiled as he opened the back compartment of the Harley, pulled out a blanket and a couple of paper bags, then handed her two bottles of water.

"Your table is ready, miss. Follow me."

It was those two last words that ended her indecision. She'd follow him to the ends of the earth just to see what came next.

He had the blanket folded like a long cushion and placed on the top step of the portico.

"Nothing like cold concrete on your backside to ruin a good meal," he said, and as soon as she was settled, he plopped down beside her and used the bottom three steps for a footrest to accommodate his long legs.

He handed her a sealed sandwich bag with her sandwich, opened a large bag of chips and put it between them, and then unscrewed the lids on the water.

"Haute cuisine, mountain-style," he said, and lifted his bottle. "To you, Sunshine."

She smiled. "Why do you call me Sunshine?"

"Because you brighten my day. Now we eat because I can't say pretty things to you on an empty stomach."

Harley nodded, then took a big bite. "Ummm, this is good."

He winked and followed his bite with a couple of potato chips. When a bird dropped down to the ground from a nearby tree, he tossed it a bit of bread crust. Another bird followed, and then a possum came waddling out from beneath a bush.

Harley ate in total silence, watching her Terminator turn into Dr. Doolittle, and wondered what other facets he had yet to reveal. She finished the sandwich, ate her fill of chips, and then slipped her hands into the jacket pockets to keep them warm. As she did, she felt something beneath her fingertips. Something round, flat, and metallic. She pulled it out.

"Brendan, this was in the pocket of your jacket."

He glanced at the small gold medal in her hand and nodded. "I guess I forgot it was there."

"Were you raised Catholic?"

"No." He picked up the St. Michael medal and rubbed it between his fingers. "Clyde broke my arm when I was ten. I had to have surgery because the bone came through the skin. One evening before Mom got off work, I was alone in the room when a priest who was making the rounds came into my room. He asked me about my injury, and being a kid, I told him." He paused, thinking back, and then looked at Harley. "The guy looked horrified. I thought I'd said something wrong, and then he pulled this out of his pocket. It was on a chain, and he fastened it around my neck. He told me that St. Michael was an archangel, a kind of warrior for God, and that he was giving it to me for protection, and then he left.

"I wore it hidden beneath my shirts for a long time. Didn't want Clyde to see it, but then of course, he did. He yanked it off my neck and slapped me. Aaron was almost twenty by then. He took the medal away from Clyde, dragged him out behind the house, and they fought until Clyde couldn't get up. Aaron came back inside, handed me my medal, then doctored my busted lip. After I got bigger, I kept it in the pocket of this jacket. Then I outgrew the jacket, and I guess I figured out that it wasn't the medal protecting me so much as the belief it gave me to protect myself."

Then he put the medal back in Harley's hand. "For protection, when I'm not there to help."

"I can't take your—"

"You didn't take. I gave. Put it in the jacket pocket, or wear it around your neck. The jacket, the mojo, and St. Michael are yours now, and I'm ready for hand pies."

Harley swallowed past the lump in her throat as she zipped the medal inside an inner pocket with her phone and watched him unwrap two perfectly browned and glazed pastries.

"Apple, cinnamon, nutmeg, and brown sugar inside. Sweet like you," he said, and took a big bite.

Harley's hands were shaking, but not from the cold.

She didn't know how she was going to make this work, but she wasn't going to lose this man. Whatever it took, wherever he took her, she wanted to be the one who loved him.

"Good?" he asked, as he watched her chew and swallow.

"Beyond good," she said, and wiped a crumb from the corner of her mouth.

As soon as they finished eating, Brendan stood up. "If you're ready to go back, I'll take you down, or you can come meet some of the old ones. They probably already know you matter to me, or you wouldn't be here, but they like to be introduced."

She glanced at the cemetery, then slipped her hand in his. "Show me," she said, so he did, starting at the front where the most recent ones had been laid to rest.

"This is Ella Pope. Up until her passing, she was the oldest living Pope on the mountain. She was everybody's aunt Ella. She saw the past, the future, and what was about to happen, just like we'd turn on the TV. Up here, they call it 'having the sight.'"

"Was she really that psychic?"

Brendan nodded. "It's not that uncommon among our people. Cameron thinks his son, Mikey, has the same tendencies. He's always speaking in future tense and past tense about things he can't possibly know."

"Are you?" Harley asked.

He glanced down at her and smiled, then lifted a flyaway curl from near her eye.

She immediately reached for the curls to push them back. "My hair. It has a mind of its own," she said.

"I think it's beautiful. It suits you," Brendan said. "And no, I'm not psychic, but I know how to pay attention to my instincts. I'd say life taught me that."

They moved on through the headstones, and as they did, he paused and picked up a piece of tiny black rock. "Look at this," he said.

"What is it? Onyx?"

"Coal. These mountains have thousands of sealed-off tunnels from mines gone bust. Unusual to see this lying aboveground, though," he said, and kept it as they moved on. "This marker is for Helen Pope, my grandmother, my mom's mother. Over there are members of the Cauley family and, over here, members of the Glass family who've passed."

Harley was reading names and dates, and not paying attention to where she was walking. She tripped on some dry vines and, before she could catch herself, was falling face-first.

Just before impact, she went airborne and found herself cradled against Brendan's chest, so close she could feel the warmth of his breath on her face.

"Are you okay?" he asked.

She took a shaky breath. His mouth was so close to her lips. All she had to do was move her head and they'd touch.

"I am now, thanks to you," she said.

He set her down on her feet and was reaching into

her hair to pull out a piece of dry grass, then stopped, mesmerized by the way the curl wrapped itself around his finger. It took everything he had to let go.

"Grass," he said, and dropped it at their feet. "The first Brendan and his Meg are at the back," he said, and this time held her hand as they went.

Harley couldn't get over the dates on the markers. Centuries had come and gone between these lives. The next time they stopped, it was in front of a large, flat rock with the name Brendan James Pope carved in it. And beside that marker, the place where Meg was buried.

Harley had never seen anything like Meg's burial site. "Is this meant to be a little house or—"

"Chickasaw tradition," Brendan said, then laid the tiny piece of coal on the graying wood on the roof before stepping back. "They put this up new at the burial, and then it's supposed to deteriorate on its own, back to nature."

As they stood, a gust of wind rose, stirring the dry leaves around them, and then it was gone.

"Maybe Little Grandmother likes you," Brendan said.

Harley's heart was pounding. She wasn't going to admit it, but she was a little spooked.

Brendan glanced up. "It'll be dark up here in a couple of hours. Gets dark early in the winter. Come on, Sunshine. Let's get you back before someone misses you and thinks you've been kidnapped."

She put her hand on his chest. "Smuggled out, taken for a ride I'll never forget, and stole my heart in the process. What's a girl to do?"

He sighed, and then his fingers were in her hair and his mouth was on her lips, and every sad, empty place in Harley's heart was full to overflowing.

When he finally lifted his head, she had a heartbeat moment of panic, like someone had just pulled the plug on her life support.

"I, uh…"

"Phase One, Sunshine. If this isn't on your agenda, now's the time to—"

She put a finger of his lips to silence him. "Where do I sign up for Phase Two?"

"I got you," he said, and took her by the hand and led her to the bike. They put on their helmets, got on the Harley, and moments later, he started the engine and toed up the kickstand. "Are you ready?"

She locked her arms around his waist. "For anything you care to hand out."

"Then hang on, honey. It's easier going down."

The big bike roared to life, and as soon as they reached the blacktop again and Brendan gunned it, he heard Harley's high-pitched shout of glee. He'd met his match with this one. Today was a day he'd been waiting for all his life.

The ride down was in total silence.

They were thinking about that kiss and the promise of what came next. When he finally rolled up at the back lot of the hotel, it was nearing dusk. He grabbed her by the hand, glanced around at the lot full of employee cars, and hurried her inside. They rode the staff elevator back to the eighth floor, and Harley had her key card in her hand by the time they reached her suite. One swipe, and they were inside without meeting a soul.

They pulled off their helmets, looked at each other, and started grinning.

"Smuggled out. Smuggled in. I'd say the operation was a success," Harley said, and started taking off the jacket.

"You keep the jacket," he reminded her.

"I'm not going to bed in it," she said.

"You're going to bed?" Brendan asked.

Harley paused, hit with doubt.

"Phase Two, remember? You took me up on that mountain, wove some magic spell around me that made me never want to leave, and I want more. I want you, Brendan Pope."

"I'll take whatever you have to give, but it will never be enough. I won't give you up easy."

"And I never quit what I start," she said.

Brendan wrapped his arms around her and pulled her close. "So, what are we starting here?"

"A fire," she whispered, as he picked her up.

"Which way?" he asked.

"Down the hall, past the half bath to the last door on the left."

Long legs made short work of the distance as he carried her into the room. "You first," he said, pointing at the en suite.

Harley walked into the bathroom as Brendan went back up to the hall to the half bath. When he returned, the bed was turned back, and Harley was gloriously naked and waiting for him at the foot of the bed.

He stopped, staggered by the sight of her. Skin like ivory. Those sea-blue eyes, and the look on her face, as if waiting for judgment.

Harley was afraid to move. Afraid to talk. Was it an illusion, or did he seem even larger without clothes than he did fully dressed? *Ah, so this is finally happening, and it feels like I've waited all my life for him. He is more than a beautiful face. So much more*, she thought, as he came toward her.

Now his hands were on her shoulders, then brushing across the surface of her breasts, and her knees went weak. Making love to him was going to change the path of where she thought she was going, and she was going to die from the want of him if he didn't hurry.

But she soon learned after he laid her on the bed that he was on a quest of his own, mapping the contours of her body, testing, tasting, learning the secrets that made her gasp, and the ones that elicited a groan, and the ones that had her reaching for him until she was begging and he was a solid ache to be with her.

Without a word, he moved over her, then in her, and the moment he took the first stroke, he was the one who groaned. She was hot and tight and wet. And then she locked her legs around his waist, and he was lost.

One stroke, and then another, and another until they were both caught up in the rhythm, chasing a blood rush that couldn't come fast enough. Time lost all meaning. There was nothing that mattered but the moment of climax.

Brendan was watching her face when it hit her. The sight of her face in ecstasy was a trigger. One moment he was with her, and then he was caught up in the wave of his own climax.

Harley was marked. Ruined for ever wanting another. Heart-bound.

Brendan was used up. Satiated. Branded for life. In complete and utter love as he raised himself up on both elbows and brushed a kiss across her lips.

"Beautiful in my eyes. Forever in my heart. How am I going to live when you leave me?"

Harley's hands were on his back, feeling scars, and then she remembered. *When he fell into the cellar and the jagged wood ripped his back on the way down.* Scars he would take to his grave, all suffered in the name of family. She wrapped her arms around his neck.

"No, love. Don't borrow sadness. I don't want to lose you, either. Just keep me alive long enough for us to figure it out."

"Giving it my best," he said, then glanced at the time. "You need to eat. It's been hours, and someone will start to worry if you don't order food. They'll think something happened to you."

"You happened, but you're right. God, I don't want to let go of you. I want to forget the mess I'm in and wake up beside you tomorrow."

He kissed the hollow at the base of her throat, then ran a finger along the curve of her face.

"I can make that happen, too," he said. "You order food. I'll go home and get a change of clothes. I have to be at work at 5:00 a.m. It's a quick hop from the eighth floor to the twelfth floor. No harm, no foul."

"Really? You would do that for me?"

He grinned. "Driving across town to get a change of clothes just so I can come back and make love to you again isn't a punishment. It's a gift." Then he threw back the covers and went back down the hall to the half bath to get his clothes.

As soon as he was dressed, he went looking for her.

"I ordered food for two," she said.

"Then what are you having?" he asked.

She grinned. "I'm having more of you."

He laughed. "I'm leaving now. Come lock up behind me."

She was in her bathrobe as she followed him to the door, and after another quick kiss, he was gone.

Chapter 12

HARLEY TOOK A QUICK SHOWER, PUT ON SWEATS AND running shoes, and went down to the lobby to one of the boutique stores with her wallet, key card, and the St. Michael's medal in hand. Once inside, she headed straight to the jewelry counter.

A clerk approached and slipped behind the counter. "Hi, I'm Keith. Is there something I can show you?"

Harley palmed the medal. "I need a gold chain for this."

Keith eyed the loop on the medal and then took a tray of chains from the display case.

"There are several styles and lengths…braided, flat links, and the finer chains like these."

"A finer chain, but one that's durable, and I think twenty-two inches. I don't want it so delicate that it's easily broken," Harley said.

"How about this one?" Keith asked, and unhooked it.

Harley threaded it through the loop on the medal, then fastened it around her neck. It fell just above her cleavage.

"This will work. I'll take it," she said, and took it off so Keith could ring it up, and then put it back on after she'd paid. "Thank you so much," she said. She could feel it against her skin.

Protection for when I'm not with you.

As soon as she got back to the room, she kicked off her shoes, replaced them with fuzzy socks, then grabbed her laptop and phone and began checking messages and emails to see if there was any news or updates from Ray Caldwell or Rusty Pope, but there were none.

She had one missed text from Liz Devon, telling her that the hotel may seem unusually crowded tomorrow, but not to worry, and that the hotel was hosting an event for country star Josie Fallin and about two hundred of her fans in the main ballroom. It would be an active event beginning midafternoon and ending after dinner that night. That meant Brendan would be involved in whatever food was being served and that he'd be on duty until the event was over.

A short while later, there was a knock at the door, and after a quick look through the peephole, she let him in, then locked the door behind him.

He dropped his duffel bag and took her in his arms. "I missed you. What are we having to eat?"

She laughed. "You weren't kidding when you said you were never full, were you? Never fear, I ordered steak and potatoes au gratin, Caesar salads, and peach cobbler. I wasn't sure about how you like your steak, so I guessed and ordered medium."

He gave her a thumbs-up, then picked up his bag and took it to the bedroom. He was hanging up his work clothes when he heard her cell phone ring, and then her voice. There were a few moments of silence, and then she was yelling.

He turned and ran.

She rolled her eyes when she saw him.

"Are you okay?" he asked.

No, she mouthed, and then lit into her caller again. "I hope you know your request is insulting. No, Dad, I will not fly to Houston. I'm working, and how dare you even suggest using me as bait to some senator in return for his vote on one of your projects! You disregard my career, and at the same time suggest I 'spend time' with a married man. And don't interrupt. I know who he is, and I've seen pictures of his wife and children. What's the matter with you?"

Brendan sighed. Her father.

She was listening again, her face getting redder by the moment.

"No, I'm not insolent. You're disgusting. Yes, you're my father, but you are no longer the boss of me."

Then she burst into tears, and Brendan lost it. He held out his hand, and she handed him the phone and left the room. Now he was hearing the derision in Jason Banks's voice when he called her a thankless bitch, and it smacked too much of Clyde Wallace for him to ignore.

"Excuse me," he said.

There was a moment of shocked silence and then the man was yelling at him instead.

"Who the hell are you, and where's my daughter?"

"I'm Brendan Pope, and I'm pretty sure she's pouring herself a shot of whiskey about now."

"What are you to her?" Jason asked.

"At the moment, assisting her in this job. Consider yourself fortunate that you are not standing in front of me right now. I'll give her your regards, and if I ever find out you called her a bitch again, or find out you made her cry, we will discuss this further. Do you understand?"

Jason was speechless, then sputtering when Brendan hung up. When he turned around, Harley was standing behind him.

"Are you okay?" he asked.

She blinked. "You stood up for me."

He frowned. "I don't want to make an enemy out of your father, but I also don't give a shit whether he likes me or not, as long as you and I are good."

She walked into his arms and hugged him. "We are so good," she whispered.

"Well then," he said, and wrapped his arms around her.

By the time room service arrived, Brendan had her laughing.

When they made love again, he saw the medal hanging above her breasts, and then saw the look in her eyes. She was reaching for him when he moved between her legs and gave her everything she wanted. Over and over, time and again, until the only need they had was for sleep.

―――――――

Brendan was on his back with his arm around Harley's shoulders. Her head was resting on his chest. This day began on an impulse that was ending at the highest point of his life. He was so deep in love with this woman that it hurt.

"Brendan?"

"Hmm?"

"This day feels like a dream," Harley said.

He touched her cheek. "Look at me." Her head came up. "This isn't a dream. I don't play house. I play for keeps. Fair warning, Sunshine. I'm falling in love with you."

"Then wipe the frown off your face, because you turned that page for me when you stood up to my father on my behalf. You're my hero forever."

―――――――

It was ten minutes to 5:00 a.m. and Brendan was ready to walk out the door when he went to the bedroom where Harley was still sleeping. He paused at the bedside, thinking of what it would be like to see this every morning for the rest of his life, and then leaned over and kissed the spot behind her ear that made her moan.

"Hey, Sunshine, hate to wake you, but I'm leaving for work, and I need you to come lock up after me."

She opened her eyes, rolled over on her back, saw him leaning over the bed, and smiled.

"I thought I was dreaming."

"Nope. I'm the real deal."

She threw back the covers and got up. Brendan helped her on with her bathrobe, and then gave her a swat on the backside as she sidled past him.

She put one finger in the air and kept walking. "That'll cost you," she said.

"Just put it on my tab. I'm good for it."

She unlocked the dead bolt, then the safety chain, and stood on her tiptoes for a goodbye kiss that made her ache.

"You're definitely good," she said. "I know you're going to be busy with the Fallin event. Don't worry about me. I'm not going anywhere."

"Pay attention to whoever delivers room service. If you don't know them, tell them to leave it in the hall."

She nodded.

He was halfway out the door when he stopped and turned around. "Love you."

Her heart skipped. "Love you, too."

And then he was gone. She quickly locked everything back up and thought about going back to bed. Instead, she started a cup of coffee brewing and headed for the shower.

Jason Banks was still reeling from being chastised by a total stranger and angry at his daughter for ruining his plans. It was eight o'clock in the morning for him, but it was 3:00 p.m. where Judith was and he needed to talk to her. He glanced in the mirror before making the call, as if it mattered whether his graying hair was in place and that he had yet to shave, and then called his wife.

It was a cold, rainy day and Judith was curled up with a book on the sofa in front of a blazing fire, with a cup of tea cooling on the side table when her phone rang. When she saw the number pop up, she put the book aside and answered.

"Jason, darling, how are you? Everything okay?"

"We need to talk," he said. "I think Harley has a man in her life."

Judith sat up straighter. "Really? How do you know?"

"I called her last night and of course we argued. She never listens to anything I say. Unbeknownst to me, she handed her phone off to this man, and when he heard me call her an ungrateful bitch, he had the audacity to read me the riot act, then add a vague threat to it before he hung up on me."

"You shouldn't have argued. Why do you always do that?" she said. "And it was despicable of you to call your own daughter a bitch. If that man is interested in Harley, at least he seems to have her best interests at heart."

"Bullshit!" Jason roared. "He threatened me."

"And you threatened someone he loves," Judith said.

"You're no help," he said.

"You're the one who called wanting absolution for being a jackass. I cannot give you something you do not deserve. I love you. Have a good day."

Jason was mumbling and muttering beneath his breath, but managed to respond in a socially polite manner. "I love you, too, of course."

Judith rolled her eyes. "Of course, you do," she said, and hung up.

But now she was excited. She wanted to know everything. Ignoring the time difference, she made a quick call to her daughter. The call rang and rang, and then went to voicemail, which irked her no end. But she left a message anyway and hung up.

Harley was on the hotel phone ordering room service when her cell phone rang. She hadn't eaten breakfast and now she was too hungry to wait for lunch, so she was having a late brunch and calling it even. She heard it ringing and checked after her order was made, but after she saw it was her mother, she guessed her dad had called her to whine. She didn't want to talk to either of them, ignored it and went back to work.

Even though the food for Josie Fallin's fan club event was coming together without issue, both the baking and cooking sides of the kitchen were running hot, trying to keep up with orders from the guests in the dining room, the room service orders, and the foods that would be in Fallin's buffet.

From Brendan's end of the line, he was pulling hot rolls and cherry cobblers out of the ovens right and left. Cherry cobbler à la mode was the requested dessert for the Fallin event, and they were feeding two hundred people at the event. Every sous-chef and junior chef on-site was double-stepping today. It was an all-hands-on-deck event.

Liz Devon was in her element. The decor was western chic, exactly what Josie had asked for, and the playlist of music was her songs. The gift bags for the attendees were at the door, ready to be handed in as the guests arrived, and Josie was texting Liz nonstop, checking and rechecking to make sure everything was perfect for her attending fans. Her event began midafternoon, and she was double-checking security for her arrival.

"Yes, our security has been notified, as well as the local PD who'll manage outside traffic as well as the vans shuttling fans from the parking lot at the music venue to the hotel and back," Liz told her.

Josie sighed. "I know I must be a pain in the neck. I don't mean to doubt your expertise, but my fans are really important to me, and I want everything to be perfect for them. I can bounce with the delays and mistakes, but they come a long way and spend their hard-earned money just to see me and take pictures with me, and, well, you know the drill. A simple dinner today is going to mean the world to them."

"You aren't a pain at all, and I admire your loyalty to the people who support you. There's not nearly enough of that in the world. I do want to ask about your brother, though. Alex, isn't it? How is he doing since the wreck?"

Josie smiled, pleased that the woman remembered. "He's doing great, but opted to stay in my bus. It has all the comforts of home and then some, and some of the guys in my band are going to look in on him. Home away from home, you know?"

"Wonderful news," Liz said.

"Oh, one last thing. Will Brendan Pope be at work today?"

"Yes, he's here."

"Sometime during our event, I would like permission to have him come to the party so I can introduce him to my guests. They all know about Alex's injuries and that a local man saved him, but I would like to honor him for his heroism."

"I'll make that happen," Liz said. "I'll be on-site for the event, so when you're ready to do that, just let me know. I'll bring him in."

"It won't upset him, will it?" Josie asked.

"Not at all. Brendan is a sweetheart," Liz said.

"Perfect. Then I'll see you later," Josie said, and hung up.

Liz sighed. Now she needed to let Brendan know that Josie Fallin wanted to introduce him during the dinner. She knew he was too busy to interrupt in the kitchen, so she sent him a text instead.

He saw it, made a mental note, and slid another three pans of rolls into the ovens to bake.

Shirley Pope was on her way into Jubilee to run errands.

Amalie was working from home today, and the moment Shirley drove out of the yard, Sean and Amalie gathered in his office for a Zoom meeting with her dad, Wolfgang Outen.

Tomorrow was the family dinner when they'd make their baby announcement, but they didn't want Wolf to be left out of the loop. They were sitting side by side when Wolf's face popped up on the screen.

"My two favorite people! Good morning!" Wolf said. "This is a great way to start the day. What's new with you two, and tell me what's going on in Jubilee," he said.

Amalie glanced at Sean.

"He's your dad. You tell him."

"Tell me what?" Wolf asked.

"That I'm pregnant with twins. You're going to be a grandfather!" Amalie said.

The surprise on Wolf's face was followed by an expression of pure delight. "Twins! Amalie! Sean! This is the best news ever! Congratulations twice. Oh wow. Grandpa. Grandfather. Naw…too formal. Papa! That's it! I want them to call me Papa."

Sean was grinning from ear to ear. "We can make that happen," he said.

"I can't wait. When's the due date?" Wolf asked.

"I'm coming up on three months pregnant, so we have a way to go. They said the middle of September, but having twins can make the due date vary," Amalie said.

"What's Shirley think about this?" he asked.

"Oh, you're the first to know," Amalie said. "Shirley is making dinner for the family tomorrow. We're making the announcement to them then."

"Then I'll keep quiet until later. This is wonderful. Just wonderful. I wish I was close. I missed all of your childhood. I would love to be near to watch them grown up."

"I guess you could, if you wanted to live in Jubilee," Sean said.

"What do you mean?" Wolf asked.

"I heard Ray Caldwell is putting the Serenity Inn up for sale because of health issues," Sean said.

All of a sudden, Wolf's expression shifted. "Really? I might give him a call to see what's up with that."

"Jubilee is a far cry from your corporate life and world travels," Sean warned.

"But it's far grander than how I was raised," Wolf said. "And none of what I have means anything without

people to share it with. You two have made me so happy.
I love you both. Take care of each other, and I might see
you soon."

"Anytime, Dad, and remember, you have an open
invitation to the extra bedroom here at Shirley's house."

"Thank you, honey, but that bedroom won't be extra
for long. You're going to have to have a nursery for two
before the year is out. Call me whenever, and if I head
your way, I'll let you know in advance."

"Okay, bye, Dad," Amalie said.

The connection ended.

Sean and Amalie were excited to have finally shared
their news, but Wolf was already calling Ray Caldwell
to get a status update about the hotel. He was already
an investor at Hotel Devon, but he'd gladly sell his
shares back to the corporation for the opportunity to
own the Serenity Inn outright. Then he could live in
the penthouse, set up an office from there and a section for his security guards, and grow old with his
family around him.

———

Once Ray Caldwell had set the federal fraud investi-
gators onto Larry Beaumont and his two associates,
he was even more anxious to get the hotel paperwork
in order. He knew there were whispers in the hotel
industry about his recent health scares, and he'd been
approached by more than one corporation regarding

other holdings he owned. His wife, Patricia, was campaigning for him to retire completely, but it would take ages to liquidate everything he owned.

The stress of it all was getting to him, and when he got a call at midday from Wolfgang Outen, he would have bet money it wasn't just to get an update on his health.

Patricia frowned when the phone rang. He blew her a kiss and winked as he answered. "Hello, this is Ray."

"Ray, Wolf Outen here. I was just speaking to Amalie and Sean, who passed on a bit of info I wanted to follow up on."

"Before you ask, yes, I'm working toward selling my hotel in Jubilee," Ray said.

Wolf chuckled. "Well, I have personal reasons for asking. I won't pressure you about anything, but before you go public with the news, would you give me a chance at first refusal? I would certainly make it worth your while."

"Of course," Ray said. "I wish I was there to give you the tour myself. It would rest easy on my mind to know someone with your integrity was taking over. I have a great staff."

"Was it your health that prompted this?" Wolf asked.

"That and the interim manager I hired. He's not working out," Ray said. "I have an auditor already on-site getting a final audit and an updated P&L statement. Profit and loss, the bane of any business owner's world."

"Your auditor… Is he nearing the finish line?"

"It's a woman. Her name is Harley Banks. She's—"

"I know who she is," Wolf said. "She's a shark, which means she's working on more than the P&L for you. Is it the manager?"

"At this moment, I can't comment on anything more, other than to assure you that by the time the hotel is ready for sale, the tangle will have been removed."

"Understood," Wolf said. "In the meantime, if I just happened to be coming to the area to visit my kids, I assume it wouldn't be misunderstood if I chose to book a room at your hotel?"

Ray smiled. "We'd be glad to have you. And if you do, maybe you and Harley could meet. For now, she knows more about what's going on there than I do. If you decide to show up, just let me know and I'll give her the okay to share information with you regarding the business. The other stuff is being dealt with as we speak."

"Thank you, Ray. I'll do that, and I look forward to meeting her. I would pay a king's ransom to have her working in my organization, riding herd on the financial aspects of my holdings."

"From all I know, she's a loner," Ray said.

"True, but one can dream," Wolf said. "Take care and I'll be in touch."

"I look forward to hearing from you," Ray said, and disconnected.

Patricia looked up. "Who was that?"

"Wolfgang Outen."

Her eyes widened. "You're kidding me."

"No. He heard the hotel might be for sale. It was a fishing expedition for sure, but he did ask for first refusal before I put it on the market."

She grinned. "What a boon that would be for all concerned."

"Agreed," Ray said. "I suppose we'll find out soon enough."

———

Ollie Prine arrived in Jubilee, Kentucky, after midnight, rented a little cabin at Bullard's Campgrounds, and slept until midmorning. But before he pulled a trigger anywhere, he had some recon to do. He had a location, but no room number. He didn't know her routine. He had to see her face to know for sure she was still on the premises, and when he did, there would be no hesitation. The silencer on his gun would muffle the act, and the bullet would do the rest.

———

After Rusty sent Harley's file to Special Agent Howard, she began digging into Tipton Crossley's background on her own. The one thing Rusty could do from her end was look into the forged papers. Harley had included photocopies of a couple of samples of paperwork with Wilhem Crossley's legal signature and some copies of the forged signatures. What she now needed was an example of Tipton Crossley's signature, and the quickest and easiest place to look for it was at the DMV.

She was in the act of pulling up the Pennsylvania DMV website when she heard a crash, then a shriek, and then the sounds of running feet and the click of Ghost's nails on the hardwood floors.

"I got it! Nobody's bleeding. We're good!" Cameron yelled.

"Thank you!" she shouted back, but it didn't stop the tattling. Mikey reached her first, but Ella was right behind him, her little toddler legs running almost as fast as her brother's.

"I had a accident," Mikey said. "Scared Sissy, but I didn't hurt her, okay, Mama?"

Rusty swiveled around in her chair and picked both of them up in her lap. "Accidents happen, buddy, and I know you would never hurt your baby sister. But what broke?"

"It might have been that old bowl on the kitchen table. The one with the apples in it."

She hid a smile. "Might have been, or for sure was?"

"For sure," Mikey said, and laid his head on her shoulder. "I'm sorry, Mama."

Rusty hugged him. "It's okay. I'm not mad. Accidents happen." Then she addressed the tears still on Ella's cheeks and started wiping them away. "Look at me, Ella. We need to wipe those tears off your cheeks because we don't need them anymore, do we?"

"Don't need 'em," Ella said.

Rusty hugged her, too. "Right. Mikey is sorry you were scared. Wanna give him a hug so he isn't sad anymore?"

Ella leaned across Rusty's lap and hugged her brother, who instantly reciprocated with a hug and a kiss.

"Sorry, Sissy," Mikey said.

"Sorry I cry," Ella said.

Rusty hugged and kissed them both. "Okay now, Daddy probably has it all cleaned up by now. You both go tell Ghost you're sorry, too. He worries when you two are upset."

They slid off her lap and ran out as fast as they'd come in.

She sighed, then refocused on the website, found a photocopy of Tipton Crossley's driver's license, then copied and pasted it to a file, added a scan of one of the forged papers, and sent them to her contact, along with instructions as to what she needed to know.

She hadn't heard back from Jay Howard. For the time being, there was nothing more she could do.

———

Josie Fallin's fan club event was in full swing. She started off by giving the attendees time to come in, get their gift bags, find the seating chart with their names on it, and visit with each other before she made her appearance.

But the moment she entered and stepped up to the microphone, the room erupted into rounds of applause.

Josie smiled and waved. "Hi, y'all. I'm so happy to get this chance to meet you. We're gonna have so much fun today. Karaoke for the brave, all kinds of goodies in your gift bags, and just so you know, this whole event is being videoed, and each of you will all be receiving a link of the entire event to save to your devices at a later date. Now, before we get started, I'm going to address the question I've been getting on social media. Yes, my brother, Alex, is healing better than expected, considering how close he came to dying in that wreck. I had planned for him to be here today, but he's not up to a party yet, so I'll give him your love, okay?"

They cheered and clapped, and then silenced as Josie held up her hand.

"While Alex can't be here, I want you to meet the man who saved his life. Brendan Pope, the head pastry chef of the Serenity Inn, and one hot biker dude. The man who turns out food fit for angels and rides his Harley like the Devil's on his tail. Get yourself on out here and say hello!" Josie said.

"This is your cue," Liz said, and gave Brendan a push. He entered the room through the same door as Josie, minus his chef coat and cap, wearing the white shirt and blue jeans he'd worn to work. He was a sight to behold as he walked out onto the stage, immediately dwarfing her diminutive size.

The oohs and aahs and the occasional whoop of

delight were enough to send Brendan packing, but he'd promised Liz he'd endure this, so he made himself wave and smile.

"Thank you for doing this," Josie said. "And thank you, sir, for saving my brother's life. As a memento of my undying appreciation, my record label and I want to give you this award for heroism in the face of danger. I don't know all the details of that day, but I know what Alex told me. The bus was smoking. The engine was already on fire, and you didn't run away. You ran toward danger. You popped the back exit to give people access to escape and then saw him standing on the overturned bus, about to pass out from blood loss, and pulled him down and carried him to safety. Thank you from all of us," Josie said, and handed him an ornately carved plaque.

The applause continued long and loud until Josie held up her hand to silence them, then Brendan moved to the mic.

"You know that old saying about being in the wrong place at the wrong time? I'm no hero. I did what any man would have done. The only difference between me and them was that I was in the right place at the right time. There were dozens of heroes there that day. Police, firefighters, and EMTs. Jubilee is good like that. We take care of our own, and the visitors who knock on our doors. Have a great day, and hope you enjoy the food."

Josie's photographer snapped multiple shots of her

and Brendan onstage, and of him receiving the award. He flashed one last smile and exited the stage.

Josie turned to the audience and grinned. "He looks as good walkin' offstage as he did walking on, doesn't he, ladies?"

After that, the party continued. Brendan was back in the kitchen with his award propped up on a shelf, getting chastised by the crew for staying mum about what he'd done, but he just smiled and kept on working.

Chapter 13

A KNOCK AT THE DOOR, AND THEN A FAMILIAR CALL.

"Housekeeping!"

Harley got up, looked through the peephole, then opened the door. It was Sophie, the maid she saw every day.

"Good afternoon, Miss Banks," Sophie said, and entered as usual with an armful of clean bedsheets and fresh towels for the bath.

"The same to you," Harley said. "I'll try to stay out of your way." She took a seat in a chair facing the open doorway.

After Crossley's warning about a hit man, this had become the time of day when Harley was most on alert. The door stayed open as the maid went back and forth to her cleaning cart, and Harley's handgun was in the kangaroo drop pocket of the sweatshirt she was wearing. She wasn't turning her back on anyone.

Sophie was all business as she began to dust, empty wastebaskets, and then go down the hall to the bedroom to clean the bathroom and change the sheets.

Another uniformed staff member arrived with the

snack cart, quickly refilled the mini-fridge and replenished snacks, and was soon gone, but today, the traffic in the hall was heavier than usual.

There were a lot more people coming and going, moving past the cleaning cart, laughing, talking, or looking down at their phones.

Harley guessed it was all due to Josie Fallin's big event and thought of Brendan, wondering how he fared during times like this. He seemed to stay calm in the midst of chaos. Even when he had confronted her father about how he was treating her, instead of shouting louder, his voice got quieter and somehow more threatening. She suspected Brendan didn't rage; he just got even. Maybe because he'd grown up in a household war, it was the last thing he chose for himself when it was over.

She glanced up at the time, thinking Sophie must have had her own busy day. It was just after 3:00 p.m. Late for housekeeping.

She would remember later how everything after that moment seemed to happen in slow motion.

Sophie banged a cabinet door.

Harley glanced toward the open doorway.

A man was standing beside the cleaning cart, staring at her. A face she remembered!

She was grabbing for the gun in the kangaroo pouch of her sweatshirt as he was reaching beneath the back of his jacket.

Sophie appeared in the hallway.

"GET DOWN!" Harley screamed, and then was diving toward the floor as she took aim and fired.

The shots went off simultaneously.

Sophie was screaming.

Harley couldn't see the man in the hall or the bullet hole in his head for the blood running in her eyes. And then suddenly, Sophie was at her side, wiping the blood from her face with one of the towels she'd been carrying, and Harley was frantically trying to push her away. "Is he dead? Is he dead?"

"He is on the floor in the hall. He isn't moving," Sophie said.

The room was spinning. Harley knew she was passing out. "Call security. Call Brendan Pope. Tell him I need him," she said, and then everything went black.

———————

Brendan was washing melted butter from his hands when a staff member came running into the kitchen.

"Brendan! Harley's room now! Dead man in the hall. She's been shot. Security is on the way."

He didn't think past ripping off his chef coat and cap as he bolted for the exit door, taking the stairs down to the eighth floor two and three steps at a time, with only one thought.

Don't let her die! Don't let her die!

Security guards were already on scene. Brendan could hear sirens in the distance. A guard stopped him at the doorway.

"Sorry, man, you can't go—"

Brendan picked the guard up by both shoulders, lifted him off the floor, and set him aside so fast the man was too shocked to argue.

Sophie was kneeling at Harley's side, holding a towel to the side of her head.

Blood was everywhere. Her blood.

Then he was on his knees beside her, feeling for a pulse. It was there, and rock steady.

"Sophie, let me see," he said, gently moved her hands away as he peered beneath the blood-drenched towel. The shot had grazed the side of her head just above her left ear. He looked up at the wall behind her head and saw the bullet hole. "Thank you, God," he muttered, and continued pressure on the wound.

Sophie came running back with a clean towel she'd taken from her cart. Brendan traded it for the blood-soaked one and kept up the pressure while talking to Harley, waiting for that first sight of her sea-blue eyes.

"Hey, Sunshine. Time to wake up. It's me, Brendan. I'm here. I'm here."

———

Everything hurt, but Harley couldn't remember why. She kept trying to open her eyes, but her head was pounding so hard that the mere thought of motion made her sick. Then she heard voices. Lots of voices, and then the one she'd been listening for—Brendan was here. She moaned.

"Easy, baby, easy," Brendan said. "I'm here. You're safe."

She felt his hands on her face before she opened her eyes, and then she saw him, panic fading on his face, worry hovering in his eyes. "Thought I'd never see you again," she mumbled, and started to cry.

"Thought I'd never hear your voice again. Hang on. Ambulance is on the way."

She tried to raise up, needing to know what happened to the man who shot her. "The man who was at the door? He had a gun. Did he get away?"

"He missed his kill shot. You didn't." Police and EMTs were on the eighth floor now and flooding the scene. "Help is here now, honey. I have to get out of the way, but I'm behind you all the way."

Then hands were on his arms, pulling him up, pulling him back. He turned around. It was Aaron.

"Little brother, you need to step back."

It was the hardest thing Brendan had ever been asked to do, but he did it anyway, for Harley. He didn't have the skills to help her, but he had the good sense to get out of the way of those who did.

───────

By nightfall, Harley was in a hospital bed, riding out the misery of a concussion and a head wound, but conscious enough to have fought with a nurse who tried to remove the medal from around her neck.

The necklace was still around her neck, Brendan hadn't left her side, and there was a police officer on guard outside her door. She kept drifting off to sleep, then crying out and waking up reaching for a gun.

Wiley's wife, Linette, had been on duty when they brought Harley in and kept checking in on them until her shift was over. She clocked out at 5:00 p.m., but came back for one last check and slipped into the room long enough to whisper a quick goodbye.

"BJ, honey, I'm going home now. Is there anything I can get you before I leave?"

"No, I'm okay, and thank you for everything," he said.

Linette eyed the readouts on the vital signs monitor, satisfied all was well. "I know this scared you to death, but her vitals are good and her fever is down. She's due pain meds again in about an hour. Have they had her up yet?"

He nodded. "A couple of times. Trips to the bathroom."

"Hopefully, they'll let her go home soon."

Brendan frowned. "Her home is a long way away. I know Harley. She'll be set on finishing her work here before she makes any other plans. After that, I'm taking her home with me. She can finish recuperating there in safety. Thanks to Sean, I have security cameras everywhere, and I'm taking off work until she's one hundred percent and they have all the bad guys behind bars."

Linette hugged him. "I would expect nothing less of you. Take care. I'll see you tomorrow morning," she said, then left the room.

———————

Harley was dreaming she was on Brendan's Harley, but no one was steering it, and it was flying down a highway with no destination. She could hear a robotic voice saying over and over, OUT OF CONTROL. OUT OF CONTROL.

She woke up crying, and Brendan was at her side within seconds.

Her tears shattered him. He could do nothing to stop the drug-induced dreams or ease her pain, but he was the face she saw first every time she opened her eyes, and he knew it eased her fears. "Another bad dream?" he asked.

"Yes. Drugs always do this to me. Either hallucinations or crazy dreams."

He wiped away the tears with a handful of tissues, then kissed the places where the tears had rolled.

"Harley, darlin'…you fought for your life today, and it breaks my heart that you had to do it alone. You're not being a baby. This is PTSD. I'm going to have them bring you some food. You're being shot up with pain meds without a damn thing in your stomach. Do you want soup, or maybe something sweet or savory?"

"If I was home, I'd be squirting cheese in a can on Ritz crackers."

He grinned. "There are cheese crackers and peanut butter crackers in the waiting-room vending machines. What do you want to drink? Pop, coffee, milk?"

"Anything cola…Coke, Pepsi, Dr Pepper. I don't care. Just something fizzy."

"I'll be right back," Brendan said. "And don't worry. Your police guard is still in the hall."

He left in long, hurried strides and was back in under five minutes with pockets full of cheese crackers and peanut butter crackers and carrying two Dr Peppers and a couple of straws.

He raised the head of her bed up just enough to keep her from choking when she ate and swallowed. When she was finally at the stopping point, he lowered the bed a little and cleaned off the wrappers and empty cans, then tucked her back in.

Harley sighed. "You were right. I feel better with food in me."

"Good. So, before you drift off again, I have a couple of questions. How far away are you from being done with the audit?"

"Half a day at most."

"Then I'm coming back to the suite with you, and when you feel ready to work again, I'll be there until you finish. After that, I'm taking you home with me to finish recuperating. Thanks to Sean, I have a state-of-the-art security system. Had it set up when Justine

Beaumont was stalking me. Nobody's going to sneak up on us there. And nobody needs to know where you go after you leave the hotel. You won't be safe until whoever is running this cleanup sweep is behind bars. You know that, right?"

"Beaumont was actually stalking you?" she asked.

"Among other things," he muttered, thinking of the knife she'd pulled on him, too.

"I can't believe what a mess I'm in, but I'd do it all again just to have you in my life and to have you bringing me into yours," she said.

He tucked a curl away from the corner of her eye. "Love you, darlin'. Now, try to get some rest so that fever will keep going down." He lowered the head of her bed, covered her up, and then kissed her. "Sweet dreams this time, okay?"

Harley closed her eyes and soon drifted off to sleep.

She was still asleep when Brendan heard voices outside the door, and then the door opening behind him. He turned to look just as his brothers walked in carrying a to-go bag from Granny Annie's bakery.

"Aunt Annie sent cinnamon rolls and sausage biscuits. Mom sends her love and prayers and the question, 'When am I going to get to meet her?'" Wiley said, and set the bag on the windowsill beside Harley's bed.

"Tell her thank you, and soon," he said.

"How's she doing?" Aaron asked.

Brendan sighed. "Concussion. Nasty graze. Bad dreams. Have they identified the shooter?"

"Oliver Prine," Wiley said.

Brendan frowned. "Do you know who sent him?"

"No, and it's now in the hands of the feds," Aaron said.

Sean slipped up beside Brendan. "She's beautiful, BJ."

Brendan nodded. "Inside and out."

"Who are her people?" Wiley asked. "Have they been notified?"

"Jason Banks, NASA scientist. Judith Banks, American playwright and screenwriter, and no they haven't, because she doesn't want them here."

Sean frowned. "Enough said, and anyway, you have family to spare."

Harley's eyes were still shut, but she quietly entered the conversation. "I can hear you," she said.

"Good. I'm Sean, the one who said you were beautiful."

Harley opened her eyes, squinted from the pain, and thought, *The brother I had yet to meet.*

"Wow, Brendan. You do all look alike."

"Sean's the prettiest," Wiley said.

Sean poked him. "Speak for yourself, dude."

"Okay, Miss Harley. I think it's time we leave you to get some rest," Aaron said. "Brendan already knows this, but there's a whole mountain full of people saying prayers for your swift recovery."

Harley frowned, then winced from the motion. "They don't even know me."

"They do now," Aaron said. "If you matter to

Brendan, then you matter to them. That's how it works here. Hope to see you again when you're feeling better. Brendan, call us if you need us."

"I will, and thanks," Brendan said, but as they were leaving, he noticed the flush on Harley's cheeks, laid the back of his hand on her forehead, and hit the Call button. A few moments later, a nurse answered on the intercom.

"How can we help you, Harley?"

"This is Brendan. I think Harley's fever is up."

"Someone will be right there," she said.

Harley threaded her fingers through his and gave his hand a little tug. "You are something special."

"So are you," he said.

She frowned. "Are you going to be in trouble at the hotel for walking out of your shift?"

"No. There are plenty of sous-chefs who know how to bake everything we make. I've trained them well. Before the nurse gets here, I have to ask. Did you recognize the man who shot you? His name was Oliver Prine."

"I don't recognize the name, but I did see him a couple of times. The only reason I remember him at all is because he looked like one of my college professors. In fact, the first time I saw him, I thought that's who it was, until he turned sideways and I realized the profile was all wrong."

"Where did you see him?" Brendan asked.

"While I was still in investigation stages, I drove by

the warehouse once just for location purposes and saw him standing outside it, and then I saw him in the parking lot of the Crossley Building another time. I didn't think anything of it. But now that I know that name, I also know he is not on Wilhem Crossley's payroll."

"Okay. That's another plus in the old man's innocent column, and maybe incriminating for Tip Crossley. I'll pass that along to Rusty. She can send it up the line."

"I just want this over," Harley said. "And I want a drink of water, too. Can you help me?"

He reached for the pitcher, poured some cold water in her cup, and then tilted the straw toward her lips so she could drink.

"Little sips, Sunshine, or you'll choke yourself."

She drank until she'd had enough. Her eyes were heavy. She'd worn herself out talking, but she didn't let go of his hand.

"Did I tell you I love you?" she mumbled.

He brushed a kiss across her cheek. "Yes, you did. Almost as many times as I said it to you."

"Forever and always?"

"Forever and always," he said, and watched her eyes finally close.

A few minutes later, a nurse came in and began taking Harley's vitals, then gave Brendan a look. "Good call. Her fever is back up. I'll check with the doctor about increasing the antibiotics, and I'll be back shortly with her pain meds."

Brendan pulled up a recliner by Harley's bed and

sat, but always with a constant eye on her face. He kept looking at the bandage above her ear and thinking, *But for her quick reaction and the grace of God, she wouldn't be here anymore.* In this short space of time, she'd stolen his heart. Losing her wasn't an option.

———————

Liz called her father that night about the shooting.

Ray was horrified, apologetic, and threatening to come back tomorrow until she finally talked him down.

"None of what happened to Harley had anything to do with you or the job you hired her to do. From the little we've been told, this all had something to do with the case she'd worked for the client before you."

"How close is she to being finished with the audit?" he asked.

"Close, for sure. The bullet only grazed her head. They hospitalized her because of the concussion it caused. We'll do everything we can to aid her after her release."

"Yes, okay. Just let me know. I want to get rid of Beaumont and sell the hotel before something else happens," Ray said.

"I will, Dad, and please don't worry. We're doubling precautions. Only a few guests on the eighth floor even knew something had happened, and there was such a large police presence in the hall that they didn't see anything specific. Nearly everyone was at an event in the ballroom, and when they carried out the body and took Harley to the hospital, they took them out the back way, down the staff elevator into the back parking lot. Once the site was released, housekeeping quickly cleaned the blood from the wall and carpet in the hall, spackled the bullet holes in the Sheetrock, and cleaned up Harley's suite. I checked for myself before I came home. You can't tell that anything ever happened there. The FBI took over the case. Apparently, the shooter was a person of interest who they'd been looking for, and we've been cautioned not to talk about it to anyone. The incident won't be reported to the public. The reputation of the hotel is still intact."

"More importantly, Harley Banks is still alive," Ray said.

———

Ollie Prine's quest was over, but Berlin didn't know. After the Jubilee police notified the FBI, they were certain Harley Banks had been targeted for the same reason Paget was dead and their special agent had been murdered. Only Harley was still alive.

According to the identification in the dead man's wallet and the phone in his pocket, his name was Oliver Prine, a current resident of Philadelphia. This was no coincidence. The feds were now digging for information that would tie him to the trafficking gang and maybe the big boss himself.

It was a little after 9:00 p.m. The hospital was mostly quiet, lights were down low, and Harley was asleep. Brendan had long ago eaten the food his brothers brought, sharing a couple of bites of cinnamon roll with her before she dozed off again.

He'd already sent a text to Larry Beaumont telling him he was taking off work until Harley was well enough to leave the hospital, and that there was no need for concern because Anthony and his other sous-chefs were perfectly capable of following through.

He didn't care whether Larry liked it or not, he knew Larry couldn't fire him and Ray wouldn't care. But the next text on his list was to Rusty Pope.

Rusty, don't know if you've heard. Harley had it out with the hit man today. She was obviously the better shot. He's dead. She's in the hospital, but will be okay. Feds have taken possession of the body. Identified as Oliver Prine. Residence in Philadelphia. Harley said she'd seen his face before. Once outside the warehouse, and another time in the parking lot of the Crossley office building. Nobody knows who sent him, but authorities are keeping a lid on the fact that this even happened. They don't want to alert anyone that the hit man failed, for fear he'd send someone else. I hope your people can link the dead hit man

to a known entity. I want this over with. I have
plans to grow old with her, and I'd like for her to
be in one piece.

He hit Send, got up to stretch his legs and check on
her again.

Her sleep was so restless that they kept the bed rails
pulled up to keep her from rolling out of bed. She still
had a fever, but it didn't feel as high. And she was still
waking up reaching for a gun. Hopefully, when her head
healed, the nightmares would go away.

He was standing at the window looking down
at Jubilee, still lit up like a circus, and then up at the
mountain, shrouded in darkness. The urge to take her
and run was huge. This wasn't over.

———————

Rusty finally had a response from her handwriting
expert. In his opinion, Tipton Crossley was likely the
person who forged his father's name, which meant he
was actively involved in what was happening at the
warehouse. She was getting ready to send the info to Jay
Howard when she got Brendan's text. Her heart sank.
Someone got to Harley before they got the answers
they were looking for, and Jay probably already knew
that, since the feds had taken over the incident.

But she still rewrote her message to Special Agent
Howard, hit Send, then went to look for Cameron. The

kids were both in bed, so he was likely in front of the fireplace with Ghost, and she was right.

Cameron looked up with a smile, then saw the look on her face, and was on his feet and heading toward her. "What's wrong?"

"Harley Banks was shot today. She's in the hospital, likely going to be okay. She took out the hit man. He's been identified. Feds have taken over the case, but nobody's talking because they don't want it known that the hit man failed. This isn't over for her. It won't ever be over until the boss is identified and put away."

Cameron took her in his arms and pulled her close. "None of this is your fault. This is a side effect of Harley's job, just like getting shot at was part of yours."

Rusty sighed. "I know that in my head, but it doesn't make me feel better."

"We have to trust the process," he said. "Maybe with the new information Harley provided, it will be the key to breaking the case for them."

"I hope so," Rusty said, then glanced down. Ghost was standing at their feet. She leaned over and gave him a hug. "Thank you for your concern, my sweet boy."

"Go sit by the fire. Can I bring you something?"

"I'll have whatever you're having," she said. "And don't forget Ghost. He needs a treat, too."

Cameron grinned. "Ghost is never forgotten, and you are his best treat advocate ever."

While the turmoil continued in Jubilee, it was spilling over into the Beaumont household in Dallas.

Karen was at work every day, while Justine pretended to job search, although the only jobs she qualified for were for unskilled laborers, and as she put it, she wasn't about to lower herself to menial labor among the unwashed. What she wanted was a rich man. But without money to squander in bars and clubs, she had no way to meet them.

She was lolling about at home, making sure she kept dishes washed and the floors clean so her mother wouldn't be on her back every evening after she got home from work, and prowling through every aspect of her mother's life in the process. Trying to find something, anything, that would get her out of this hole.

She'd already gone through the jewelry box and found nothing but worthless costume jewelry. There was a small safe on the floor of her mother's closet, but the door was ajar and there was nothing in it, so she moved to her mother's office and began digging through the neatly color-coded filing system in the side drawers. There was one for repair receipts. One with tax information, incidentals she didn't even understand.

And then there, at the back of the last drawer, a file marked Insurance Policies. She pulled it out and began sorting through the contents. Homeowner's insurance. Car insurance. Health insurance. And then *bingo!* A last will and testament and a $500,000 life insurance policy.

Her eyes widened as she read the will. She was her

mother's heir. Then she read the life insurance policy. She was the recipient of the payout.

"Thank you, Mother, for your concern," she crowed. She put everything back the way she found it and began thinking of all the ways Karen Beaumont could die.

That evening when Karen came home, Justine had done the best she could do with a box of Hamburger Helper and made a salad out of lettuce and tomatoes with croutons on top. The table had been set, and everything was in its proper place.

Karen came into the house from the garage and could already smell food as she passed through the utility room and into the kitchen. She saw a covered dish warming beside the stove and Justine loading pans into the dishwasher.

"Wow!" Karen said.

Justine was all primed for her act as she glanced up. "Oh, hi, Mom."

"Hello, yourself!" Karen said. "Something smells good."

"It's done whenever you want to eat," Justine said.

Karen walked up behind her and gave her a quick hug. "Thank you for this. I want to get out of these shoes first."

"No problem," Justine said. "Sweet tea or coffee?"

"Sweet tea," Karen said, and hurried away.

Justine filled two glasses with ice and filled them with the tea she'd made, then put them at the table. She carried the casserole to the table and set it on a hot plate, removed the lid, and put a serving spoon beside it, then took the salad and the bottle of salad dressing from the fridge and put them on the table, too.

She was sitting primly at her place, waiting, when Karen returned and sat down.

"I feel like I need to give thanks for your help and this food before we eat," Karen muttered.

Justine frowned. "Just don't, okay? That prayer stuff freaks me out."

"That's the devil in you, scared of the Word," Karen said, and then winked.

"Maybe so," Justine said. "Maybe so. But I still don't like it."

Karen was still laughing as she scooped out a generous helping of the hamburger and noodles, added a serving of salad, and then took a sip of her tea and leaned back, waiting until Justine had filled her plate.

"Enjoy," she said as she picked up her fork.

Justine smiled as she took a bite, blithely adding a little salt to the casserole and some pepper to her salad—eating, drinking, and watching every bite her mother chewed and swallowed.

Justine poured the rest of the dressing onto the lettuce that was left and gave it a toss, then added another helping to her plate.

"More salad?" she asked. "It's not good left over and will go to waste if we don't eat it."

"Good thinking," Karen said, and put the rest of it on her plate, added another handful of croutons, along with a second helping of the Hamburger Helper. "Coming home to the wonderful supper is such a treat. Thank you, darling." Then she started on her second helping.

Justine smiled. "You're so welcome. And thank you again for coming through for me. I can promise you, that will never happen again."

Karen was chewing and smiling, and then she wasn't.

She reached for her throat, her eyes widening in panic, but Justine was looking down at the salad on her plate and didn't notice.

Karen banged the flat of her hand on the table and then shoved her chair away from the table and tried to get up.

Justine looked up, then flew out of her chair. "Mom! Mom! What's wrong?"

Karen was visibly choking now, and waving her hand toward the hall.

Justine grabbed her mother around the waist and started doing the Heimlich maneuver over and over, trying to get whatever was stuck in her mother's throat to come up. One minute passed that seemed like an hour, and then another, but nothing happened, and then all of a sudden, Karen went limp in her arms.

Too heavy for Justine to hold up, she fell with her. Her hands were trembling as she felt for a pulse, then leaned over her mother's face.

Karen's eyes were frozen in a wide-open stare, bloodshot and bulging. Her tongue was swollen and protruding from the side of her mouth. Her skin was flushed and hives were visibly apparent.

Justine leaned over, checking to see if she could feel breath on her cheek. No pulse. No air coming out.

Now she was crying and screaming as she ran to get her phone to call 911.

"911. What is your emergency?"

"My mother, my mother," Justine kept saying between sobs. "She choked while we were eating. I tried to help her cough it up, but it didn't work. She fell on the floor and she's not breathing anymore. Help me. Help me!"

The 911 operator verified the address that came up on the call and dispatched help, then kept talking to Justine.

"Do you know how to do CPR?" she asked.

Justine was sobbing. "Yes, but her tongue. Her tongue. It's…it's…it's so swollen that it's sticking out of her mouth."

And that's when the dispatcher guessed it wasn't food the woman had choked on. She'd eaten something she was allergic to.

"An EpiPen. Does your mother have an EpiPen? Does she have allergies?"

"Uh, nuts…some kind of nuts. I don't know about the pen. I've been living with my father for the past four years and just moved home. Should I go look?" And then she began hearing sirens. "Oh wait, I hear sirens. I need to unlock the door!" she cried, and jumped up running, still talking to the dispatcher as she opened the door. "In here! In here!" she cried, and then ran back to where her mother was lying.

It was obvious to the EMTs that the woman was dead, even though one of them immediately jabbed an EpiPen into her arm before they loaded her onto a gurney. They were putting an IV into her arm when the ambulance took off. It would be up to a doctor to pronounce time of death.

Police were already arriving on the scene and Justine was in hysterics, barely able to answer their questions, but volunteering all the information to the detective on the scene.

"How was your mother when she came home?" he asked.

"She was good. I made Hamburger Helper and salad. She was happy. Went to change her shoes. We both started eating. We both had seconds."

"Is she allergic to anything?" the detective asked.

Justine wiped her eyes and blew her nose as she nodded. "Some kind of nuts, but I forget if it's all of them or a certain kind. I thought she choked on a bite of food. I began doing the Heimlich maneuver." She shuddered. "I kept doing it and doing it, but nothing came up. And she got heavy and I couldn't hold her up. We both fell on the floor. And that's when I saw her face!"

"You didn't go look for an EpiPen then?"

Justine was rocking back and forth, staring off into space as she shook her head. "I didn't connect that...

that... Oh God, her eyes!" Snot was mixing with tears until the detective handed her his handkerchief. She wiped and blew. "I thought she looked like that from choking. Like I told the dispatcher, I've been living with my father for the past four years. I just moved home a couple of weeks ago. Online job hunting." She took a slow breath and then looked up, straight into the detective's face, and shuddered. "She's dead, isn't she? My mommy is dead."

He didn't answer, but he kept asking questions.

"You said you made the food. Can you show me everything?"

She nodded. "It's all either in the trash or still on the kitchen counter."

"Who does the shopping?" he asked.

"Mostly Mom. I don't have a car. Sometimes I went with her, but not often. She shops for the cheap stuff. We're watching...were watching how we spend the money. It's tight right now."

She got up and led the way to the kitchen.

"Don't touch anything. Just point out what you used. The forensic team will deal with gathering it," the detective said.

She nodded, still trembling, staring blankly at everything for a moment, then pointed to the open trash can.

"That's the box the Hamburger Helper came in. That's the tray the hamburger meat was on. And the wrapper with the seasonings. I'm no cook, so I just followed directions. The pan in the sink is the one I cooked it in. The leftovers are still in the casserole dish. The empty bowl is where the salad was. The rest of the head of lettuce is in the refrigerator, and the handful of cherry tomatoes I put in the salad are from the container in the refrigerator. The open bag of croutons on the counter are the ones I used on top of the salad. The bottle of dressing on the table is the one we used. One of Mom's purchases. They're all her purchases. I just used them. We drank sweet tea. The rest is in the pitcher in the refrigerator." She stopped, swaying where she stood. "We were eating and laughing, and then we weren't." Her eyes rolled back in her head.

She fainted.

The detective caught her before she hit the floor.

When she came to, there was a cold, wet cloth on her forehead and a female policewoman sitting in the chair beside her. The house was full of people she didn't know.

And Justine was playing it to the hilt.

"Is there anyone you can call?" the policewoman asked.

"Not anymore," she said.

"You mentioned living with your father prior to this."

Tears rolled again. "He didn't want me. Mom came and got me. It was temporary. Until I could find work and get my own place."

"Is there somewhere else for you to stay tonight?"

Justine panicked and sat up. "I don't have any money. I don't have any friends here. This is home. Why would I have to leave?"

"The techs from the crime lab are still—"

Justine came off the sofa like she'd been launched. "Crime lab? My mother's death is a crime? I didn't kill her! I didn't kill her! I just cooked supper. Oh my God! Oh my God!"

She started screaming and crying incoherently, to the point that other officers came running.

"What the hell happened?" the detective said.

The officer was flustered. "I was just asking her if she had somewhere to go, and this happened."

"Exactly what did you say to her?" he asked.

"That as long as the crime lab techs were here, she—"

"You called this death a crime? We don't know that. And at this point, I have no reason to believe it was. The coroner will figure out why she died. We'll figure out the rest. Dammit it, Officer. You know better than this."

"Yes, sir. It was just a slip of the tongue. I didn't mean to infer that she'd killed her."

"But she's obviously taken it that way. Has anyone called her father?"

"I asked if we could call him for her, and she said it was no use. He didn't want her. Her mother is the one who went after her and brought her home."

"Well, she's an adult, and if she doesn't want to communicate with him, she doesn't have to. We found out Karen Beaumont has been divorced from Justine's father for years. So, there's no law that says he must be notified."

The officer nodded. "Yes, sir."

"Then there's no law that says she can't be here. The end. Go tell her. She's had enough shocks for one day, dammit."

"Yes, sir."

In the end, it was the detective that delivered the news. After that, Justine crawled back onto the sofa, pulled the blanket up over herself, and watched in wide-eyed horror until every person had left the property.

Then she lay there for an hour or so longer before going to the kitchen. They'd carried off the casserole dish, the pan she made the food in, the bowl the salad was in, and half the food in the refrigerator, and tracked stuff all over the kitchen floor.

She started gathering up the mess in a garbage bag, carried it out the back to the garbage can, and then got a mop and a broom and went to work, removing every trace of the police presence in the house, made sure everything was locked up, set the security alarm, and then went to take a bath.

She was exhausted, both physically and emotionally.

Murder was hard work, after all, but the guilt would never fall on her shoulders because the grocery receipt for those cheap-ass buttered croutons had been part of the contents of the garbage they'd taken. And they'd been paid for with Karen's own credit card, along with the rest of the food she'd bought two days ago on her way home from work—while Justine had been logged onto her laptop, filling out job applications.

It had been nothing short of fortuitous that Justine

had noticed something about the croutons that Karen had not. They'd been deep-fried in peanut oil for extra crunch before the artificial butter flavor had been added. The way Justine looked at it, the rest was nothing more than Karen's karma for being such a cheapskate.

———————

Liz made sure that Harley's suite at the hotel had been sealed until her return. She didn't want Larry slipping in with a passkey to nose around. She knew Harley had added her own password to the hotel computer, so there was no chance of anyone else snooping, either. For now, she was still registered as a guest in that room, and no one had any further need to go inside.

But the next morning, bright and early, Larry was knocking on Liz's door and waving his phone in her face about Brendan's message.

"He's taken off work to be with that woman…that auditor."

"I know. He copied the same text to me. Didn't you see?"

Larry frowned. "No, I guess I didn't notice. But that doesn't change the fact that we no longer have a boss in the bakery section."

"Yes, we do. Anthony. He's Brendan's second-in-command and has been for almost two years. The team is well trained. They're efficient. We're fine. How's Justine?"

Larry glared. "I have no idea. Her mother came and got her. I have work to do."

"So do I," Liz said and winced when he banged the door behind him as he left.

But Liz knew something that Larry Beaumont didn't. She'd had an email from her dad last night when she got home from work.

Darling daughter,

What a mess my health issues have caused, but I think we're finally on the downhill slope. The fraud division of the FBI who's been working with me found money trails from both new vendors to a Dallas bank account in Larry Beaumont's name. Payments into that account varied according to money rendered by us, but the timeline was always the same. Three days after the vendors received payment from the Serenity Inn, half of the overage they were charging wound up in Larry's account. Larry has been defrauding me to the tune of thousands, and at any time within the next few days, federal agents will be coming after him with an arrest warrant. Don't worry about what happens next. I have it covered.

> *Love, Dad…*
> *Mom says hello.*

Liz read the email twice in disbelief. First a hit man,

now the feds coming to arrest their manager. It was a hotelier's worst nightmare.

"Oh my God… Michael! Come read Dad's email."

Michael stopped what he was doing and joined Liz on the sofa, leaned in to read, then shook his head and gave her a hug. "The underlying chaos is unbelievable. A fraudulent manager. A crime boss trying to tie up loose ends. It's hard to know who to trust anymore," he said.

"It's sure taking the joy out of my job. I feel responsible because I'm the owner's daughter, and yet I'm caught in the middle, knowing everything that's happening, without the power to fix it."

"Maybe Ray will sell, and you'll have a new and capable owner."

"I can only hope," she said.

Michael kissed the back of her neck. "Come to bed, love. You need a cuddle and I need my wife."

"Best offer I've had all day," she said, and left work and worry behind as she followed him to their bedroom.

═══════

It was Sunday morning.

The police had finally taken her statement the day before.

Harley had just been released from the hospital.

She and Brendan were going to stop by his house to get some clothes on their way back to the hotel. As they were riding, Harley reached across the console and put her hand on Brendan's thigh.

"Thank you."

He gave her a quick glance. "For what?"

"For standing by me. You're putting yourself in danger because of this."

He shook his head. "When you find your place in the world, you do everything you can to keep it. And when you find your forever person, you do whatever it takes to keep them. You're my forever person, Sunshine. I was baking bread when you nearly died. That's not happening again. We do this together. Understood?"

"Understood," she said, and then shifted focus as he pulled up in a driveway and drove into the garage, then helped her out of the car and into the house.

"I'm going to pack some clothes. You can either rest on the bed while I'm doing it or here on the sofa," he said.

"With you," Harley said.

He swooped her off her feet into his arms and carried her to the bedroom, then eased her down on the bed.

"I could get lost on this thing. Big bed for a big man," she said.

He grinned. "Trust me, if you get lost, I'll find you. As for big beds, they are a necessity in our family. When my brothers and I were growing up, our feet were always hanging off the foot of the beds. We got used to sleeping that way, but it was hell in the winter—never could keep our feet warm enough. Now we all have beds made to fit."

"I had a canopy bed when I was little. I called it the princess bed because it looked like something out of a Disney movie. But the canopy aspect of it always freaked me out a little. Felt like something was hovering above me, just waiting to fall."

He winked. "The trials of childhood. Our beds were too short and yours was intimidating."

She laughed, then groaned. "Crap, it hurts to laugh."

He frowned. "Sorry. No more talking. Lie back on the pillows. I'll hurry."

He pulled a suitcase out of the closet and opened it up on the bed, then grabbed underwear and socks from a dresser drawer, then T-shirts and sweatshirts from another.

"Don't pack much," she said. "I shouldn't be at the hotel more than two days, counting this one."

"Noted," he said, and took a couple of pairs of jeans off their hangers and a couple of shirts, and added them to the mix. He was in the bathroom gathering up toiletries when his cell phone began to ring. He ran back to the bed, picked it up, and answered.

Sean and Amalie's faces popped up on video call. He sat down beside Harley, showed her their faces. They waved at her, and then Brendan moved it back to him.

"Hey, you two. What's up?" he asked.

"We have news we're going to share with everyone at dinner today, but we didn't want you left out of the loop, so you're the first brother to find out. Amalie's pregnant...with twins."

Brendan let out a whoop, and Harley laughed at his delight.

"This is awesome news! Congratulations to the both of you!" he said, and glanced at Harley. "Harley is sending you two thumbs up."

"Thanks, little brother. We're both really happy and excited."

"You should be, and Mom's going to brag all over the mountain about the babies being twins, so prepare yourselves," Brendan said.

"Yes, we know. The only other person who knows is Wolf. And we had to tell him via Zoom, too. Gotta go. I hear cars driving up. The onslaught has begun."

The call ended, and Brendan was still smiling. "This is the kind of news that reminds you good still happens, isn't it?"

She nodded, watching the delight spreading over his face. She'd never had siblings, but seeing that relationship through him made her envy that bond.

"You're very blessed by the family you have," she said. "I can't imagine how it would feel to know there were people who always had your back."

"You have me," he said.

She sighed. "I do now...to a degree. But we can't start being us until we get rid of the me I was before."

He shook his head, frowning. "I fell in love with that person. I don't want her gone."

"But I brought the ghosts of my past with me, and that hinders everything, including your safety. That's something I can't forget."

He dumped the rest of the stuff into his bag and closed it, then leaned over. "My lady," he whispered, and brushed a kiss across her lips. "I'm going to take this suitcase to the car and then come back for you. Bathroom's there if you need it. Don't go wandering about. You still wobble when you walk."

She poked him in the arm for the comment.

He grinned, then started singing at the top of his voice as he walked out of the room with the luggage.

"AIN'T NO SUNSHINE WHEN SHE'S GONE…"

Harley started to laugh, and then winced again. "That still hurts," she muttered, and got up and wobbled her way to the bathroom.

———

Up on the mountain, Shirley Pope was busy in the kitchen. She was skipping church today because her family was coming to dinner—everybody but Brendan, but that was okay. Right now, he was right where he needed to be, and she'd sent him a text this morning, giving him her love and sending best wishes to Harley for healing.

The year was moving them closer into spring, but they'd have to get through the irascible month of March before she could count on better weather. It was still cold, but the sun was shining and the sky was clear. A day for gathering to her those she loved.

Sean had run a dust mop over all the floors. Amalie had gone behind him with a dustcloth to wipe off the furniture, and Shirley was in her element in the kitchen. She'd baked pies yesterday so the oven would be free for the ham baking now. Vegetables were being prepped. Two kinds of salad were in the refrigerator, and rolls on the sideboard were ready to pop in the oven at the last few minutes.

Aaron and Dani were on their way up.

Wiley, Linette, and Ava were on their way down.

She was as happy as any mother could be.

But Sean and Amalie were even more excited. Today they were sharing baby news, and none too soon. Amalie's morning sickness had been hard to hide. After calling Brendan earlier, the itch to tell the world was the only thing on their minds.

When they heard a car coming up the drive, Sean looked out the window and saw Wiley and his family pull up and park, and started announcing a play-by-play.

"It's Wiley and his crew. The back car door opens… and…there she comes…the fabulous Ava, flying out of the gate before the starting bell rang. She's got Pinky under one arm and a little tote bag in the other. I hope it's not hair bows and barrettes. They do nothing for my hair."

Amalie burst out laughing, remembering when Ava was going through her hairstylist phase. Nobody was safe.

"Ava is always in a hurry to get to Grandma. The rest of us are side pieces. I wonder what she's going to think about babies."

Sean hugged her. "No worries, darlin'. She'll love them, and then hold it over Mikey Pope for becoming an aunt, when his only claim to fame is being a big brother."

Before they could get to the door, Aaron and Dani drove up.

"Looks like the gang's all here," Amalie said.

Ava came shooting through the front door, dumped her stuff at the end of the sofa, and was yelling as she ran through the house.

"Grandma! We're here!"

Wiley and Linette were right behind her, with Dani and Aaron on their heels. Coats came off. Sean put another log on the fire, and the laughter in Shirley's voice had already begun to echo throughout the house.

Dinner was a hit, and Shirley sat at the head of the table, thinking of how coming home had saved them. Her sons were men to be proud of, and she loved their wives like the daughters she'd never had. Ava was the little cuckoo in their nest, and no better surprise could have happened. She was Shirley's little shadow.

They had eaten their way through the main meal and were clearing the table and making coffee in preparation for dessert. Shirley was at the sideboard, getting ready to cut pies.

"Cherry pie and apple pie. Ice cream in the freezer if you want it à la mode. Who wants what?" she asked.

Sean stood. "Hey, Mom, before you cut the pies, Amalie and I have something we need to tell you."

All of a sudden, the room went silent. Even Ava's chatter ended.

Sean reached for Amalie's hand. "Amalie's pregnant. With twins."

Within seconds, the room was alive again with shouts of delight, congratulations, and hugs and kisses all around. Shirley was beside herself. There were going to be babies in her house. Her mother would have been so proud. And then in the middle of the chatter, Ava piped up.

"You do know the baby business is a lot of trouble, right?"

Linette grinned. "As much trouble as you and Wiley are?"

Ava giggled. "Bubba causes it."

"Hey…I can hear you two talking about me," he said, and then picked her up and kissed her.

Ava was in Wiley's arms, eye to eye with him. "I guess you and Linnie are gonna get in the baby business, too. And then Aaron and Dani, and Grandma will have a whole house full of crying babies. I'm just sayin'… I've heard how they sound."

Wiley grinned. He got Ava like nobody else. They both said what they thought.

"I don't know about baby business," Linette said. "Right now, I have my hands full dealing with monkey business."

"Ava, do you know what happens to you when the babies are born?" Sean asked.

Her eyes widened. "What?"

"You will be their aunt. Aunt Ava. That's really special. Kids your age hardly ever get to be an auntie that young."

Her eyes widened. "Is Mikey Pope an auntie?"

"No," Sean said. "Girls are aunties. Boys are uncles. But Mikey isn't anybody's uncle."

"Right. He's Ellie's big brother. Not an uncle."

Sean winked at Amalie. "I told you. Mikey's gonna get an earful at school on Monday."

———

After a text from Brendan, Liz was waiting at Harley's suite to let them in as he brought her into the hotel from the employee entrance. But as they came off the staff elevator, Harley staggered. Seconds later, Brendan had her clutched tight against his side, his arm around her waist.

"I got you, Sunshine. Lean on me. We're almost there."

Liz ran toward them and grabbed Brendan's bag. "I've got this. You take care of her," she said and headed back to the room to unlock the door, while Brendan picked Harley up and carried her.

"I thought I could do this," she muttered.

"Just hush, you and I are good," he said, and kissed the top of her head as they went.

Her arm was around his neck, her head against his shoulder as they walked into the suite. Liz shut the door behind them and waited while Brendan took Harley to her bedroom.

As soon as he laid her down, she breathed a huge sigh of relief.

He took off her shoes and covered her with a blanket. "Rest, darlin'. I'll be up front. You will not be left alone again."

"Love…" she mumbled.

"Love you, too," he whispered. "Going to talk to Liz."

"Liz."

He hung up his coat, then hurried back to the living area where Liz was waiting. She handed him a key card.

"This is your card. Harley's is on the dresser in her bedroom. We found it on the floor when we were cleaning up. Her purse and money are safe. I made sure. Everything is shipshape, except her," Liz said. "What's the prognosis?"

"Actually, it's good from a healing standpoint. Concussion will heal. The head wound wasn't serious, but between the two, she's dealing with a constant and pounding headache and some balance issues. They will pass. She said she was about a half day away from finishing the audit, so maybe we'll be out of here by tomorrow night."

"Don't let her overdo it," Liz said.

"I won't. What's happening with the hotel sale?"

"Dad's beyond ready. This thing with Beaumont and his daughter were bad enough, and then the hit man slipping past our security sent him over the edge. We already have someone interested enough to ask for first refusal. Hope it works out. He seems keen enough."

"Is it confidential, or can I ask who?" he said.

"Probably confidential, but you know how to keep stuff to yourself. Wolfgang Outen."

"Whoa! Really?" And then he smiled. "Oh, wait, I'll bet I know why he's willing to give up his jet-set lifestyle for Jubilee."

Liz was surprised. "Why?"

"He's about to become a grandfather. Sean and Amalie are having twins. They just announced it."

Liz beamed. "Oh wow! That's wonderful. Twins. Two more little Popes in the world is a good thing. Dad and I will pretend we don't know that, and Mr. Outen can tell us himself if he wants to. I better get back to work and leave you two to get some rest. Room service is ready when you are, and security is on high alert until you're out of here."

Brendan walked her to the door, then locked up the suite before taking his bag to the bedroom. He kicked off his boots, went to wash up, and then eased down on the bed beside Harley.

The moment he curled up behind her, she sighed. The last conscious thought he had was of the sound of her breathing, and the first thing he heard as he was waking was her mumbling in her sleep, "Brendan, get Brendan."

"I'm here, Sunshine. I'm already here."

Harley woke with a jerk, her heart pounding, then saw him lying beside her and groaned.

"I was dreaming. God, will this ever go away?"

He cupped the side of her face and then brushed a kiss across her forehead. "Yes, it will, darlin'. Eventually, the bad stuff we live through is sorted and stored away in a part of our memory we choose to forget. It's self-preservation and you're already good at that."

"And you know this because?"

He didn't flinch or look away from her gaze. "It's how we survived Clyde Wallace. The miracle is that we didn't turn into him, and we have Mom to thank for that."

She was silent for a moment and then clasped his hand. "Why did she stay with him? Why didn't she pack all of you up and come home sooner?"

"Well, she tried once, when I was just a toddler. I don't remember it, but I know the story. Clyde followed her, loaded us all back up and took us back to Arkansas, and told her if she ever did that again, he would kill her and us, and then go back to Pope Mountain and kill Grandma. And Mom knew he meant it."

"Oh my God. That's awful. She was trapped, wasn't she?"

"Right up until the moment Clyde murdered those people. His life sentence freed us," Brendan said.

"What a remarkable woman she must be to have endured all that and not be bitter. My mother is never happy for long. Dad gives her everything but himself. I grew up knowing there was a great divide between them. It's why I was so gun-shy about boyfriends when I was younger and why I stayed single. I never met anybody I wanted…until you. Now, I can't think of life without you in it."

"You don't have to. I'm your guy. I already gave you my heart. The rest of my life is yours, too, when you're ready." He glanced at the clock. "It's time for you to take your meds, but you need to eat so they won't make you sick. Can you think of anything that sounds good?"

"French fries and any kind of pie."

"Noted…and extra ketchup, so you're not double-dipping in mine again."

She grinned. "You weren't using it, and I don't like to see things go to waste."

He helped her sit up, then hesitated. The thought of leaving her on her own, even for a moment, felt risky.

"I'm going to get the menu. I need more than fries. Can you get to the bathroom and back on your own?"

"Yes."

"Don't try to come down the hall on your own. Promise me. I'll come get you in a few."

"I promise," Harley said, and then watched in silent wonder at how a man that size could move that quietly and quickly, and how a random job that nearly got her killed was the reason they even found each other. "Meant to be," she muttered, and eased herself up and off the bed, while Brendan was calling in their orders.

Chapter 14

HARLEY HAD MOVED BACK TO HER WORK AREA AND was going through her figures for the audit, refreshing her mind as to what she'd been working on and what she had left to do. Her head hurt, but it hurt doing nothing, too, and she wanted this over.

Brendan was kicked back on the sofa, watching TV with closed captioning and the sound on mute, killing two birds with one stone. Staying quiet for her, and watching cooking episodes of Gordon Ramsay. Seeing all that manic yelling and shouting without sound was a new viewing experience. Hysteria and anger in mime. Since coming back to Jubilee, he had not missed even one day of that life.

Then two knocks at the door, and someone called out, "Room service."

Harley jerked, startled out of the numbers rolling through her head, but Brendan was already up and striding toward the door. He recognized the server and opened the door.

"Hi, Keith. Thanks for the quick delivery," he said.

The young redhead nodded. "Our pleasure. The staff sends their regards."

"Just put it on the end of the table. I'll deal with the rest."

Keith pushed the cart into the room as Brendan watched from the foyer, then let him out and locked them back in.

Harley was standing when he turned around.

"Wash up first?" he asked.

"Read my mind," Harley said, and slipped her hand beneath his arm to steady herself as they went.

A few minutes later, she'd taken her meds and was dunking fries in ketchup, with an eye on her piece of chocolate meringue pie.

"Is that a BLT?" she asked as he took his first bite.

He nodded. "Want some? I'll share." Before she could answer, he put the other half of his sandwich on her plate and kissed her cheek. "What's mine is yours."

She blinked away tears, managed a sheepish smile before biting into it, then gave him a thumbs-up.

They were getting close to pie time when Harley's cell phone rang. She glanced at caller ID and groaned. "Mom, again."

Brendan frowned. "Answer it, and don't think about anything but the sound of her voice. One day she'll be gone, and you'll wish for it."

Harley blinked. "Oh my God, mister. You sure know how to get to the heart of a matter," she said, but she picked up the phone. "Hello?"

"Finally!" Judith said. "I thought you'd dropped off the face of the earth."

"No, Mom, I didn't go quite that far, but I came close. I can't talk to you right now because you always make me angry cry, and crying will make my freaking head hurt worse than it already does, so will you please talk to my Brendan instead?"

Judith gasped. "What aren't you saying? Why does your head hurt? And why have I not heard about this Brendan person?"

"I know you've already talked to Dad. And if he told you enough of the truth, you'd know Brendan is helping me with this case, and we fell in love. What Dad doesn't know is that two days ago, a hit man tried to kill me in my hotel room. His shot only grazed my head. I, on the other hand, did not miss. And now you can get details from Brendan because I passed out after that and don't remember shit."

Judith was shrieking in Harley's ear as she handed him the phone. "Darling man of my heart, meet my mother."

And once again, Brendan got an earful of what talking to her parents was like. "Mrs. Banks... Mrs. Banks, excuse me, but if you'd care for further details about Harley's welfare, you're going to have to stop screaming in my ear."

A deep, sexy voice with a slight hint of sarcasm was not what she expected to hear. Her silence gave Brendan permission to continue.

"Much better. Thank you. My name is Brendan Pope. I was asked to look out for her by the man who hired Harley for this job, and may I say, you have raised a most remarkable woman. Yes, she's beautiful, but she's also the smartest, most persistent female I've had the pleasure to meet, and skillful at her job. The hit-man issue turned out to be residue from the job just prior to this. It's being dealt with. We had been warned the possibility was real, so when it did happen, Harley was prepared. They shot at each other at the same time. His shot grazed the side of her head, which resulted in a concussion and a great deal of pain from both injuries. He's dead. She's not. Okay?"

He could hear Judith crying softly. "Don't cry. You've already heard her voice. You heard the sass, and she's eating her fries and half of my lunch as we speak, so she's doing great. There isn't a lot more we can talk about, because that case is still open and it would be in Harley's best interests if the world did not know she's still alive and the hit man is dead, so just don't talk about it right now, okay?"

"Yes, yes, of course, but can I ask you something now?" Judith said.

"You can ask me anything."

"She called you 'my Brendan.'"

"And I call her 'Sunshine' because she lights up my life. Yes, she loves me, and I love her. So much."

"You have family?"

He grinned, then winked at Harley, who was licking mayo off her thumb.

"Ah…we're gonna do this now, are we? Okay, yes, I

have family…upward of two hundred or more aunties and uncles and cousins and three brothers, one little half-sister, and three sisters-in-law, and one mother. I'm the sixth generation of the man who settled this place. You can't throw a rock here without hitting a relative. Two of my brothers, Aaron and Wiley, are police officers. Sean is a tech wizard, and my brother Wiley is the legal guardian of our seven-year-old half-sister. As for me, I'm the head pastry chef at a hotel. I trained in New York City and studied some in Europe and was so homesick for the mountains that I came back here to work. That was a little more than three years ago. So that's the ancestry of the man who's going to be your son-in-law."

Silence.

"Are we cool now, Mrs. Banks?" he asked.

Judith blew her nose. "Call me Judith. We are cool. I want to come see Harley now."

"You can't. Not until the threat to her life is over. If the bad guy finds out she's still alive and can't get to her, there's every likelihood he'd target people she loves to draw her out. The best thing you can do for her is abide by the authorities' requests." Then he winked at Harley. "Harley, darlin', wipe the mayo off your fingers. Your mama wants to talk to you."

Harley blew him a kiss and took the phone. "So, Mom, to quote the man…are we cool?"

"Yes. Is he as yummy as he sounds? What does he look like?"

"Yes. Six feet, seven inches of Scottish and Chickasaw ancestry. I'll send a picture. Not of me. I still have the bandage above my ear and bacon grease on my face."

Judith groaned. "You are such a brash, outrageous thing, and I'm beginning to realize I might be a little envious of your dash-and-be-damned attitude."

"Hang on a sec," Harley said, and pulled up the camera feature. "Brendan, turn just a little bit this way and smile for the camera. Mom wants to know what you look like."

"Where's my biker gear when I need it," he said, and then put his hands on his hips and grinned.

Harley was laughing aloud when she snapped the picture, imagining what her mother would have thought if her first sight of him had been in Terminator gear.

She glanced at the photo, gave him a thumbs-up, and hit Send, then went back to the call. "I just sent you a picture."

"Hold on, I want to look," Judith said.

Harley waited, but not for long before her mother was back, and then all she could say was, "Oh. My. Lord."

"I know. Listen, Mom. You know how Dad is. I'm not asking you to lie to him, but if he disregards any aspect of what you've been told, I'll wipe the freaking floor with him. I have all I can handle without him turning into bully boy. Do you understand?"

"Implicitly," Judith said. "I love you. Please, one of you keep me in the loop…and I can't wait to plan the biggest wedding on the planet."

"Oh. Are you and Dad renewing your vows?" she asked.

Judith laughed. "No, silly. I meant yours."

"Well, don't even start, because that's not how it's going to happen, and I'm not arguing about it. Love you. Gotta go."

Brendan had seen the angry flash in Harley's eyes again, but didn't ask why. The war between her and her parents was too old for him to understand the nuances of her caution, and as long as no one was messing with her, he wouldn't interfere.

She pointed at her pie. "I'm saving this for later, so when I put it in the mini-fridge, it doesn't mean it's leftovers. It's still mine, okay?"

He burst out laughing, then wrapped his arms around her.

"Why do I feel like there's more to your reaction than what I said?" she asked.

"Because that's basically the same thing my mother and three brothers always said to me when they began putting leftovers away. 'BJ, just because we didn't eat it now doesn't mean it has become your property,' so I promise it will be safe. I'll clean up. Lie down for a while if you need to."

"No, I'm so close to finishing this. I want to work for a bit more. If my head starts hurting worse,

I'll quit...and thank you for enduring the family interrogation."

He shrugged. "It was inevitable and it's over with, honey. And I promise my mother will love you on sight before you even open your mouth, because she loves who her sons love."

He began clearing off the table as she went back to work.

———————

It was coming up on 4:00 p.m. when the sounds of an inbound helicopter filled the air.

Liz quit what she was working on and headed for the lobby.

Larry Beaumont was finishing up a report and paused to listen, wondering if the chopper was landing here or at Hotel Devon.

Brendan heard the chopper and walked out onto the balcony to make sure it wasn't a Medi-Flight heading to the hospital. Those were the chopper flights nobody wanted to see.

Harley walked out behind him, slid her arms around his waist, and laid her cheek on the middle of his back. He turned. "You're gonna freeze out here, honey," he said, and wrapped her up in his arms.

"The fresh air feels good on my face."

"And you feel good in my arms, but you're still going back inside." As soon as he closed the sliders, he noticed her computer was on screensaver.

"Quitting for the day?" he asked.

"Quitting, period. I finished. I'll need to do a print-out tomorrow or just send the files to Ray. I'll need to call and ask him his preference."

"Way to go!" Brendan said.

"I'm glad to be finished. And I'm a cheap date. I just want to watch TV tonight, eat junk food, drink pop, and fall asleep in your arms."

"How's your head?" he asked.

"Sore, still hurting but not as much. I think—"

Before she could finish, the hotel phone rang. Brendan answered.

"Hello. This is Brendan."

"Hi, it's me, Liz. How's Harley?"

"Some better, why?"

"Because a prospective buyer has just arrived, and Dad had already given him permission to talk to Harley about the financial aspects, but after what happened, I didn't know how to approach this. It's just a few questions."

"Hang on a sec," he said, and put his hand over the receiver. "It's Liz. A prospective buyer for the hotel has arrived. They had planned to speak to you a bit before you were shot. Are you up for a couple of questions?"

"Sure," Harley said. "Bring him up."

"Liz, did you hear that?" he asked.

"Yes, and thank you. We won't linger, I promise. See you in a few."

Wolfgang Outen heard enough of the conversation to know something had changed. "What's the issue? What do you mean, after what happened? If she's ill or injured, I don't want to interfere."

Liz sighed. "It's not that. But Harley Banks, our auditor, was shot the day before yesterday. It had something to do with a prior case she'd worked on. She helped take down a human trafficking ring, and they arrested everybody on-site and freed a lot of women and children. But the boss man was never identified, and it seems he's been picking off the people connected to the takedown ever since."

Wolf was no stranger to the dark side of corporate crime. "Picking off others…besides Harley?"

"Two so far that I know of. She would have been the third."

"What happened to the hit man?"

"He got off a shot that grazed her scalp, and as they say in the movies, she took him out."

"Then there's more to her than I even knew. I am impressed. I can't wait to meet her, but you're sure it's okay?"

Liz smiled. "Brendan said it was."

"Brendan Pope?"

"Yes."

"Then this is my lucky day. Getting to see Brendan again and finally meeting Harley Banks."

"She's famous?" Liz asked.

"Her reputation precedes her in the world of

corporate shenanigans. Lead the way. We can do the tour of the hotel after we talk to her."

═══════════

Harley was waiting with her feet up and a cold drink at her elbow when their visitors arrived and knocked.

Brendan checked to see who it was and then let out a little whoop. "You've got to be kidding me," he said, and opened the door wide. "Wow…what a surprise! Good to see you!"

Wolf was all smiles as he gave Brendan a quick hug, then let them lead the way, but he'd already seen the woman sitting on the sofa and was trying not to stare. Even with the bandage on the side of her head, she was stunning.

Harley stood as the trio approached, but the buyer was walking behind them, and she had yet to see his face. Then Brendan stepped aside, and she was face-to-face with Wolfgang Outen. Shock left her momentarily speechless. She'd seen countless pictures of this man, but they hadn't come close to the real thing.

"Miss Banks, I have been wanting to meet you for years, but you keep a low profile. Thank you for agreeing to speak with me under such adverse conditions."

Harley shook the hand he extended. "Brendan is giving me that look. I'm still a little wobbly on my feet, so please sit with me. Oh…Liz, I finished the audit this evening, so I can freely answer any questions regarding the financial stability of the hotel."

"Wonderful! Does Dad know?"

"I intend to email him tonight. Now, Mr. Outen, you ask, and I will answer your concerns."

Wolf fired off questions and Harley responded without hesitation, expanding when he needed clarification until he was satisfied, while Brendan sat in the background, watching in admiration at Harley's acumen. Finally Wolf seemed satisfied with what he'd been told.

"Miss Banks, you have been most helpful, and it's obvious why you're the first name on the lips of anyone in need of your services."

"Harley, please, and thank you. I like numbers. They don't make mistakes. They don't lie."

He smiled and then leaned forward, his elbows resting on his knees.

"I didn't get where I am today by hesitating. I have a question to ask you that has nothing to do with the hotel. May I?"

"You can ask," Harley said.

He laughed. "Which means I may or may not get an answer. Fair enough! Okay, here's what I want to know. If I were to buy the Serenity Inn, I would be moving my main headquarters to this hotel, and if I did, would you consider coming to work for me as my global finance manager? I have holdings all over the world. I know it's a lot, but we would begin salary negotiations at a million."

"A year?" she asked.

He nodded. "You'd be earning it. My holdings are vast. A couple of years back, I lost an entire refinery in South America because of an embezzling employee. He was trying to cover up his crime, set the office on fire, and in turn, the refinery caught fire and blew up. Men were killed. The fire was still burning weeks later when I relinquished it. And none of that would have happened if I had someone like you who would not have missed the details when invoices and payments didn't add up to the amount of crude oil being shipped out. The accountants I already have at each location would still be employed, but you would be overseeing all of them all over the world, but from this location. Don't say anything. I don't own the hotel yet, but will you at least think about it?"

Harley was trying not to giggle from the glee of the offer. "Yes, sir. I will give it serious consideration, and thank you for the vote of confidence," she said.

"Awesome," Wolf said, and then shifted focus to Brendan. "Now that business is out of the way, how do you feel about becoming an uncle?"

"Excited for Sean and Amalie, for sure. And for Mom. She's beside herself. Probably bragged it all over Pope Mountain already. Are you ready to be a grandfather?"

Wolf laughed. "Papa. I'm going to be a Papa. And don't tell them I'm in Jubilee. I want to surprise her. I'll be talking to her tonight. Oh, I have a suite in this hotel, so mum's the word, please."

"No problem," Brendan said. "And mum's the word on Harley, too. The whole event was hushed. The feds are dealing with it. We don't want the wrong people knowing she's still alive."

"Of course," Wolf said, then stood and shook Harley's hand. "Please don't get up. Get well and come work with me instead."

Liz escorted him to the door, and Brendan locked up behind them, then turned around and saw the smile on Harley's face.

"So, Sunshine…what an opportunity, or is it too far out of your wheelhouse to consider?"

"A million dollars a year is never out of my wheelhouse. It's a dream job. Living here in this town and working where you work, and for Wolfgang Outen? Pinch me. I think I'm hallucinating again…but he has to buy it first."

"You don't know Wolf. If he says he's buying it, then it's already in the bag. He'll outbid any other buyers until he gets what he wants and then turn this hotel into a showplace," he said.

She frowned. "Will he expand, do you think?"

Brendan hesitated. The one secret he couldn't tell until she was his wife.

"I don't think that's possible. The town and the land it's built on are all property of a corporation. They have rigid rules about the land, all in order to maintain the natural beauty of the place and not outgrow the original footprint. They don't want Jubilee to get any bigger, just maintain the status quo, so to speak. The way I understand it, the building will always be a hotel, to do with as each owner chooses, but the footprint of the building itself can't change."

"Interesting business concept," she muttered, then shrugged. "Anyway...I'm telling you now, if he buys it, I'm working for him. I can only imagine the scope of his holdings. It won't be a breeze, but it will be a challenge, and I like being challenged."

"I know you do. You also like pie, and it's still sitting in the mini-fridge. I'm not sure it'll still be there by morning, though. Wanna share?"

"What's mine is yours," she said, echoing his declaration when he'd given her half of his sandwich.

"Stay right where you are. I'll get the pie and the fork."

They sat side by side on the sofa with Brendan holding the pie and feeding her a bite, and then himself a bite, back and forth, quibbling about the size of his bite compared to hers.

"Your bites are bigger than mine," Harley said.

He faked surprise. "Really? I hadn't noticed. I guess because I'm bigger than you."

She rolled her eyes. "Seriously? Is this going to be your argument for the rest of our lives?"

He paused, staring into those beautiful eyes, and then he leaned over and kissed her, softly, slowly, tasting chocolate and her. "I sure hope so," he said. He forked one last bite for himself and then handed her the plate. "You earned a whole damn pie, and as soon as I get you home, I'll make you one."

"I'm not much of a cook, but I'm hell on wheels about cleaning. I'll be your sous-chef and dishwasher, okay?"

"You're going be wheeling and dealing with Wolfgang Outen, and I'm going to be the proudest man ever. As long as I get to fall asleep beside you and wake up with you in my arms, my life will be complete. Now, finish off that pie. I'm going to make coffee."

Harley took another bite and then waved her fork in the air. "I don't think you realize how quickly you have devastated my chi."

He arched an eyebrow as he popped a coffee pod into the Keurig. "Is that a good thing or a bad thing?"

"Oh, it's a good thing, but I have reveled in my autonomy for years, and I am still shocked by how quickly I succumbed to your charms."

He laughed. "You're a mess, and I just realized I don't know your middle name. I'm going to guess it's Harley Chocolate Banks? Is that it?"

Now she was laughing. "It fits, but that's not it. Harley Jo…without the *e*. Dad wanted a boy."

Brendan nodded. "Harley Jo. I like it. Good thing he leaned toward an American ride, or you might have wound up Yamaha Banks."

Harley burst out laughing, then winced. "Oh oww… I made my own head hurt. God, I love you. Nobody makes me laugh like you do."

"There's a little bit of wiseass in every Pope," he said.

She was still giggling at the thought of going through life as Yamaha, and after she finished off the pie and coffee, stretched out on the sofa and fell asleep with her feet in Brendan's lap.

He covered her with the blanket she'd brought from the bedroom, then sat watching her sleep, all too aware their momentary peace was tentative, as a rumble sounded in the distance. He glanced toward the balcony and then to the mountain and the sky beyond. Storm clouds were gathering. Rain was coming. It felt like a portent of the days ahead.

━━━━━━━━

Rusty was wiping pudding off Ellie's face, while Ghost was licking up the splatters on the floor at her feet. She made a mental note that the floors needed to be mopped, but she would do it after she got everyone in bed tonight. It would be useless to do it beforehand.

Cameron and Mikey were on their way home from Jubilee, and she was anxiously watching the weather, hoping they'd get back before the storm hit.

"Mama, I play with Ghost now," Ellie said as Rusty helped her down from her booster seat at the table.

"You go read him a story. No dress-up. No makeup. Ghost doesn't like that, okay?"

"Okay," Ellie said.

Ghost looked up at Rusty as if to say, "I got this," and trotted along behind her.

The storm clouds were already gathering on the mountain, announcing their arrival with the rumblings of far-off thunder.

As soon as Rusty finished cleanup, she grabbed her laptop and went into the living room to join them. Ellie was holding her audience of one hostage with a vivid rendition of "The Three Little Pigs," and as Rusty listened, she realized Cinderella had joined the trio and was fighting off the Big Bad Wolf on her own.

Rusty grinned. "That's my girl," but then her cell phone rang, and she lost track of the story.

It wasn't Cameron checking in. It was Special Agent Jay Howard. "Hey, Jay, what's up?"

"Got a minute?" he asked.

"Yes."

"I need you to call Harley Banks. Ask her if she has received a phone call from Tipton Crossley since she arrived at the Serenity Inn."

"Okay, but why?"

"Two things have happened since we last spoke. One of the men from the raid at the Crossley warehouse obviously had a beef with a couple of the men within the gang, and it turns out they weren't on-site when the raid went down, so he's named them in some deal he's made. He says they know who the big boss is."

"That's fabulous!" she said.

"Yes and no. One of the men named was Oliver

Prine, so we know he's not talking. The other is Phil Knickey."

Rusty frowned. "That name seems familiar."

"It should. He was a big-shot pro hockey player until he messed up his knees. Apparently, he was getting paid big money to become bait for the trafficking ring... You know, famous face and name, good-looking, flashing money around. He was the lure who picked out the victims, and others would make the snatch."

"Good lord! How low do you have to go to do something like that?" she muttered.

"Takes all kinds," Jay said. "So, we have a warrant out on him. If we can find him, we may learn more. The reason for my request is that we have Prine's phone and the rest of his gear from a cabin out at Bullard's Campgrounds in Jubilee. We're going backward from his phone records trying to find a connection to who sent him to Jubilee. We were already looking at Crossley as a possibility, but the phone records we requested on Crossley aren't revealing much. His personal calls aren't ringing any bells, and we have no way to access burner phones.

"There were calls on Prine's phone to Tip Crossley's private number, but we don't know what about, and there was one personal call Tip made to Harley Banks. We need to know what that was about, and where she was when she took that call. If she was already at the hotel, then Tip would have been able to locate her geographically. And that could have been how Prine found her."

Rusty frowned. "The boon of technology always has a downside. I'll call and ask her, then get back to you, okay?"

"Yes, thanks. I'll be waiting."

Rusty ended their call and immediately made a call to Harley.

———

Brendan was texting a message to his mom when Harley's phone began to ring. He jumped, trying to get it before it woke her, but he was too late. She'd already roused and was sitting up to answer. "Hello?"

"Harley, it's Rusty. Got a sec?"

"Sure," Harley said, rubbing sleep out of her eyes.

"I have a random question to ask you. I won't go into the details of why just yet, but this is at the request of one of the agents working the Crossley case. He wanted me to ask if you have personally spoken with Tip Crossley since you arrived in Jubilee."

"I didn't speak to him, but he did call me and left a message, which I heard afterward."

"What was the message?"

"Some big story about just finding out about what was happening, sorry he'd never had a chance to meet me. Offering special security on behalf of the Crossley company to keep me safe, and all he needed was my location so he could send security guards."

"And that was the only time?"

"Yes, just the once," Harley said.

"Okay, thanks, honey. Take care. Big thunderstorm brewing."

Harley glanced toward the mountain. "Oh wow. It sure is. Thanks," she said, and disconnected. "It was Rusty. The feds wanted to know if I'd ever spoken to Tip Crossley since my arrival. You heard what I said. I wonder what's going on?"

"No telling, but I sure see what's coming. I hope it stays rain, and not sleet or snow."

———————

The moment that call ended, Rusty called Jay Howard back.

Jay answered with a question. "So?"

"You were right." And then she told him everything Harley said.

"Perfect," Jay said. "Now all we need is to find Knickey and squeeze him until he talks."

Rusty's call ended at the same time Ellie started jumping up and down at the living room window. "Daddy's home! Daddy's home!"

"Thank goodness," Rusty said, and saw them pulling in beneath the big carport only seconds before the heavens unloaded.

Wind and rain slapped the window where Ellie was standing. She screamed from the sudden shock, then slapped back, leaving a little handprint on the window.

Rusty ran to get her and picked her up. "Ellie, honey, we don't hit windows. They're made of glass, and glass will break. And that would cut your hands and make them bleed, and then the wind and rain would come into the house and make a mess."

Ellie frowned. "Scared me."

Rusty rolled her eyes. "Yes, but no hitting windows," she said, then shifted Ellie to her hip and headed for the kitchen to help with the groceries.

Mikey came in with a paper bag from Granny Annie's Kitchen, and Cameron was right behind him with the grocery bags. He paused to give Rusty a quick kiss and then tried to kiss Ellie's little cheek, but she was having none of it.

"What's the matter with baby girl?" he asked.

Rusty put her down. "Sissy, go see what Mikey has."

Ellie ran to see, while Rusty started helping Cameron unload. "She's mad. The wind and rain came suddenly and slammed against the window where she was standing. It scared her. But did she cry? No. She just hauled off and slapped the window for scaring her."

Cameron grinned. "Someday I predict that attitude will save her life...if we survive her raising."

"What did you get from the bakery?"

"Cookies and brownies. Cookies for the kids and brownies for you," he said.

"You didn't get anything for yourself?" she asked.

He winked. "I'll have some of both and you for dessert."

A shiver of longing slid through her. Cameron Pope…her Soldier Boy…still held the key to her soul. She brushed a kiss across his lips. "Definitely on my agenda for later. In the meantime, I'll fill you in on what I've learned about the case," she said, and began going over the details as they put away the groceries.

Chapter 15

THE STORM THAT BEGAN ON THE MOUNTAIN SWEPT down through the valley, thoroughly drenching Jubilee's nightlife. When the power went out in the area nearest the music venues, they were forced to shut down for the night.

The hospital was running on generator power, and the police department was on high alert for the possibility of thefts and flooding in the low-lying areas. Josie Fallin was tucked in tight in her tour bus with her brother, Alex, and her assistant, Trinity, and the men in her band were in the bus parked beside them.

Wolfgang Outen was on the phone in his suite. He'd already alerted Amalie to the fact that he was in town and would see her tomorrow, and was on the phone now talking to Ray Caldwell.

"Yes, the hotel tour went great. Liz had all the answers I needed," Wolf said. "I spoke at length with Harley Banks. I understand she'd finished your audit, so I'm assuming you've had time to look at the figures."

"Yes. I am going to sell the inn, and I have a figure in mind."

"I'm listening," Wolf said.

Ray told him what the asking price was going to be, and Wolf didn't hesitate. "The price is acceptable. I want it. I want to live close to my daughter and watch my grandchildren grow up."

Ray was beaming. "Then I accept your offer. I'll have my lawyers draw up the papers, but I'm giving you a heads-up. Even before you take possession, you'll be without a manager."

"I don't need a manager. I'll be living on-site. And I offered Harley Banks the job as my global finance manager. If she accepts, I'm moving my main office to the floor just below the penthouse level and she'll be there full-time."

"How is this going to play out with Hotel Devon? I know you're an investor."

"I'll have to relinquish my seat on the board and step away, and now that the inn will be mine, I'll be informing them of that fact."

"Good enough," Ray said. "I know this is a little unorthodox, but you and I have been friends for a long time, and I honor your word. If you want, I'll agree to you moving into the penthouse to take over management even before the paperwork has been finalized."

"Really? But what about your manager? What's his timeline for leaving?"

"Whenever the feds show up to take him into custody, which should be any day now."

Wolf burst out laughing. "Okay…so it's like that,

then. No problem, my friend. I know nothing until I hear from you, and then I'll make sure the hotel is secure for you until we sign the sale papers."

"That's a load off my mind," Ray said. "And I know I can rely on your integrity to keep this between us."

Wolf was still grinning when he disconnected. Apparently, Harley Banks found a skunk in Ray's woodpile. He couldn't wait to get that woman into his organization and set her to ferreting out the employees who were cheating his system. He knew they were there. He just had too many irons in the fire to find them on his own.

There was a knock at the connecting door to the adjoining suite where his personal security team was sleeping.

"Come in."

Joe stood in the doorway. "Tex is taking the night shift in the lobby. Rafer and I are up here with you."

"Thanks. Did you eat?"

"Yes, Boss."

"Get some rest. Full day tomorrow, and then a flight back."

"Yes, Boss," Joe said, and shut the door.

Wolf scrolled through his contact list and then called Michael Devon.

Michael was in the bedroom watching television, and Liz was in the shower when his cell phone rang. He started to let it go to voicemail and then saw who was calling and quickly answered. "Wolf, you're working late tonight," he said.

Wolf chuckled. "Aren't I always? Listen, I need to update you on some business moves I'm about to make. Ray Caldwell is selling the inn, and I bought it. Paperwork yet to be finalized, but it's happening."

"Oh wow!" Michael said.

"I know, which is why I'm calling you. I'm relinquishing my seat as an investor for Hotel Devon and stepping out. This isn't just business. It's personal. Amalie is pregnant with twins. I'm going to be a grandfather, and I'll be moving my headquarters here so I can watch them grow up. I lost every bit of that joy with Amalie, and I'm not letting her down again."

Michael sighed. "We'll be sorry to lose you, but I understand. Family should always come first in our lives. And it's actually a relief for me to know that Liz's new boss will be someone I trust. She loves working there and has been worried about Ray and what might happen to the hotel if he sells. This is good news. However, I'm going to leave that news for Ray to share with her, and I'll let Dad know about your decision tomorrow."

"Good enough, and my best to Marshall as well."

"Of course," Michael said, and hung up. When he heard Liz turning off the water, he upped the volume on the TV.

———

Harley finished all of her messaging and transferring files just before the storm hit. She'd seen the gathering clouds and had already heard the rumble of thunder, but when the vicious blast of wind and rain finally slammed into the sliders, it made her jump, and then she went to look out. The sky was black and streaked with intermittent lightning, and the deck was awash in rain.

"Oh my lord! My heart's still pounding. I wasn't prepared for that."

Brendan walked up behind her, then pulled her close. "We're good, honey. All bark and, except for rain, no bite. I already checked the weather. It's above freezing, so except for minor flooding of a few streets, we should be okay."

She leaned against him, listening to the deep rumble of his voice as she fingered the medal around her neck and then turned in his arms.

"Something you said after the shooting has been bothering me. How you said you let me down because you weren't here to protect me when I needed you, that you'd been baking bread when it happened. I didn't think that then, and I don't think that now, and I don't want you to feel like that. Ever. And then today, I kept wondering how a professional hit man could miss at such close range, and that's when it hit me. I was wearing the St. Michael medal you gave me when it happened. And I will believe for the rest of my life that you did save me when you gave that to me, and that when I needed help most, I was protected."

The emotional impact of those words left him speechless. He shook his head in disbelief, slid his hands up the sides of her neck and then to her face, and kissed her. Slowly. Softly. While a storm of their own began to build.

"Ah, Brendan…how I love you. Make love to—"

"Already on it, Sunshine," he said, and picked her up in his arms and carried her to the bedroom, undressed her, and then himself.

Outside, the psychedelic flashes of lightning were so close and so bright that each flash painted a graffiti-like image of itself upon the walls and onto their naked bodies.

Harley was lost somewhere within the pounding blood rush of her body, holding on to Brendan to keep from flying away. From their first kiss to this moment, now and forever, she'd finally found where she belonged.

And for Brendan, she was always going to be his first thought in the morning and his last thought at night. She made colors brighter and life worth living, and making love to her was the wildest ride of all. No matter how fast he went, she kept up, holding on, trusting him to take care of her.

And like always, the one stroke needed came without warning. The last push. The final thrust that shattered composure and restraint, leaving them spent and breathless, and then the laughter, from the utter joy of such a feeling.

———

The next morning, they packed and left without a word, taking the back way out again for safety's sake. He was carrying their luggage, and she was bundled up against the cold. As they approached his car, Harley paused.

"What's that sound?"

He put the luggage in his trunk and then cocked his head to listen. At first, he didn't know what she was talking about, and then it dawned on him.

"That's water, running down from the top of Pope Mountain. Big Falls probably looks like Niagara Falls this morning."

"That's a frightening sound. It's almost a roar," she said, and then got into the car.

As they were driving away, she thought about the day she'd arrived at the inn. She'd come in the front door, and now as they were leaving, they were sneaking out the back.

"I hope you're ready for all this," she said.

"All what, darlin'?"

"To have your bachelor world invaded."

"Way past ready. I'd say I'm at the impatient stage. I've been waiting for you all my life. I didn't know your name or what you looked like, but I was ready. Am ready," he said. "We'll be home soon, and now that you've finished all the work for Ray, this is your down-time to heal before you enter the melting pot of Wolf Outen's world."

"If he buys the inn," she said.

"He'll buy it," Brendan said, and then braked for a red light.

As they were waiting, Harley's phone signaled a text. She dug it out of her purse and read the text, then started smiling.

"Good news, I take it," Brendan said.

"He bought the Serenity Inn. He'll be in touch."

"Fantastic! Congrats, honey!"

Harley was still smiling and leaning back in the seat, just enjoying the ride, when she remembered. "You know what I left behind? That darned rental car I never used. Will you remind me to call and deal with that tomorrow? Ray was paying for that."

He nodded. "No worries. They can come get the keys from you and retrieve it themselves. For now, I just want to get you comfortable and settled in the house."

She glanced at his profile as he drove, thinking how important he'd become to her, and the thought of putting him in another hit man's crosshairs was horrifying.

"I hope to God the feds figure out who the boss man is. I don't want you hurt on my behalf. Ever."

He gave her a quick glance and frowned. "That's not how love works for us. We take care of our own. Brendan Pope never got over losing his little Meg. We know, because after she disappeared, there were few entries made in the journal. He never remarried. He lost the best part of himself when he lost her. That's how a man thinks, Sunshine. That's how I think of you. We're going to have a long and happy life together because you will always be first in my heart."

She sighed. "Message received."

"Good, because we're home."

———

The autopsy on Karen Beaumont was confirmation of what the police suspected. She did die from anaphylactic shock due to an allergy to peanuts, which were found in her system.

The lab at the medical examiner's office traced the peanut issue to the salad croutons recovered from the scene. They'd been fried in peanut oil before finished off in commercial ovens. And they'd recovered a grocery receipt from the trash listing that same product only four days prior to her death. The purchase had been made with her own credit card, within the hour after leaving her job. But Detective Freeman still wasn't buying the story, so they sent an investigator from the lab to view security footage from the parking lot of the supermarket to see who was driving Karen's car and who did the shopping on that day.

Based on the timeline from the receipt, they quickly found her on the footage. Karen arrived alone. Came out and loaded her groceries alone and drove away. The daughter was still in the clear.

But it wasn't until the full background check on Justine Beaumont came through that Detective

Freeman knew he'd been right and took it to Lieutenant Wakefield, his superior.

"Boss, I need to run something by you."

Wakefield leaned back at his desk. "What's up?"

"It's about Karen Beaumont, the woman who died from the peanut allergy. I just found something in the daughter's background history that concerns me."

Wakefield sat up and leaned forward. "Like what?"

"She spent two stints in rehab for alcoholism, and during her last stay, one of the doctors became concerned about her violent outbursts and, with the mother's consent, ran some psychological tests on her. She scored off the charts as a narcissistic psychopath. I think we need to find out what she did that made her father kick her out before we accept this as an accidental death."

"Do we have his contact information?" Wakefield asked.

"Yes, sir. She gave it—reluctantly, I might add—but at the time, I attributed it to nothing more than family issues. I'm going to phone him now. I'll let you know what he has to say."

"Then do it," Wakefield said.

Freeman went back to his desk, pulled up the notes he had on Justine's interview, and then called Larry Beaumont.

Larry Beaumont was on his way back to his office when his cell phone began to ring. When he saw Dallas PD come up on caller ID, his gut knotted.

"What now?" he muttered, bolted for the office, then shut himself in. "Hello, Larry Beaumont speaking."

"Mr. Beaumont, I'm Detective Freeman with the Dallas Police Department. I have some news to share with you, and then I will need to ask you some questions. Are you free to speak?"

Larry's heart was pounding. "Yes, what's wrong?"

"Your ex-wife, Karen Beaumont, suffered an allergy attack a few days ago and passed away from anaphylactic shock. Peanuts, I believe."

Larry felt all the blood draining from his face and, for a moment, thought he was going to pass out. "Oh my God, my God. Where was her EpiPen? She always carried one."

"I'm afraid it happened during a meal at home. We later recovered the pen in her purse and another in her bathroom."

"Where was our daughter? Where was Justine?"

"She thought her mother was choking on a bite of food and began performing the Heimlich maneuver. The evidence of that act was left in the bruising on her upper torso, so we have no doubt that did occur."

Larry's shock turned to horror and then unexpected grief, and he began to weep. "I can't imagine… I'm so sorry…so sorry. Why didn't Justine call me to let me know?"

"She refused our offer to notify you, so we assumed she might have chosen to call you herself, although we had indications there had been a falling-out between you and her before she came to live with her mother."

Freeman heard Beaumont crying and waited a few moments before proceeding. "I'm sorry, sir. I know this must be difficult for you, but I need to know what happened with Justine when she was with you. What happened that caused the problems?"

Larry wiped his eyes and started talking, unaware he was confirming Freeman's suspicions about Justine Beaumont's intentions.

"So, she's always been...you said, unsettled?" Freeman asked.

"Yes, and sometimes completely irrational for no reason other than something didn't go her way. The last stunt at the bar and grill was it for me. I would have left her in jail and hoped it taught her something, but Karen couldn't bear the thought. I did give Karen the money to pay off the damages Justine caused, but I kicked my daughter out of the hotel. It wasn't just her pulling stunts anymore. It was my job on the line and the reputation of the hotel to consider."

"So, Karen and her daughter were close?"

Larry still didn't see where this was going and answered honestly. "Not really. The older Justine got, the more she challenged her mother's authority. It's why she came to live with me. But in the end, it was her mother who bailed her out of her last mess and took her back to Dallas." Larry kept crying and talking, as if trying to reassure himself he wasn't responsible for this. "You know how it goes. Sometimes, you can do everything right in raising a child, and they just don't respond."

"One last question," Freeman said. "Were you aware of her psych evaluation at her last rehab stint?"

"What psych evaluation?" Larry asked.

"Your wife never shared it with you?"

"No. By the time we divorced, we were not on the best of speaking terms."

Then Freeman told him what they'd learned.

There was a long moment of silence and then Larry's voice was trembling as he asked, "You think Justine killed her, don't you? You wouldn't be asking all this if you didn't."

Freeman didn't answer; he just asked another question. "Did your wife have life insurance or a substantial amount of money? I ask because Justine mentioned they were buying cheap food because they were short of money. Money seemed to be a sticking point for her."

Larry was sick to his stomach, thinking of all the money he had stashed and how selfish he'd been because he was mad. "I wouldn't know about insurance policies now. She used to. You'd have to check that for yourself, but money in the bank? No."

"Okay, Mr. Beaumont, thank you for your time, and again, I'm sorry for your loss. Please do not contact your daughter in any way. Don't tell her we've contacted you. Understand?"

"Understood," Larry mumbled, then left the office and headed for the penthouse. He was crying before he walked in the door.

───────

But this information had opened a new line of inquiry for the Dallas PD. After a discussion with the rest of the team, they began searching for life insurance policies in Karen's name and found one, for $500,000, payable to her only daughter, Justine Beaumont. But after further research, they also learned that Karen had recently lapsed on payments and the policy was no longer in effect.

It was then that Detective Freeman realized there might still be a way to crack her story. If this was why Karen was killed, and if Justine was unaware of the policy lapse, she just might screw herself. So, he called her to set up an appointment tomorrow, on the pretext of returning her mother's personal effects.

───────

Justine was up by 7:00 a.m., setting the stage for the visit, dressed in worn-out sweats with a hole in the knee, a baggy sweater, and no makeup. She hadn't washed her hair since her mother's death. It was her nod to being a grief-stricken daughter.

She'd never seen a dead person before her mother's untimely demise and was mildly curious as to what happens after someone dies. Did they really go to this heaven place, or do they just roam the earth like a ghost, or disappear forever like they were never here? It was the latter that worried her most, and what drove her to snatch at whatever this life had to offer while she still had the chance.

Even though she'd dressed herself down, she had cleaned and straightened up the house and was calmly waiting for the doorbell to ring.

"Curtains up," she said, when the police finally arrived. She composed herself and then opened the door, pausing on the threshold for effect as they assessed her demeanor.

Both detectives flashed their badges, and then she stepped aside for them to enter. "This way," she said, and led the way into the living room and sat.

They chose chairs facing her.

"Good morning, Justine. Thank you for seeing us," Detective Freeman said. "This is my partner, Detective DePlaine. She is going to go through your mother's belongings with you, and then you'll sign off on them, okay?"

"Yes, sir," Justine said, then watched as DePlaine emptied the packet onto the coffee table.

Justine immediately teared up. "Mom's wedding ring? She hasn't worn that since their divorce. Why do you have it?"

"I believe it was on a chain around her neck," DePlaine said.

Justine's surprise was real. "I had no idea she still had feelings for Dad."

DePlaine had the checklist. "There's not a lot else to identify. Her watch and the earrings are the ones she was wearing. If you are satisfied these are hers, I'll need you to sign here."

Justine took the offered pen and signed the itemized list. "I don't know what to do next or how to do it."

"Well, the coroner has ruled anaphylactic shock as the cause for your mother's death, related to the peanut contamination," DePlaine said. Justine frowned. "What peanut contamination? We didn't have nuts in anything."

"The salad croutons…apparently, they were deep-fried in peanut oil before being roasted. It was listed in the ingredients on the packaging," Freeman said.

Justine gasped. "Oh my God. I didn't think to look. I guess I assumed that if she bought it, she had deemed it safe."

Neither of them commented or commiserated with her as Freeman shifted the subject. "As soon as the investigation is complete, the body will be released. They'll call you and ask what mortuary you plan to use so they can have them pick it up."

"I don't have any money yet," she said.

"Yet? Are you coming into some? Your father gave us to understand that your mother came to him for money to pay the damages you caused at Trapper's Bar and Grill in Jubilee, Kentucky, so she could get you out of jail."

All of a sudden, she was in defense mode. "Why did you call my father? I told you not to."

"We needed confirmation on some things that popped up in your background check and—"

Her voice rose a whole octave. "You ran a background check on me? I did nothing wrong!"

"It's procedure when a person dies at home, unattended by a physician. You were with her. It's how we clear a case," DePlaine said.

Freeman could tell Justine was rattled, and pushed. "You have a history of instability. A DUI, two stints in rehab for alcoholism, and then the most recent incident in Kentucky. There's even a stalking report that was made on you there."

Her eyes narrowed, and her fingers curled into fists. "Stalking. That's ridiculous. I never—"

"They have a threatening note taken from the man's property that has your fingerprints on it, and a list of witnesses who saw your continued harassment for the time you were at the hotel where your father worked, and a statement from the person who filed the report that you'd pulled a knife on him and cut his neck. The complaint is still on file and pending."

All of a sudden, she was lightheaded and seeing flashes of light before her eyes. "I left town. All that's over," she mumbled. "When do I get my mother's death certificate? I'll be needing some copies."

"The Department of State Health Services files the death record, and eventually the mortuary issues copies to the families," Freeman said. "You have the freedom to ask for as many copies as you need, but extra ones aren't free. You should be asking your father for help in all this."

"I don't talk to him! He doesn't want me. Nobody wanted me!" she screamed, and then stopped, realizing what she'd just said, and recomposed herself. "Actually, it was Mother's current boyfriend back then who didn't want me. It's why I went to live with Dad. But that boyfriend is gone, and Mom is the one who came to get me when I needed help."

Neither detective was talking, which made Justine nervous, and she started rambling to fill in the silence for fear of what they'd ask next. "I know I'll need one copy for Mom's life insurance policy. I'll need that money to pay for her funeral and pay for probating her will."

Freeman frowned. "What life insurance policy? We were given to understand she didn't have any."

"No, no, she does! I can show you. It says a copy of a death certificate is required." Then she leaped up from the sofa and bolted out of the room.

DePlaine arched an eyebrow at Freeman but said nothing, and moments later, Justine was back. "This is her policy," she said, and handed the file to Freeman and sat down.

Freeman glanced at it. "Oh! This policy! When we

have a suspicious death, we always run checks to see if there are existing life insurance policies and which heirs benefit most from the death. I know it sounds terrible, but it's just procedure. We feel we owe it to the deceased to check off all the boxes. We know for certain that your mother let this policy lapse a few months back. It's no longer valid."

Justine froze and then began mumbling and leafing through the policy as if a different answer would fly off the page. "Can't be. Why would she…stupid bitch…all for nothing…"

Detective Freeman stood as he and DePlaine pulled Justine to her feet. "Justine Beaumont, I'm arresting you for the murder of your mother, Karen Beaumont. You have the right to…"

Justine heard his voice, but the words meant nothing. She was laughing maniacally, and then screaming and spitting rapid-fire invectives at both parents, and blasting threats at both detectives as they walked her out of the house.

———

That same morning, six federal agents walked into the Serenity Inn and asked to speak with Liz Devon.

The moment Liz got the call from the front desk, she bolted for the lobby. It was finally going down. Within moments of her arrival, they asked if Larry Beaumont was on-site. She called Larry's cell to get his location.

Larry's sleep had been tortured. He was still coming to grasp with the information the Dallas detectives had given him and was slow getting ready for the day. He was finishing up his last cup of coffee when Liz called.

"Hello?"

"Larry, this is Liz. I need a word. Are you in the office or still in the penthouse?"

"Penthouse, but I was just getting ready to leave."

"I'll come to you," she said, and hung up. "We're going up," she told the agents and led them to the private elevator.

Nobody was talking. Nothing needed to be said. Everyone in the car knew what was about to go down. When they exited into the foyer, Liz led them to the door and rang the bell.

Larry didn't bother to look first, but it wouldn't have mattered.

The six agents already had their badges in hand and were identifying themselves as they walked in.

"Larry Beaumont, you are under arrest on federal charges for theft, fraud, and intent to deceive your employer, Ray Caldwell. Your accomplices, Joe Ellis and Louis Freid, are being arrested as we speak."

His mouth dropped as they were reading him his rights. The look of satisfaction on Liz Devon's face punctuated the end of his scam. They took him out in handcuffs.

Liz rode down with them and walked them through the lobby, then watched them walk him out the door. The staff at the front desk were in shock, but they could tell by the look on Liz's face that this came as no surprise to her. They didn't ask. They didn't comment. Word would spread soon enough.

Liz went to her office and sent a blanket memo to the staff divisions that they no longer had a manager and were to come to her for problems, but otherwise carry on.

Chapter 16

BISCUITS WERE IN THE OVEN AND BRENDAN WAS frying bacon when Harley walked into the kitchen. He paused long enough for a good-morning kiss.

"Hey, sleepyhead. How do you feel this morning?" he asked.

"Like a well-loved woman with a groove in her head should feel," she said, and snagged a piece of bacon.

He grinned. "You're welcome. Eggs? Scrambled or fried?"

"You make them, I'll eat them. Just no runny yolks, please."

"There you go again, darlin', proving this was meant to be. I don't do soft yolks, either. Coffee's ready. Help yourself."

She took a cup of coffee to the table and then held it between her hands, waiting for it to cool, watching the fluidity of his movements within a space most women were left to inhabit and thinking how much she loved him. But this man, her renaissance man, was also wild when it mattered, especially in bed.

Brendan caught her staring. "What?" he asked.

She blinked. "Er… I, uh, I was just thinking of what a well-rounded man you are. That's all."

He shook his head. "And I'm thinkin' you just skirted the question with a well-rounded answer."

"It's all good, love… No, better than good. Fantastic. Aren't those biscuits done yet? I dreamed about them when I had them at the hotel," Harley said.

"Coming out now," he said.

A few minutes later, he made their plates and carried them to the table, got butter and jelly from the refrigerator, and topped off her coffee before sitting down with her.

"Here's to a good day with my Sunshine," he said, and they began to eat, talking about everything from how she was going to get her things moved from Chicago to the time when their families could meet.

She laid down her fork and folded her hands in her lap, trying not to be despondent. "I hate that everything hinges around finding the rat in the barrel before we can get on with our lives."

"The rat being the man behind the hits?" he said.

"Yes, and at this point, all of my hopes are pinned on the feds. It's maddening not to know what's going on, or if they're gaining ground."

Before he could answer, his phone rang. "It's Aaron."

Harley waved at him to answer and got up to refill her coffee.

"Hello."

"Hey, little brother, I have something interesting

to share. If you want your girl to hear it, put this on speaker."

"Okay, just a sec," Brendan said. "It's on speaker, so what's up?"

Harley came back to the table with her coffee, but instead of sitting in her chair, she sat in Brendan's lap to listen.

"Your stalker, Justine Beaumont, has been arrested for the murder of her mother. I'd say that knife she pulled on you and the threatening note she left on your door weren't as innocuous as we assumed."

The skin crawled on the back of Brendan's neck. "You aren't serious."

"Dead serious, just like the mother. Chief Warren told us at roll call. Apparently, the Dallas PD was running a background check on Justine. Something about the mother's death was suspicious, and when they saw Justine's rap sheet, they began following up. The chief said they called to ask about the incident at Trapper's Bar and Grill. And then the chief found out today that she'd been arrested. From what I gather, she kind of told on herself. She's crazy, as in psychopath crazy. You kept saying something was wrong with her. I guess you were right."

"I wonder if Larry knows." Brendan said.

"He knew Karen was dead, because the detective told him, and he knew they suspected Justine," Aaron said. "I don't know if they notified him of his daughter's arrest or not."

"And I thought we had a messed-up family," Brendan said.

"We did, until they hauled Clyde off to prison. Hey, I gotta go. Yancy's waiting for me. Take care. Hello to your pretty lady."

The call ended, but Harley was still sitting in Brendan's lap. She slid her arm around his neck and hugged him.

"She pulled a knife on you?" Harley asked.

He nodded. "She was aiming for my face. I ducked, and it caught the side of my neck instead, before I knocked it out of her hand."

"Good lord! I know this is stating the obvious, but you sure dodged a bullet with that one," she said.

He lifted a curl away from the healing wound on her head and then kissed her cheek. "Dodging bullets seems to be a thing," he said. "But yours was real." Then his phone signaled a text. "I guess this is the morning for news," he said as he scanned the message and then handed her the phone. "Look at that."

"Federal agents just arrested Larry Beaumont? Ray didn't waste time nailing him to the wall, did he? I wonder how all that is going to play out now. No manager on-site and a new owner who has yet to sign final papers. Kind of puts you all in the twilight zone for a while," Harley said.

"We'll be fine. Liz will keep her finger on the pulse until Wolf can take possession."

"What are we going to do today?" she asked.

"You're going to lie around, watch movies, eat stuff, nap, take your meds, and heal."

"And what will you be doing?" she asked.

"Ah, Sunshine…whatever your heart desires."

———————

Two days later, Wilhem Crossley woke up in the morning and realized that ever since the raid, he'd been coasting from the shock of everything Harley Banks had uncovered. Even the warning he'd given her had been a guilt-ridden impulse. He wanted to forget it had ever happened, but he couldn't.

Things had been left undone. The head of the snake that had swallowed women and children whole and hidden them in his warehouse was still unknown. He needed answers, but no one was communicating. He feared it was because the federal authorities still viewed him with suspicion, and that alone made him sick.

Daily, he went over everything Harley had told him and shown him, and he was still puzzled by how long this had gone on right under his nose. The attention to detail had been meticulous. Fake companies, fake invoices, ghost merchandise, and money being funneled elsewhere. She had discovered the deceit, but not who was responsible or where the stolen money went. It was making him crazy, going through employee names every day, trying to make one of them fit. But none of them had access to all of it but him and his son. Who within the organization had the power and know-how to pull this off without rousing his suspicion?

It was with a heavy heart that he went down to breakfast. He was in the morning room with a waffle and coffee when he heard Tip coming down the stairs and talking on the phone. Wilhem couldn't hear the words, but the angry tone in Tip's voice was apparent.

———————

"I don't want to hear that! No, that's not going to work! Never mind. I'll deal with it myself, like I should have done at the outset," Tip said, and hung up as he entered the morning room.

"Good morning, Son," Wilhem said.

Tip didn't even look at him. "For some, I guess," he said, and poured himself some coffee. "There isn't any bacon on the sideboard! You know I want bacon for breakfast. This shriveled-up link sausage isn't going to fly, dammit!"

Wilhem frowned. "The staff knows it. They've gone to get more. Calm down and sit down."

Tip didn't see the look of disapproval on his father's face and was still ranting. "Worthless bunch of employees! I've a good mind to fire them all!"

Wilhem slapped the flat of his hand on the table, rattling the fork on his plate. "That does it! Enough! I don't know what's going on in your personal life, but it's nothing that happened under this roof, so shut it down.

As for hiring and firing, you're not in charge yet. You're the one tripping off to the foreign market all the time. You don't have the first notion of how the business here runs!"

Tip stopped, shocked by the chastising he was getting. "Sorry, Dad. It's just a lot going on right now. All the merchandise we had on hand went up in flames, and I'm thinking I need to make another trip oversees to—"

"To do what?" Wilhem roared. "We're short a warehouse as it is. The other ones are full. We don't have a place to put new merchandise. And if we did, you don't need to go on a buying trip. Just contact the prior vendors and reorder, for God's sake. You keep saying you want to help, and then you talk about leaving? You stay put and run the business as is, or if you don't want to take it over, I'll sell! Either way, I'm not putting up with your shit."

Tip panicked. "No, don't sell it! I never meant to imply—"

"Then go to work!" Wilhem said. "Go to the office. Business is happening. Tend to it! Or not! Either way, I don't want to see your face in this house before dinner."

Then Wilhem got up from the table and stormed out of the room, leaving Tip in utter shock. But it didn't take long for the shock to be displaced by frustration. Playing tit for tat, Tipton stormed out of the house, unaware Wilhem had gone to the library and was on the phone, calling Harley Banks.

Harley was in the living room with her feet to the fire, going through email on her laptop when her phone rang. She glanced at caller ID and frowned. Wilhem Crossley? Should she answer? If she did, would he tell Tip? If he mentioned it to Tip, and he was the one issuing hits, then he'd know she wasn't dead.

So, she let it ring and wondered what he wanted. Whatever it was, she was done with him and his son. A few minutes later, fresh from a shower and shave, Brendan joined her.

"Did I hear the phone?"

She nodded. "It was Wilhem Crossley. I didn't answer."

"Good move. That would have been proof to someone that the hit on you failed."

Wilhem didn't know what to think when Harley didn't answer, and then chided himself for even making the call. She didn't know any more now than she did when she was debriefed by the special agents before the raid.

When he heard Tip leaving, and then the screech of tires on pavement, a sure indication of his displeasure at being called down, Wilhem sighed.

"Act like a fool, get treated like one," he muttered. "At least he's out of the house, instead of skulking around like he used to do when he'd been caught breaking rules." And the moment he said it, a whisper of something dark slid through his mind, insidious even in thought, and so horrifying he couldn't speak it aloud. But the longer he sat, the more impelled he felt to go look, if for no other reason than reassurance.

I'll see for myself. Nothing will be off. And that will be that.

But his heart was pounding as he left the library and returned to the central part of the house, pausing in the grand foyer.

It's not too late to let it go. Shame on me for even thinking it.

And yet he stood, considering the consequences that he might be opening a Pandora's box of trouble.

To the right was the north wing of the mansion where Wilhem lived, and to the left, the south wing where Tip's suite and office were located. He never intruded into Tipton's world, and Tip never intruded into his. It had been an unwritten choice by the both of them when Tip moved back into the family home and went to work for his father.

But the longer Wilhem stood, the more random incidents he could recall that seemed odd at the time or seemed off. All of the times he'd ignored the obvious or taken Tip at his word, the more certain he was that secrets were being held under this roof. Unwritten rules or not, privacy issues or not, this was still his house. He turned to the left and walked up the grand staircase and into the south wing, trying to remember how long it had been since he'd set foot on these floors. He went straight down the long hallway and opened the door into his son's space. He paused on the threshold, staring about the suite in shock before walking into the room.

The decor was pure luxury, with furnishings Wilhem had never seen. White drapes. White furniture. A clear, bloodred vase strategically placed on a small table in front of a window to catch the last gasp of sunlight from each day.

Glass-topped tables in shiny chrome frames. Fine art and ancient wall hangings displayed on every wall, and bookshelves filled with things Tip had obviously collected from his foreign travels, and ancient, illustrated books depicting graphic poses of sex and porn. A copy of the Kama Sutra bookmarked to a particular page that even shocked a man as old as he was.

His hand was shaking as he put it back on the shelf and moved into the bedroom. By now, he was beyond surprise as he eyed the opulence of the black satin bedding as more of the same and the largest flat-screen television he'd ever seen as overindulgence.

"What the hell?" Wilhem muttered. "Where did this come from? How did I not know this existed?"

He thought of all the long hours he'd spent at the business and never once thought of what Tip was doing on his own. The single, horrible thought that had sent him on this quest was growing into a possibility he didn't want to consider. Taking care not to displace a thing, he left the suite and walked farther up the hall until he found Tip's office. He reached out to turn the doorknob, and at the same time he realized it was locked, the door swung inward.

He frowned, looked down to see an oversized bull-dog clip stuck at the corner of the door. It must have fallen from a file Tip had been carrying and had kept the door from going all the way shut.

Wilhem pushed the door open and turned on the light.

Multiple computers blinked on tables lined up against a wall. Images on video screens from multiple security cameras were running in real time in places he didn't recognize, showing women bound and gagged being paraded through narrow hallways. He could see a massive safe inside a cloaked alcove and cabinets every-where, all of them with coded locks.

In a sudden panic that he would show up some-where on another video screen, he kicked the bulldog clip beneath a table, pulled the door shut behind him, and ran out of the south wing, scrambling down the stairs faster than he knew he could move. Grabbing his coat on the way out, he jumped into his car and started driving.

He couldn't be there when Tip came back home. The look on Wilhem's face would give him away, and if what he believed was true, he didn't know to what depths Tip would go to keep his secrets safe. For the first time in his life, he was afraid of his son.

Wilhem was crying as he drove and finally pulled over to gather his emotions, then set his GPS for the FBI field office and drove through the city. Then the moment he arrived, he lost his nerve. He was shaking so hard he couldn't breathe, but he couldn't run away. He couldn't hide this. Not even from himself. Finally, he called the field office's main number instead.

"Federal Bureau of Investigation. How may I direct your call?"

"My name is Wilhem Crossley. I need to speak with the special agent in charge of the raid at the Crossley warehouse that broke up a human trafficking ring. I may have new information."

"Please hold."

He sat with the phone on speaker and his head down on the steering wheel, trying not to puke. Moments later, a man answered. "Mr. Crossley. I'm Special Agent Jay Howard. How can I help you?"

Wilhem choked on his first words and then took a breath. "I'm in the parking lot in front of your field office. Late-model white Lexus. I have just discovered some very shocking evidence that may pertain to your case."

"Come into the lobby. I'll have someone waiting to escort you to my office," he said.

Wilhem's voice was shaking. "I don't think I can walk that far. I feel like I'm going to pass out."

"Stay there. We're coming to get you," Jay said.

"Yes, thank you," Wilhem said, then fixed his gaze

on the main entrance and started counting the minutes and looking constantly to make sure he was still alone.

———

The minute Jay Howard took the call, he knew in his bones that was going to be the break they needed, and as soon as he hung up, he said, "Somebody! Anybody! With me now!"

Two other agents followed Jay through the building and then out of the lobby onto the sidewalk. "There! White Lexus," Jay said, and they took off running.

Wilhem opened the door to get out and then staggered and grabbed onto the door to steady himself. Seconds later, the agents had their arms beneath his shoulders, steadying his steps as they walked him in out of the cold. Nobody spoke until Wilhem was safely seated at Jay's desk, with the rest of the team gathered around him.

"Can I get you some water or a coffee?" Jay asked.

"Coffee would be good," Wilhem said. "I can't quit shaking, but it's not from cold. It's shock."

A cup of coffee was put on the desk in front of him, and then they waited for the old man to get a few sips under his belt.

"We're going to record this," Jay said.

Wilhem nodded, and after that, he began to talk.

They listened without interruption, hearing the truth and the shock in Wilhem's voice. Masking their emotions when he started talking about the office and all of the high-tech equipment and seeing the live videos of women bound and gagged.

"I guess there are none so blind as those who will not see, but I never once considered that he could have had anything to do with the theft from my company or using our property as part of trafficking humans."

Jay leaned forward. "We had a tip from one of the people we arrested at the raid. He gave us the names of the two people closest to the boss. A man named Oliver Prine, and a man named Phil Knickey. Oliver Prine was killed in a shoot-out in Jubilee, Kentucky. The woman he was sent to kill took him out."

"Oh my God! Harley Banks? Please tell me she's all right!"

"Wounded, but recovering," Jay said.

Wilhem covered his face and started weeping. "Because of me. Because of me. I got her into this mess when I hired her to audit my company. I will never get over this shame."

"She wasn't seriously injured and is as capable as advertised. She took him out with one shot. However, we did pick up Phil Knickey. He said he's spoken to the boss more than once, although never seen him, so I'm going to ask you, sir… Do you know anyone by the name Berlin? Mr. Berlin?"

Wilhem frowned, trying to remember if he'd ever met anyone by that name, then finally shook his head. "No, I'm sorry, Berlin doesn't ring any… Oh God."

"What?" Jay asked.

The stricken look on Wilhem's face said it all. "When my wife and I were first married, we lived in Berlin, Pennsylvania. Tip was born in Berlin. My parents were German-born. My great-grandparents were Amish. My father left the sect after he and mother married. She didn't want that life, and he wanted her enough to leave it. My wife and I moved away from Berlin when Tip was about three, maybe four…as he was getting old enough to begin school. She wanted him in bigger, better schools."

Jay added another facet. "What we now know is that the money stolen from your company wound up in bank accounts in three different locations outside of the United States, all belonging to a man named Dale Wayne Berlin."

Wilhem moaned. "I am Wilhem Dale. My son is Tipton Wayne. I can't go home."

"Where is your son now, Mr. Crossley?"

"I'm not sure. We had an argument this morning. I told him I was going to sell the company if he wasn't interested in running it. He begged me not to sell it. I shouted at him. I told him to go to the office and work instead of hanging around me, and I didn't want to see his face in the house before dinner."

"You think he's at the office?"

Wilhem shrugged. "I can't speak for him anymore. I do not know who he is. But I do know our fight this morning was because of him talking about needing to make another buying trip. I told him we didn't need more merchandise because we had nowhere to put it. But I would not put it past him to jet off somewhere anyway."

Jay began issuing orders. "Get his picture up at all the airports. Do not let him get on a plane. Get some men over to the Crossley building and see if his car is there, and if it is, sit on it and him until we get there. Get a car to the Crossley residence in case he goes back there. If he's in the wind, I want bulletins out on his vehicle. Find it. Find him."

"We?" Wilhem said.

"You're coming with me," Jay said. "If he's at work, he's in your building. I need to know all of the exit points, and you're going to help us."

Wilhem nodded.

———

Tipton Crossley entered the company offices through the rear entrance and took the elevator up to the top floor where the main offices were. He nodded at Margaret, the secretary he and his dad shared.

She looked up and smiled. "Good morning, sir. I left your mail and a few messages on your desk."

"Do I have any appointments this morning?" he asked.

"Yes, sir. A new client for the company. Eleven a.m."

"Do we have a file on him?" Tip asked.

"Yes, sir, on your desk."

"Excellent. Bring me a cup of coffee and any sweet roll lying about," he said, and entered his office, closing the door behind him as he went. He hung his coat in the closet, then sat down at the desk.

He stacked the mail into a neat pile for later and opened the file for the new client and began to read. A few moments later, Margaret came in with his coffee and a cinnamon twist on a paper plate.

"Thank you," he said, took a bite of the sweet roll, then followed up with a sip of coffee, then wrinkled his nose. Too hot and a little bitter. It's what he got for storming off without breakfast at home.

As soon as he was caught up on the new client's details, he finished off the roll and coffee as he went through mail. There was a letter from the insurance company, informing him of a payoff date for the warehouse and a separate payoff for the loss of merchandise.

He nodded, and laid it aside for his father to see. Money in the bank was always good news. Once the mail had been dealt with, he turned on the TV. It was always on the local news channel, and after adjusting the sound, he went back to work. He focused better with background noise.

He was glancing toward the clock, making sure he had everything cleared from his desk before his eleven o'clock appointment, when regular programming was interrupted by a news bulletin. Curious, he turned up the volume.

"Unnamed source has reported that retired hockey star Phil Knickey was taken in for questioning by special agents of the FBI. Speculation is high as to what charges, if any, might be pending. In other news…"

"Holy shit," he muttered, then jumped up and went to get his burner phone from an inner pocket in his coat and began scrolling through calls and messages. He didn't have any new messages, but he did have four calls he'd made that were never answered or returned. He needed to lose this phone, and something told him he needed to disappear. He was standing in the middle of the room and staring out the window when the door opened behind him.

He turned, then frowned. "Dad, what are you…"

Wilhem stepped inside as four men walked in behind him, flashing their badges as two of them pulled Tip's arms behind him and cuffed him, while Jay Howard flashed an arrest warrant.

"Tipton Wayne Crossley, a.k.a. Dale Wayne Berlin, I have a warrant for your arrest for fraud, human trafficking, arson, money laundering, theft of property, and with the possibility of further charges being added at a later date."

Tip knew the Miranda warning, but he'd never had it directed at him before, and hearing it now was a death knell. He didn't argue. He didn't deny. He didn't admit. It didn't feel real until the handcuffs pinched his wrists.

"I want my lawyer," he said.

Wilhem shook his head. "You don't have one

anymore, and I won't share mine with the man who stole from me. Conflict of interest, and all that."

Tip couldn't look his father in the eye. He couldn't argue with the truth.

"Mr. Crossley, a team is en route to take possession of everything in this office and everything in your son's office at your home. Anything not pertaining to your son's crimes will be returned at a later date," Jay said.

Wilhem nodded, watching as the agents put Tip's coat over his shoulders and walked him out of the building. He followed until he reached Margaret's desk, and then stopped.

Margaret was stunned, but when she saw the devastation on her boss's face, in a moment of empathy, she reached for his hand.

"I'm so sorry," she whispered.

Wilhem gave her fingers a quick squeeze. "So am I, Margaret. So am I."

Chapter 17

On Saturday morning, Rusty Pope could hear the kids playing and the back door slamming as Cameron came back inside with Ghost. They'd been out on their morning run. She knew she would walk into chaos when she left the office, but she had news to share.

Cameron was getting fresh water for Ghost when she walked into the kitchen. He looked up, set the water bowl on the floor, and went to meet her.

"What?"

"Jay Howard just called. Tipton Crossley was the boss man after all. He's been arrested. But that's not the best part. When they were going through evidence they'd gathered from the family estate, they were also able to close out another case." She put a hand in the middle of his chest. "Cameron…it was our case. Crossley was the man we couldn't find when we busted that trafficking ring happening here. He would have been the man who would have sold Lili to the highest bidder. The big man pulling strings on all the puppets he was controlling across the nation. Interpol has been notified. They have enough information to shut down reception points across the globe."

"My God," he muttered. "And what are the odds that this would ever come full circle?"

Mikey was sitting on the floor, building another tower for Ellie to kick over, but he'd been listening.

"Not odds, Daddy. Poison. The snake got greedy and bit itself. It will die."

They both turned and looked at him in disbelief.

"Why did you say that?" Cameron asked.

Mikey shrugged. "Heard it."

"Right," Cameron muttered, and looked back at his wife. "Every day, it's something. Swear to God, we might have named our daughter for Aunt Ella, but her spirit is with our son." Then he wrapped his arms around her. "This is what you get when you marry into this family."

At that moment, the tower toppled before Ellie got a chance to kick it. She threw back her head and screamed. "No, Mikey! I do the kickin'!"

Rusty sighed. "And that's what you get for marrying me."

"And I'd do it again without blinking. Now, go tell Harley she's off the hook. I finished the quarterly PCG reports last night. Money coming in. Dividends going out. And if you want, bring back some ribs and fixings from Emory's Barbecue."

"Deal," she said, and went to change clothes.

It was nearing noon when Rusty started down the mountain into Jubilee. Brendan and Harley weren't the only people she was going to talk to. Sonny Warren and his officers had been knee-deep in Rusty's trafficking case, and she wanted them to know that loose end had just been tied in a great big knot.

But she was telling Harley first. She needed to know she was no longer under the gun. She made a quick call to Brendan to let them know she was coming.

———

Brendan was putting a load of clothes into the washer, and Harley was folding the clean towels he'd just taken from the dryer, when his phone began to ring. He glanced at the screen and then answered. "Morning, Rusty."

"I'm almost at your house. I have news you are never going to believe. And don't panic. It's all good."

"What's happened?" he asked, then frowned. "Dang it. She hung up."

Harley heard just enough of the conversation to worry. "What's happening?"

"That was Rusty. Nothing bad, she said, but she said she's almost at the house. She has news we're not going to believe."

"All I want to hear is that this madness is over," Harley said as she put the last washcloth on the stack and started to shove her hair back from her face when she remembered the healing wound. She'd taken the bandage off yesterday because it kept coming unstuck. The area that had been raw was already dry and healing and hidden by her curls, and it felt good to have it off.

Brendan walked up behind her, slipped his arms around her waist, and kissed the back of her neck. "You taste as good as you smell," he said.

Harley turned in his arms and kissed him. "Hmm, so do you," she whispered. Moments later, the doorbell rang.

He groaned. "Hold that thought. I'll get the door. You get first dibs by the fire," he said, and went to the door as Harley took a left into the living room.

Rusty breezed in, bringing the cold air with her. Brendan took her coat and hung it on a hook by the door, then ushered her into the living room. "Can I get you some coffee?" he asked.

Rusty shook her head. "No, and quit fussing. Come sit. I'm fit to busting with news."

As soon as everyone was seated, she unloaded.

"First off, Harley, you are officially safe. Tip Crossley has been arrested. You were so right to suspect him. He *was* the man behind it all, and it was his father who found the proof. Special Agent Howard didn't go into details because this case is pending, but he said the old man was so devastated by what he'd discovered that by the time he got to the field office to tell them what he'd found, he was too shaken to get out of the car, so they came out to get him."

"Poor Wilhem," Harley said.

"So, Harley is truly safe now?" Brendan asked.

"From all of this, yes. Besides what Wilhem found and the other evidence they have uncovered, they also have the testimony of two gang members. Tipton Crossley's reign is over. But there was a huge shock at the end of this for me as well. Harley, you won't have known about this. It's even before Shirley moved back to Jubilee with the boys, but I first came to Jubilee as an undercover agent for the FBI. Single women had been going missing from this area for months, and there were suspicions that because of the number of tourists funneling in and out of Jubilee, that it might have been targeted as ample shopping grounds for women who came on their own.

"As it turned out, that was happening, and between me, Cameron, and the entire Jubilee police department, as well as County Sheriff Rance Woodley, we were instrumental in bringing the gang down. We even recovered some women before they disappeared in the chain of command, but we never found the head of the snake, so to speak." Rusty paused, thinking of what her son said about the snake biting itself, and then continued. "The feds have physical proof that that gang was part of Tipton Crossley's combine. Having his headquarters in his hometown was risky, but convenient because of international shipping. What he never counted on was his father noticing something wrong or foreseeing that he might hire an auditor like you. You didn't just crunch numbers; you followed the money and found out about the crime. The fact that you and Wilhem took it to the feds was the break they'd been searching for. They send high praise and thanks to you."

Harley was speechless. "How many years ago was that?"

"Eight, nearly nine years ago, I guess. Mikey is seven, nearing eight. And all that was right before Cameron and I got married."

"I've heard people talk about it," Brendan said. "And about Cameron's run up the mountain to rescue Lili from the kidnappers."

"They were taking babies?" Harley said.

Rusty nodded. "She was just a toddler, and they already had a buyer waiting for her when she was snatched. But that's a story for another day. I'm heading to the police department to tell Chief Warren about this, too. The Jubilee PD was instrumental in helping bring it to an end here."

Brendan frowned. "Didn't you wind up getting shot before all that was over?"

"Yes, but again, that's also a story for another day." Then she gave Harley a hug. "Thank you for coming to me. For trusting me to help you."

"I'm just grateful you were willing to get involved," Harley said. "Now we can get on with our lives."

Rusty had been watching the expressions coming and going on Brendan's face and knew he'd become involved with Harley, but she didn't know to what level and wasn't too shy to ask.

"So, what are your plans, if you don't mind me asking? I'm going to be selfish enough to hope they include sticking around."

"She's sticking," Brendan said.

Harley leaned against him. "He's right. I am so stuck on this man. I'll also be going to work for the new owner of the Serenity Inn as the global financial advisor."

"So, Ray did sell the inn? Who to?"

"Wolfgang Outen. He's moving here to be close to Sean and Amalie. He wants to be a hands-on grandfather," Harley said, and then shivered with relief. "God, I'm glad this nightmare is over."

"I'm happy for you, for the both of you," Rusty said. "Don't get up. I'll see myself out." She grabbed her coat off the hook and was putting it on as she went out the door.

"It's finally over," Harley said.

"And we're just beginning," Brendan added. "Best day ever. And now that we're no longer under wraps, how about going to lunch somewhere? You've seen next to nothing of Jubilee."

Thinking of the wound she'd just uncovered, Harley reached for her forehead, but Brendan caught her hand, then turned it palm up and kissed it.

"You're fine, Sunshine. Nobody can see that for all the curls, but if they do, just remind them that the other guy looks worse."

She burst out laughing. "You are so good for my soul."

"And other things," he drawled.

"Lord, yes, those other things," Harley said.

"Put on some shoes and get your coat. I can't wait to show off my pretty lady."

A few minutes later, they were in the car and backing out of the garage. "Brendan, what's your favorite place to eat at?" she asked.

"Mom's house, but here in Jubilee, probably Cajun Katie's, or the Back Porch. Back Porch is just down-home southern cooking. Cajun Katie's speaks for itself. The shrimp and grits are killer, and so is the gumbo, or the blackened fish. Which sounds best to you?"

"Gumbo sounds really good in this cold weather," Harley said.

"Then Cajun Katie's it is," he said, and headed uptown. He found a place to park and then hurried her inside out of the cold.

"Brendan! How did you escape the hotel kitchens?" the hostess asked.

"Took a few days off," he said. "Paula, this is my girl, Harley Banks. Harley, this is my cousin Paula Cauley. One of Aunt Annie's granddaughters."

"Aunt Annie who makes the cinnamon rolls?" Harley said.

"The one and only," Paula said. "Table or booth?"

"Better make it a table," Brendan said. "My legs don't fit under your booths."

She led them to a table by the window and left their menus. "Enjoy your meal," she said, and hurried back to the front, but Harley kept looking out the windows and at the diners, getting her first glimpse of the tourist section of the town, and was impressed.

"This place is charming, and unique, and amazing, but there isn't much of a residential area. Where do all the people who own and run these shops live?"

"Over half of them live on Pope Mountain, and almost all of them are, in some way or another, people who've grown up in this area. Usually, the only strangers in town are the tourists or people connected to the music venues."

"A unique approach to small-town living," Harley said, then picked up her menu and started reading.

"You'll have a big adjustment to make living here," he said.

She looked up from the menu, then reached across the table and took his hand. "No, love, I won't. I haven't had roots since I left home for college. My home will always be where you are."

Wishing for privacy, all he could do was give her hand a quick squeeze. "I don't know how I got so lucky, but you fill up every crack in my heart."

She sighed. "You are as pretty as you talk. What am I going to do with you?"

"Feed me?" he drawled.

"For sure. I'm having gumbo, jalapeño hush puppies, and sweet tea."

"I'm going the shrimp-and-grits route, and if you don't eat all of your hush puppies, I'll help," he said.

She laughed. The waiter came, took their orders, and brought out little mini cast-iron skillets of crackling corn bread hot from the oven—one for each of them—and ramekins of whipped butter.

"What is this?" she asked.

"Pones of crackling corn bread. Cracklings are deep-fried pork skins. Back in the day, it would have been standard fare on any table in the area. Now it's a hot commodity with the tourists."

Harley cut a piece out of her pone, slathered it with butter, and took a bite. "Ohmygodthisissogood," she mumbled, talking around the bite.

He grinned. "We'll make a southern woman out of you yet."

A short while later, their orders came, and she waded through the gumbo and hush puppies like she'd been starving. Brendan ate his, and then her leftovers, and was finishing his drink when he saw Amalie walk in.

Almost instantly, they locked gazes. She spoke to Paula, the hostess, then wound her way through the diners to their table and slid her arm around Brendan's neck and hugged him.

"Hey, BJ. Did you leave anything for me to eat?"

Brendan stood up and gave her a big hug. "Congratulations, Sister. You're just in time to meet my Harley. Harley, darlin', this is Amalie Pope, Sean's wife and Wolf Outen's daughter. She is a CPA and has an office on Main Street down by the bank. Amalie, this is Harley Banks. You two are in the same line of business, except you don't pack a gun when you go to the office, and she does."

Harley was smiling. "It's the PI license. It'll catch you every time. I've heard so much about all of Brendan's family. It's wonderful to get to meet you, and congratulations on your blessed events."

Amalie immediately put a hand on her tummy. "We're excited, and I also heard from Dad that you're going to be working for him here at the hotel."

"That I am," Harley said.

Paula came up behind them and touched Amalie on the shoulder. "Your to-go order, honey," she said, handed it off, and hurried back to her post.

"Oh, thank you," Amalie said. "I guess this is my signal to get back to the office. Good to see you both," but as she put her hand on Harley's shoulder to say goodbye, her eyes widened, then almost went out of focus.

Harley froze, unaware of what was happening until Brendan whispered, "Sunshine, don't move."

"Look for the stag to make your bed. Look for the stag to lay your head," Amalie said, then blinked, glanced at her watch, and tightened her grip on her to-go bag. "Gotta go. Tax preparations piling up. Come see us," she said, and left.

"What just happened? What did that mean?" Harley whispered.

He shrugged. "We're all so used to it, I forget how startling it can be to some. Amalie just gets visions...

or hears voices… I don't know what it means. Maybe something to do with the future. She just knows things. Kind of a mixture of precognition and psychic abilities."

"Was she always this way?" Harley asked.

He frowned. "I don't think so. You saw her scars. You saw the white streak in her hair. All of that was from a car wreck. She nearly died. The car was on fire, and she was screaming for help when she heard a voice in her head telling her it was going to be all right, and seconds later, she was pulled from the fire. She survived it and came away with scars, a white streak in her hair, and precognition."

"Good lord," Harley muttered. "She's as phenomenal in her way as Wolf Outen is in his." She reached toward her healing head wound, then stopped. "I'm never going to complain about this again."

"You own the right to complain," he said. "And I think it's time we got you home. You need to call your parents and let them know it's safe to visit now."

She sighed. "Oh lord. More drama."

"Hey, it's all good. Just remember, I survived Clyde Wallace. Cranky parents won't even put a dent in my attitude."

"Well, they still put a dent in mine," she muttered.

Brendan stifled a smile. Harley Banks was so much more than just a pretty face. She was genius-level smart and full of more grit and determination than she could hold. As long as he stayed on the good side of this woman, he was gold.

As soon as they got home and settled, he pointed to the phone she was holding. "I'm going to give you a little privacy to call your mother. She can relay all the pertinent information to your father. You won't even have to talk to him directly, okay?"

"Stay with me, please."

It was those eyes of hers, locking into his gaze. He was never going to be able to tell her no. So, he sat, put his arm around her shoulders, and pulled her close.

She leaned her head against his chest. "Sorry for treating you like my security blanket, but I love you for tolerating it."

"You're fine, Sunshine. Make the call."

"Fine, but I'm putting it on speaker," she said, then pulled up her contact list. A couple of clicks later, the call began to ring, and ring, and ring, until finally Judith answered in a sleepy, frustrated tone.

"Harley Jo? Do you know what time it is here?"

"Sorry, Mom. It's just that I have good news. All of the threats to me are over. The FBI has everyone under arrest, and I'm out of the hotel and recuperating at home with Brendan."

Judith sat up in bed and turned on the lamp. "Darling! That's wonderful! Just wonderful! So, I can come see you now?"

"Yes, the danger to anyone connected to me is also over. You can tell Dad, but I'm not having another conversation with him until he apologizes to me, and you can tell him I said so. You can make reservations at either the Serenity Inn or the Hotel Devon, and the closest air-port is in Bowling Green, Kentucky. You can rent a car to get the rest of the way here or charter a helicopter and fly in. Both hotels have landing pads."

"We can't stay with you?" Judith asked.

"No room. Take it or leave it," she said.

Judith sighed. "I'll call Jason and let you know what he says."

"I don't need to know what he says. He'll either come or he won't. All I need is the day and time of your arrival. And neither Brendan nor I will be available for lengthy visits. As soon as the doctor releases me, I'm going back to work."

"Harley! After all you've been through, you're going back to that?"

"Yes and no. Same kind of job. Different location. I'm going to work as the global financial advisor for the new owner of the Serenity Inn, so Brendan and I will be working in the same hotel."

"Global finance? My God, who's your new boss? Wolfgang Outen?" And then she laughed aloud at the joke she'd just made.

"Yes," Harley said.

Judith choked in midlaugh. "What? What are you saying?"

"Yes, Wolfgang Outen just bought the Serenity Inn. He's moving his headquarters there because his daugh-ter lives in Jubilee and he wants to be close to family. Don't worry. You'll meet them all. Brendan's brother Sean is married to Mr. Outen's daughter."

"Oh my freaking word!"

"And you don't need to tell all your friends just for bragging rights that you're going to meet him."

"No, no, of course not," Judith said. "Anyway, I can't wait to get there and meet your Brendan in person. My love to both of you. I'll see you soon."

The call ended.

Harley looked up at Brendan.

"See, that wasn't so bad, was it?" he said.

She rolled her eyes. "Let's you and I be honest here. Your connections to one of the richest men on the planet have shifted her opinion of you, me, and Jubilee. That's why it wasn't so bad."

He'd already figured that out, but it was enlightening to see how fast Harley had seen through it. "This is why you're such a good investigator. You know how to find the truth, no matter how deeply it's been buried in bullshit."

She blinked. "And this is why I love you to forever and back. Because it's me you love. Not my mother's fame or my father's scientific renown. Me. Number cruncher...heat-packing...hardheaded female."

"Ah, darlin', when I look at you, all I see is sunshine, sea-blue eyes, and beautiful, soft black curls that wrap around my fingers as readily as you have wrapped around my heart. Come to bed with me, love. I have this constant and abiding need of you."

So, she did.

It was just after 5:00 p.m. when Brendan and Harley started up Pope Mountain. Shirley Pope had issued an invitation they weren't about to refuse. All of her sons had already met Harley. Shirley knew about the moratorium on visiting, and understood why, but it had been hard to know what they were going through and not be able to help.

By the time they left Jubilee, the sun had long since disappeared behind the mountain. Everything was slowing down for the arrival of nightfall—even the cold wind had laid.

It was one of the few times in Harley's life when she'd felt out of her element. She'd never loved a man like she loved Brendan, and she wanted his mother's approval. No amount of reassurance he'd given her was going to count until she and Shirley Pope were face-to-face. As they started up the mountain, she took a deep breath and then exhaled slowly, willing herself to relax.

"Harley, darlin', she's going to love you."

"You can't know that," she said.

"Yes, I can. Mom knows us better than we know ourselves. If we love, then she's satisfied. She has always wanted nothing more than happiness for all of us because she had so little of it for herself. Our joy is her joy. You'll see. All I can say is, she's nothing like your mother. You will not be judged."

Harley smiled. "Good to know."

The headlights continued to light their way and, now and then, reveal a furry little denizen scurrying across their path or catch one ducking into the underbrush at the side of the road. Harley thought about living among things unseen and realized she felt safer up here with Brendan than she had on the streets of Chicago.

But when he began slowing down, anticipation made her shiver. As he took the turn off the road, she caught a glimpse of the name S. Pope on the mailbox, and then they were driving up a one-lane road through what felt like a tunnel of trees. She saw a glow of lights and then they drove into a clearing and she saw the house, lit up in every window like a church at Christmas, and the long front porch that ran the length of the house, and the porch swing, and all the chairs against the wall, and cars lined up along the front.

"Looks like the brothers are already here," Brendan said as he parked.

The scent of woodsmoke was in the air, and there was the sound of music coming from inside as they got out.

"Somebody's dancing with Mom. Probably Wiley, but we've all done it in our time. She pretends she doesn't like it, but she does. Come on, darlin'. We're the guests of honor. Let's go make an appearance."

He clasped her hand as they walked up the steps together and were heading to the front door when it suddenly swung inward, and Harley saw a woman standing in the doorway and knew without asking that was Shirley. The faces of her sons were evidence of her DNA.

"Come inside out of this cold!" Shirley said, and then clasped both of Harley's hands. "Harley, finally I get to meet you. I'm Shirley. Welcome to our home."

"Uh, I'm here, too," Brendan said.

Shirley laughed as she hugged him. "You already know you're loved. Harley's new to this madness. We're all in the kitchen, of course. Come introduce your girl to the rest of us. Ava is beside herself at the thought of getting another sister."

"She's not a thought, Mom. She's a for-sure," Brendan said. "Come on, Sunshine, let's do this."

Harley was swept up into the family as if she'd always been there, and meeting Ava was a surprise. She hadn't expected a tiny blond in a household of dark-haired giants, and then remembered Ava wasn't related to Shirley. Only to her sons, but it didn't appear to have ever mattered.

Everything out of Ava's mouth was Grandma this, and Grandma that, and Wiley was her Bubba, and her brothers' wives were her sisters, and that was Ava's world. And now, she'd added Harley's name among them. Brendan was right. She'd had nothing to fear.

But it wasn't until they got the food on the long, wooden table and sat down to eat that Harley saw the true beauty of family.

Three generations in one place, and two more babies waiting to be born, all talking and laughing, and teasing and sharing food and stories without missing a bite or a breath. It was like watching a tennis match on speed, and in the middle of it all, she saw Brendan in a new light.

He was the youngest brother, but the tallest brother. He was the quietest brother, but his delight in being among them was written on his face, and he kept up a running monologue for Harley's ears only, constantly explaining the connections between everyone at the table and the people they were discussing.

Finally, Shirley raised her hand. "If I might get a word in..." They immediately hushed. "Thank you. I needed to make sure Harley's ears weren't about to fall off."

Harley grinned. "No, ma'am. I've loved every minute of this. I'm an only child and my parents haven't lived under the same roof together more than a week per month in all my days."

"Whyever not?" Shirley asked.

"My father, Jason Banks, is a scientist at NASA. My mother, Judith, is well known in her field as a playwright and screenwriter. I am an only child. I don't think becoming parents was ever on their radar, but you know how that goes. Once I aged out of tolerating being put on display, I was sent to private schools, then off to college, and out on my own. Not a sad thing. Just how I grew up. Only now, thanks to Brendan, I see what I've been missing."

Wiley piped up. "We think little brother is all that

and a bucket of beer, but you'll have to watch out when it comes time to eat. He's never full."

"Oh, we've already had words over a piece of pie," Harley said, and when they all burst into laughter, Brendan felt obliged to explain himself. "She let it sit in the mini-fridge nearly a whole dang day. I couldn't stand the suspense."

Laughter rolled around the table again, and as it did, Brendan reached for her hand beneath the table and gave it a quick squeeze. She glanced up at him, her eyes twinkling in delight.

"Harley's parents are coming to visit," Brendan said.

"Bring them up for a meal," Shirley said.

Harley rolled her eyes. "I'm not subjecting any of you to that. I'm not speaking to my father at the moment, and I don't even know if he'll come, because he'll have to apologize to me first, and after about three hours, Mother becomes intolerable."

"She speaks the truth. I've spoken to her father once over the phone and to her mother a couple of times. They are unique, and they made the most perfect daughter, for which I will be eternally grateful, but they're a handful on a good day."

"You're the best judge of that," Shirley said. "But I have survived far worse than people who've forgotten to be happy. So never feel uneasy about someone hurting my feelings, okay? Your comfort is what matters. And none of that 'ma'am' business. I'm Shirley, or Mom, or Grandma. Take your pick."

"I choose Grandma," Ava said.

"We all know that," Wiley said, then hugged her until she giggled.

Shirley was in her element with her family at the table, and supper wasn't over yet. "Who wants dessert?" she asked, and saw everybody raise a hand.

"I'll help," Brendan said.

"Aaron and I will clear the plates," Dani said, and pointed at Harley. "Stay seated, honey. Tonight, you're the guest. Next trip up, you'll just be one of the crowd."

Harley sat, and watched, and knew in her heart she'd found her people.

———

A short while after the meal was over and everything cleaned up and put away, the family began to separate.

Ava had fallen asleep on the living room sofa, and Wiley and Linette began gathering up their things.

"Brendan, you did good. Harley, honey, you've got more grit than you have a right to. Glad you're going to be part of our family. Mom, thank you for the great meal, but it's time we got this baby girl in bed," Wiley said.

"I'll get the door," Linette said as Wiley swaddled Ava in her little coat, then picked her up and carried her to the car, with Linette beside him.

Aaron and Dani were the next to leave, with hugs all around, and soon afterward, Sean and Amalie retired to their rooms.

Shirley still had something to show Harley, and something she wanted to say to both of them. "The two of you…get your coats and come out to the back porch with me."

Brendan went to get them, and once they were on, Shirley led them out the back door and then walked to the edge of the porch, took a deep breath, and looked up at the vastness of the star-studded sky.

"Harley, what do you see?" she asked.

"I have never seen such beauty, or felt so small and transient," Harley said.

Brendan put his arm around Harley's shoulders and pulled her close.

Shirley nodded, but kept looking up. "For as long as I can remember, this was my world. And then I grew up and left it to follow a man I thought I loved. That decision nearly destroyed us. I used to dream of coming home because I knew I'd be safe here. But coming home would have also meant bringing trouble with me, and we don't bring trouble to this place. Sometimes it finds us here, but it's not of our making. The saddest part of our homecoming was that it took the deaths of three people to make it happen. The two people my ex-husband murdered freed us of his reign of terror, and the death of my mother gave us sanctuary."

She sighed and slipped her hand beneath Harley's elbow. "You are a wise and courageous woman, and I'm so very happy for you and Brendan. You don't need my advice. You don't need my guidance. But if you want it,

I will give Brendan and you five acres of this land to put your own roots in this land. It will always be yours, but it can never be sold out of the family. That's how the land works on Pope Mountain. And if you don't want this kind of life, it won't hurt my feelings. It's not for everyone, but for the people who need it, it's where we thrive."

Brendan was stunned. From the first moment they'd come to live in this house, he never wanted to leave, and yet he had. Like Shirley, coming home to Jubilee had settled his soul.

Harley reached for Brendan's hand. She didn't know what he was thinking, but she felt the depth of this gift all the way to her soul. "A place to call home," she mumbled, unaware she'd even said it aloud.

Shirley smiled. "Yes, sweet child, a place to call home."

Tears were thick in Brendan's voice. "Oh my God… Mom… I don't know what to say. I never saw this coming, and I don't know how Harley would feel about living up—"

"Like she just won the lottery," Harley said.

Shirley nodded. "Then it's yours. You come back tomorrow…before you both go back to work. We'll take the ATV and drive the property until you find the spot. I'll have five acres surveyed, and then the rest is up to the both of you. And there's no hurry about anything. Only that you'll know it's there and you'll know it's yours."

Then they kept hugging her and thanking her over and over, and all Shirley could think was how blessed her life had become.

And all the way home, Brendan and Harley kept talking about the remarkable gift they'd just been given.

"You're sure you'll be okay with this? Sometimes weather makes it slow going, trying to get home."

Harley laughed. "Brendan! I'm from Chicago! Snow is a way of life."

"Yes, but your roads get plowed and sanded and salted. We make our own ruts in the snow and go from there," he said.

"But it's never quiet in the city. Ever. And standing on that porch tonight with your mom... I didn't know until then that silence had its own sound. And I can only imagine the view in the daytime. Honestly, it sounds like heaven."

He sighed. "Okay then, we're good to go. Mom said to come when we're ready. She's not going anywhere."

"Let's go after breakfast, okay?"

He nodded.

"We'll have to dig a well, won't we? What if we pick out a place that doesn't have water?" she asked.

He shook his head. "Stop worrying. We'll just get Uncle John to come witch it. He always finds water."

Harley's eyes widened. "Do what?"

"We call it witching for water, but he uses a dowsing rod to find water," he explained.

"Oh. Right. Okay… I am officially out of my depth here, so I'm not going to worry about one more thing. You all have hundreds of years of knowledge about things I've never thought of, let alone done. My street smarts aren't going to go very far up here."

He grinned. "Maybe not, but they sure wrapped me up in a box and tied me with a bow."

Harley just smiled. "And when we get home, I know exactly how to unwrap you, too."

"Just like Christmas," Brendan said, and down the mountain they went.

Chapter 18

As promised, they were back at Shirley's house just before 10:00 a.m.

She had her four-seat ATV already parked in the backyard waiting for them to arrive, and a basket packed with bottles of water she'd tied down with a bungee cord to one of the back seats. When they arrived, she welcomed them inside, beaming from the excitement.

Sean came out of the kitchen carrying a cup of coffee on his way up the hall to his office. "Hey, guys! Mom told us the news this morning. I can't tell you how happy Amalie and I are for you. Don't let Mom drive. She goes too fast."

Harley laughed. "Oh, so that's where Brendan gets his love of speed. Ever ride with him on that Harley?"

"Well damn, I forgot about that," Sean said. "Maybe I should—"

Shirley swatted at him. "You go chase computer viruses, mister. We're fine."

They could still hear Sean laughing as they went out the back door.

"It's a chilly day, but we have sunshine. And just so

you know, Uncle John said he'd come by later today and dowse for water around the place you pick so you'll know where to set the house," Shirley said, and then climbed into the back seat beside the basket.

Brendan winked at Harley as they got into the ATV. One of her concerns was already being dealt with.

"Buckle up, Sunshine. We aren't going to go fast. We're taking the scenic route. Mom, is it okay if we look on the east side of the property, like behind the tree line on the blacktop, somewhere where's there's already cleared land? We like the idea of having the house out of sight of traffic, like yours is."

"Of course, it's okay. And like everyone else up here, you can drive all the way up and over the peak, and all you'll see are mailboxes and roads leading up into the trees. No houses are visible from their roads, and those roads were first cleared when most of the trees standing now were only saplings. The old growth are the giants that were here before white men ever set foot on this land. It's good you don't want to cut any of them down, because the root systems are myriad beneath the surface and hundreds of years old. You couldn't dig deep enough in this forest to even set a fence post."

They took off through the yard, past the old chicken house and barn, and then took a hard right just before they reached the pond and began to drive east, following the edge of the clearing.

The first hints of green were just beginning to show

beneath the winter-brown grass. Harley pointed to a huge bird circling high in the sky above them.

"Eagle," Brendan said.

"Wow," Harley said.

Shirley tapped her on the shoulder and pointed into the trees they were passing just as a bright-red cardinal dropped down from a limb.

Harley nodded to indicate she'd seen it, but didn't know where to look next. Everything was new and beautiful and just the tiniest bit intimidating, but she loved challenges, and this was going to be life-changing. She was about to become a part of the history of Pope Mountain, and their children would continue a legacy she would never have known existed. Taking the job for Ray Caldwell had forever changed her life.

They kept driving and looking and talking until in the distance, Harley saw a small cluster of trees out in the clearing, and then as they came closer, a huge animal stepped out of the shadows.

Harley grabbed Brendan's arm. "Stop! Stop!"

"What's wrong?" he asked.

"Look!" she said, pointing toward the trees.

"Oh my!" Shirley said. "What a magnificent elk, and it still hasn't shed its antlers."

"Look for the stag to make my bed. Look for the stag to lay my head," Harley said.

"Yes! Amalie!" Brendan said.

"What am I missing?" Shirley asked.

"We saw Amalie when I took Harley out to lunch.

As she was about to tell us goodbye, she put her hand on Harley's shoulder, and suddenly she's staring off into space. That's what she told Harley. To look for the stag. We didn't know what it meant, but now we do. I think this is the place. This is the land we're supposed to choose."

"Perfect," Shirley said. "And you're less than a quarter of a mile from my house. You can use my driveway to enter the property and then we'll build a road from there and gravel it all the way to your place. If Uncle John can find water, of course."

"Is this it, Sunshine?"

"Yes, this is it!" Harley whispered.

"Then the water will be here, too, because the stag marked the spot," Brendan said.

"I brought a couple of stakes," Shirley said. "You two go put them in the ground to mark your land. They're in the back, Son. You and your girl should do the honors."

Brendan found the stakes with strips of red fabric tied to them and a small sledgehammer to drive them into the ground. He handed the stakes to Harley, then took her hand and walked about thirty feet ahead.

"You first," Harley said, and handed him a stake.

He drove it into the ground with two blows, then they walked a short distance further, where Harley set her stake—hammering until it was securely in the ground.

When they turned around, the stag was gone.

"If it's meant to be, we'll see him again. He was here

for a reason," Brendan said, then wrapped his arms around Harley and gave her a quick kiss and a hug to commemorate the moment before they started back to the ATV.

Shirley's eyes were tear-filled as she watched them, walking back hand in hand, animated and laughing, so full of joy they were almost bouncing with each step. "I did it, Mom. Thanks to you, I did it. Four good boys turned into four amazing men. Daddy would be proud to know his grandsons are carrying our name."

―――――――

By the time Brendan and Harley were home, they had a tentative plan for their future. Harley was still waiting for Wolf Outen to take possession of the inn, and they were awaiting her parents' arrival, neither of which was within their control. But Brendan had plans of his own, and now that he was about to meet her parents, he didn't intend to leave them guessing as to how he felt about their daughter.

So, while Harley was in the kitchen, he snuck a ring from the travel pouch of jewelry she'd brought with her and dropped it in his pocket. When he went back up the hall, Harley was already in the living room with her feet to the fire and her laptop open.

"Hey, honey. I'm settling in here for a while. I need to go through my email, pay some bills, and check on the details of moving me from Chicago to Jubilee."

Brendan leaned over and kissed the top of her head. "And I have some errands to run downtown. Anything special you need while I'm out?"

She glanced up, her eyes dancing. "Cheese? The kind that squirts out of a can?"

He grinned. "Cheese it is. Any particular crackers that please your gourmet palate?"

"Anything but saltines. Those are the ones I use for peanut butter," she said.

He shook his head. "If I hadn't already lost my heart to you, this would have been the tipping point. I don't suppose you like Vienna sausages?"

"Dipped in whole-grain mustard? Yum."

"Well, now we know what to serve at our wedding. Be back in a bit."

Harley's laughter followed him out the door.

Brendan made a quick run through the supermarket and then headed for the Serenity Inn. He parked in the visitor parking lot and went into the hotel, and through the lobby to the boutique jewelry store on-site. They didn't have huge selections of fine jewelry, but they had some. He knew what he wanted and was hoping they'd have it in her size, and after a diligent search, he found it.

As they were ringing it up, Liz Devon walked in.

"Brendan! I'm so glad to see you. How's Harley?"

"Great now that the feds finally found their man. She's still got a groove in her scalp, but it's healing, and she's regained her balance, which was huge. For a while there, she was bouncing off chairs and walls like a ball in a pinball machine."

Liz shuddered. "I won't soon forget them taking her out on that gurney. I was so scared for her, and I know you were, too." Then she eyed the small bag he was holding. "Anything interesting in there?"

He grinned. "I couldn't say. Tell the crew in the kitchen that I'll be back soon, and I appreciate their help more than they know."

"Of course," Liz said. "Oh…Wolf Outen is due to move in tomorrow and step into the managerial role, and it's none too soon for me. I don't know how he plans to integrate the security he travels with, but that's all on him to figure out now."

"Good to know," he said. "Gotta go. See you soon."

They walked out of the boutique together, then went their separate ways.

Brendan noticed the wind picking up as he headed for his car. It didn't seem to matter what time of year, or what the weather was like, tourists still came to Jubilee. It was good for business, and even better for the families on Pope Mountain. PCG Inc. had turned Jubilee into the tourist attraction it was today and saved their way of life.

By the time he got to the car, he was running. The first drops of rain were beginning to fall, and he had the sudden urge to hurry. He dropped the bag from the jewelry store into the seat beside him and then started the car and headed home. Just knowing Harley would be there waiting for him made his heart skip a beat. Tonight, he was putting a ring on her pretty finger— one step closer to being his wife.

As he was driving, he got a call from his mom. He answered on Bluetooth so he could keep his hands on the wheel.

"Hey, Mom. You're getting rained on, aren't you?"

"We sure are, and it's really coming down. Good thing we went out this morning to look at land instead of waiting...and that's why I'm calling. Uncle John came with his dowsing rods. I drove him out to the place, and it didn't take him any time to walk the area. He swears there's good water under your land. You'll drill deep to get to it, but it will be a strong, continuing source."

"Great news, Mom. Can't wait to tell Harley. We're both still in disbelief at such a loving and generous offer. Love you. Tell Uncle John we said thanks."

"Will do. Take care. Love you, too."

———

Unaware of Brendan's plans, Harley had been wading through emails and making plans of her own. She'd contacted the leasing company about her Chicago apartment, informing them that she was moving out of state. With only a month left on her existing lease, and the fact that she'd been a tenant for almost eight years, they agreed to let her go without a penalty. She informed them she'd be sending her furniture to an auction house, and she would forward the name of the company so they could give them access to the apartment, and that another company would be packing her clothes and personal belongings to ship to her. And, after she mailed back her personal keys to the place, they would refund her deposit.

She'd just shut a door to her past, and without one regret. No more lonely days and nights in the apartment. No more solitary walks down the block to the local sports bar. Her solitary life was over, and Brendan Pope had made it worth the wait.

She was getting hungry and wondering when Brendan would be back when she heard a rumble of thunder and, at the same time, the garage door going up. She got up and headed for the kitchen. The man had timing down to an art, in more ways than one.

He was already coming in through the utility room with his arms full of grocery sacks when she walked into the room.

"You went after groceries and came home with rain, too. Was that on sale, or did it come for free?"

He put the sacks on the island, turned on the radio and swooped her up in his arms, and started dancing her around the kitchen. "Everything I have is yours, including this slow Kentucky rain."

"Did you bring me canned cheese?" she asked.

He laughed, gave her one last turn around the room, and then stopped and began digging through the sacks.

"Voilà! Cheese, peanut butter, two kinds of crackers,

a jar of spicy mustard, and a couple of cans of Vienna sausages. Also, a bucket of fried chicken and sides from the deli."

She threw her arms around his neck and kissed him, and then kissed him again and again, until Brendan groaned.

"You're killin' me, Sunshine. All I want is to take you to bed, but we didn't eat before we went to Mom's, and you need to take your meds, but you can't take them on an empty stomach, so hold that thought, okay?"

He was right, so she tried to lighten the moment for both of them. "I happily wait when it matters, although I've been put on hold while waiting for a computer tech, and that pushes every button I have."

"Well, you'll never have to suffer that again. We have Sean."

Her eyes widened. "Right! I'd forgotten about that. Your family is as handy as a pocket on a shirt. A saint for a mother. A darling little sister. A computer guru, and two cops for brothers. Three of the nicest women I've ever met who are going to be my sisters-in-law. And my man… the best chef in the history of ever. I'll get the plates."

"And I'll get the groceries put up and the food on the table," he said.

Minutes later, they were eating together, listening to music in the background and rain on the roof, while Brendan doled out her antibiotics.

She smiled her thanks and downed them, then took another bite of fried chicken.

"Mom called," he said. "Uncle John says we have good water under the property."

"Fabulous!" Harley said.

He nodded. "Agreed. Also, I saw Liz Devon. She said Wolf Outen moves into the inn tomorrow. She also thinks he'll probably rearrange some offices to accommodate his needs and set aside some suites below the penthouse for his bodyguards."

"I'm excited and also a little nervous at tackling the job he's given me," Harley said.

"It's nothing new, just more of it. That's what I tell myself when we bake for guests every day and then add private parties and holidays to it. We're still doing the same things. Just more of it."

Harley frowned. "That's a good way to look at it. Nothing new. Just more of the same, and you're right. I know how to do my job six ways to Sunday."

"I'm not going to lie. I'm really glad he won't be wanting you to do investigations on your own anymore," Brendan said.

"I'm not going to lie, either. Getting shot took the thrill out of that chase. I'll happily find the flaws and holes and let him deal with the criminal activities on his own. He's certainly equipped for it," Harley said.

Brendan nodded and went on eating, but her engagement ring was burning a hole in his pocket. He wanted to just give it to her now, but this wasn't the time.

"I'll make some good dessert for you tomorrow, but

I did bring home some candy bars and ice cream, if you want to save room," he said.

"I am going to resist the urge to clap my hands. My penchant for sweets is my downfall," Harley said. "That and squirt cheese."

They finished their meal and, after cleaning up the kitchen, headed for the living room with bowls of ice cream to eat by the fire.

"How did you know Rocky Road is my favorite?" Harley asked as she settled into her spot on the sofa.

"I didn't. But I figured I couldn't go wrong with chocolate ice cream that came with almonds and marshmallows."

"Oink," she said, and took her first bite, then another and another, until her bowl was empty. "I'm stuffed and that was so good. Thank you."

Before he could answer, her cell phone rang. She glanced at it. "It's my mother," she said, then answered. "Hey, Mom."

"Harley darling, your father and I are coming to Jubilee the day after tomorrow. We have reservations at the Serenity Inn. We wanted to see where you both work, so we chose that hotel. I'm already in Houston with Jason. We've chartered a helicopter at your suggestion. It seemed the better choice. Depending on the weather, our scheduled arrival is just after twelve noon. We'll let you know when we've arrived, okay?"

"Yes, that's great," Harley said. "Safe travels. See you then." And she disconnected. "Both of them. Day after tomorrow. Reservations at the Serenity Inn, likely hoping for a glimpse of you-know-who."

He grinned. "Are they really that impressed with fame?"

"Yes."

He sighed. "I guess I'd better hang up my award for saving that kid's life in the wreck."

She wadded up her napkin and threw it at him. "You are such a fake. You aren't the least bit worried about what they think of you…thank God. So, I guess that covers the updates for today."

"Almost," he said. "Sit tight. I'll be right back." He was trying not to run as he headed down the hall to his bedroom, got the ring from his coat pocket, and returned to his seat.

"Harley, darlin', as brief as the time has been since I first saw you, you have become the most important person in my life. I already think of you as mine. My love. My woman. My heart. We've talked about marriage. We've picked out land for a house. We're living together already, and I've never said all the right words, in the right order, all at once."

Harley's heart was pounding. She was so locked into the dark eyes staring into her soul that she couldn't breathe. She felt it coming. Thought she knew what he was going to say, and even when she finally heard them, realized she'd been waiting for them all of her life.

"Harley Jo…my Sunshine…" He opened the box and removed a white-gold, two-carat, round-cut diamond ring. "I pledge everything I am and will be to you. Will you marry me?"

"Yes, yes, a thousand times, yes," she said, and her hand was trembling as he slipped the ring on her finger. "Oh, Brendan, it's beautiful!"

"Just like you," he said, then cupped the back of her neck and leaned forward until he felt her mouth beneath his lips and kissed her.

———————

Larry Beaumont was handcuffed and shackled and on his way to a visitation room for a conference with his lawyer. He knew he was going to prison. There was no way to deny what he'd done. The surprise was that he'd never seen it coming. Maybe because he'd been so wrapped up in Justine's misbehavior that he'd missed all the clues. In hindsight, he should have been wary about the auditor, but her unassuming manner and pretty face had fooled him.

When they reached the room, the guard walked him inside, seated him at the table with his lawyer, then left the room.

"So, Mr. Manheim, I assume you have updates, or you wouldn't be here," Larry said.

"I do, but I'm afraid they're personal, rather than legal."

Larry's stomach knotted. "Well, hell. Then just get it said."

"The official word on your ex-wife's death is that she was murdered. Your daughter, Justine, gave herself away after she had a meltdown about your wife's lapsed life insurance policy. She is, at the present time, in a holding facility for the criminally insane. I can't say what the courts are going to do with her, but she's been labeled as untreatable. In other words, there are no meds that will help or fix her."

Larry felt sick. "And you're telling me this because...?"

Manheim frowned. "Human decency? The assumption that you might want to know? Pick one."

"Fine. So now I know. But see where I am? I can't even help myself, and there's no one left to bury Karen."

Manheim sighed. "I do know that Karen Beaumont's will is being carried out according to her wishes by her lawyer. He will see to her burial and to the sale of her house. The money will be banked. The will stated your daughter as the beneficiary, but if she was deceased or incapacitated, you would be next in line. So whatever money is recouped from her estate will be yours once you've served your time."

"What am I looking at?" Larry asked.

"I'm guessing a minimum of ten years, but again, since you've abdicated a jury trial, the sentencing will be up to the judge."

Larry sighed and looked down at the cuffs on his wrists. "Anything else you need to share?"

Manheim frowned. "No."

"Then that's all the good news I can take for one day. I think we're done here," Larry said.

The lawyer left. The guard took Larry back to his cell. The clank of metal to metal as the door locked behind him said it all.

———

Justine Beaumont was now residing in Vernon, Texas, at the North Texas State Hospital for the criminally insane, and for those with mental issues too severe to stand trial. She had a room with a bed and a chair and a window. And a television high on the wall with controlled content, and a tiny adjoining bathroom with a toilet, a sink, and a shower. Every aspect of her life was being monitored and controlled, including the daily meds for psychosis.

Her reality was what she needed it to be on any given day, and anything else contrary to those needs caused her to react with violence or hysteria.

Today, she'd been taken to the psychiatry wing for a "visit" with the doctor, and she'd gone to great lengths to brush her hair and clean her teeth. They'd taken away her makeup and pretty clothes, but she kept asking for them anyway. And today, she was reliving her time in the Jubilee jail, waiting for her parents to come bail her out.

Dr. Yellin was reading through her file when she came into the office. She was new to the facility, and this was her second session. He was just reminding himself of her diagnosis, why she was here, and prior offenses. When the guard knocked, Dr. Yellin called out, "Come in," and then closed the file and turned on the recorder to tape the session. It was old school, but still in practice because cassette tapes were more difficult to tamper with or alter than digital recorders and needed to be foolproof when taken to trials.

"Good afternoon, Justine. Please sit down."

She sat in the chair indicated, then smoothed down her hair and folded her hands in her lap.

"How have you been?" Yellin asked.

"Do you know when my parents are coming to get me? I don't much care for it here."

She seemed calm, but her whole body was on alert. Stiff shoulders, straight back, and one knee bouncing as she sat. She had a tic at the corner of her eye, and he could tell she was biting on the inside of her jaw.

"Do you know why you're here?" Yellin asked.

She wouldn't look him in the face and looked at a point above his head instead. "They're coming to get me," she repeated.

"No, your parents can't come."

She frowned, her voice rising an octave as she asked. "Why not? Daddy has money."

"Your father is in jail. He stole money from his boss."

She pounded a fist on her knee. "He wouldn't let me come home. Mama will get me. Call her."

"We can't call your mother, remember?"

She shook her head. "No, no, I don't want to remember. Just call her!"

"She can't come to the phone anymore. Do you know why?" Yellin asked.

Justine covered her face. "Shut up! Stop talking. Just call her!"

"She's dead, and now this is where you live."

"No money…no money. Waste of time. I need to leave now. Tell the man to take me home."

Yellin signaled the guard. "Miss Beaumont is ready to go to her room now," he said, and turned off the recorder.

Justine was talking to the guard as they walked out the door, giving him her address back in Dallas, but Justine Beaumont was already home. She just didn't know it.

═══════

Tipton Crossley's "come to Jesus" moment happened when the door to his cell slammed behind him. His heart was pounding, and he'd broken out in a cold sweat. He'd already asked for a criminal defense lawyer and had given them the name of one he'd met before. He knew they'd find out everything now, and he had no hope of getting leniency, but he wasn't going down without a fight.

But the longer he stayed locked up, the more he began to realize the irony. He'd stolen women and children and locked them up to sell. He knew some of them died before they reached their destinations, and the ones who survived probably wished they had not. But they hadn't mattered. They weren't real to him. He saw them as merchandise and sold them for what they were worth on the open market. Now he was locked up and going to pay a fortune to someone in an effort to keep himself off death row.

His first night in prison had been horrifying, and he kept thinking of the home he'd had with his father and the luxuries they'd enjoyed. All that was over, including his relationship with his father. He would die remembering the look on Wilhem's face as he'd stepped aside for the federal agents swarming into his office. It was shame. He'd brought shame to the family name.

After his arraignment, Tipton was moved to a federal lockup and was now awaiting notice of a trial date.

Then just when he'd begun to assimilate within the population, someone recognized his name from news reports, and word of his reputation began to spread, and all of a sudden, his safety was at risk.

There were inmates who'd had their women disappear, and their sisters, and their children, and even their mothers, and he became the face and the reason. He began looking behind him everywhere he went and staying to himself in the common room, until one day a man walked up behind him, wrapped his arm around Tip's neck, and whispered in his ear.

"What did you do with my woman?"

And then another inmate hit him in the face and

broke his nose. "My daughter. You unholy bastard! What did you do with my baby girl?"

And a third, and then a fourth joined in, and Tip couldn't scream because he couldn't breathe, and the blows kept coming, and his flesh kept ripping, and when they finally dropped him, he'd bled out all over them and onto the floor.

And no one saw a thing. Not even the guards.

Prison justice had happened because prisoners had nothing to lose.

———

Wilhem Crossley was notified of his son's death the next day, but he had no tears left to weep. In his heart, his son had died the day he found the hidden room. He didn't understand how Tip had taken that path. Was it a weakness in him? Was it all greed? Or had there been something sinister within him from the day he'd been born?

Finally, Wilhem's common sense prevailed. He knew he'd been a good father. Tip was the one who'd failed to be the good son. He was just a bad seed.

It happened now and then in families.

It happened in his.

———

Special Agent Jay Howard sent one last text regarding the case to Rusty Pope.

Tipton Crossley was jumped and murdered in prison. Prisoners found out why he was there. Case officially closed.

As Rusty read the text, she kept thinking what Mikey had said. "The snake got greedy and bit itself. It will die." And Tipton Crossley was dead.

Chapter 19

JASON AND JUDITH BANKS WERE COMING TO THE END of their flight and eyeing the massive mountain looming above the town of Jubilee below. "Lord, Judith. It looks like Disney recreated something from the 1800s. Log-house shops. Cobblestone walkways. Cedar-shake roofs. Three hangar-like metal buildings with neon signs. Wonder what the hell those are for? Little buildings everywhere and nowhere to park."

"Stop whining, Jason. It's like Disney World but smaller. You don't drive there. You walk for days. At least we won't need a map to figure out where we are," Judith said.

Jason snorted. "I can't believe Harley thinks this is a good idea."

"Harley found a man she loves, and from all appearances, he loves her, too. I envy her that," she said.

Jason frowned. "What are you saying?"

Judith shrugged. "That you love your rockets more than you love me?"

He flushed, but the chopper was descending to land, and he said no more. As soon as they were down, the pilot helped them out, then carried their luggage to the hotel shuttle waiting nearby.

"Thank you for flying with us," the pilot said. "We'll be back to pick you up in three days. Confirmation of the time will be forthcoming."

"Thank you," Jason said, then watched as the pilot ran back to the chopper. "I predict this will be the longest three days of my life."

"And I'm already sorry you came with me," Judith muttered, and got in the shuttle van. Jason was right behind her and sat in the seat opposite her. "So you'll have more room," he said.

Judith turned to look out the window. "You are so thoughtful," she muttered as they drove away.

A few minutes later they were checking in at the front desk, while a bellhop took their bags to their suite. The desk clerk did a double take when he saw their names.

"I don't suppose you are any relation to Harley Banks?" he asked.

They looked surprised. "Yes, she's our daughter," Jason said.

"You must be very proud of her. She's an amazing woman. The elevators are down that hall. Enjoy your stay," he said.

"Thank you. I'm sure we shall," Judith said, and slipped her hand under Jason's elbow as they started across the lobby.

The ride up to the seventh floor was smooth and quick, and once they walked into their room, the first thing they noticed was the balcony and the view over-looking Jubilee and the other hotel in the distance.

"It's hardly the bright lights of Houston," he said.

"Unpack your clothes, Jason," Judith said, then sat down on the sofa and called Harley to let her know they'd arrived.

―――――――――

Brendan was watching Harley dress as if she was going to war. Her expression was solemn, sometimes stern. She'd opted for the black leather pants and boots she'd first arrived in, and was standing in the closet staring at two different sweaters as if the wrong choice would be the end of her.

He would have teased her but for the seriousness of the moment, and he kept thinking, *This is what they've done to her—made her doubt her own choices.*

"Personally, I like you naked best, but those black leather pants are dangerous. You are more beautiful than a woman has a right to be."

She turned, eyeing the boots, dark slacks, and gray cable-knit sweater he was wearing. His hair was as thick and black as hers, but where hers curled, his was bone straight with a tendency to feather across his forehead. He looked like he'd just stepped off the page of a *GQ* magazine.

"So says your hunky self," she said as she pulled a butter-yellow sweater from its padded hanger and slipped it over her head. "Three days," she said as she finger-combed her hair back in place, careful of her still-healing head wound.

"It's not a prison sentence, just a family visit," he said. "And you got a text while you were in the shower."

She snagged her phone from the dresser and pulled up the text and frowned. "It's from Wilhem Crossley. Tip's dead. Killed in prison. Can't say I'm sorry."

Brendan pulled her down onto his lap. "That's good. No danger of you ever having to testify at his trial now."

Shock spread across her face. "I never thought of that."

"Well, I did. Fate stepped in and took that worry away."

Her phone rang while it was still in her hand, startling her enough that she nearly dropped it, then she answered. "Hi, Mom. Are you here?"

"Yes, we're just now in our room and unpacking."

"Have you had lunch?" Harley asked.

"No, and I'm starving," Judith said.

"What's your room number?" Harley asked.

"We have suite 702."

"Then get yourself fluffed. We'll come get you and escort you up to the main dining room. It's on the tenth floor. See you soon."

Then she hung up before Judith could argue.

"I need a kiss for fortitude," Harley said.

"Happy to oblige," Brendan said, then cupped her

face and kissed her until she was breathless. "Let's go do this," he said.

"A little war paint," Harley said as she dashed into the bathroom for a bit of lipstick and then grabbed her coat and her Dior clutch bag on the way out the door.

Soon they were on their way across town and Brendan was on the phone, reserving a table for four by the windows.

———————

The moment Harley hung up, Judith hurried to the bedroom. "They're coming to our room and taking us to lunch here at the hotel. I'm so glad. After all the flying, I didn't want to go out again so soon."

Excited that this day was finally here, she began rushing to freshen her makeup and hair, then quickly emptied her suitcase and hung up her clothes. She and Jason were on the sofa and waiting for the knock when Judith reached for his hand. "Please be nice. I need for him to like us."

Jason frowned. "He's the one who needs to be nice. We're the ones he should want to impress."

Judith sighed. "No. The only person he cares to impress is our daughter. I have a feeling this man won't lose a wink of sleep if we disapprove. So, in the spirit of unity, if you get a wild hair to be an asshole, think twice. This matters to Harley, and I don't want her to draw away from us any farther than she already has. She hasn't forgiven you for calling her a bitch, and I won't forgive you if you shame us in his eyes."

Jason blinked, startled by the tone in her voice. "Oh, stop worrying. I told you I was sorry, and he's just one man. Not God."

She sighed. "You apologized to the wrong person, and you don't believe in God."

And then there was a knock at the door. "I'll get it," Jason said.

She frowned. "Then the first words out of your mouth better be, 'I'm sorry, Harley.'"

Jason wasn't accustomed to being in the wrong and was defensive as he strode to the door, but when he opened it, he almost didn't recognize his own daughter. She looked beautiful in love. Then he had to look up at the man standing slightly behind her.

"Come in," he said, and then gave Harley a quick hug. "I owe you an apology. I'm sorry I was rude, and I'm so sorry you were hurt."

"Thank you," she said, but it was Brendan's hand on her shoulder that steadied her most as they entered the room. "Mom. Dad. This is my fiancé, Brendan Pope. Brendan, my parents, Jason and Judith Banks."

"Your fiancé?" Judith cried, and then saw the ring on Harley's hand. "Oh, honey! It's stunning. Congratulations to the both of you."

"It's a pleasure to finally meet you both," Brendan said. "Although we've spoken to each other on the phone before, a face-to-face meeting is always better."

Jason heard the challenge. He remembered their talk. And wearing shoes, Jason Banks was still two inches shy of six feet tall. They used to make jokes about how Harley wound up taller than both of them, but this man was huge and intimidating, and Jason didn't do intimidating.

"How was your flight?" Brendan asked.

"It was fine," Judith said, "and we really appreciate you being thoughtful enough to choose to eat here. It's just an elevator ride to get where we need to go."

"Yes, ma'am," Brendan said. "I've made reservations, and Harley needs to eat pretty soon. She's still on antibiotics and can't take them on an empty stomach."

Judith paled. "Oh my God, I didn't even ask about your wound. I didn't see a bandage and I guess I thought it was healed."

"Not yet. Just hidden in all these curls," Harley said, and gently pulled back the curls enough so they could see.

Jason was horrified at the long, shallow groove at the side of her head.

Judith teared up. "That's where you were shot."

"He missed. I didn't," Harley said.

The meaning of those words shocked Jason to the core. His daughter had shot and killed a man in self-defense, and yet was so matter-of-fact about it.

"The concussion she suffered was far worse than the wound," Brendan said. "Besides headaches for days, she lost her sense of balance."

Harley laughed. "Every time I stood up, the room spun around me. I don't know what I would have done without Brendan."

"We would have come," Jason said.

"He carried me everywhere for days. You couldn't have done that. Besides, all your presence would have done was put us in danger. I was in lockdown. The federal agents managed to keep the news of the hit man's death a secret, in the hopes that whoever hired him would assume he was still looking for me, or that I was dead. But you two showing up would have blown that cover and put all of us in danger again," Harley said.

"It wasn't personal. It was a necessity," Brendan said. "Now, sir, what do you say we go get our ladies fed?"

Jason glared. Harley was his, and Pope was claiming her.

Brendan saw his flash of anger. "She'll always be your daughter. But she's going to be my wife," he said quietly.

Jason sighed. "Yes, of course. Lead the way. We're right behind you."

Harley reached for Brendan's hand as they started up the hall toward the elevators.

Judith saw him look down and smile at her and, in that moment, knew her daughter was so precious in his eyes. She glanced at the dour-faced man beside her and sighed. Jason was out of his element and out of sorts, but he'd get over it. As soon as he got back to his propulsion lab, he'd be fine.

She had a moment of regret that there would be no

lavish wedding to plan, no trips to the dressmaker, no wedding showers, no pastor to reserve, no church to pick out. Then she shrugged it off. She and Jason had a wedding like that, and in the end, all it had amounted to was a flash in the pan. Frenzied joy that didn't last.

But looking at the quiet devotion between her daughter and her man gave Judith hope for a deeper, lasting love between them, and as a mother, there was nothing more she could ask.

As soon as they reached the dining room and she saw how warmly Brendan and Harley were greeted, she was beginning to be impressed.

"Chef Pope! Welcome back, Chef! Great to see you, Chef!" and "Miss Harley, we were praying for you. Miss Harley, so good to see you back on your feet!"

The comments followed them all the way to their table and as they were being seated. As soon as they were alone again, Judith commented. "It's wonderful to see how revered you two are."

"No, ma'am. 'Revered' is the wrong word. We don't elevate people by rank. It comes from respect. And that's earned. Harley gained their respect with her diligence in uncovering ongoing theft and fraud. And I didn't earn it from being good at my job, which I am. I earned it by being good to my team. And mentoring them as I was mentored—to become skilled at their chosen professions."

"All of the great chefs I have encountered have a reputation for being vocal," Jason said.

Brendan's gaze shifted. "I don't have to raise my voice to be understood." Then he slid his arm around Harley's shoulder. "Sunshine, do you see anything on the menu that sounds good to you?"

"What are you having?" Harley asked.

"I'm thinking about chicken pot pie with the puff-pastry crust, and whatever you don't eat."

Harley laughed at the startled expression on her father's face. "He's not joking. There are no such things as leftovers at our house. Brendan's mother, Shirley, swears he's never been full."

Brendan shrugged. "It's a long way from my mouth to my belly. Even farther to my toes. And being the youngest of four brothers made it worse. I learned at an early age not to be late to the table and not to waste food."

Judith giggled. "Your mother must be a saint."

"Yes, ma'am, and a phenomenal cook and baker. She inspired my love of baking," he said.

"It runs in the family," Harley said. "There's a little bakery down in the tourist area of Jubilee called Granny Annie's Bakery. She's Brendan's great-aunt and her cinnamon rolls are to die for."

"I like cinnamon rolls," Jason said.

"Then we'll take you there tomorrow," Brendan said. "And weather permitting, if you want to sightsee, we'll be happy to show you the sights. The atmosphere in Jubilee is like stepping back a couple of hundred years into the way life used to be here."

Their waiter appeared and took their orders. Then as they were waiting, they heard a flurry of excitement at the door.

Wolfgang Outen had just entered the dining room and was scanning the area when he stopped and then headed straight for their table.

"Oh my God. That's Wolfgang Outen," Jason mumbled, but Brendan was already on his feet, and Wolf was hugging him.

"Brendan! They told me you and Harley were here. Harley, so good to see you up and about. I'm having offices revamped especially for you, with quiet and privacy at a premium. Later, you must go over it with me, and anything else you need will be provided." He paused, and only then did he shift his gaze to acknowledge the other two people at the table.

Harley quickly introduced them. "Mr. Outen, these are my parents, Jason and Judith Banks. Mom and Dad, this is Wolfgang Outen, the new owner of the Serenity Inn and the man who's going to be my new boss."

Wolfgang smiled. "I am honored to have snared the shark she is. Her reputation in the corporate world is renowned."

Jason stared at Harley in disbelief, then stood to shake his hand. "It's a pleasure, sir."

Wolf kissed the back of Judith's hand instead of shaking it, and forever sealed her opinion of him as not only handsome and debonair, but also the perfect gentleman.

Then Wolf clapped Brendan on the shoulder again. "My best to Shirley, as always. Tell her I'm open for another invitation to her table any time she feels called."

Brendan laughed. "I'll tell her. You know she loves your company. Your daughter. Her son. Living under her roof. Her world is just about perfect."

"And with the twins on the way, I might be just the tiniest bit envious that she'll be with them daily."

"You might want to rethink the every-day aspect," Brendan said. "According to Ava, babies are noisy."

Wolf threw back his head and laughed. "I look forward to being interrupted. Now, pardon me for the interruption to your meal. Jason and Judith, it was a pleasure to meet you. Enjoy your stay."

He left as abruptly as he'd appeared, but Jason was seeing Brendan in a whole new light.

"Outen knows your mother?"

"He knows all of us. He's part of our family now and enjoys all of the benefits that come with that," Brendan said.

"Benefits?" Jason asked.

Harley glared and leaned forward, her voice angry and verging on a hiss. "That's enough out of you. You've belittled and berated me my whole adult life, but you shut your mouth about Brendan and his family. You came to visit, not dissect. If you can't figure out how to separate the two behaviors, then feel free to fly your ass back to Houston. Mom's used to being on her own. We'll see to her care without you. Now, here comes our food. Sit up straight like a big boy and use your fork while you eat."

Brendan choked back a laugh, and to ease the tension, he tucked his napkin into the neck of his sweater, picked up his knife and fork, and held them upright in his hands on either side of his bread plate.

Judith took one look at him and giggled.

Harley rolled her eyes.

Brendan caught Jason's eye and winked. "I already know that when the fire's coming out of her ears, it's easier to do what she says."

Reluctantly, Jason grinned at the absurdity of this huge man pretending to be cowed by his daughter's ire and held up his hands in defeat. "Message received loud and clear, Harley Jo. I'm not going anywhere until I have myself a cinnamon roll."

Harley yanked the napkin out of Brendan's sweater and kissed him on the cheek. "I do not deserve you, but I am grateful you are mine."

"Forever and a day, Sunshine. Forever and a day," he said.

———

That night, Judith was in their suite getting ready for bed, and Jason was standing out on the balcony of their suite looking down into the streets of Jubilee. The parking lots at the music venues were full. All of the eating and drinking establishments were open, and shops were still lit up. People were bundled up against the chill and still walking about as if it were a balmy summer day. He didn't understand the fascination with the place, but it was obvious it attracted a lot of people.

Today had been a revelation for him in more ways than one. Harley's love for Brendan Pope was real, and it seemed to be returned. They were protective of each other, and yet the man had known instinctively when to step back and let her shine. And shine she did. Love had softened all of her hard edges without dampening the fire within her. He could go back to Houston without further concerns and pat himself on the back for raising a brilliant child. For Jason, success mattered more than love.

Judith was enjoying a bath in the jetted tub and aimlessly popping bubbles as she soaked. She was satisfied with the man Harley had fallen for and tried not to think of what she herself had sacrificed for the pleasure of Jason's money and the cachet of his name.

Life was a trade-off, and she'd traded love for money and would take that secret to her grave. Harley had Jason's name, but she was not his child. Only Judith knew that, not even the man with whom she'd had the affair. But every time she saw her daughter, she saw his face and remembered love.

———

Harley had been following up on details of getting her things moved out of her Chicago apartment when Brendan left her sitting by the fire and went to shower. The day had been long and stressful, and tomorrow would be more of the same. But even after he'd showered and washed his hair, he was still standing beneath the flow of hot water with his head down and his hands braced against the wall.

Suddenly, he felt a rush of air, and then Harley was behind him. She slipped her arms around his waist and laid her cheek on his back.

"Thank you for today. For enduring my father's digs and my mother's constant inquiries into your bloodline."

Without a word, he turned and lifted her off her feet.

Anticipation shot through her as she wrapped her legs around his waist. His hands were on her backside as he pinned her against the shower wall. Water was running in rivulets down his back as he eased her down on his erection.

Harley moaned.

"Hold on, Sunshine. I've been thinking about this all day, but I can't last long. You're gonna think you've been a victim of a hit-and-run."

She tucked her head against his shoulder and closed her eyes. "Just love me," she whispered.

"I already do."

═══════════

The day before Jason and Judith were to leave, Brendan and Harley took them up the mountain, and again, his family had come through for him. They were all there waiting to meet Harley's parents, just as they'd waited to meet her. What they didn't know was that Wolf Outen was also there, waiting for them to arrive.

———————

"This mountain is a bit intimidating," Judith said as they drove. "No houses in sight. No traffic on the road."

"There are multitudes of homes here," Brendan said. "Everywhere you see mailboxes, there are roads and houses connected to them, and if there are multiple mailboxes at one road, that means multiple families live on the same property and the roads fork later to go to their respective houses."

"Oh! Well, that makes sense," Judith said, and laughed at herself. "I am definitely out of my comfort zone up here."

"Mother, your villa in the south of France is on the edge of a cliff. You drive up three miles of a narrow, winding, one-way road to get there," Harley said, and laughed.

Judith giggled. "Touché. I guess because I'm familiar with it, I didn't see the similarities."

Jason was silent. He just wanted this trip over with. He wouldn't have to come back until their wedding, whenever they decided that might happen.

When Brendan took the turn off the blacktop and started up the road to his mother's house, both of

Harley's parents went silent, and when the house came into view and Jason saw the assortment of cars lined up in front of it, he frowned. Then he glanced up in the rearview mirror and caught Brendan watching him. He flushed and looked away.

Harley was talking to her mother as they got out and started toward the house. Brendan and Jason were right behind them, but then Brendan moved up beside Jason and lowered his voice.

"I put up with your snide insinuations for Harley's sake. But you don't get a break here. This is my mother's home. You make even one condescending, denigrating remark about her, or this lifestyle, or her home, and you and I will have a discussion behind the barn. Is that clear?"

Jason stumbled. Brendan caught him by the arm. "Careful where you step," he said lightly, then looked up smiling as the front door opened.

Shirley Pope appeared, tall and elegant in her stance—a female version of her sons. "Welcome to my home. Come inside where it's warm."

And the moment they entered, three other men appeared wearing varying versions of Brendan Pope's face, and Jason Banks knew he'd entered a world where only giants dwelled.

Introductions were made, and Judith was charmed by the brothers as much as she had been by Brendan. Then Wolf Outen came out of the kitchen and shook their hands. "We meet again. Prepare yourself to be charmed by this beautiful lady and her food. She's a real steel magnolia and cooks like an angel."

Shirley laughed. "You, sir, are a sweet-talker, just like my Wiley. Brendan, would you please hang up your coats for me? Amalie, would you be my hostess for a bit? I need to check on something in the oven."

"I'll help," Wolf said, and followed Shirley.

Amalie stepped up to Shirley's request and introduced herself. "I'm Sean's wife. Wolf is my father. These are my sisters-in-law. Dani is married to Aaron. Linette is married to Wiley, and this tiny little blond is our sister, Ava."

When Ava found out her grandma was having another party, she had asked to wear her pinkest dress, and so now she stood before them like a little pink fairy with a Band-Aid on her knee and a tiara on her head, delighted to have been singled out.

She eyed the two strangers carefully, then pointed to the sofa. "We sit there, and when Grandma hollers 'It's ready!' we'll sit in there," she said, and pointed to the kitchen.

Jason was leery of kids, but Judith was instantly charmed. "Thank you, Miss Ava. Will you sit with me? You can tell me all about your tiara, and what you like to do best."

Ava plopped down between them and looked up at Jason. "You're Harley's daddy?"

He nodded.

Then she looked at Judith. "And you're Harley's mama?"

"Yes, I am," Judith said.

Ava nodded. "You did a good job. Harley is gonna be my new sister. She's pretty and smart and really nice, and Brendan loves her forever. Sean and Amalie are having babies. The babies will cry a lot. I'm gonna have to teach them stuff because I'll be their auntie. Linnie is my mommy/sister. Wiley is my Bubba/daddy. Aaron is my oldest brother, and his Dani is my sister/teacher, and my grandma loves me. I'm a keeper."

Judith was enchanted. "Amalie, I believe this one's a charmer."

Ava frowned. "No. I used to be a Dalton, but now I'm a Pope."

Everyone laughed, even Jason.

Brendan and Harley were hanging up coats when they heard the laughter. "Ten to one, that's because of Ava," Brendan said.

"Really?" Harley said.

He nodded. "She and Wiley are just alike. Neither of them has filters."

"Good. Maybe between the both of them, they'll squash my dad's ability to insult."

He slid a hand across her shoulder. "Not to worry. Jason and I have already discussed that."

Harley paused, startled by the news. "Really? When did all that happen?"

"Within the ten seconds it took for us to walk from the car up to the porch."

Harley grinned. "Did you scare him good?"

"I scared him enough," Brendan said. "We don't bring discord into our mother's house. She already escaped that life. This place is her sanctuary."

Harley hugged him. "Thank you."

"I'm always here for you, tough stuff. Never forget it."

━━━━━━━

By the time the meal was over, Harley's parents were certain that their daughter's welfare was in good hands. They were impressed with the people and their chosen lifestyle, and were beginning to understand the draw of anonymity. Even Wolfgang Outen, a billionaire countless times over, found comfort here.

They were quiet on the drive back into Jubilee, just sitting in the back seat of Brendan's car and listening to him and Harley talking and laughing together. Hearing the fire in her voice and the quiet caution in his.

They're suited, Judith thought.

When Brendan pulled up at the front entrance to the inn to let them out, Judith finally spoke up.

"Thank you both for the most wonderful evening I've spent in years. Brendan, your family is lovely. Harley, I honor your wisdom in all things. You are a better woman than me. And when you two decide to tie the knot, unless you plan to elope, let me know. I want to hear you say the words 'I do.'"

"Of course we'll let you know what we decide, but

it won't be any time in the near future. We have plans. And why do you need to hear me say, 'I do'?"

"Because not once in your entire life have you ever said, 'I do,' or 'I will,' without prefacing it with an 'if,' or a 'when,' or a 'why,'" Judith said.

Brendan burst out laughing.

Harley blushed.

And even Jason was grinning as they got out of the car.

"Safe travels," Harley called out as they were on their way inside.

They turned and waved, then entered the lobby.

Harley reached across the seat and took Brendan's hand. "Let's go home."

He eyed the dark circles beneath her eyes and the pain on her face. "You hurt, don't you, darlin'? You did too much and worried too much while they were here. Home it is."

As soon as they got home, Harley showered, took her meds, and crawled in bed. Brendan tucked her in and then kissed the side of her cheek.

"Sleep well, darlin'. I won't be long."

She snuggled down beneath the covers, listening as he moved around the room getting undressed, and heard him when he slipped into the bathroom. She heard the shower come on and then nothing.

She was sleeping, and then dreaming.

Becoming Harley Jo Pope, wife of Brendan James Pope and of a house yet to be built, and babies yet to be born, and then in the dream, he was in bed beside her, pulling her close. Keeping her safe. Keeping her warm.

———

When Brendan came out of the bathroom, all he could see was the top of her head on her pillow and covers pulled up to her ears.

Mine, he thought, and then turned off the last of the lights and slipped into bed beside her, curled up behind her, and put his arm across her waist.

"Love you forever," he whispered, then closed his eyes.

Epilogue

SOMETIMES THE ENSUING MONTHS FELT ENDLESS. Other times, they slipped past so fast it felt like life was trying to buck Harley and Brendan off the ride.

The grand opening of the renovated Serenity Inn happened just at the height of summer. Brendan was back at work in the hotel kitchen, and Harley was in her office, methodically cleaning Wolfgang Outen's financial house.

On their first day off, they went up the top of Pope Mountain, to the little Church in the Wildwood, and said "I do" with Brother Farley officiating from a wheelchair. He'd married his last Pope and was retiring and moving away.

A new preacher would come, but they didn't yet know his name, and it wouldn't matter. Brother Farley had stood in the shoes of the Wildwood church's pastor long enough. It was time for someone else to claim them.

And that day, after Brendan and Harley were finally alone, he was finally able to share his last secret with her.

"Mrs. Pope, come sit with me. I have a secret to share that only members of our family can know."

Harley plopped down on his lap, smiling. "As long as you aren't going to tell me you shape-shift under the light of a full moon."

He laughed. "Oh, way better than that. I know when you were auditing Ray Caldwell you saw the payments going to the company who controls Jubilee, right?"

"Yes, and the same now that Wolf has taken over, why?"

"Well, every business in Jubilee has the same agreement, because PCG Inc. owns the land outright, and all of the business owners pay PCG to have shops here."

"Yes, I know that," she said.

"Well, what you don't know is that we are PCG Inc.—Pope, Cauley, Glass—PCG. We own Jubilee together, all of us on Pope Mountain."

Harley gasped. "What? Wait. How?"

"Cameron is the CEO. He and a lawyer in Frankfort manage the corporation. A couple of generations back, they incorporated when Jubilee began turning into what it is today. It was a way to control our way of life, and with no one knowing, we aren't constantly invaded with complaints from tourists or shopkeepers. We, as in every voting member of the corporation, get quarterly dividends paid into personal accounts in banks outside of Jubilee. No one outside the families know this. So now you do, and you are part of the secret."

Harley just kept staring. She heard the words coming

out of his mouth, but could hardly grasp the extent of the revelation.

"Good lord, honey! That has to be millions of dollars yearly."

He nodded. "And you all share in the profits."

She started to smile. "Amazing. Who knew?"

"Just us, is who."

"Right, and we'll keep it that way." And then she threw her arms around his neck. "We all own a town. A whole freaking tourist industry. This is one of the smartest business moves I've ever heard of. My lips are sealed."

"Not too tight, I hope. I still want my kisses."

She was laughing as he carried her to bed.

———————

Months later, Amalie gave birth to twin boys. They were born on Labor Day, which seemed fitting, because she'd labored long and hard to bring them into the world. Sean held both of his sons in his arms for the first time, looking deep into their faces, seeing pieces of him and pieces of her. But their dark hair, long legs, and long arms were a given.

Aidan Pope and Dillon Pope had entered the world.

The seventh generation of Popes had just been born.

———————

The last nail went into Brendan and Harley's new home almost a year to the day from when they first met.

They spent their first night on Pope Mountain in a home of their own and woke up to a sight they would never forget.

Brendan looked out the window and then quickly called out.

"Harley! Darlin'! Come quick."

She ran to his side, and as she pushed aside the curtain to look out, a chill ran through her.

A magnificent stag was in the clearing, standing between their new house and the clump of trees where they'd first seen him.

"Oh, Brendan! It's a welcome home sign! We're meant to be here."

He slid his arm across her shoulders. "We were always meant to be here, Sunshine. We just didn't always know it."

It was a Sunday in April, about a month after Brendan and Harley moved in. It was also their day off, when they began hearing cars and trucks coming up their driveway and seeing people piling out of vehicles, carrying shovels, and plants in pots, and trees in tubs.

Brendan and Harley came out smiling. "What's going on?" he asked.

Shirley came up the steps smiling. "Impromptu

housewarming," she said. "But don't worry. All of this, including us, stays outside."

They looked across the yard in disbelief as Aaron and Sean came across it dragging a tree with the root ball still wrapped in burlap.

"All you two have to do is tell us where you want stuff planted. We brought shovels. We'll do the rest," Aaron said.

Harley started clapping and jumping up and down and running from flowering pot to flowering bush, and tree to tree, and back again.

"Brendan, oh my gosh… You do the trees. I'll pick where the shrubs go."

"Deal," he said, and off they went in different directions.

Harley grabbed Shirley's hand. "You have to help. I've never grown anything in my life. What needs shade? What needs full sun? What might grow too big too close to the house?"

Caught up in the excitement, Shirley began sorting and pointing, and Harley was listening and learning.

The yard was full of aunts and uncles and cousins and neighbors, and every Pope on the mountain, big and small. Dirt was flying, water hoses were strung out, and one by one, all that was green and flowering was going in the ground.

And when they were done, they gathered in a crowd and stepped back to get the full effect of their landscaping as Sean appeared with a fancy camera on a tripod.

"Brendan and Harley, go stand on your front porch, just above the steps." So they did, Harley standing with her arm around his waist, and Brendan standing with his arm across her shoulder, while Sean took photo after photo. And then he paused. "Okay, now everybody get in the picture. Stagger yourselves on the steps, and then spread out along the front porch. We're going to take a panorama shot of all of us."

The crowd moved as one toward the house, sorted themselves out, and then Aaron waved at Sean. "Here, Brother, I saved you a place. Do your thing and come a-runnin.'"

Sean nodded, focused the lens, grabbed his remote, and bolted.

He was standing in place when he called out, "Everybody say, 'Jubilee'!"

And as they did, he pressed the button on the remote control at least a dozen times.

A few weeks later, Sean gifted Brendan and Harley with two framed 18-by-24 pictures.

They hung the group picture in the dining room, and the one of them alone over their fireplace. Their hearts were full of the love looking back at them.

And there the pictures would hang as time flew by, and the planted trees grew tall, and birds nested within them, and the bushes flourished and bloomed.

Over the years, the apple trees bore bountiful fruit, and what fell to the ground was left for the stags and the does, and shrubs grew tall and spread out as shelter for the little woodland creatures of the night.

And for all the generations to come, the beginning of Brendan and Harley Pope was on the wall for them to see.

About the Author

New York Times and USA Today bestselling author Sharon Sala has over 140 books in print, published in seven different genres—romance, young adult, western, general fiction, women's fiction, nonfiction, and children's books. First published in 1991, her industry awards include the Janet Dailey Award, five-time Career Achievement winner, five-time winner of the National Readers' Choice Award, five-time winner of the Colorado Romance Writers' Award of Excellence, the Heart of Excellence award, the Booksellers Best Award, the Nora Roberts Lifetime Achievement Award, the Will Rogers Gold Medallion Award, and the Centennial Award in recognition of her 100th published novel. She lives in Oklahoma, the state where she was born.

Website: sharonsalaauthor.com
Facebook: sharonsala
Instagram: @sharonkaysala_

Also by Sharon Sala